C000162784

vicious *little* snakes

USA Today Bestselling Author
TRILINA
PUCCI

Cover: Ashes and Vellichor

Formatting: LJ Designs

Editing: Erica Russikoff of Erica Edits

       Rebecca, Fairest Reviews Editing Services

       Sandra, One Love Editing

Proofreading: Rumi Khan

Printed in the United States of America ISBN-13:979-8709850767

vicious *little* snakes

recap

Need a recap? I've got you. Sit down and let me spill all the tea. Okay, let's see where we left off—

Grey and Liam seemed at odds, one of them fighting to win Donovan's heart, the other to ensure it didn't get broken. The battle for Donovan finally came to an end with the only choice to be made. It's no surprise it was Grey. You can't fight fate. Let's be real. They're meant to be.

Now, where does that leave Liam, you ask? Well, I can't tell you... spoilers. But there's nothing worse than being a third wheel. And to a girl whose heart he set out to win. Or maybe, someone already caught his eye? (Psst...I'm talking about Caroline.)

Speaking of the devil herself, is anyone even speaking to Carebear after the shit she pulled to set Grey off and make Liam hate her?

God, cafeteria drama is always the best. This one time, my junior year—never mind, sorry. Back to the book.

If you ask me, Caroline Whitmore is on shaky ground, even though she delivered Donovan straight to Grey's library and promised peace, begrudgingly. But truces are as fickle in this world as Facebook relationship statuses. It's safe to say "it's complicated" doesn't quite cut it.

And let's not forget that our beloved Dray? Gronovan? Grey and Donovan. They need to stay on the downlow. Thanks to too many whiskey shots, a smidge of toxic masculinity, and a burnt-down tree. Oh, McCallister, I do love a broody bastard, but a possible appearance in Page Six complicates everything. #fuckpaul #fuckredoak

Here's the thing: there are more questions than answers—an insane amount of scandal and lots of goddamn angst. But there's also Liam. So much Liam. *swoons*

Welcome back to Hillcrest. Best to buckle up for the ride.

If you would rather fall into a coma before rereading a book...I got you.

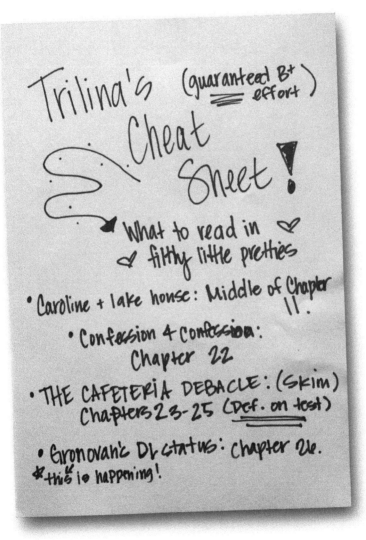

Trilina's (guaranteed B+)
effort

Cheat Sheet!

What to read in ♡
♡ filthy little pretties

• Caroline + lake house: Middle of Chapter 11.

• Confession 4 Confession: Chapter 22

• THE CAFETERIA DEBACLE: (skim) Chapters 23-25 (Def. on test)

• Gronovan's DL status: chapter 26.
☆ this is happening!

vicious *little* snakes

"All that glitters
is not gold."

-William Shakespeare

vicious *little* snakes

Prologue

Liam—The Red Oak Race

"L oser."

"Where the fuck have you been? We won. By a lot." I huff at Caroline's smug expression.

The crowd is up the hill by the bonfire, but I'm still trying to get my legs to work. Grey definitely carried us over the finish line because I think I died a click back.

"No, I mean your little competition with Grey. It just became a forfeit on Donovan's part. So…" She shrugs with a smirk. "Loser."

Caroline stands in front of me, wallowing in my expected misery as she pushes to her tiptoes to boop my nose.

My head draws back from her hand as I stare down and shrug. "What the fuck are you talking about? Grey's in the boat. I'm not in the mood for your little games."

A quick laugh shoots from her lips. "Look for yourself."

She turns, pointing, and my eyes lift over her head to see Van straddling Grey in the boat, obviously having just kissed him. Son of a bitch. Honestly, I'm surprised it took them this long.

My gaze narrows back to Caroline.

"I wouldn't count me out just yet."

"It's pathetic you ever thought she counted you in, Brooks."

I tuck my hands under Caroline's armpits, enjoying her squeal as I curl her, bringing us eye level.

"You're a mean little bitch, aren't you?"

She scowls. I can feel her nails dig into my shoulders, but I don't give a fuck.

"Doesn't matter. Because now I'm going to kiss that girl stupid. Just to irritate the fuck out of you. My mouth will be covered in cherry."

I almost wince, feeling her claws dig deeper.

"And why would you think that mattered to me?"

"I don't know. And I don't care. It's enough that I piss you off, Carebear."

I drop her without warning, letting her almost fall on her ass.

"Make sure you get a good seat."

Chapter One

Caroline
Last Thursday

I hate her. That's all I can think of while standing in the middle of the empty school hallway. Donovan stares back at me, hand on hip, chain Chanel bag across her body, shining almost as much as the highlight on her face. God, I hate her so much I could cry. In theory only. In real life, I never cry.

You have to feel to do that, and I swore off that shit a long fucking time ago.

Donovan's giving me that look, the one with the smugness she reserves for when she thinks she's won. It's bad enough my plan in the cafeteria didn't work, but now that the crowned prince of Hillcrest and his princess are back together, I'm checkmated.

"I said, get, bitches," she snaps.

Nice line. More me than her. But this is Donovan's shining moment— the one where she tells me who's boss. Puts me in my place, like in a mediocre mean-girl movie where one of us is a morally high-grounded virgin. *Whoopsies, Donovan, all these bitches are sycophants and whores, kitten.*

Feet scurry around me, jumping into high gear, leaving Laura and me alone with Queen D. The nickname makes me smile. She is the queen of D, considering what a little prossie she was in Spain. Donovan's overly shiny blonde hair sways with the tilt of her head, and those boho bracelets—Jesus, they make me want to weep for fashion's sake.

"Laura, I was going to speak to Caroline about you, since you don't seem to have a mind of your own, but I think you should hear this firsthand. Stop allowing yourself to be used by boys…"

Her voice turns into one of the parents from Charlie Brown, causing me to drift off until her red-hued lips lift into a smile. "…I want you to ask yourself one question, Laura. Who's my queen afraid of?"

Not you, Cherry. God, I knew she'd draw on her inner bitch, the one buried deep down, for this moment. But I'd like to show Donovan how to do it properly. Fortunately for her, Grey's already beat her to this plot twist. And my brother—he always gets my loyalty, as well as my acquiescence.

Only fools and masochists cross Grey McCallister. I'm neither, at least not for his brand of torture. I'll play nice because it evens the score. After all, this is my penance for the trouble I concocted. I eat shit and let the Cherry stay on top.

Maybe then, he'll forgive me. The other him, I mean—*the only him.*

Laura's eyes nervously dart to my face. I'm trying my best to seem contrite and not think about Liam. I must be convincing because Donovan exhales a heavy breath, "This is the last time we have a conversation like this. Consider your 'get out of jail free' card used up. Next time, it's all consequence. Okay, girls. You can go. We're all done."

I almost roll my eyes because *boring.* That was weak at best. Before Donovan can catch my callous regard for her, I turn around and begin walking away. Donovan's done, now that her tongue-lashing is complete, but Laura's voice grabs my attention, and I look over my shoulder to see her open her mouth to speak. I'll kill her.

"How can you love him when you know who he is?"

God, shut the fuck up, peasant. This is why you don't get to be a real friend.

Donovan turns around, just as I do, locking eyes with me but answering Laura, "Because even a villain is someone else's hero."

"*Bitch!*" I'm screaming it, but only on the inside because it's a perfect label for her and me.

Donovan, because she still holds the heart of the boy I love hostage, and me, because I got bested by an Upper East Side Kate Hudson. Now I'm the villain, and undoubtedly, I'll never be Liam's hero.

I swear to God, if I didn't hate her so damn much, we'd be best friends. Almost were. Until she stole from me—twice. And like that saying, fool me once blah blah.

No. Always shame on you. Always.

"You and I—" She points at me, pulling me back from my memory, but I cut her off, unwilling to sit through another monologue where she flexes. It's too fucking cliché and basic.

"We're good, kitten. I see you."

"Keep it that way."

I know she thinks I call her "kitten" because of her nasty little claws, but it's not. It's because I'd like to put her in a pillowcase and throw her in the river. Donovan turns around, walking away as the sound of her boots echo off the walls until we're alone.

My eyes cut to Laura's, and I shove her shoulder. "You couldn't keep your hayseed mouth shut? It's bad enough you turned the cafeteria thing into a spectacle, but then you had to go and what, seek forgiveness? Look pathetic? Try to befriend her? *Putain de perdant.*" *Fucking loser.*

Laura winds a hand around her wild red hair as she straightens out her bunched sleeve.

"Jesus, Caroline. You don't have to shove me. And that's not fair. You told me to."

My glare intensifies as my eyes widen.

"What? You did. I did all that stuff with Grey because I thought you wanted to stir up shit between them—"

My hand shoots up in front of her face. "Please. Shut. Up. Just go home. In fact, take a few days off. I could use the vacation from your stupidity."

Laura lowers my hand and stares at me incredulously.

"I have a chem test today. And a partner in that class. I have to be here."

My smile slides out over my lips as I tuck a strand of her hair behind her ear.

"I'm sure your partner won't mind your D average going missing. Sometimes it's nice to let the dead weight sink. Try not to drown."

Laura's frown grows as I speak, but her mouth stays shut. Smart, because I'm feeling especially mean right now. She takes a step back, pulling on the strap of her backpack that's slung over her shoulder.

"Fine. Okay, fine. See you in a few days."

I turn away, not bothering to answer or look at her. I should feel bad. It's not all her fault. I did tell Laura to play nice with Grey. I offered her Kardashian-sized ass up as a fake love interest. She was supposed to make Donovan mad with jealousy so she'd leave and eventually man up to choose the only boy she's ever really wanted—Grey.

But not before Liam watched her crumble over Grey. Her choice would've been out in the open, murdering whatever hope Liam was clinging to and shredding the connection between them. But instead, the debacle made Liam hate me and Grey burn down a fucking tree.

The worst part, though, is Liam chose Donovan, right to my face. He meant for it to cut deep, and he got his wish.

My face drifts toward where Donovan walked as my fingers gently tuck under the opposite sleeve of my crisp white button-down shirt. The raised scar on the side of my wrist still sits there, bumpy and protruding from my skin, the pain lingering in my memory. Close enough that if I close my eyes, I can almost feel the sting, not from the cut but from what happened after. I blink, pulling myself from the moment before I remember too much.

None of them understand. I wasn't trying to make Grey hate her, not forever, at least. I don't even care that much that Donovan loves Liam. It's Liam's undying loyalty and affection for her that genuinely makes me sick to my stomach.

It's unbearable—the weight of his affection for someone else because it's something that used to be mine. For a brief apocalyptic moment, I was the only thing in his existence, and then that life died, and I woke up in a world in which he occasionally visits but never stays.

Laura's eyes are still on me, but I ignore her, leaving her to wonder why I haven't moved. I don't care because all I've been thinking about for the last few minutes is that Donovan headed toward the art room.

And that's where Liam is. It's always where he is.

Despite all my better judgment, I head the same way, following Donovan's footsteps or in her shadow—depending on the opinion. With each step, my body becomes tenser. Why do I do this to myself? It's like emotional cutting. I slice a piece of my heart open and watch myself bleed, but unlike the times I've done it to my flesh, my heart never heals. It just shrivels up and dies, more and more.

The closer I get, the clearer I can hear voices. My hand skims over the silver metal lockers as I slow to a stop and listen. Soft, hurt-filled voices squeeze through the crack in the door. The noise begs me to spy, but I can't look inside the room without being seen, so I lean back against the concrete, eavesdropping.

"What does that mean?" Donovan questions.

Liam's voice sounds frustrated as he answers, "It means, this is what you do. You always have. Grey does something atrocious, and you forgive him. As if it never happened."

Silence hemorrhages between them, and I close my eyes, laying my head back against the wall. I hate the way he sounds. Like he's already lost a friend. Liam won't survive this. As much as I wish she'd disappear again, I'll kill her if she doesn't make this right.

"In the cafeteria... He treated you like dirt, Van. Likened you to a whore and..."

She is one, but not because she fucks randos.

"Then fucked me like one..." Donovan sounds gutted as she continues. "You don't have to say it. It's written all over your face."

Ha. Great minds.

There's a harsh exhale, and I imagine Liam's rubbing his hand over his shorn head the way he does when he's the most frustrated. I hear him say, "Why can't you hold him accountable?"

Because she's a whore. We covered this.

Their voices grow quiet, robbing me of discerning what they're saying. I roll my shoulder closer to the door, blinking my eyes open to stare at the hinges. My fingers barely touch the cold metal, moving centimeters closer, hopeful of making out any shred of a syllable.

"Fuck you," rings out, and my eyes go wide as my head pops up off the wall. "I only forgive him blindly. Only him. So pay attention to what you say to me."

I can't help my smirk. Liam must've told her some truth. God knows Little Miss Perfect doesn't like that thrown in her face. Good for him. I lift my eyes to gamble a peek inside the window, but Liam's shoulder comes into view through the pane on the door.

Shit. I draw back, pressing against the wall, my eyes fixed on Liam. Shit. Shit. Shit.

His angular jaw is tense as he grips the strap of his black backpack.

"No. I'm done, Van. If you want me as a friend, then that doesn't include Grey."

Fuck. I look around for an escape, taking two side steps away from the door, but it swings open too quickly and slams closed just as fast behind broad, muscular shoulders. Oh my God. Caught. I drop my head and squeeze my eyes shut, hoping I'm suddenly invisible.

A deep throat clearing—"Ahem"—lingers in the air, but all I can manage is one eye opening as I tilt my head to the side to peek. Those unmistakable shoulders squared off in my direction serve as more evidence that I am not, in fact, invisible.

I close my eyes for a millisecond more before pushing off the wall to face him, lifting my head as if embarrassment isn't something I would entertain. A smart-ass remark readies on the tip of my tongue, but tortured hazel eyes lock to mine, gluing me to my spot, and render me stupid.

Walk away, Caroline. Now. But I don't move. I couldn't walk away, even if I wanted to try…harder.

Liam swallows, bobbing his prominent Adam's apple, staring down at me. He crosses his arms as his head tilts, and he licks his goddamned perfect lips—the actions of a bastard.

He's always acting this way with me. Like I'm a snack he hasn't had yet. It's infuriating and addicting. I hate it, but like the fucking beggar I am, I'll take it. Just not without disdain for myself.

"Carebear."

I roll my eyes as he says "Carebear" in the way he does—it always makes me feel like Liam's caught me doing something I shouldn't. And in this case, I am.

Liam takes a step forward, so I take one back. But he doesn't stop, forcing me backward quickly into an alcove, flanked by lockers. He halts me, hand on my waist, just before my back touches the cold wall.

"Eavesdropping is beneath you, Caroline."

My eyes narrow while my arms cross. "Well, we both seem to want to stoop to new lows today." I add a pout as I say in a baby voice, "Be my friend, Donovan."

I need to shut my mouth. My snark isn't going to make Liam forgive me any sooner for the cafeteria.

The side of Liam's mouth tips into a crooked grin, but his fingers press tighter into my waist as he gives me a tiny push against the concrete.

"What are you doing here? Stalking? Missed me that much, huh."

"I was walking by," I snap, shoving his hand from my waist. "But since I overheard your little chat, why not talk about you. I never thought you'd beg for her attention. It's pathetic."

He huffs an empty laugh and steps back to pull out a toothpick from the front embroidered pocket of his school blazer. Popping it between his impossibly white teeth, he looks me up and down.

"I've never begged for her attention. And what would you know about begging?"

That damn toothpick wiggling, set against his grin, God, it's making me all flushed. I can't stop staring. He leans in closer, and my lips part ever so slightly. "I wonder what a begging Caroline would sound like?"

"You'll never know."

"Right. Because you've got everything you want."

I don't answer, opting for a lackluster scowl that seems to amuse him because he adds, "Come on. Think hard. There has to be something you want but don't have."

The way his mouth moves around those words—fuck. I'm losing all focus, unable to whip out a response when he does stuff like this. Goddamn him.

"Nope."

"How about a truce."

My eyes lock to his.

"Me and you—we could kiss and make up." His tongue darts out over his bottom lip. "Tell me something, Carebear. How badly do you want that?"

More than I should.

"Enough that you'd beg for it?"

I have been.

His eyes shift between mine as if he sees through me. But he doesn't. I've mastered the art of staying invisible, even in the spotlight. If he did see me, he'd know I'm full of shit. But my attitude serves me well. It hides the fact that all I want is a hit—an argument, crude flirting, being teased. I'll take all or any of it, even knowing that it's empty and meaningless.

That's the worst part of unrequited love—knowing you're the fool and being unable to stop yourself.

His fingers brush the top of my ear as he tucks a stray piece of hair behind it, just as patronizingly as I did to Laura earlier.

Liam's intoxicatingly closer. So close that I think I can feel the prick of the toothpick.

"Nah, you're too posh to beg. Right? Plus, what's the point when you want the one thing you can't have."

Nope. Wrong about which prick was stabbing me. My hands shove Liam backward, barely gaining any room, as he chuckles.

I make a gagging sound. "Keep flattering yourself. You're no prize for me, Brooks."

He gives a tip-of-a-hat gesture. "It was almost nice talking to you again, Carebear. I won't make that mistake again."

My lips press together to stop whatever "can't come back from" words I'm about to say from spilling out. But seeing Liam saunter off gets the best of me, and I hurl venom at his back.

"She'll never choose you. You're a fool."

He answers over his shoulder, "I don't expect that she will, but I chose her, remember?"

Yes, I remember, you dick. It was the only thing you said to me during my cafeteria failure last week. I stare at Liam's back, hating him for making the memory of his hateful words come back.

"And you"—Liam scowls, looking directly at me—*"you aren't the girl I thought you were. I don't know what you did, but I choose Van."*

Chapter Two

Liam

The violent beeping of my alarm yanks me from my sleep as I groan and pull the pillow over my face. I was up half the night, trying to finish my painting—evidenced by my oil-stained hand that shoots out, knocking the alarm from my nightstand. I only manage to warp the sound rather than kill it.

"Too early," I mumble.

Three sharp "tsks" precede my mother's voice.

"Liam, please stop ruining your alarm clocks."

My mom's voice has the pillow lowering and my eyes opening. No matter how old I get, she still wakes me up—every damn morning. One day I'll thank her for keeping me on time, just not today. Or tomorrow.

Soft footsteps pad on the floor before I feel her rub my back. "What's this, number four, darling? People should buy stock in alarm clock companies. You'll make them wealthy. Now, get up." A sharp slap to my bare shoulder sheds any leftover procrastination.

"Easy, killer."

I drag the pillow across my body, rolling over, and throw it at the alarm, missing altogether.

"Good thing you don't play basketball. You have an hour and a half before school starts. Get moving, little prince. And please figure out how to put that thing out of its misery."

The beeping sound grows more warbled, sounding cartoonlike.

Grumbling, I rub my face. "Serves it right. The beeping is fucking traumatic."

"Liam. Language."

I smile, pushing against the mattress to sit up and stretch my arms overhead.

"One day, Mom, I'll become the gentleman you always hoped I'd be. Promise."

"I won't hold my breath," she teases, walking away and yelling over her shoulder, "Don't make me come back in there. Monday is my busy day—I have the Nudes benefit for the Academy of Art. Please get it together, or I'll disown you."

"Nudes? Want me to help?"

"Never mind. I'm disowning you."

Her threat makes me chuckle as my bedroom door is closed. She's tiny, as in barely five feet tall and a hundred pounds soaking wet. But Babe Brooks is a force of nature, and I love her. So I almost always listen.

I throw my blanket off, tossing my legs over the side of my bed, and roll my shoulders, feeling my tired muscles ripple as I do. Between my crew schedule, school, friends, and my secret art project, I'm spent.

The yawn that's been waiting in the wings breaks free as I stand and shove my hand down the front of my basketball shorts to rub my half wood. I reach back to my nightstand and grab my cell, kicking the jacked-up alarm out of the way, silencing it for good. Heading to my bathroom, I don't look up as I crack my neck and shoot off a text to Grey.

Me: Up late. Grab me a coffee.

Grey: Pussy or painting?

Me: The only girl I stay up late for is your girlfriend. So tell her she should sleep in today.

My phone buzzes almost immediately with his response, but I ignore it in favor of scrolling through my playlist. When it stops and starts again, I smirk. Now that Grey and Donovan are an unofficial-official thing and the three of us made peace, I especially love throwing out jabs to make Grey lose it.

He's too easy. And it's always fun.

I hit Shuffle, bobbing my head as music fills the room, place my phone on the counter, and cross the black-and-white heated tile floors to turn on the shower. The double showerheads rain down as my hand cuts through the water, testing it before jumping in. The minute the hot water washes over my tired muscles, I groan, rubbing my head and wiping down my face.

"Fuck."

A familiar song begins to play, one that moves me to turn on the Bluetooth speaker inside my shower. Marcy Playground, an old band Kai introduced me to, dances around with the steam, inviting me to lean into the memory of the last time I heard this song. I grab the washcloth, soaping it up, and scrub over my chest as I hum along.

Damn, I was drunk that night, too drunk, or maybe not enough, but that whole party at the cabin was crazy. There are parts of the night that are hazier than others, but I do vividly remember dedicating this fucking song to Caroline—bathed in the light of a bonfire with a bottle of Jack in hand and that ever-present scowl on her face.

Riling that girl up should count as a hobby, considering how much I do it. Or used to do it. It's been a week, and I still haven't forgiven her for that cafeteria setup. I was beyond pissed when it all went down, but after Grey shared all the details, I got even madder.

Outside of one hallway encounter, I've been treating her like she has the plague. It's fucked-up and unfair to forgive Grey and not her, but recognizing that doesn't change how I feel.

What she did meant more.

I whisper the lyrics to myself, running the soapy washcloth across my stomach before submerging my whole body under the stream. The water pours over me, cascading down around my eyes, keeping them shut as I give in to the daydream.

"You're drunk, Brooks."

I'm nodding as I stare at her. I am drunk. Very drunk. Drunk enough to be standing here, messing with the queen of mean. But her hair is pretty, so chocolate that it looks black. I like it this way, her real color. I drop the bottle from my mouth with a pucker, sucking the liquor from my bottom lip.

"But you love me drunk. Admit it."

She waves a hand, dismissing me.

It's what she always does. Although, every once in a while, I get an honest conversation and a smile. Glimpses of Caroline.

"Come on, admit you secretly love me," I drawl, moving in closer.

I already know the answer. It's been definitively "no" since our sophomore year and Kai showed up to take my place as her favorite. A fact that still grates my nerves and makes me mean—but only sometimes, because I crave her more than I hate her.

"I tolerate you at best, Liam. And only because you're Grey's best friend, which means I don't have a choice, now do I."

I laugh as someone comes up beside me, slapping my back while I'm mid-swig, announcing, "I think Grey and Donovan just got here. And Kai is looking for you, Caroline."

She starts to walk off, shrugging. "Kai's calling."

I grin. "Whatever. Your replacement's here, anyway."

She narrows her eyes as I smile broader. I know she hates it when I say shit like that, even though I always tell her I'm fucking with her. But something about her reaction—like she wants to be my favorite. I don't know. It makes me keep doing it—acting like an immature prick. I can't stop.

This time I don't reduce my words down to just a joke. Instead, I stare at Caroline, mentally daring her to do something.

She doesn't. So I cave.

"Hey, you wanna know something? A secret?"

My body moves in closer, plucking at her white cropped T-shirt that's hanging right above her belly button. Her chin lifts, and she's still glaring at me, but I feel like a giant looking down at her. God, she's so tiny. I want to pick her up and rub her all over me.

"No."

The bottle in my hand dangles from my fingers, rubbing against her hip.

"You sure?"

I let my eyes drift over her body. It's an indulgence I try to limit. But I fail.

Her voice is barely above a whisper. "Yes, loser."

Without thought, I begin to play with the ends of her hair. "Liar."

Soft strands slide between my fingertips just above the slope of her right breast. I shouldn't touch her like this. Not that Kai would care. They aren't exclusive, but it's still a dick move. An even bigger dick move is that she'd rather be in whatever-the-fuck kind of relationship she's in with Kai than give me the time of day.

"Your hair's soft," I say idly, forgetting why we're standing here.

Caroline rolls her eyes as her chest lowers, releasing the breath she's been holding. "That's not a secret."

"I know."

Am I making her nervous? Before I can ask, she answers the thought by snapping her teeth at my fingers. I laugh but don't move. The joke's on her. I'd let her bite me if she wanted to.

Caroline smooths her hair over her shoulder, removing it from my grasp, stopping my fun.

I raise my brows in question, and she raises hers back.

"Just spit it out already because you won't leave me alone until I listen."

I'm drunkenly mesmerized by her lips, wondering how soft they'd be against mine. I almost feel guilty, seeing as I've been flirting my ass off with Donovan, but I'm too drunk to think about that right now.

I should stop fucking with Caroline. I'm a dick. Maybe I'm that guy who can't get over a loss? I mean, I'm a human boy—we tend to fixate on the pussy we don't get. And like I said, immature prick.

My weight shifts unsteadily to the left, so I grab her waist to anchor myself, and her body tenses.

"If you fall, I'm leaving you in the dirt."

I take another pull off the bottle, grinning, knowing that she would. Nah, it's not about winning. Caroline has this power over me, and it fucks with my head and my life. It makes me do dumb shit, like use Donovan against her.

"If I do, I'll take you with me, and then I'll finally get you all dirty."

She swallows, pressing her lips together, and I keep staring at her skin, wishing I could bruise her neck with kisses, then wrap a hand around it while she comes.

"Are you going to tell me or what?" she huffs.

Somewhere between thinking about how her eyes almost look violet in this light and fucking her raw, my head makes one more dumbass decision tumble out of my mouth.

"I promised back in the day that I'd never let you replace her. Did I ever tell you that? But the thing is, Carebear, I didn't think about her once that whole week."

Caroline looks up, unreadable. Her small palms come to lay against my chest, and for a brief moment, the urge to kiss her almost kills me. But she pushes me away.

"One whole week? Generous. My memories are different." I don't miss that she rubs the scar on the side of her wrist. "Also. Why do I care about this?"

Shut the fuck up, Liam. Now.

"No reason, just drunk talk."

A speaker someone's brought outside begins blasting music, busting our bubble. I stumble backward, grinning from ear to ear, recognizing the song, and spread my arms.

"This song reminds me of you, Carebear. You're like peppermint candy, and well, I wouldn't mind helping you smell like the sex part—"

My hand finds the wall of the shower as the other grips my cock. I'm hard. "Fucking Caroline." I groan.

But that's my problem—I want to fuck Caroline.

She never took me up on the offer that night, opting to hang all over Kai and ignore me. Later, I got so drunk that I semi-fucked my best friend.

Not my finest moment but just another skeleton in the closet for me. I seem to have an endless supply of bad decisions surrounding the girls I know.

Tugging upward, I moan and then push back into my hand. My fingers are curling against the stone shower wall, trying to hold my ground as my mouth falls open. This is what always happens when I let myself think about Caroline for too long.

My hips roll, the sides of my ass indenting, picturing her laid out, legs spread and begging for my cock.

"Wider," I whisper, eyes closed, drunk on my fantasy, imagining she's running her tongue across those pouty lips, ready to suck me off.

The end of the song drags out over the speakers, but it could be Jauz's "Baby Shark" playing because, at this point, I can't hear anything except my own panting.

I lower my head, letting the water bead down my back. The veins in my forearm swell as I pull faster, teeth grinding, while mentally fucking Caroline Whitmore's perfect mouth. Goddamn, I want to feel every fucking inch of her. Fill every single hole and watch her come undone.

My chest begins to burn from the breath I've been holding as I chase my release. Defined lines in my six-pack deepen in an intense moment, and I feel my balls draw up before my whole-body shudders and "yes" hisses between my teeth accompanied by warm cum shooting up onto my tan skin.

Collapsing my cheek onto the cold tile wall, I lazily wipe at my stomach, removing the evidence of my obsession.

"Sex and candy," I breathe out heavily. "You're fucking Sex. And. Candy."

Chapter Three

Caroline

"**I**'m starving. What's for breakfast?"

Grey's voice is too chipper for a Monday morning. But that's my faux brother. Everything about Grey is larger than life—even the way he walks into a room.

"A little decorum," I snark. "It's Monday morning. Please act accordingly."

He laughs, plopping down into the chair next to me at the Versailles-inspired dining table. Maeve, a relatively new addition to the staff, places a gold-rimmed coffee cup down next to Grey, the steam rising off in wisps.

"Tea not your thing?" I grin as Maeve walks away.

He deadpans, not answering before looking over the newspapers, artfully arranged on the table. I lift my teacup, hearing it rattle the saucer before bringing it to my lips.

Grey's not looking at me as he questions, "So little step-monster, what can I expect this weekend?"

I know what he's asking, but I answer sarcastically anyway.

"Expect? Oh, for everyone to adore me and ultimately decide that it's me they worship, and you're no longer required to show your face. Is that what you're aft er?"

He smirks, rustling the *New York Post*, opening it to check Page Six. "Not quite."

I watch him let out a heavy breath, probably relieved not to see his name for once. Last week's drama hasn't made anything easy for any of us.

Grey picks up his fork, stabbing the sausage on his plate, like a Neanderthal, and shoves it into his mouth, but it's hot, so he says, "Paparazzi?" while chewing fast.

I smile but say, "Eww. Chew your food first. With your mouth closed." The humor behind his eyes isn't unnoticed as I continue, "But yes, only out front. Not inside."

He nods, wiping his mouth, and swallows, then takes a drink of his coffee before adding, "Cell phones?"

I let out an exasperated breath, even though I'm not.

"Taken at the door. Is this some kind of test to rule out that I'm not an amateur? I'm offended."

Grey sits back in his seat and runs his hand through his boyishly tousled hair. He looks stressed, so I stop playing around, placing my cup down, and lean in.

"I took care of everything, Grey. Not one single photo will release showing you and Donovan together. Frankly, I expect people to stay focused on me for my birthday. But I've got your back. Nothing will stop you from signing those papers next week and being New York's youngest tyrant billionaire. Least of all the rightfully deserved beating Paul received."

After Grey went nuts, there were just too many videos and witnesses to keep it quiet. To her credit, Donovan's plan was genius. And although a few Instagram videos popped up here and there, anyone that mattered—people that could give the story wings—kept their collective mouths shut. Because that's how this world works—the same rule that let Paul become a monster keeps Grey safe: never bite the hand that feeds you.

Power is the only real currency in life. And people like Grey, Liam, Donovan—me, we have that in spades. But to stay off the radar and not play Russian roulette with a multibillion-dollar company, he and Donovan have to lie low another week.

He stares at me, deep in thought. And I swear I can read them. We may not be blood, but Grey and I are cut from the same cloth.

"Stop looking for holes. You'd think you'd have found enough, seeing as how you spend all your time with your Cherry. Plus, I've been saving your brawling ass since we were twelve. It's going to be fine."

That garners a smirk. Grey taps the table, raising his brows. "Don't toot your horn too much. I'll start to think you want me to like you."

"Like me? Never. I'm a monster. A horrible sister."

"The worst." He winks. "Speaking of family, have you heard from your gold-digging mother?"

"No. I expect Vivienne will stay hidden until after my birthday. God knows she wouldn't want anyone to witness her as a degenerate parent."

Grey's shoulders shake with a laugh as I take another sip of my ginger tea.

We drift into a comfortable silence. I like it when Grey's home. This place feels as empty as it is massive when I'm here alone.

Grey reaches out, nabbing a croissant. "You're especially wicked today. Almost happy. Did you fuck another staff member? Kill a puppy? Bring down a princess somewhere to ensure your golden ticket to that fucking ball?"

I roll my eyes.

The International Debutante Ball is the most significant and prestigious introduction into society. Forty girls received invitations for consideration— an interview that narrows the list to the final chosen twenty-four. Anyone not on that list had to submit an application, along with a hundred other hopefuls, for the chance into contention. I applied.

My power comes from my associations, not my name. Everything I achieve, I claw and maim to attain.

"Please shut up. Since when are you interested in the Deb Ball?"

"Since I'm dating someone on the short list." He goes back to his paper. "You'll have to clue me in on what's expected of me. I managed out of escorting anyone until now."

Of course Donovan received an invitation. Of fucking course. I bet she was the committee's first fucking call. It's like the devil's just sitting in hell laughing at me. Cunts, both of them. There goes my good mood.

"Ask Kai. I realize my dick is typically bigger than yours, but you'll have to do your own research this time."

He coughs, slapping his chest. "Jesus, Caroline. Do you have an off switch?"

My lips thin before I slap my palms down on the table. "You should stop making everything about you. First, with my birthday. And now with the Deb thing."

He could at least pretend to be contrite. But he's Grey.

My eyes narrow. "I'm going to need some fawning and petting right about now. And make it good."

Grey laughs, shaking his head, "That's more of a Liam job. I'm the asshole brother, remember?"

Just the mention of Liam's name shuts my mouth. Liam and I haven't spoken since last week—when I eavesdropped on him. I know he's mad that I schemed, that I hurt Grey and Donovan. I bet that a tiny bit of Liam even blames me for being the loser in the Donovan games.

And he'd be right too. Who knows how much longer it would've taken her to see what we all saw—it may have been long enough for Donovan to fall just a little bit deeper for Liam.

The thought makes me sick.

Liam and I have been many things to each other over the years, but we've always been something to each other—crushes, bullies, allies, friends, but never enemies. Naively I thought he'd forgive me the moment I apologized, but I'm still waiting.

"I said I was sorry, Liam. For fuck's sake, I brought the fucking cherry for Grey to top. Shouldn't that count for something?"

"No. Sweeping up the ashes doesn't erase the fact that you set it all on fire."

I don't mean to be myself so often, but of all people, he knows that. Grey looks up from the attack on his food, noticing my silence.

"You two haven't made up?"

Where the fuck have you been? Oh, wait—inside Donovan.

"I thought he was your best friend. Why are you asking me?"

The clink of the fork has me avoiding the glare that I can feel burrowing into my skull.

"Caroline. Look at me."

I do, and he nods for me to keep talking. I stand, dropping my napkin down next to my plate.

"If you want to ride in my car, then I'd finish your food, Grey. I'm leaving."

He pulls his phone out and begins texting, and my panic sets in. My hand darts out, swatting at him.

"Don't you dare text Liam."

Grey draws back, tensing his jaw, and shoves his phone inside the front pocket of his blazer. Pushing from the table, he stands to his full height and looks down at me. It's intimidating, but I'm not intimidated.

"I texted Cherry about your party this weekend, Caroline."

I swallow, feeling exposed and stupid. Grey steps closer to me, looking me up and down. "Did you eat today?"

My lips press together, securing my silence. I hate how easily Grey slides inside my head. He raises an expectant brow, so I speak.

"Why are you so concerned about my eating habits?"

I turn away, grabbing my Birkin from the chair adjacent to me. Grey's words are spoken to my back, but they hit just as hard.

"Because I know when you feel—anything—you actively seek out your own demise. Now, answer my question."

I spin around, smiling the fakest smile I own.

"Who the fuck bothers with feelings anymore? You're getting soft, brother. Shame, really. You were one of the greats."

Grabbing an apple off the table, I wave it at him. "Leave the heavy lifting of my baggage to my therapist."

I walk away, knowing he's behind me, but I won't look back. The last thing I want anyone to know is that Liam makes me feel. I make my way out to the waiting limo and climb in, Grey doing the same. As he does, my phone buzzes—Laura. Thank fuck.

"Hi, Laura."

After what I said to her last week and making her stay home, she's been calling me daily, and I haven't been a dick. That's not to say that I'm warm. But I wish I got credit for the things I don't say because those might put me in the running for fucking sainthood.

"Hey," she breathes. "I know you're on your way, but you're never going to believe what I just heard."

She pauses for dramatic effect.

I look out of the window and cross my black-tight-adorned legs.

"I can't decide until you tell me."

"Right. So, do you remember Hunter? Hot lacrosse player at St. Simeon? He basically followed you around that whole party last summer."

A vision of a guy we met at some party in the Hamptons comes to mind, and I nod. "I think so…dark hair, sexy brown eyes, killer body."

"Thank you." Grey smirks to himself, staring at his phone. "Perfect description of me."

"Crazy small dick energy—" I add.

"Definitely not me, then," he answers again, not looking up.

"Hold, Laura." I pull the phone away from my mouth and look at Grey. "Please shut up, narcissist. Not everything is about you, remember?"

He grins, reaching into his pocket and producing one of his signature smokes, and rolls down the window, looking like some Ralph Lauren model depicting the rich and famous.

"If you say so," rolls off Grey's lips with an exhale of smoke.

There was a tiny moment when I tried to ruin our parents' marriage by offering myself up on a silver platter, but it wasn't well thought out. I wasn't even attracted to Grey. I hadn't even fucked anyone then, just had the reputation—thanks to some piece of shit freshman year.

He got his later. I made sure of it.

Moments like this make me glad I didn't ruin the marriage because then I'd never have *this* brother. Because not just any idiot would've done.

I wave him off, turning back to my conversation.

"Continue, Laura."

She goes into a whole story about Hunter taking some girl's virginity, giving her crabs and a possible bun in the oven, blah, blah. I listen, not really surprised, just happy to escape from another conversation with Grey about Liam.

"Honestly, it reminds me of a certain guy we both know."

She whispers *Liam Brooks* the way people whisper terrible maladies before adding, "Obviously minus the crabs and baby, but like the whole being an overall manwhore with girls lining up part—amiright?"

I swear I can't escape him today.

"I have to go." My words are curt, and I don't care.

I fucking can't with his goddamn name right now. I hate that I want Liam's forgiveness, that it even matters to me. But it does, and he does. He never stopped since the day my pride met his prejudice.

"Wait. You need to hear the point."

I exhale heavily, "Get to it, Laura."

I snap for Grey to give me a cigarette, but he shakes his head no, so I flip him off. Laura clears her throat aggressively, and I wince. I hate when she does that.

"Hunter fucked one Tiffany Astor, and everyone is talking about it. I heard the story is going to run tomorrow on Page Six. She can say goodbye to an invitation to the Debs. That girl was a shoo-in. She ticked off every box, but this scandal will make her a human plague."

I'm silent, thinking a mile a minute.

"Care. Do you know what that means?"

A chance to have something people like Donovan take for granted? A permanent place at the table? Silencing my fucking mother? All of the above.

"Don't jinx it by saying it out loud. I'm going to go. I'll see you in a minute."

Laura goes silent, then says, "Okay. Meet at the front steps?"

"As always."

I hang up the phone, smiling from ear to ear.

Grey locks his hands behind his head after tossing the barely smoked cigarette out of the window.

"A smile. Do tell, what made this miracle happen?"

I shrug, stretching my arms in front of me before placing my hands on my knees.

"Oh nothing, just slaying princesses."

Grey barks out a laugh. "Fucking Deb season. Blood in the water is an understatement."

Chapter Four

Caroline
Past—eleven years old

Sunshine dances through a slit between two airy cathedral drapes that hang along the sunroom wall. I like that they're sheer because they're always closed, giving only a glimpse of what's hiding behind them. On the other side is the garden patio, where blooming rosebushes and perfectly trimmed green shrubs create my very own secret garden.

Julia, my nanny, and the girl that stays too long in my father's office, slicks my hair back with her palms, neatening the ponytail on my head.

"Stop fussing over me," I snap, swatting her hand. "It's annoying. I'm not three years old."

Julia looks nervous. Her eyes dart toward the doorway, opting to smooth the shoulders of my garnet Fendi tea dress. It's my favorite because the color on me always makes my mother happy.

"Miss Caroline. Your mother was clear. You are to accompany them to the Plaza for brunch, and she wants you 'impeccably' dressed. They're meeting an 'important family,' and as you know, social circles are critical in Manhattan society. So you need to make a good impression."

My eyes roll involuntarily. The only time they include me in their plans is when we need to look like a real family. Otherwise, I'd be a living, breathing version of *Home Alone*.

"Here's a bright side. They have a daughter your age," she offers.

I slap at Julia's hand again, forcing her to take a step back. "I said, stop it."

"Please cooperate, Miss Caroline."

"Why should I—" My indignation is silenced by the sound of my mother's heels clicking against the imported Italian marble.

Julia and I both look toward the sound's direction just as Vivienne Rycroft Whitmore turns the corner. Her presence immediately sucks all the air from the room. My mother is beautiful, with modelesque jet-black hair and a body just as enviable, and she knows it.

When she was fifteen, she moved from Paris without a dime or a purpose, and now she lives in one of the largest mansions on the Upper East Side, married to one of the wealthiest men in the world. But unlike the orchid Cavalli dress she's wearing, she'll always feel like a fake, and I get to pay the price for her insecurities.

Her discerning eyes drift over my outfit. "Caroline." Then they drop to my shoes. "Ballet flats? Surely you have something with a heel. A lift will help you to look slimmer."

She bought me these flats last week as a reward for losing three pounds.

"Julia, I thought I was clear. First impressions are important today. Shall I interview new help? Or are you only ineffective for me? *Salope stupide.*" *Stupid bitch.*

"No, ma'am. I apologize."

"Fix it. We leave in ten minutes. I won't wait a minute longer."

"Yes, ma'am."

My mother turns her back to me as Julia grips my hand too hard and jerks me toward the stairs. I pull back, but she doesn't let go, trudging up the side stairs, towing me behind in silence.

"Ow. Let me go," I gripe as we land at the top of the staircase and walk down the hall toward my bedroom suite.

Her head shifts over her shoulder—"Shh"—as she opens my French Louis XV hand-painted bedroom doors, ushering me in and closing them behind us. Julia dashes into my closet, vanishing for a moment before reappearing with black Mary Janes that have a small heel. I despise those shoes.

"I don't want to wear those. They're uncomfortable. I don't think they fit anymore."

I lift my hands to the end of my ponytail. It still feels dry from the bleach used to make it blonde. My mother said the new color would give my skin the warmth that I was lacking. I hop up onto my bed, lying back onto the soft cashmere throw, and look at the underside of my canopy.

"Caroline. You have to put them on," Julia insists, holding them out as I lift my gaze, but I scowl, shaking my head.

"No, Julia. Choose another."

Julia grabs my foot, but I kick them loose, sitting up.

"Quit it," she snaps, gripping my ankle, her long nails digging in.

"Ow. You're hurting me. Stop," I yell, but Julia ignores me, lying over my lap to hold my legs still as she pulls off one of my flats. She's murmuring to herself as I struggle underneath her. "I'm not going to lose my job over this, you entitled little shit. Fuck your ballet flats."

My eyes grow wide as she shoves the shoe on, fastening the strap over my foot. I've never heard anyone speak so crudely. My lips quietly mouth the word *fuck*, trying it on for size, unable to stop it from bouncing around in my head.

In the scuffle, she'd dropped the other Mary Jane, so she leans over and grabs it before pulling at my other shoe. My hands push against her shoulders as vicious words hurl from my lips.

"I'm telling my father. And not even extra time in his office will save your job."

The words barely leave my lips before a sting scorches my face—Julia's hand connecting with my cheek. I reach for my hot skin, tears welling in my eyes instantly as I stare at her.

"Put the damn shoes on, or next time I'll really make it hurt."

***

My feet hurt. They hurt the whole ride over to the Plaza and all the time we've been seated. Because they're squeezed into shoes that don't fit anymore. But at least there's a heel.

I didn't say anything when I came back downstairs. Truth is, I don't think anyone would've believed me, or even if they did, I would've been ignored because they wouldn't want to lose Julia.

"Sit up straight," my mother whispers even though I am. "And don't forget to smile. When you don't smile, your jaw looks full, and you look less pretty."

The corners of my mouth lift obediently. My mother stands alongside my father as the guests my parents are entertaining for brunch approach the table. I didn't bother to listen to the whys for our lunch because it's always business.

I look up, watching as the seemingly happy family stops in front of our table. A girl that looks my age stands just behind her father in a white knee-length tank dress that has little suns embroidered on the hem. The dress is almost too young for her but stylish. She's holding her father's hand with both of her own, smiling brightly, with blonde bangs almost hitting her eyelashes. She's pretty, just like her mother.

I don't look like my mother. She says I got my father's genes. I glance at him—short, portly, but refined features. I guess she's right, but Julia once told me that if I lost some more weight, I'd look just like Audrey Hepburn, and then we watched *Breakfast at Tiffany's*. Maybe that's why I didn't tell on her for the slap. She's more nice than not.

"Caroline, this is our daughter, Donovan," my father's new friend says, drawing my attention up. "I understand the two of you will be attending Dalton together next week. I'm sure she can help you acclimate. I bet it'll be a big change from your boarding school."

I nod, not forgetting to smile. "Thank you, it will, but I'm looking forward to spending more time in the city with my family. I also hear Dalton has an excellent music program."

"It does." He grins.

Donovan leans against her father, staring at me with big wide eyes—like a Disney princess. She seems nice. It might be good to have a friend at school. The girls were exceptionally cruel at my boarding school.

I'm "smart"—they hated me for it. I'm "fat"—they hated on me for that. My father's extraordinarily rich and powerful, and they had to be nice to me—for that, they made my life hell.

Donovan's father smiles down at me. "I don't think anyone would ever believe you're eleven."

"Well, I do turn twelve in a couple of months," I offer with all the charm I've learned to have.

He looks up at my parents. "What a mature, articulate young lady you have."

My mother smiles. "Yes, boarding school is wonderful. But it will be nice to have her home."

My smile doesn't falter, even though it's all a lie. She's done nothing but complain about my presence since I've been back. And I'm articulate because I haven't got any friends and spent all my time with either the headmistress or whatever tutor I was provided. They don't kick children out of boarding school for bullying. They just isolate the victim.

Donovan's still staring at me, playing with the hem of her dress. As if on pretension's cue, my mother compliments Donovan's clothing, to which Donovan replies, "It's vintage. I got it from a thrift store."

I can't help shifting my eyes to my mother to see her response. Vivienne Whitmore would never, ever be caught dead in a thrift store.

"It's so chic. Bohemian. Exquisite taste for such a young age."

Unbelievable. This must be a really important contact, like an invitation to the Met Ball contact for that kind of compliment.

Donovan shuffles her feet on the floor, and my eyes lower—ballet flats. I grin for real this time.

Everyone begins to take their seats. Donovan is ushered in next to me, taking her napkin into her lap and smiling over at me.

"Do you like them? I just got them." She smiles back at me, noticing that I was staring at her shoes.

I nod, opening my mouth to speak, when my mother cuts me off.

"Donovan, they're fabulous. Our Caroline will need a friend like you. Someone so in tune with fashion; Caroline's hopeless, really." My mother leans over toward Donovan's mother, smiling like a jackal, her French accent thick. "She insisted on wearing a pair of truly garish heels. Girls— what can you do?"

My mother laughs. Donovan's mother laughs. Everyone laughs, except for me.

I just smile, not wanting to be any less attractive than I already am.

The waiter approaches the table, quieting the cackling as our drink orders are taken. It's no surprise that my mother orders champagne. She'll have plenty more throughout the morning until she'll need a nap.

"Great," Donovan whispers as her mother requests the same. She rolls her eyes and then turns in her seat, all her attention on me. "So, what was boarding school like? Please say it was a little like *Harry Potter* but without the magic. Although the magic would make it better. Right?"

I can't speak. I'm staring at her. She's so bubbly, bright—everything I'm not. And suddenly, I feel mean.

"Mieux qu'ici." *Better than here.*

Her eyes blink, and she giggles before rubbing her glossy lips together. If Donovan asked me, instead of blankly staring at me, I'd explain that at least with the mean girls, I knew why they hated me. But at home, with my mother, the reasons change like the seasons.

"I don't speak French. I chose Mandarin." She lets out a groan. "Or my father chose it. So dumb, right? I'm never going to use it. Business is gross. I want to grow up and write a column for one of our newspapers. Or be a photographer. Or maybe a zoologist. What do you want to be?"

Oh my God. She won't stop. Is it possible to dislike someone because they're too nice?

I give a shrug and look away. I don't know why I'm mean. Maybe it's because Donovan laughed too when my mom made her critique. Or perhaps because she didn't have to do anything to gain all my mother's interest. Either way, disliking her feels better than wishing for her to be my friend.

"Donovan, what adorable bracelets," my mother coos. "Miles, your daughter is just so stunning."

My mother's voice is saccharine, and I wish I could scream. *We get it, Mother. Donovan is the daughter you've always wished for. Just take some pills and shut up.*

"Thank you." Donovan smiles, her impossibly perfect white teeth shining brightly as she fiddles with the braided string bracelets cluttered on her arm.

Something inside me snaps, and I turn toward her, reaching out and touching the clutter on her wrist.

"They're *Sweet Valley High* meets *Baby-Sitters Club* chic. Very Greenwich of you. Bold choice," I add, keeping my smile.

"Thanks?" she answers quietly with a furrowed brow, and I almost feel bad, but I bet this is the first time anyone's ever said something that isn't a five-star rating.

Our parents begin speaking, but Donovan and I sit side by side, quietly.

"Donnie," her father interjects quietly, patting her hand.

Of course he calls her a boy's name. As if anyone would ever confuse her for anything but a damn angel. Donovan smiles at her father as he points across the room, then looks at me. "The dessert cart is out if you girls would like to have the first look. It's brunch, after all. No rules."

My stomach involuntarily growls over the idea.

Donovan grabs my hand, pulling me up. "Come on. Let's go. The meringues are delicious. I could eat a hundred."

But my mother halts my movement, gently patting my stomach. "*Peut-être des fruits, petit cochon.*" *Maybe some fruit, little pig.*

I don't answer her as I walk away with Donovan, letting my smile fade now that my mother can't see me. Donovan glances at me as my hand slips from hers, and she begins playing with her dumb bracelets. "What did she say to you? You look sad."

My face stills, all the well-placed barriers I've perfected slipping into place.

"If you weren't such a primitive, maybe you'd actually speak another language, and then you'd know without having to be so nosey."

Her eyes grow wide, then narrow.

"Excuse me. You don't have to be so nasty. I was just trying to be nice."

She turns away, picking a cube of fudge to place gently on a dessert plate before looking back at me.

"That was me being polite. But you stay precious, Donnie." My finger lifts, tipping the plate and knocking the fudge onto her pristine white dress. Fuck your vintage.

Chapter Five

Liam

I walk out of my room, dressed in my uniform, head still damp, orgasm relaxing my shoulders as I trot down the hallway and toward the red-bricked chef's kitchen. Our home has a private kitchen for the staff, which has a great room attached. It's like a regular house inside our brownstone. It's also where I spend most of my time, not in my bedroom, because it has the most life.

I may have parents that resemble the most normal roles parents play, especially in this world, but they're still busy with benefits, galas, and running companies. So while they love me, in our family, it's definitely quality over quantity of time.

As soon as I enter the room, I see my mom enter the opposite end, from the main house. She's speaking animatedly on her phone, probably to the event planners. A list is handed to our private chef, Simon, before she turns to notice me. She motions with her head to the plate sitting on the island full of eggs and bacon before returning to her conversation.

"Thanks, Simon," I say to the person who actually made it.

"*Bonne nourriture pour un garçon qui grandit.*" *Good food for a growing boy.*

He knows I don't speak French, but he's been trying to teach me for years. So I respond back with the only thing that ever stuck.

"*À quelle distance est le bordel?*" *How far away is the whorehouse?*

Simon barks out a laugh, and I grab the bacon, shoving a piece in my mouth as I give a wave. My mom's pointing a finger as she snaps orders into the phone, but I sneak around the island and nab her hand, spinning her around, and plant a quick kiss on her cheek.

"Bye, killer."

"Liam, you need more than that—" she complains, covering the phone and smiling, pointing her chin at the plate. "Eat more, darling."

I give a wink as I make my getaway, holding up the other piece of bacon before descending down the staff stairs, hoping to cut past my father's office without him noticing.

He's been on my back lately about schools, expectations, and legacy. And by lately, I mean my whole life. This year, however, his lectures feel like they're on a fucking loop. I don't have it in me to have another "I know what's best for you" conversation. He's too much sometimes. There's no compromise, only what he sees for me. It's crazy that nobody ever asks my opinion about my own life.

My feet hit the bottom of the stairs like I'm walking on marshmallows. I'm moving fast but also so quietly that I could seriously become a ninja. *Be one with the floor. No sound, Liam.*

I cut around the banister so close that my jacket bunches, dragging against the newel post. I'm staring at my father's office door, and that means that now isn't the time to take any loud chances. Just in case he's home.

My shoulders ease once I'm about ten feet away, turning into the hall that leads to the foyer.

I glance over my shoulder, the side of my mouth ticking up—*Fuck yeah. I'm in the clear*—as my chin swings back toward the front doors, victorious, when something shifts out of the corner of my eye, forcing me to do a double take.

Shit.

A voice booms from the library, "Liam. I'm glad I caught you."

The mountain of a man called my father stands in the doorway wearing his signature navy crewneck sweater, monogrammed with our family crest.

I stand straighter and give a tight nod.

"Dad. I mean, sir," I say, to his immediate frown. "I didn't realize you were out of the office this morning."

I can't pinpoint when he stopped being my dad and became someone I called "sir." But that's where we are, and it feels like another burden I have to carry.

When I was ten, he took me to work with him. I remember being so excited because I couldn't wait to see what he did and sit at his colossal desk that faced the windows. Ones that had a complete view of the city. It was better than going to Disney World.

He was better.

But like every other ten-year-old, I got bored quickly and started wandering around the office floor. I got turned around and scared, even though Dad had told me to stay close, but thankfully, one of the security guards found me.

As we walked back to my dad's office, the guard showed me a framed poem by William Ernest Henley—"Invictus." It was given to my father by the staff during an anniversary party for the company they'd had months prior.

My father is esteemed, revered by everyone, and they'd given it to him out of respect for his leadership. At that moment, he became the greatest man I knew and everything I wanted to be.

He was *my* hero. That's who he'd always been for me. The one man I have to help me through life's storms—to lead me.

Until now—now it feels like we're always at war with each other, and I kind of wish I could go back and not get lost so he'd just be a man. Not a hero. Maybe then I'd have enough fucking backbone to be my own.

"Sorry, sir." My father smirks at me as my eyes dart to the door and back. "I was just heading out to school."

"This'll only take a moment. Good thing I was in the library, or I may have missed you."

He's aware that I was trying to make an escape. The amusement in his eyes is almost obnoxious.

"Your timing is impeccable."

My father steps forward, his arm landing across my shoulder as he turns and guides me into the library.

"I decided to take the day to help your mother with her benefit. And cards on the table? I figured you'd try to avoid me after our last talk, so I bested your strategy and cut you off at the pass."

I smile. "That you did. But I really am going to be late. I have to hustle to be at school on time."

"Son—"

A frustrated groan leaves me. "Seriously, Dad. I don't have time. Can't we suffer through this tonight?"

His eyebrows rise, and I add, "Sir. Would you mind if we did this tonight?" because my tone is braver than preferred.

I may be eighteen, but I know my place.

"I just wanted to say I'm proud of you."

My head pulls back, his arm dropping from me as we face each other, me totally confused. I thought this would be another conversation about my college application—not plural.

He wants Harvard. Not in a "consideration" kind of way. In a "this is where you'll go" kind of way.

But I never sent it. Even after I was ordered to do so.

It was the boldest move I've ever made against my father, even if it's a secret. Art isn't a hobby for me, and business isn't an interest. I don't want Brooks Industries. Besides, the idea of leaving the city is off the table. Vacation is one thing, but for six years—never happening.

He shifts to open the cabinet of the Wooton secretary desk he won in a Christie's auction in London last year, rummaging around for a moment before shutting the door again. When he turns around, he's looking down, gently tapping an envelope against his fingers. My heart starts racing as I register what it is. His eyes lock to mine, and he extends the crimson envelope with pride on his face.

My soul leaves my body. There's no way.

"Go on. Take it, Liam."

Hesitantly, I reach out, looking down at the envelope with its neat writing addressed to me. It's actually handwritten. I've heard of these—a legacy acceptance letter. Harvard only sends these to the most compelling early admissions.

People like me.

But I wasn't supposed to receive one because I never fucking mailed my application. Dread pulses through my system. I try to swallow, but my throat is the goddamn Sahara.

"How—" My eyes lift to his.

He doesn't even look guilty.

"Mail's lost all the time, Liam. Did you really think your stunt would stop this from happening? The dean of admissions, John, is an old friend and was more than happy to look at your records. You're a Brooks, son. Apparently, that means something to everyone but you."

I only needed a couple of weeks. All my pieces would've been done. I could've submitted to the Columbia art department and been able to present a similar letter to my father—with the exception being that it would've been something I want.

Fuck. Fuck. Fuck.

Say something, you pussy. Tell him no. Say fuck off. Scream. Anything.

I stare down at the envelope in my hand. My future is so intricately detailed and planned, like the calligraphy used in the address.

"So this is it."

Those are the words I choose to speak. And they barely make it out of my mouth before I'm bounding toward the front door.

"Liam," my father calls out, following me. "I know you harbored a wish for something art-related, but I thought seeing this…Liam, stop—"

But I don't stop. Not until I'm sliding into the back of the black town car and slamming the door shut. We pull into traffic, and I chance a glance out of the window, seeing my father on the stately concrete steps that lead to the front of my home. I should've said more, stood up for myself, yelled, refused. But it was as if I couldn't even breathe.

My fist meets the leather seat next to me. "Fuck!"

I hit the seat over and over until all I'm left with is heavy breaths and a disheveled tie. I dig in my pocket for my phone, texting the familiar number.

Me: The Harvard letter came today.

Van: I thought you didn't apply…am I missing something? You trashed it, right?

Me: Yeah—what you're missing is that my dad sent it for me.

Van: Whoa. That's more of an Evan move.

Me: It's fucking over, Van. That's it. I might as well torch all the evidence.

Van: Don't you dare. I'll kill you. You've worked too hard.

She's right. I have. I'm pretty sure I've studied the likes and dislikes of the Columbia committee more than any test I've ever taken.

Me: What the fuck, Van. I'm so pissed.

Van: We need a plan b. Let's put our heads together and see what we come up with. We'll ditch and go to that ramen place you love.

Me: It's morning. Nobody eats ramen at the crack of dawn. Plus, Grey will kill you for disappearing without an explanation.

Van: Grey will survive. I'm worried about you, Brookie.

I love her for trying to make me feel better, but drowning my sorrows in Van only makes for trouble and forced explanations of why I need cheering up. I don't want either.

Me: Don't be, Van. I'll figure it out. I just need to clear my head.

Van: Promise?

Me: Pinkie.

Tossing my phone to the side, I look out of the window, wondering what it would be like to be one of the bazillion people not related to Tucker Brooks. My life would be ordinary. I could choose any school, study any major, have any kind of life. Not something preplanned and measured out for optimal success.

I should just fucking bail on college. Drop out before I begin. Good ol' Tuck would love that. Buzzing sounds off against the black leather, another message coming through. I flip my phone over, reading it.

Van: Hey, Grey just reminded me that we have Caroline's birthday this weekend. I think I was trying to forget. LOL. Let's go together! We can drown your sorrows and then reformulate whatever terrible plan you're already thinking about.

I chuckle because this girl definitely knows me.

Me: Not a chance in hell.

The phone rings. I knew it would. I hit Decline because I'm already in a foul mood, and talking about Caroline Whitmore isn't going to make me feel any better.

I should add my fucked-up morning to the plethora of reasons I have to hate Caroline.

She's the reason I fell into art. I always doodled a lot. Too much if you ask some of my middle school teachers. Something about it always helped me make sense of the world. But if it weren't for that fucking field trip to the Met in seventh grade, I may have always just been a doodler.

The car cuts over a lane, the driver lowering the privacy window to tell me we may have to take another route because of traffic. I nod, looking back out of my window, feeling suffocated by my goddamn thoughts.

People are packed onto the organized chaos, also known as the New York sidewalk, rushing to their destinations, not taking a moment to look around.

I feel like that's all I do—look around, noticing everything that everyone else ignores or misses. I can't help it. This is why my shit day is ultimately courtesy of Caroline Whitmore. I noticed her—the way Eve saw the apple and took a fucking bite.

The car slows to a stop, and I look up from my checked-out thoughts. We're stopped directly in front of the Met. *Come on.* A flag advertising a showing of paintings on loan from the Tate in London brings a frown to my face.

Of course that's the showing. Fuck traffic and fuck life's cruel jokes.

I reach into my bag for a toothpick.

Caroline was my first muse and doesn't even know it. I saw her here, at the Met, hands fastened behind her, staring at John Everett Millais's *Ophelia*. A painting on loan from the damn Tate.

She looked so small, hair pulled back by a ribbon that matched her eyes, standing so still, not at all like the other kids running around the museum during our field trip. Caroline was never like the other kids, always more of an adult in a child's body.

God, she seemed almost as immovable as the woman floating in my favorite painting. I don't think she even blinked.

Caroline's all I remember about that day.

It was that moment—me staring at her and her at that painting—that's when I was filled with this overwhelming desire to draw her. It wasn't so much desire, more like I was possessed by the need. So I did.

Looking back, I think I did it partly because she looked so pretty but mostly because it felt like I would be able to keep a piece of her.

That's when my doodles became art and a way for me to save all the details, the memories, the perfect fucking moments, forever.

I only managed half a sketch before almost getting caught by Grey, but it was enough to ensure that every painting I've ever done since has a piece of Caroline in it.

My phone vibrates, pulling me back from the memory. I smirk, swiping it and hitting the speaker.

Kai's deep bass vibrates through the phone, making me actually smile.
"Bitch ass."

Music's playing in the background, loud enough that he's talking over it.

"What's up is that I was just booked by the Good Room for Sunday—which officially makes me the coolest person you know. That place is a whole experience. It's gonna be a perfect after-the-party party."

Kai's started making a name for himself over the last few months, which is cool because we get to go to dope-ass parties but even cooler because he's good at it. All my best playlists are curated by him.

"Sweet. Celebrity kid DJ looks good on you, man. Mark me down with a plus-one."

"Plus-one? I'm proud. Who says second place has to lose?"

He's joking—*maybe*. Either way, I shake my head, grinning.

"Fuck you."

His horn blares as he yells expletives before coming back to our conversation, laughing. "Come on, Duckie. Don't get mad."

"Who the fuck is Duckie?"

He chuckles. "*Pretty in Pink*—the skinny boy in wingtips obsessed with the redhead, where he waits for her to figure out she likes him too. That's you with Donovan."

My shoulders shake. I'm going to kick Kai's ass when I get to school. I look up to see my car pulling through the Hillcrest gates and smile.

"I'm gonna take a hard pass on that reputation. Fuck that. And, you know, the joke's not funny if you have to explain it. I'm disappointed in you."

"Well, I have to save all my good material for the girls—they're smarter."

"You're an asshole. Just for that, I'm ghosting. And I'm gonna buy all the tickets so that you have to sit and spin by yourself."

He barks out a laugh. "Stop pretending the idea of watching me deejay doesn't make you want to *come.*"

He whispers the last word in the creepiest, most suggestive way, making me tip my head back and laugh hard.

"All right, let's stop jerking around," I tease, saying the last part with a high-pitched moan. "Because I'm definitely coming."

He's still laughing as I say goodbye. Shoving my phone into my bag, I throw my arm through the strap as the car slows to a stop. Opening my own door, I give the driver a nod. My foot hits the ground, and I push out to stand, locking eyes across the pavement with Caroline Whitmore.

Damn those icy blue eyes for burning right through me and instantly making me think of my shower.

Joke's on Kai—I'll never audition for "heartsick friend" to Donovan. I already landed that role three fucking years ago, except my Molly Ringwald liked me back.

Chapter Six

Caroline

Every time Liam walks by this morning, it takes a concerted effort on my part to pretend I don't notice him. I never see him before my classes, but today he's everywhere.

His voice carries from a few lockers down, prompting the tiny baby hairs I've swept up into my tight ponytail to prickle. He's like an irritating fly buzzing around from girl to girl, making them laugh and allowing them to think they have a chance.

It's all a lie, bitches.

I suppose now that Donovan's occupied with Grey, Liam's trying to make up for lost time—gross. Why do I care? I shouldn't. We aren't friends or anything else anymore. He's making that abundantly clear with his insistence on ignoring me.

It's absurd. Liam's made up with Grey. Forgave him for his crimes against the little tart. Why still choose her side? The thought makes my skin burn. When he refused my apology outside of Grey's bedroom, I'd hoped that he'd finally be satisfied Donovan got to put me in my place.

But no, it's "I hate Caroline Whitmore" all day, every fucking day now. *Jesus, how long until he forgives me?* I'd say that like a prayer. If I thought it'd help.

My eyes drift against my better judgment, watching as he leans his shoulder against a locker and speaks to some inconsequential. I drop my gaze to that fucking toothpick and tilt my head, mirroring Liam as he cocks his own to the side.

He's beautiful—all shine and no tarnish.

A high-pitched, bubbly laugh yanks me back to reality. I'm paused, like I'm glitching, the book in my hand hovering mid-pull before I aggressively shove back inside, rattling the metal.

I swear to fucking God, if I hear one more giggle or swoony sigh over Liam's wearing-on-my-goddamned-nerves charm, I'll drive that little twat to jump off a bridge. Just. For. Fun. She won't even need thirteen reasons.

My focus returns to my locker as I let out a breath, trying to relax my shoulders. Shit. I stare at the books. I don't even remember what the hell I was doing here in the first place—*duh, trying to avoid him but being too cracked out to leave.*

Oh God. That's what I am—cracked out. My brows knit together as my lips part. I'm fucking Gollum, and Liam's my precious. I'm doomed to die in a cave on the Upper East Side, old and shriveled, obsessed over someone I can't have. He's turned me into an ugly troll.

"Good morning, gorgeous."

My shoulders jump as I'm jerked from my inner spiral. Kai hands me an espresso—thank God for small miracles—as he leans in, taking my lips between his.

"Mmm. You taste as good as you smell...Gucci?"

"Ew, poor Chanel."

I swipe my tongue over my bottom lip. "You have unicorn blood all over you."

"Beg your pardon?"

I shut my locker and turn around to face him, holding only my coffee.

"My lipstick. It's called Unicorn Blood. It's smeared on your bottom lip—"

"What a perfectly depraved name for your mouth."

I wink as Kai wraps his arm through mine, leading me down the hall. We're meandering rather than acting out my secret desire, which would be to run past Hillcrest's infamous manwhore.

Don't look at him. Don't look at him.

"How does it look on me?" Kai asks, bringing a thumb to his lip and giving me a place for my focus as we walk by.

"Stunning. Then again, your goddamn skin color makes everything look good. To be so lucky."

"Well, one of us has to be the pretty one because you've cornered the market on mean."

I shrug, giving a chuckle—not a giggle because I'm not four—as I look up at him.

Kai is striking. I noticed him the moment he set foot on campus sophomore year. Everyone did.

First of all, his mother is Oscar famous and on the cover of every fucking tabloid. Second, he's gifted with the face of an angel and a mind straight out of hell. It's the perfect pairing for his chiseled bone structure and body carved from the gods. But the most delicious attribute is the gorgeous hue of his skin. It's a caramel spotlight in a sea of preppy whitewashed legacies.

He's a breath of fresh air—and I knew we'd be best friends. Mainly because he was wearing the new Prada loafers, a smoky black eyeliner, and smelled like women's Dior perfume. And yet, so comfortable in his manhood that it was captivating. I'd never met anyone like him. Kai was so quintessentially him, unabridged, and for the second time in my life, I found that I was jealous of someone.

"Oooh," he rasps, looking over at some lacrosse players. "Did you invite Mark to your party? I was hoping he could be your present, from me, that I could share."

I ignore his gaze, looking at my glossy red nails. "Pass. His dick is small—'roids. Everyone knows that. Plus, lacrosse is so pedestrian."

"It's not the size of his stick that matters."

"Says a boy with an oar."

"Fair."

Kai's never been in any "closet," so to speak. He was bisexually proud from day one. He's also too built for any overly conservative homophobe— and there are many at Hillcrest—to fuck with.

Not that anyone would've dared, considering Grey and Liam took to him immediately. Of course, they did. Greatness is always recognized when mirrored.

Kai earned their friendship because he's audacious—always the life of the party. They respect him because he rows like a beast. And their loyalty is cemented because he understands what it's like to be someone others want to know—it's all false friendships and double-crossers behind big, bright smiles.

Except nobody gets by Kai, which is why I never leave his side. The steep edge of that thought overlooks a deep black hole. One I'm unprepared to fall down right now, so I look up at him, ready to change the subject until he beats me to the punch.

"What's got your frown lines doing overtime, gorgeous?"

I slap his hand. "Take it back. I don't have frown lines."

Kai laughs. "You do when Liam Brooks is around."

My eyes roll involuntarily.

"We aren't speaking about that. Ever. You promised."

Some time ago, when I was high and too fucked-up to care, I told Kai all about my obsession—how it began and *almost all* the gory fucking details in between. It was the truest test of our relationship.

Kai is my person, my best friend. My soul mate. He's just not the love of my life. Then again, I'm not his.

"Okay. But you can't avoid this conversa—"

My eyes snap to his, cutting him off. "Please don't make me Laura you."

"I dare you to try."

I can't help the smile that sneaks out as we stop at the fork in the hall because I never would.

"Now, bloody my mouth again, baby."

He leans in, but I draw back, thwarting his attempt to ruin my lipstick.

"Don't be cruel. How will I make it through the most boring fucking history class ever invented if I can't daydream about you sucking my face?"

"You'll survive"—I blow a kiss at him—"You can think about Mark's tiny dick."

One of his brows rises as I feel our arms slip away. He's still grinning at me, walking backward, probably thinking of a snappy comeback, as I turn, walking directly into the one person I thought I'd successfully avoided.

"Where the hell did you come from?" I gasp, surprised by the closeness of our bodies as I take a step backward.

I attempt to look less flustered than I feel by giving him a stern look before smoothing my blazer to make sure I didn't spill my coffee. Liam's all broad shoulders and a devious grin, and damn, is that keeping me anxious.

"Carebear."

"Don't call me that."

Feet shuffling next to him draw the ire behind my eyes as I dart to the familiar pile of hair and clothes Liam is draped over. The locker girl.

"What in the freshman is that under your arm?"

Liam smiles like he's taunting me. At least that's what my irritation feeds me. Hate is so handy when you need to mask disappointment. When he doesn't answer, I shift my gaze back to her. Her—the compilation of big dumb eyes, hidden by a mess of overly highlighted hair, and a school skirt rolled too many times.

I smile, motioning a finger to her skirt. "Word of advice. If they can see your ass, sweetie, they'll want anal."

She blinks back at me like a big stupid— "Jesus, you're like a deer in headlights." I snap my fingers. "What a perfect idea. Maybe I'll hit you with my car later."

Her mouth drops open before she looks up at Liam for help, but he isn't paying her any attention. He's staring at me with that damn look on his face like he's amused at my dissent. It's how he used to look at me. *Is this us, getting back to what we do—who we are?* I internally cross my fingers, hoping that it is.

Without a word, he reaches for my hand, staring down as he brushes my fingertips with his. It lasts all of a second, but it's long enough for me to forget there are other people around.

"Come on, Carebear, stop making empty threats. Everyone knows that you don't drive."

There he is.

As much as I chant "don't smile" inside my head, I do. But only a Mona Lisa. I won't give him the satisfaction of knowing he's actually funny. Where's the fun in that.

"Perfect alibi," I counter with less snark than before. His hazel eyes crease in the corners.

It's the friendliest moment we've shared in a week, and I don't want it to end. Suddenly I feel nervous, almost scared the longer we stare at each other.

Forgive me, Liam.

He tips his chin, eyes growing colder. "See ya around, Caroline."

Fuck.

Bambi wraps her arms around Liam's waist, giggling as they walk away, saying, "Why did you call her *Carebear*?"

I don't hear his answer. Not that he'd ever share the truth. The bell rings, echoing off the walls, and I look to my right and then back, only catching a glimpse of Liam with that girl, turning the corner.

Chapter Seven

Liam

I turn around, taking the body attached to my side with me, with lazy steps. It's getting harder to walk away from Caroline, so this time, I need to fucking stay gone.

Why did I have to touch Caroline's goddamn hand? Fuck me. But she was just there, in all her *her-ness*. All her beautiful, cold, exquisite elegance, holding me hostage, with each cruel jab and scowl only serving to remind me that I want her.

So I fucking brushed her hand like an idiot, and now it feels like I'm losing my goddamn mind.

"Why did you call her *Carebear*?" freshie speaks, interrupting my thoughts.

"Huh?"

Her hand squeezes my waist. "*Carebear*…you called her that."

"Oh. Um, because I do. You should go to class, Bambi."

My arm falls off her shoulder as I step out of her grasp.

"It's Amber, and I thought—" She points awkwardly down the hall.

"Do you want my number?"

With an apologetic smile, I head toward the side doors.

"You know what? You don't want mine. Trust me, I'm a dick."

My palms smack the bar on the door, throwing it open as I exit. I can't do school today. Just being in the same building with Caroline is too much. It's melodramatic, I know, but everything feels bigger when it's about her. Like all rational thought gets tossed out of the fucking window.

The air is chilly as I stalk across the commons, heading for the parking lot. I don't care if I get in trouble or my father is called. I need to breathe.

Caroline makes me feel like I'm fucking suffocating on all the shit I won't say. I can't even trust myself not to be a grade A prick to her. Fuck. The surprise on her face though, when she thought we'd accidentally bumped into each other was priceless, and I enjoyed it too much.

What the fuck is wrong with me?

I look around the parking lot, trying to remember where I parked my Ducati.

The entire morning, I made it a point to make sure Caroline saw me. It was obnoxious, even for me. But something about her breezing down the fucking hall like she owned the place, and that stupid Duckie joke, it just pissed me off. She acted like I didn't exist. As if me ignoring her wasn't eating her alive.

Of course she acted like that. I'm ignoring her, but what if she doesn't actually care. That's the thought that makes it hard to take a full breath.

I've always harbored the idea that I may not mean as much as Kai, but I still mean something. And now, I'm fucking positive that *something* feels a shit ton better than *nothing*.

"Fuck," I shout, only now remembering that I took the car in rather than driving myself.

I search the parking lot, spotting Grey's beloved little speedster. *The keys are inside—I'd put money on it.* Nobody would dare to even stand next to it, let alone steal the shit. Weaving around cars, I'm snapping my fingers, grin on my face, as I come to his car and try the door.

"Bingo."

Sliding inside, I flip the visor, and his fucking keys fall out. "The arrogance," I laugh to myself. I'm also appreciative that he's my best friend because I know he won't actually have me killed for what I'm about to do. Desperate times.

The car purrs as I turn it over, but instead of enjoying it, I tear out and leave Hillcrest in Grey's rearview. Trees streak by as I drive, probably too fast, down the entry, kicking up dust, putting as much distance between me and it as quickly as I possibly can.

***

The sun shines off the river as we walk back up the dock, sweaty from practice. I'd made it back to school just in time because the coach's wrath is never something I seek. But rowing was something I wanted to do—it always clears my head. Not as much as painting, but since one makes me think of the girl I'm trying to forget, I chose the other.

"If there's even one scratch, dick," Grey grumbles, tossing his duffle over his shoulder.

I'd run down the hill, tossing his keys to him, giving myself away, instead of leaving them in the car. It was funnier in my head.

"Calm down. I put gas in it, and I only jerked off on the passenger seat."

The truth is, I did nothing. I drove a mile down the road, parked, and lay on the hood, staring at the fucking sky and overanalyzing every fucking piece of my life. Surprisingly, I thought a lot about art and my conversation with my father since it's what kicked off my shit day.

Kai barks out a laugh, shaking his head as Grey stands staring at me. Grey slams his duffle down, ready to have my head, but I can't stop smiling. He's so uptight.

Backing away, I toss more gasoline on the fire. "Dude, you left the keys inside—it was begging to get stolen; at least I returned it. But cards on the table? I may have hit the parking block, but I'm sure it'll buff out."

"You're going in," he shouts, pointing at the river.

Shit. Grey starts off toward me, but Kai tries to block him, unsuccessfully, because he's hot on my six. I dart over the planks to the grass, laughing.

"Run, bitch. Or you're getting drowned."

I'm hauling ass up the hill, Grey on my heels, as I spot Van coming down from the stump. Before she can say anything, I wrap an arm around her waist. I hoist her up in front of me, using her as a shield.

"Time-out. Time-out."

"Liam," she screams, gripping my arms.

"Take one for the team, Van. Your boy's crazy."

Grey stops, breathing hard, looking over at the water and back to us. "Time-out? What are you, six? Cherry won't save you. I'll throw her in too."

She kicks her feet out in front of her. "Don't you dare, Grey McCallister. He stole your car. Not me."

My eyes grow wide with amusement.

"Traitor. I should've known you'd tell on me," I laugh. "For your information, I put gas in it and returned it back in perfect condition."

Grey crosses his arms and looks at Donovan. "So the plot thickens… you knew he stole my car? And didn't tell me?"

She squeals in my arms, covering her face. My shoulders shake, as do Grey's because she's caught in the act. Donovan must've texted me a hundred times once I didn't show up at lunch, so I'd told her I needed some time to clear my head, and then I sent her a selfie of me in Grey's car.

Kai's caught up and comes to stand next to Grey. "Well, it seems your Cherry has decided to turn on both her boys today." He wags his finger at her. "Donovan, you've been a naughty girl."

She sticks her tongue out at Kai, and I heave her up, adjusting her, making her giggle again.

"Question is—what do we do with the turncoat?" I tease, feeling a pinch on my arm. "Ow. First, you withhold evidence and now assault. We should call the cops."

Grey closes the distance, and she puts her hands over her eyes, trying to wiggle out of my arms. He stands over her and removes them from hiding herself, shaking his head. Kai smirks at me because we both know

Grey is about to fuck with her.

"There's really only one thing we can do," Grey offers in a severe tone.

"What does that mean?" she whispers as I set her on the ground, caged in between us.

Her face shifts between Grey and me, landing on mine.

"What happened to ride or die?"

I give her a wink before, "I ride, you die. You're a good swimmer, right?"

"Liam—"

Grey grabs her waist, but she breaks free, running, and he chases. Kai and I laugh, watching as she screams, and Grey follows, much slower. He's not going to actually throw her in, but it's funny to watch her freak out.

"Hey"—Kai smacks my arm—"I heard you made a big impression on some freshman meat today."

"How the hell do you know about that?" I laugh.

He gives me a look. "How do you think?"

I don't want to think about it.

"It was nothing. Just some fun. I don't even remember her name."

Kai looks over my shoulder, and my gaze follows, locking on Caroline standing with a few of her lackeys.

"Speak of my little devil," he says. "I'll see ya tomorrow, dude. Oh, and bring your no-name freshman on Sunday."

We slap a hand, bumping shoulders as I smile. "Never happening. But when were you going to tell me it's all the way in Brooklyn?"

I'd figured that tidbit out when I googled the venue, wasting time this afternoon.

"Live a little, Brooks. Chicks over the bridge give good head"—he shrugs—"at least the ones that Caroline shares do."

I chuckle. But it's not funny. I hate that Kai shares her. If I can't have her, he should monopolize her time and body.

Kai walks away, and despite my better judgment, I watch them. He comes to stand in front of the concrete ledge she's standing by, hands gripping her waist, lowering her down for a kiss.

It never gets easier seeing *anyone* with her, but when that anyone is

Kai, it makes me feel like a shit friend because I all but shoved her into his arms. I start off back to the dock to grab my bag, passing Grey and Donovan, who are almost dry humping, hiding over by the bank.

Good luck staying incognito.

"Get a room," I shout, answered by Grey's middle finger.

My shit is scattered on the ground from when I dropped and ran, so I bend down, scooping it up, as I glance again over at Caroline, watching her smile and laugh at something Kai's said.

She's pretty when she smiles, not that I get to see it much. When we were kids, she never really smiled, and on the rarest of occasions when it happened, it was definitely never aimed at me—*except once.*

I shove my shit inside of my duffle, grimacing over the memory.

Once we got older, there was a time when smiling was all she ever did when she looked at me. I still haven't found anything that rivals that feeling—being a person Caroline smiles at. But being that close to the sun never lasts unless you want to get burned, and with Caroline, I was fucking scorched.

Over the last year, those burn marks left us in this weird place where we took as many jabs as we played nice—but the nice, that was really fucking spectacular. Until Donovan showed up, and then Caroline was all blows to the head.

My eyes obediently seek out my desire, seeing her staring at me this time. She's rubbing that damn scar on her wrist, chewing her lip. *Fuck you for looking contrite—as if that's something you'd have the fucking audacity to feel.*

I look away, shoving the sweatshirt into my bag harder. Goddamn her. She's fucking selfish, mean, cunning, and ruthless. She doesn't deserve my forgiveness for almost turning my best friends against me or treating me like shit like I didn't matter. *To her—like I didn't matter to her.* I stamp the goddamn voice out of my head, blowing out a heavy breath.

Fuck her.

Ethan's voice comes from behind me. "Hey, what's up, Brooks?" He scoops up my towel and tosses it to me.

"Hey," I offer, unable to stay away from her fucking face.

"Coach was pissed that you skipped classes but showed to practice, but I smoothed it over."

My head shoots back to his. "And how would he know that, Ethan? Unless someone ratted."

It was probably him.

Before he can answer, Grey and Donovan join us.

"What's up, E," Grey says, letting go of Donovan's hand.

That's fucking torture for him. If it were me, I'd—*I'd what? Fucking nothing.* I'd watch the girl I was obsessed with date my friend because I'm a fucking idiot.

My train of thought pauses because Caroline's still staring over at me. I know because I'm doing the same, like a dick. *Stop.*

Goddammit, this girl's fucking with my head. Why can't I just stop looking at her? It's gotta be that song and the fucking shower from this morning. It's still lingering in my mind and messing with me. That's why. Gotta be.

Patting the pockets of my sweatpants, I pull my phone out of my pocket and scroll through my playlist.

I'm going to fix this shit right now.

I hear words being said around me, but I'm on a mission. "Sex and Candy"—delete. "Bloody Valentine"—delete. "Do I Wanna Know"—delete. "2002"—delete. "Driver's License"—delete. And fuck you, Taylor Swift—all of it, delete, delete, delete.

"What the hell is Brooks doing?"

I glance up, hearing my name, as Van peeks over at my phone. "Looks like he's cleaning out his playlist. Also—T Swift? I'm impressed, Brookie."

"So lame. That's chick music." Ethan laughs until I look up.

I shake my head. "Taylor's hot and a dope musician. Don't hate on excellent women, E. This is why nobody touches your wiener."

Ethan flips me off. "Plenty of girls have touched my dick."

Van coughs, surprised, and Grey looks irritated as fuck.

Ethan looks at her and grimaces. "Sorry, Van."

"Watch your mouth," Grey growls. "Nobody needs to hear about your wiener. Have some fucking manners."

"Stop calling it that," Ethan complains, looking between us.

It's too easy. My lips tip up, enjoying fucking with Ethan. As our coxswain, he's boss, but off the river, we even the score—all the time.

"But E," I interject, "wiener's the name for small penises. I don't make the rules. Look at it this way, maybe one day you'll grow into it, and then you'll be proportioned."

Van giggles, reaching out to slap my arm, but Ethan looks to Grey for back up, holding up a protesting hand.

"Seriously. No help here, Grey?"

Grey crosses his arms over his chest. "Don't look at me. It's your father's fault your dick is small. But I can help with music deficiency. *1989*'s on my playlist. I'll have Coach add it to our workout track tomorrow—that way, you can learn to appreciate Taylor."

"You guys are assholes. You know that?"

Grey and I grin at each other before I go back to deleting all the music on my fucking phone.

"Speaking of Coach," Ethan segues, "why were you over in the East Hall this morning, Brooks? Isn't your third-period class on the other side of campus?"

So he is the one that ratted about me ditching. Asshole. I don't answer.

"Uh, okay, good talk," he throws out, turning his attention away from me.

This is so dumb, I think to myself. I can't erase all of it, and let's be real, a stupid old-ass song isn't what coerces me into jerking off to Caroline Whitmore. If I delete anything, it needs to be my memory.

"So what time are we all hitting up Caroline's party?" Ethan questions Donovan.

Come the fuck on.

He nudges my shoulder as he continues. "Did you see she's trending on Twitter? This party is going to be epic."

I exhale harshly, looking up, brows knitted together, irritated that I can't just erase this fucking conversation.

"We had to relocate. There's a leak in the ceiling of Trig."

"Huh?"

"Why I was in the East Hall this morning. You asked, and I'm answering."

Ethan nods, thrown off by my change of subject. I can feel Van staring at me. That girl can read my mood from a mile away. Luckily for me, I'm positive she's worried about my conversation with my father and thinks I feel the same. I'll never correct her. I don't need the Donovan-sized headache that would come with an admission of my thoughts or the ten thousand plus questions Grey would have.

Because my friendships are complicated, and I'm a coward.

"Dude, you know what's above your Trig class?" When no one answers, Ethan starts to laugh. "The men's bathroom. How funny would it be if Mr. Issacs were teaching and the ceiling broke open and doused him in shit?"

"He'd deserve it. Class is boring as fuck," I mumble over the joint laughter from Grey and Van.

With a grin on my face, I look out of the side of my eye, sneaking another peek, getting a full view of Caroline's perfect ass. There's definitely no looking away now. *Damn you, hormones.*

"Liam? Hello? Earth to Liam."

I jerk my eyes away but not fast enough because Ethan says, "Oh shit," then starts laughing.

His gaze followed the line of mine.

"Were you just checking out Caroline?" His laughter builds. "I'd watch out. She might freeze your dick off. I mean, no offense, Grey, but your stepsister is an ice queen."

Ethan bristles as I tense my jaw.

"What the fuck did you just say?" Grey's already got a hand on my chest, but I'm pushing forward. "Repeat it. I fucking dare you. And then we'll see how far I can toss your ass."

Ethan holds his hands up by his face, stepping backward. "Whoa, Liam. No hate, man. It was a joke—obviously, a bad one. I'm sorry. I didn't know you guys were hooking up."

Yeah, you fucking idiot, he didn't know you two were hooking up because you aren't. Get it together.

I swallow hard, forcing myself to cool, pushing Grey's hand from me.

"I'm fine. And we're not. Caroline doesn't mean shit to me, but show some fucking respect. That's Grey's family."

Ethan looks sheepishly to Grey, who's staring at me. Fuck, this is all I need. Grey's head swivels to retrack my gaze. He's not so sure I wasn't looking either. I look back at my phone, feigning nonchalance, hoping everyone buys it.

Whatever Grey's debating doesn't seem to stick because he turns to Ethan, saying, "E, I'd listen to Liam's advice, or next time I won't hold him back."

Damn. That was too close for comfort.

Van's raspy voice interjects, "Yeah, and don't talk about girls like that. It's a bad look, Ethan. Plus, we don't hate Caroline." I look up from the screen, right at Van.

It's the way she says it, like an accusation, that makes my eyes dart away. She keeps her eyes on me, picking at her bracelets. "Do we, Liam?"

Fuck this. Sliding my phone into my pocket, I give Grey a nod.

"I'm out. I've got some pressing business."

He smirks when I motion to a random flock of girls sitting by the stump. I give Van a wink, hauling my duffle over my shoulder, and pat Ethan's back a little harder than I should before popping a toothpick between my teeth and making a chill goddamn getaway—picture-perfect reputation in place.

The irony is it's a reputation that makes Caroline hate me but also lets me hide in plain fucking sight.

Chapter Eight

Liam
Past—twelve years old

Grey: You awake?

Liam: Yeah. Did you see?

Grey: Yeah. All her socials are gone.

Liam: Her number is disconnected too. They probably took her phone.

Grey: I don't care. She'll be back.

Liam: Dude. Van's gone.

Grey: Shut up. I mean it.

Liam: I'm scared we aren't going to see her again.

Grey: I know. But she has to come back. She just has to.

Liam: Don't tell anyone, k, but I can't stop crying. And don't call me a pussy.

Grey: You aren't. I won't.

Liam: The messed-up part is she would know how to

make us feel better. You know what I mean?

Grey: …..

Grey: …..

Grey: I don't want to talk about her anymore. Can we just not for a while? It hurts too much, Liam.

Liam: Yeah.

Grey: Yeah.

Liam: But we won't stop missing her.

Grey: Never.

***

"Mr. McCallister, please sit down."

Aw shit. Here we go. I grip the front of my desk, pulling myself forward onto my forearms as I look up to where Grey is standing in the middle of the aisle. He's so mad—madder than Mr. Green for sure.

"No. Put it back where it goes," Grey grits out, stabbing his finger to where Donovan's desk used to be. His voice cracks a little, but he doesn't care.

I get it. I felt the same way. The minute I walked into the room and saw the empty space where her desk used to be. It hurt so badly.

"Mr. McCallister, sit down."

Grey shakes his head. "No. Put it back where it belongs, and then you can teach."

Mr. Green's hand slams down on his large oak desk, making the girl's shoulders in front of me jump. I feel nervous, not scared but amped up, as my eyes switch between Grey and our teacher.

"Mr. McCallister, you will be seated, or you'll see the headmaster and be suspended. Your choice, boy."

The room is dead silent, watching the stand-off, but I already know what Grey'll choose.

"Just sit, Grey. It's not worth being suspended," some girl whispers.

I can see Grey's hands balled into fists, and I know there's no coming back. If they don't put that damn desk where it belongs, he'll go crazy.

There's no way Grey will sit in this room for hours with the reminder that we lost her. He's not like me. He can't compromise, sacrifice, or accept defeat.

Right now, for Grey, it's about the desk—because it was hers and she's ours. And they can't just erase her.

Paul, a dumbass new kid that's seated across from Grey, whispers, "McCallister, just sit down. Who cares about Donovan Kennedy? She's gone. Get over it. There are plenty of other girls for you to obsess over. This is dumb."

Instinctively I reach forward for Grey, but I'm bound by my desk. Doesn't matter because he's already on top of that dumbass, slamming his fist into Paul's face. Fuck that kid. He deserves it. The room breaks out in pandemonium. Books falling to the floor, and girls squealing as boys begin to chant, *"Fight, fight."*

More clamoring happens when Paul tries to swing back. Kids begin standing on their chairs to watch the beatdown from a better vantage point, but I've already scrambled out of my desk, closing the distance, and wrap my arms around Grey before I strain to pull him backward.

"Dude. Chill."

Grey struggles back toward Paul, spit flying from his mouth as he groans so hard his voice breaks again, but I yell in his ear.

"Quit it, Grey. Enough, dude. Enough."

Paul's bloody nose invades my vision, the rich red color smeared over his face mixing with the darkening eye that will eventually turn purple. He's already muttering about telling his father while trying to wipe his tears. Pussy. I should let Grey go and watch as he makes the other eye black. But I don't. I keep tugging backward, giving enough distance for Grey to chill out.

Mr. Green's voice is loud, cutting through the adrenaline buzzing in my ears, reprimanding the students before directing his words at Grey and me. "You two are a disgrace to this school. Grey McCallister. You're out. For good. Get out now, or I'll happily throw you out."

He steps forward angrily as Grey shoves me off, but I insert myself in between them, holding up my hands. I don't even know what I'm doing, but it's an instinct. I can't leave him alone in this.

"One more step and I'll call my father."

My chest rises and falls too fast as I try to catch my breath. I'm willing myself to look brave, worried I'm failing.

Mr. Green's reddened face glares down at me like a bull. My insides are shaking underneath all my contrived confidence because I've never spoken to a teacher this way. That's Grey's job. I'm the "good" one.

Mr. Green's jaw is tensed as he crosses his arms, making his muscles look bigger than they are, but I stand my ground.

"Stand aside."

I don't.

"Mr. Brooks, I said to stand aside."

"Respectfully, sir, you'll lose your position here if I do."

His eyes harden, and I suddenly feel as if this is one of those defining moments. The kind that lets you try on manhood before you're actually there. My dad tells me about moments like this all the time—the ones that will decide who I'll become as a man. I guess I thought they'd all happen later.

"Are you threatening me?" he sneers.

I stare back, swallowing, hoping to produce some spit for my dry throat. It is a threat. One I'm not sure I can back up, but one that's still a possibility. My father, unlike Grey's, cares about me. He can be strict and bossy, but he'd never tolerate anyone calling his son a disgrace. Not when our last name's stamped on the bricks the city is built on. I take a deep breath and glance back at Grey, who hasn't stopped looking at the empty space where Donovan sat.

"No, sir. Just stating the facts. But that doesn't have to happen. Grey will go to the headmaster. He'll take his suspension, but you'll put the desk back. And keep it there. Empty."

The silence stretches out for an unbearable wait until Mr. Green nods, saying, "Escort him to the office before I change my mind."

"Yes, sir."

Instant relief floods my body.

Mr. Green turns his back to us, quieting the students again, and I motion for Grey to get his bag as he nods, retucking the bottom of his shirt. I grab my own bag, just in case I'm getting in trouble too, before my attention turns back to Paul, who's waving his hand in the air.

"What about my nose? Grey should be expelled. There's a zero-tolerance policy at this school."

I'm going to kill that kid myself.

Caroline Whitmore—Van's archnemesis and the girl with a mean tongue but beautiful icy blue eyes—jerks his hand back down, hissing her words.

"You deserved it, you whiny baby. Now shut up before I tell everyone you're on scholarship here because Daddy's a drunk and lost it all."

Paul snaps his mouth closed, looking down at his desk as she tosses him some tissues from her bag. Our eyes connect for only a moment but long enough for me to give her a small unreturned smile.

***

An hour later, I'm back in my seat. Grey was sent home, and I was given a stern warning, but it all feels like a dream. The rows of desks are arranged neatly, back to the way they were before the classroom turned into *Lord of the Flies*, and everyone is back to their tasks as if nothing ever happened.

The only difference is Grey's desk is empty, and Donovan's is back.

Heads are down, focused on the journal entries we're supposed to be writing, but I'm finished. I drew a picture instead of writing. Mr. Green never checks them, so nobody will ever know. Propping my elbow on the table, I rest my chin in my hand and think about how weird this day is.

My gaze drifts to my right, grinning as I see the bruise on Paul's cheek, and then over to Caroline. She looks up, and I dart my eyes away.

She's never seemed nice. I'm surprised that she helped us. *Whatever.* Donovan made us promise not to be friends with her, so there has to be a good reason. I chance another look, lingering this time, watching her chew on the end of her baby blue pencil.

Donovan never told us why she hated Caroline. It was enough for us that she did, no explanations needed, but right now, I kind of wish I knew. Caroline's unexpected. She's not like the other girls.

I lean sideways, reaching into my pocket, and pull out a small puffy sticker. I took it from the nurse's office without asking.

Grey and I sat there, him holding an ice pack on his knuckles, saying nothing but feeling everything. Some friends know each other well enough to know when to be quiet, or maybe I didn't have anything to offer. I wasn't going to tell him everything would be okay. That felt like a lie. So I said nothing but thought about Caroline.

I'm flipping the sticker between my fingers over and over as my head shifts to Caroline's again. Hers is down as she writes. I watch her pencil move as if it can't keep up with her thoughts. *What kind of things make her write so fast? What does she think about? Is she writing about me?*

My arm stretches out over my desk, providing a pillow for my head as I place the sticker on my desk, brushing my finger over the picture. It's a bear with two hearts on its belly—one of those Care Bears from that movie. I had a nanny who played it for me once. I remember acting like it was dumb, but I secretly liked it.

That's not why I swiped it though. Actually, I don't really know why I did it, only that I didn't want to risk being told no. I just couldn't stop staring at it.

Each time the nurse would come into the room, I was scared she was going to take the basket to the other room and give Paul his choice of a sticker since he wouldn't stop crying about his fucking bloody nose. But she never did, and the sticker sat there, all alone, in a basket full of yellow stars.

It's weird, but I kind of felt bad for it. I wondered if anyone had ever stuck their hand in the plastic basket and ignored it, opting for a star. It seemed dumb to me that nobody picked it because it was special—different, a completely unique sticker in a basket full of stars. So I shoved it in my pocket when nobody was looking.

I've never stolen anything. Ever. I have everything I've ever wanted. No need.

But even as I think it, I lift my eyes, and Caroline Whitmore is staring straight at me. Everything she's thinking written all over her face.

Like a Care Bear in a room full of stars.

Chapter Nine

Caroline

Thank fucking God it's Thursday. One more day and I can stop looking over my shoulder every three seconds. Monday's run-in with Liam set the bar for the week— really fucking low—and yet, it hasn't gotten any better.

I've done nothing but avoid him in the hall, the cafeteria, and even this shared class, but today I'm stuck. One day pretending to be sick and skip was doable, two manageable, three's pushing it. Four—forget it.

So here I sit, in World Econ, like a bundle of nerves, constantly checking the door for those hazel James Dean-y eyes to drift in.

I don't know why I'm worried though. Liam hasn't so much as looked in my direction. Whatever happened on Monday after he touched my hand felt as if bricks were stacked, creating a concrete wall between us. I hate it because that's not the Liam I know.

A high-pitched whine interrupts my thoughts.

"Miss Whitmore, could you tell us what CAGE stands for?"

Yeah, the thing I'm trapped in, unable to escape Liam Brooks.

"Yes," I answer. "It stands for culture, administration, um…" My words trail off as I notice Kai waving at me through the pane in the door. I shake my head, pulling my eyes back to the teacher's back.

What was I saying? Shit.

"Sorry, it stands for culture, administration, geography—"

My focus wanes again because Kai's pointing to the screen on his phone, tapping it over and over. For fuck's sake.

A loud tap of Mrs. Pearson's hand on the desk pulls my attention, just as she looks toward the window. But it's empty. A laugh escapes my lips, so I press them together, hoping to seem clueless. But picturing Kai ducked under the glass is making me do a poor job of hiding my smile.

Her attention turns back to me. "What's funny, Miss Whitmore? Your inability to answer the question? Because I'm not laughing. Maybe if you'd been here the last few days instead of in the nurse's office, this question wouldn't be so difficult for you."

Settle down.

"Culture, administration, geography, and economics."

"Thank you," she huffs, turning around back to the board to write my answer.

Kai's head comes back into the frame, smirking at me before he dramatically wipes his forehead like *phew.*

"Stop," I mouth.

The teacher instructs everyone to open to page 114 as I shoo Kai, but he points at me and acts like he's going to strangle me, which has me catching myself again so that I don't laugh. He's so dramatic and cute.

Kai lifts his cell again, glaring at me, and I scowl but lean down to my Louis, rifling through until I find my phone. Swiping my screen, I glance up to make sure I'm not going to get caught, then read.

KG: GET OUT HERE. NOW. We're ditching.

KG: Don't say no, or I will come in there and get you.

KG: I MEAN IT, GORGEOUS. This is NON-NEGOTIABLE.

I sit up, tucking my phone into my lap, and type back a message as incognito as I can.

Me: Calm down with the shouty caps. Go away. I have

class. You're a pest.

No sooner do I hit Send than the door handle squeaks. Oh my fucking God. If he walks in here, Mrs. Pearson will have both our heads. My arm shoots up as I cough into my fist for attention, putting on my most miserable face.

"Mrs. Pearson. Excuse me."

She looks over her shoulder midsentence. "Let me guess, Miss Whitmore. You don't feel well. Again."

I lower my hand and nod, trying to ignore the theatrics happening on the other side of the door. Kai's flicking his tongue and being obscene, pretending to kiss someone imaginary. I hate him.

"Truly. I don't. I think it's best that I go and maybe call our family doctor. God knows what I could have. I could be contagious."

She frowns, but I'm already gathering my bag and my book in my hands. "I'll make sure to make up any work."

I'm trying to leave as if I'm feeling pitiful, but she glares at me and snaps her fingers as I walk past. My head swings over my shoulder, eyebrows raised. *Did she actually fucking snap her boney, unmanicured fingers at me?*

"This time, I want a note back, Caroline. No excuse equals no grade for today. Am I clear?"

Fantastic. I'm going to kill Kai.

"Absolutely."

I pull the door open, my eyes wide as I jerk my head for Kai to stay invisible. He ducks under the glass window as I close the door, grabbing my waist and pushing me forward.

"What the hell?" I rush out, swatting at him.

"Shh. No time to waste."

He's laughing, and it's so quiet that he seems maniacal. He is. We move another few feet from the door before he stands up to his regular sixish-foot height and wags his eyebrows.

"I could kill you, Kai. Now she wants a nurse's note."

He shrugs. "That's it? Piece of cake."

Kai grabs my hand, pulling me down the hall, the opposite way from the entrance, and I look back over my shoulder, confused. "Where the hell are we going? The exit is back that way."

He doesn't answer, dragging me behind him. We come to a door labeled Boys' Locker Room, and I jerk my hand from his.

"Are you crazy? I'm not going in there. I can only imagine the smell."

Kai chuckles, looking around the hall, and holds a finger to his mouth. "You aren't going in. I am. Be quiet and stay put. I'll be right back."

A whispered "What the fuck" is ignored as he blows me a kiss and slips behind the metal door. Oh my God. What am I doing out here, alone? My head shifts from side to side as a smile graces my face. Nobody's here to see me, so I let it bloom. He's crazy.

I cross my legs, shoving my hands inside my blazer pockets, and look down. I hope I don't get caught out here while he does God knows what in there. That's all I need—getting suspended doesn't scream *debutante*. Then again, the committee's busy with crabs and unplanned legacies.

Still, my head swings back to the door. "Come the fuck on already, Kai." I stare for seconds longer, feeling like minutes before I cave. Screw this. I'm leaving and going back to class.

I take a step forward when my ass is bumped by someone exiting the locker room. It sends me stumbling a few steps and almost hitting the ground. A strong arm hooks around my waist, saving me.

"Trouble standing?"

I right myself and wiggle free, recognizing the familiar voice. "You almost killed me. Who walks through a door so aggressively?"

Grey laughs. "Shut up. What are you doing out here? Trolling around the boys' locker room? Don't you have class?"

"Don't you?" I counter.

He crosses his arms. "No. Free period. I was working out."

Of course you were.

I straighten my jacket. "Well, if you need to know, I'm waiting for Kai."

As I say it, the door behind Grey swings open, and I lift my hand to point out Kai, but I'm not that lucky. Fuck my life.

Liam's pushing through, shirt half over his head, school blazer in hand. His tan, bare chest is on display. His head pops through the top as his stormy eyes land on mine. Time slows to a snail's pace, and I suddenly feel cornered.

I look away, trying to pretend to be unaffected, but I'm having trouble counting all the ways my stomach is flipping. Liam tugs the T-shirt down over his perfectly defined chest and comes to stand next to Grey.

It's almost too much.

"Okay, byeee. You don't want to be any later," I snark, even though Grey just told me it was his free period.

Grey doesn't answer. He's too busy looking at his phone, engrossed in what is probably his seven hundredth message to Donovan. Just as I start to snap on my fake brother, he looks up.

"Start times are a suggestion, Caroline. We saw Kai inside. I was fucking with you. He told us to make sure you don't chicken out. Whatever that means. We'll wait."

Great. Lucky me. I glance up at Liam, who's staring at me with a hint of a smirk on his face, and it infuriates me. Don't fucking turn that arrogant grin at me when you act like you hate me.

"Can I help you?"

He jerks his head. "Yeah, move. Like you said, I'm late for class. Grey can wait with you. I don't babysit."

Move? I look around and back to him—eyebrows hitting the ceiling. There's an entire empty hall, but he wants me to step aside for him?

"Walk around."

He makes no attempt to move, but neither do I.

Grey chuckles, turning his attention back to his phone. "When are you two going to make up?"

Neither of us answers. We're in a game of chicken, staring at each other until the other breaks. Liam tugs his blazer over his defined shoulders, tilting his head from side to side as he straightens it.

I stare.

Sweeping my long locks over my shoulder, I lick my lips.

He stares.

I'm not breaking first, asshole.

Grey pockets his phone, letting out a breath. "Fix this shit between the two of you. It's inconvenient for me."

Footsteps sound as Grey walks away, mumbling about making a call and giving us the space to have a conversation. Not that I expect we will. Liam has so much contempt for me, and I'm trying to be patient, do the time I deserve, but he needs to get over it already.

I won't keep apologizing—okay, maybe I will, but he shouldn't keep making me. A small voice inside of me speaks the words I'm terrified of— that even if I keep apologizing, he'll never really forgive me.

I'm searching his face for any sign of the boy I know as he glares at me.

The one that always tells me jokes and says the crudest things just to make me blush. The one that saves me from being myself. I'm looking for the boy that always, ultimately, forgives me for being mean when he's nice.

His face grows colder, the smirk contorting into a sneer, and just like that, all my hopes are dashed. Again.

"There's more space in the hall now. Walk that way," I spit with narrowed eyes, trying to protect myself.

Liam pulls his school tie from his back pocket, popping his blazer collar and draping the striped polyester around. He folds the collar back down and lets his eyes drift down my body. God, so fucking arrogant.

"Is this the new boys' uniform? A T-shirt, blazer with a hint of a tie... Let me guess, it's called Peter Pan."

Liam licks his lips, not even acknowledging what I've said.

"You look good, Caroline. Wanna find a dark hallway?"

God, he's such an ass.

I cross my arms, trying not to do what I want to do—bite because it's what he's baiting me to do. But when his eyes reach mine again, I say precisely what I'm thinking.

"Why can't you forgive me? You let everything else go with everyone else. Why do I have different rules? And stop looking at me like that."

I all but stomp my goddamn foot. Thank God I don't, or I'd have to immediately transfer, but he's making me crazy and fucking petulant. The muscles in his jaw ripple as he looks sideways down the hall. He's squinting his eyes as if he can't stand to look at me, and all my anger instantly sours, turning into fear.

"Because you don't mean what they mean to me."

There's a funny thing that happens when people hear mean things— even when they're facts. After a while, you learn how to take a hit. I know he doesn't feel the same way about me as I do him, but it still stings to hear it from his lips. Lucky for me, I trained with the best, so no tears will be shed, my throat won't get tight, and I won't crumble.

Liam Brooks will never know how that felt like a knife in my goddamn heart.

I huff a laugh, covertly running my finger over the scar on my hand. "Bad guy isn't a good look on you, Liam. Leave it to the professionals. Can we please stop this charade?"

Liam leans down toward my face, wiping a hand over his mouth and pinching his bottom lip between his fingers before releasing it. "Who told you I was a good guy?"

I glare into his cold eyes, unwilling to be intimidated, even though I trust what he's saying is true. Because I've seen this Liam before.

He's not the angel his precious Donovan thinks he is. Liam is more than anyone ever gives him credit for—good and bad.

"You've been living in my good graces, Caroline. Basking in my undeserved charm. But after all your shit, those perks just don't exist for you anymore. Can you really blame me? You've given me plenty of reasons over the years."

I frown as he steps in closer, hating hearing my thoughts spill from his lips. But no matter what he just said, my body begins to betray me. My eyes land on the area right below his throat, where his collarbone is, where it's kind of indented. It's so smooth and male and in my face.

"Should I list them, Caroline?"

Nope. I know them by memory.

His finger traces under the lapel of my school blazer, flipping it up.

"Stop it, Liam."

"Maybe I should start with the end of our sophomore year?"

My eyes lock to his, and the bastard grins. I know why I feel guilty for that moment—but I'll never apologize for it. And he has zero reasons to make it one of my sins, especially seeing as he can't throw any fucking stones.

I fix my collar and push his face back with my finger against his forehead.

"Funny how our memories are always different. I seem to remember you saying you 'dodged a bullet,' or maybe I imagined that conversation."

Liam turns away, holding back his words. Chicken.

He starts off in the direction he's looking, but I reach out, nabbing the back of his blazer. He freezes, exhaling harshly before interlocking his fingers behind his neck.

I hold him in place, my lips pressed, not knowing what I'm going to say. He stares at the ground for what feels like forever, and I swear I can't let him go, but I also can't admit what's on the tip of my tongue.

I want to plead, *"Forgive me. I'm sorry. I'm scared if I lose you that I'll never get even a glimpse of me anymore. You're the only one that makes it all make sense. You're the boy I love, and I'm desperate for you to look at me like you did before I ruined you."*

But I don't. Instead, I whisper, "Forgive me or forget me."

He lifts his tortured gaze to me from over his shoulder. "Are those my only options?"

My hand falls from his blazer as my chin jerks toward the sound of the door swooshing open.

"What up, assholes," Kai calls out with a smile.

I step back as Liam walks to Kai and slaps his hand.

Kai's hand engulfs mine. "Thanks for watching my girl, but we gotta jet."

I see Liam nod, and without acknowledging me, he turns and walks down the hall.

Grey says something as he walks up, but I don't even register because I've already turned my back to them. They finish, and Kai begins pulling me along, and although we've only taken a few steps, I swear it feels like I have to catch my breath. What other options are there—to torture me? Hate me?

"You okay, gorgeous?"

I nod, putting on my brightest smile. No point in looking the way I feel.

"Perfect, because I got 'em." He grins.

Kai's looking at me like I know what the hell he's talking about, but my brain is still trying to recalibrate.

"Got what?"

I glance over my shoulder, seeing Liam and Grey walking the opposite way, shoving each other like they're playing around. As if nothing ever happened.

Kai's chuckle brings my attention back as he holds up a stack of nurse's slips. And the vision is like a shot of adrenaline, bringing me back to the present.

"Did you steal those?" I squeak out.

He wags his brows. "Right off Coach's desk. Now, let's go have some damn fun."

***

"How the hell did you find out about this?" I smile at Kai as he shrugs off his peacoat, sitting down into the booth.

"I have my ways."

"Come on. A secret concert in the middle of the day wasn't floating around Twitter."

He takes his coffee mug in hand and has a sip before answering, "I'm full of surprises. And duh, my mom's publicist told me."

I grin against my cup, saying, "I still think it's crazy they don't allow phones," as I look around the off-the-beaten-path venue. I thought Kai was crazy when we crossed the bridge into Brooklyn, but I have to admit, it's a vibe.

Kai tilts his head toward me. "Well, gorgeous, it's a secret concert— doing a live would give away the secret."

"Whatever," I laugh, setting my mug down, letting my thumb skim up and down the warm surface. "When do we find out who's playing for us?"

He offers me a delicious-looking cookie, but I shake my head, so he takes a bite out of it. *If that were Liam, he'd make you eat it.* Ugh. Get out of my head. I need a priest, stat.

I give my head a little shake, trying to refocus. Which isn't easy. After I was left in "Liam purgatory," waiting to be forgiven or forgotten, I can't seem to concentrate. Maybe that's his plan—to fucking consume me.

Kai's voice bleeds into my thoughts. "You assume I don't already know?"

"Huh?" I say absentmindedly.

"I'm disappointed in you—" Kai presses with a mouth full of food.

"I'm lost. What are we talking about?"

Kai leans back, wiping his mouth with a napkin. "The secret performance…you asked when we'd find out who was playing, and I said—you know what, forget it. Where have you been this last hour? Because I'm almost certain that it's still in the fucking hallway, gorgeous."

I frown.

"Yeah. I noticed. It was hard not to. What the fuck did Liam say now? Did he forget to say you were pretty? Or are we mad that he said you were pretty?"

Now I scowl, but Kai smiles.

"I'm kidding, baby. Tell me what happened."

"It doesn't matter. We're here, and I'm happy—so why let Liam ruin another moment." I place a palm to his face. "You have my full attention."

He turns his head, kissing my hand.

"This is us, Caroline. You get to be a mess with me."

I stare into Kai's eyes. I love him. He's everything I wish I could want—my life would be so much easier if I could just be *in love* with him. But instead, we're best friend–soul mates that occasionally fuck—each other and a curated approved list. It's actually the healthiest and least complicated relationship I've ever had. No jealousy, zero judgment, and a handsome plus-one.

There's just the whole "I'm hooked on Liam Brooks" problem.

"There's no mess here. I promise. Now," I say, sitting up straighter, looking appropriately excited, "come clean. Who's performing?"

Kai begins to answer, but I cut him off.

"It better not be that guy that looks like a dirty baby. You love him."

Kai throws his head back and laughs before saying, "I promise it's not Post Malone. You'll have to trust me. This little outing is well worth your time."

My hands fall into my lap, and I grin up at him. Today was seemingly going to shit, and he's saved the day. He's the best boyfriend/not boyfriend ever.

I shrug. "Well, I suppose a secret concert in the middle of the day, plus a stolen stash of nurse's notes, makes you a legend. So I'll trust you just this once."

Kai's ignoring me, showing off his profile before he turns back, gleaming.

"What?"

He kisses my cheek and points toward the stage. "Happy early birthday, Care."

I follow to where he's pointing, but nobody's taken the makeshift stage. I search the space, confused.

"Am I missing something?"

He groans, taking my chin and guiding my face to a couple sitting toward the front. I grip his wrist, bringing my eyes to his, almost bouncing in my seat.

"No. Is that...?"

"Yes."

"Kai. Oh my God, if you aren't careful, I might fall in love with you, for real."

His fingers release me, then take my hand, kissing the top.

"Don't be ridiculous. We could never stoop so low as to fall in love— homies over matrimonies."

I smirk, shaking my head at the stupid saying. "You know that's never going to be a thing, right? Please stop."

He wags his brows, kissing the tip of my nose.

I push my hair over my shoulder. "Okay, give me a once-over because I need to make my way to the front and introduce myself to the second most powerful woman in New York society. The goddamn personal assistant to the chair of the International Debutante Committee."

Chapter Ten

Liam

"I wish you were coming. Are you sure you won't change your mind?"

I'm not looking as Donovan holds up the millionth outfit for me to vote on. I don't know why she's asking because she already knows the answer. She walks back inside her closet, bringing back three more outfits. She's holding them up one at a time, and I shrug.

"Shouldn't Kai be doing this? He loves clothes. I don't care what you wear, Van. I'm only here because you said you had donuts."

She texted me after practice asking me to come over. Told me she'd feed me snacks, but all I've gotten is air and irritation. I should've known something was up when Grey couldn't "make it." Fucker.

"Whoa there, dick. You're so grumpy, Brookie. You need a night of fun…just saying."

I'll kill her. I'm not doing this again.

I glance up at Van, who's got her bottom lip pushed out, pouting to add some pressure. This girl won't quit. She's been pestering me about Caroline's damn birthday party since the beginning of the week, and now that it's Friday, she's going for broke.

"You're killing me, smalls." I groan from where I'm seated on the edge of her bed. "Go ahead, give me your best pitch. You're dying to. But after, you have to feed me, or I'll start choosing all the shitty outfits."

"Deal," she squeals, adding, "There weren't any bad outfits."

I laugh, wrinkling my forehead. "Lies. There was some real shit in there."

Her mouth drops open. "You're the worst friend."

"Whatever," I laugh, "Speak now or forever hold your peace, pest."

She tosses some sparkly green thing on a chair and jumps up on her bed, crisscrossing her legs to look at me.

"Okay, listen." She takes a deep breath like she's preparing. "It's not the same without you, Liam. And if I have to, I'll stoop to peer pressure and call in the troops. I'm not above it. If it gets me what I want, then so be it. I've never pretended I wasn't selfish."

"Is that it?"

Her hand darts out to pinch me, but I put my own in her way to protect myself.

"No, that's not it. That's just my warning in case my speech doesn't work. Now, shut up so I can give it to you."

I pretend to lock my lips as she starts fidgeting with her bracelets. She sweeps her bangs from her eyes, then smacks her hands down onto her knees. "I have three *excellent* reasons why you have to come. And they're debate-proof. Are you ready?"

I open my mouth to say, "Then why the warning?" but she narrows her eyes, so I just motion with my hand as an invitation for her to begin. I lie back, tucking an arm behind my head.

"Okay. Number one—" she starts.

I chuckle at the way she says it, like she's giving me a presentation.

"Stop laughing at me," she snaps playfully, so I give her a thumbs-up.

"Number one. I'll have nobody to dance with."

"You have Grey," I counter, staring up at the ceiling.

She shoves my leg. "No talking. And we aren't supposed to be a thing, remember? Also, don't you remember our junior cotillion classes?"

The memory of eleven-year-old Grey stepping all over her feet makes a brief appearance, making me laugh.

I lift my head. "Your second part is solid, but as to the first—Grey made sure the party is camera-free. Good luck even going to the bathroom alone."

She giggles as my head falls back again.

"Okay. True. But that doesn't solve my dance partner issue. You're my best friend. You can't let me die out there. And never tell him this—you're a better dancer."

"Straight facts. He may have a small amount of rhythm, but I have an enviable amount of swagger. It's hard to be the better one, Van. It's a real cross to bear."

Donovan shifts to her knees, bouncing on the bed, ignoring my funny. "See? You have to come."

I shake my head. "Nope. Move on, beautiful. Solving your Carlton problems is not on my list of to-dos."

She scrunches her nose. "'Kay, fine. Be that way. Excellent reason number two."

Despite the topic, I'm starting to enjoy myself. The whole week has felt heavy, so it's nice to have an easy moment. After yesterday's run-in with Caroline, my head's been underwater.

Even when I manage to put Caroline out of my mind, she crashes back into my thoughts each time I picked up a brush or a pencil. I haven't drawn a decent goddamn thing all week, and I'm running out of time for my submission to Columbia.

I roll over to my side, propping my head up.

"Hit me with this undebatable second reason."

Van locks eyes with me. "If you don't come, it won't go unnoticed."

Her face is serious, too intentional, and I don't like it. At all. There went nice and easy.

"And I care why?"

She scoots closer to me, lying down onto her side so we're eye to eye.

"People will talk, Liam. Are you ready for the rumors and gossip to swirl? We've kept all this drama on lockdown mainly because we're a united front. This fucks with that. And for what?"

"For reasons. Good ones." My voice is devoid of any generosity from before as if urging her to let it go.

But Van pushes anyway. "Why are you still angry at Caroline? I forgave her. Grey forgave her. Why can't you?"

"Because," I huff, rolling onto my back again.

It's a dumb thing to say—because. But it's all I have—the other words won't come out. Donovan's eyes are searching over my face. I hate when she does that, looks for all the puzzle pieces.

"Is all this out of some allegiance to me?"

God, I wish it were that easy.

"You're the most loyal friend I've ever known, Liam, but even loyalty has a limit."

"Since when, Van? You expected my loyalty to you and Grey, despite what I felt. Remember? So tell me something—am I your friend or hers?"

My eyes stay trained on the ceiling, unable to look at Van. It's a low blow, using all the shit that went down between us against her, but I'm that desperate for this conversation to end.

"Who said you had to choose between us? I never did between you and Grey. Remember?" She swings the last word back at me like a machete.

I level my eyes to her narrowed ones. "You did. You told me who to choose, sitting on Grey's bed, with tears in your eyes while holding my hand. And you did again when you showed back up this year and took your seat between us. So don't start with me. I'm allowed to be pissed off for however long I'd like to be."

I push myself to sit so she's staring at my back. I'm a dick, the biggest, and I don't want to witness that on her face. It's like all the shit I'm shoving down is starting to burst over the surface. Why can't I ever seem to say what the fuck I mean? Or say what I actually want to say?

Jesus, Liam, just tell her you can't forgive Caroline because she broke your heart too many times. Tell her you're scared that if Caroline cared back, you'd never be the friend Donovan was to you and refuse to choose between them. You'd be the kind of bastard that let your friend go for the girl you've obsessed over for what feels like your whole damn life.

Donovan's hands press against my shoulders.

"That's fair, Liam. I did ask you to choose me. Because I saw that there was a choice."

My fist gives a few light punches into my thigh before I answer, "No, there wasn't, Van."

Liar. All lies. Fucking say it, you coward—Caroline's always been it, even though you can't have her.

Van wraps her arms around my neck. "And so much has changed. Do I love her? No. But she's family to Grey, and that means she's ours too."

I let out a breath, pulling her arms from around me.

"I'm just done with her, Van. She's toxic and doesn't give a shit who she hurts." *And it hurts too much.*

I feel her fall back on the bed as she lets out a frustrated groan.

"That's it, Liam? Toxic? We're all fucking toxic. Have you met Grey? And me?"

"You asked, I answered," I say, tilting my head up, feeling like I can't breathe.

"Bullshit, Liam." I look over my shoulder at her as she continues. "That reasoning is light at best. You forgive her for everything." She points her finger at me. "In fact, it's the one thing that makes me crazy. I never understood why you held her to a different standard. Then I started to think, maybe it's because you felt sorry for her. But now—"

I'm on my feet, shoving my hands into the front of my hoodie as I walk into the expanse of Donovan's room. I know she's right. My reasoning is light. Because the cafeteria is just the straw that broke the camel's back.

Donovan's staring at me, watching me wander around aimlessly. I stand at her desk, taking a hand from the front pocket, moving some paperclips around as I think.

My fingers tap against the smooth surface, coming to a photo of the three of us as kids, next to one that she and Grey must've taken together recently.

How do I explain to someone who has their person? What do you tell someone to help them understand that each time you watch a piece of yourself fit with someone else, it breaks you? Caroline's a piece of me, but I don't ever get to be whole.

If I don't hate her, I hate myself, and I don't want to do that anymore.

"You can't understand it, Van. I don't feel sorry for her," I say, breaking the silence. "I mean, sometimes I feel sorry for her, but I don't pity her. I wouldn't do that to Caroline."

Donovan's arms slip around my waist from behind, surprising me. Her head is pressed against my back as she squeezes.

"You won't pity her, but you'll punish her?"

I try to pry Van off me, but she doesn't let go this time. Sometimes I forget we aren't twelve anymore because in moments like this, Van is still the little girl with bangs that shields her eyes, and I'm the gangly curse-word sayer that needs a hug but pretends not to.

"I'm not trying to punish her, but Caroline and I have a complicated history. A history you weren't around for and one I'm not explaining. Why are you suddenly a fan of Caroline's anyway?"

I feel her laugh. "I'm not. But I'm a Liam fan. And I know you— maybe better than you know yourself, Brookie."

I stand there wishing what she just said is true because then I wouldn't be struggling to tell my best friend all of my fucked-up thoughts, knowing I never will. I lean my head back, laying it on top of hers.

"I know that I'm unfair, Van. But I can't forgive her anymore. Don't ask me why—I just can't."

She doesn't say anything, but I can feel her breathing. It's soothing. So I say more.

"Even if it's fucking eating me alive."

Donovan yanks on my hoodie, twisting me to look at her.

"Liam."

Her brows are drawn in, a frown on her face. Donovan's hands come to the fresh stubble on my cheeks.

"Talk to me. What are you holding on to so tight? This is me and you, Brookie."

How do I do that, Van? Her eyes almost break the seal on my tongue, but I swallow all the words down. Maybe another day. I grin, leaning in to brush her nose with mine, trying to change the subject. "Hey, that was two—what's excellent reason number three?"

Her expression doesn't change as her cheek rests against my chest.

"You'll break her heart."

"She'd have to have a fucking heart to break. Plus, I only have room in mine for you."

My lips brush the top of her forehead in a soft, chaste kiss. But she shakes my body, barely moving me, locking those big blue eyes on mine.

"One day, Pooh, one day you'll forget that you loved me most and find another bear."

Chapter Eleven

Caroline

"Happy birthday to me," I whisper to myself, winding through the well-placed couches and cocktail tables in the atrium ballroom upstairs. Every detail is elegant and posh, including the three bars scattered around the room, fully stocked. It's amazing how many rules simply don't apply when you have the right last name.

I lift my eyes to the glass ceiling, adorned with what seems like a million twinkle lights, and smile. Tiered crystal chandeliers hang down from everywhere, and tonight, the full effect will resemble a star-filled sky on a rainy night. It's perfect.

Clipped footsteps sound against the stamped concrete floors, grabbing my attention. Our house butler, Bradley, is hastily making his way to where I'm standing, hands behind his back and a stern look fixed on his face.

"Miss Whitmore, you have a call from your mother."

The staff calls me by my given name rather than lumping me into the McCallister clan. I've never been offended—quite the opposite. I appreciate the distinction because it separates me from my gold-digging mother.

Absentmindedly, I slide my hand down the fabric of one of the club chairs, still admiring the room. "Why is she calling the staff line for me? Tell her to call my cell."

He stands in place, unmoving.

"Did you hear me, Bradley?" The question is rhetorical, but he answers.

"Your mother called to handle house business and doesn't want to be inconvenienced, miss. She requests that you come to the phone. Now."

He shows me the courtesy of looking straight ahead so that I don't have to see the pity in his eyes. Because how sad—poor little Caroline in her mansion, all by herself, with no one that loves her. I've never known the difference. I'm confident that my mother loathed me in utero. If I could only manage that same kind of hatred toward her, my life would be so much easier.

I motion with my hand for him to lead the way, walking out of the bedecked room, but not before I take one last look.

It was an almost happy birthday.

We make our way down the long hallway that leads to the room, passing the elevator, opting for the stairs. Bradley never says a word as we pass through the formal dining room and the foyer, getting closer to our destination.

My white Jimmy Choos slice through the chandelier-cast rainbow on the marble floor as I follow Bradley to the staff offices.

Bradley stops, stepping aside to open a door camouflaged to look like the wainscoting on the wall. It opens to a hallway that leads to Bradley's office. I've only ever been here once before. Grey and Liam used to sneak into the staff quarters when we were younger to steal cigarettes from Bradley. Liam always made me come with them by daring me I wouldn't.

But that's back when Liam liked me enough to speak to me, and I didn't despise myself for believing he was real.

As I walk through the door, I ready myself for the call. "Bradley, let's not pretend my mother is calling to wish me a happy birthday. Did she tell you why she's beckoning me?"

He shakes his head, retaking the lead. "I apologize, but no, miss."

He opens another door, this time to his office, and motions for me to enter. A faint smell of cigars wafts out, and the strangest picture develops in my mind. Bradley in a sweater vest, smoking a cigar like a grandpa. He's old enough to be my grandfather, I guess, and truth be told, he probably knows me better than my own parents, but thinking of him outside of his work persona—stiff upper lip and a penguin suit—is weird.

"Miss," he says, holding the black receiver out to me—not even a cordless phone. Jesus, the staff exists in the Stone Ages.

I take it, glancing at the door and back to Bradley. He gives me a nod.

"I'll be outside the door if I'm needed any further."

"No need. I'll find my way out when I'm done."

I watch him leave, but I don't put the phone to my ear until the door has closed behind him. The only thing I hate more than conversations with my mother is other people witnessing them.

"Mother."

"*Maman*," she corrects, hating my English, but continuing in it. "You sound winded. Was the walk down the staff hall that exhausting? You should consider shedding some more weight, Caroline. Fat women sound like hogs. After all, it's debutante season, not that it means much for you, but if you ever had hope, you can kiss that gold envelope goodbye if you look the way you sound."

Well, shit. Vivienne's coming in hot today, I see. Cunt.

"*Je suis en parfaite forme, Maman. Tout essoufflement est causé par mon excitation pendant cette conversation.*" *I'm in perfect shape, Mom. My shortness of breath is caused by my excitement over this conversation.*

"I see we should stick to English too."

My lips press together, damning the words I'd like to say from escaping.

"I'm calling because your father and I just landed."

"Evan's not my father."

"*Faites attention à vos manières, petite salope.*" *Pay attention to your manners, little bitch.* "Evan puts a roof over your head, clothes over your wide ass, and too much food in your belly. And he also paid for that extravagant fucking party you're throwing tonight. You should be begging to call him papa."

I hate her, and it gets the best of me, despite years of training to shut up and be pretty.

"You know, Maman, if you'd released my inheritance early, I could pay for everything myself. Even a diet program for my super-fat ass."

When my father left, he disowned us to start a new family. It was quiet, discreet, but my mother found herself thrown out like the trash. It was very "full circle" for her, I'm sure, except this time she was stuck with me.

Frankly, the only thing that saved her, elevating her back into this cult of society, was marrying Evan McCallister. And although my father is a bastard who's never acknowledged my existence, he was decent enough to put money aside for me. However, my mother has control of it until I'm twenty-one.

"Enough of this uncouth talk. Have the house ready. I've already given clear instructions to the staff. However, I requested you for a particular matter that's more delicate. Evan wants our rooms joined, but I think it's best they stay separate. As you can imagine, this is delicate. Handle it, Caroline. It doesn't come from me. Comprenez-vous?" *Understand?*

Unbelievable.

"Yes, Mother. I completely understand."

But what I really want to say is, *"Does Evan need you to hold him while he sobs at night? I'm sure losing your status, credibility, and a company can be emotional. Almost as emotional as the idea that you may have to put out for your dinner now."*

"Caroline. Are you there? Caroline."

I nod. "Yes, sorry. When should Grey and I expect you... Today?"

"Please try to not be completely stupid. Of course not. You know things are tense between Grey and Evan. Evan has an important dinner tonight with Miles Kennedy and a few others. We'll be by tomorrow after brunch—make those arrangements and make sure Grey joins us. Oh, and I hear Donovan was invited by the Deb Committee to interview. Take notes, Caroline. She is what a debutante looks like."

"I'm writing it all down."

I don't even attempt to hold my fucking sarcasm back this time, but it would feel better to deliver if my chance encounter with that damn personal assistant had gone better. I was dismissed politely before I'd made much of a case for myself.

"Always such a disappointment. It's a pity to have such an opportunity wasted on you. Try not to cause more trouble, and ensure my items are completed before I walk through the door, Caroline. I mean it."

Her voice is sharp. It's always sharpest when she's speaking with me.

"See you Sunday, Mother."

The line disconnects without a goodbye, and my eyes lower. As much as I wish it didn't bother me or that I was used to this treatment, my mother's words always sear my flesh. She excels at placing them in the perfect position to cut so that you bleed long after she's left the room.

Bradley clears his throat. "Miss Whitmore. I'm sorry to interrupt, but Miss Laura is here for you."

I hang the phone up and turn to face him, my smile gliding into place.

"Bradley, Mrs. McCallister has requested that you join her room with the senior McCallisters, and also, if you could make it 'romantic,' that would be amazing. She'd like this to stay as private as possible, which is why she entrusted the task to me, and I'm charging it to you, Bradley."

The look on his face is nothing past surprised, but I shrug innocently, adding, "It's like another honeymoon for those two. They're just so in love. I'd like it to be special."

I should feel bad...and I do, just not about what I'm doing.

Bradley gives a tight nod as I walk past, retracing my steps back out to the house. I slide my hair over my shoulder, feeling its softness, trying to shed her hatred. Out of the corner of my eye, I catch my reflection. I stop in the middle of the entry, staring at myself in the oversized Victorian mirror.

Why is it that a hundred people can tell you that you're beautiful, but you'll only hear the one voice that says you're less? I run my hand over my flat stomach, sucking it in more.

I haven't been watching what I eat or working out. I've been so busy with school and planning my birthday— My thought morphs into something uglier. My mother's right. None of that's an excuse to let myself slip. I can be better, just like the girls chosen before me for the Debs.

"Caroline. Oh my God."

My head snaps to Laura, who's bounding toward me like a Labrador, pulling me from my self-hate.

"You are never going to believe who tweeted about your party tonight. It's insane—incredible."

She's practically buzzing with excitement, and I feel allergic to it.

"Guess! Oh my God. You're never going to guess. It's major."

Eww. I don't answer, just raise my brows.

"Arden. Arden fucking Livingston. She's like the original badass socialite but even better. Apparently, she's back from London, and she's coming. Arden's the crème de la crème. Nobody's more important than her."

My eyes narrow, making Laura shut her trap before she offers, "Sorry, you know what I mean. But like, wow. Right? You're so getting a ticket now, Care. No way do the Debs ignore this. Arden is still beloved."

Now? She said, "Now"—because before, on my own, I'd never been good enough for an invitation.

"Is that chocolate on your face?" I question with a smile.

My comment seems random, but it's not. Nothing ever is when I speak.

Her hand reaches for her mouth, and laughing, she says, "Oh whoops, I had the most delish artisan chocolates. I brought you some for your birthday."

So happy. Without a care in the world.

I cross my arms. "Maybe if you cared more about avoiding diabetes or not looking like a disheveled hick, you'd be excited about getting your own ticket instead of riding on my coattails. Wipe your face, Laura—it's disgusting."

I don't stand there to see her reaction. I can't. I'm afraid that my reflection in her eyes will be my mother's face and not my own.

***

A quiet knock on my door lifts my attention over my shoulder. Kai pushes through my door, looking handsome as usual in his suit. His hunter velvet jacket perfectly complements my Dolce netted illusion tulle dress.

"You're early." I smile, pushing the small silver cigarette case back into the drawer it hides, spinning to sit sideways on my chair.

My heartbeat flutters over at almost being caught.

Kai doesn't seem to notice anything, saying, "Well? Let me see you."

I smooth my hair, pretending to put on the finishing touches before I stand. My hair is styled with a deep middle part, giving me a sleek look to go along with my dress. Kai circles a finger, so I do a twirl.

His hand covers his mouth like he's shocked by my beauty. "You look like a goth queen. Gorgeous and deadly. You're perfect, baby."

Leave it to Kai to pull the first smile out of me today.

"Oh, wait," I say, clapping my hands together. "These beauties are the best part." I tiptoe with dainty hops over to my bed, lifting my toe-to-heel crystal pumps. "I'm like Cinderella."

"Except tonight, you're a queen, not a princess."

I'm smiling as the shoe brushes my hip, igniting a tiny sting from the bandaged wound. I half blink, turning to set the heels back on my bed and sit, my happiness replaced with shame. I've never felt less like a queen in my life. *Queens don't bleed on their gowns.*

Kai's weight sinks the mattress as he sits too. "Hey." When I don't answer, he pulls my face to his. "What's got my beauty so down?"

I stare into his eyes, not even knowing where to start.

"Is this because your prince isn't coming tonight?"

I blink once before catching myself. *Liam isn't coming.* I shake my head, turning back to my heels.

"No. I don't care about Liam. I'm tired. I think I'm finally feeling the exhaustion over planning and school."

I know Liam's angry and holding a grudge, but I never entertained the thought that he'd skip tonight. Missing my birthday is tantamount to saying, "I don't want to know you anymore."

Does he really never want to know me again?

Kai grabs my hand, bringing the back of it to his lips. "Well then, I have the perfect gift."

I roll my eyes. "Your dick is not a gift. You take it back with you. How many times do I have to say that?"

"Shut your pretty mouth. It's something pink."

I'm about to say *pussy*, but his finger shushes me.

"It's not that either, you little whore." His grin is contagious. "Now you can't have it."

I take his finger in my mouth and suck, letting it go with a pop. Kai groans and wags the wet finger at me. "Not fair."

He reaches into the breast pocket of his jacket, pulling out a small clear bag and shaking it in front of my face.

My eyes shoot open. "It's pink!"

"Like I said."

I grab the lapels of his jacket and bring my lips to his. "It's the perfect present."

Since I'd like to forget the night before it even starts.

He gives me a wink. "But you know the rules. You only do this with me, and you stay by my side for the night."

"Of course. Done."

Kai stands, walking over to my mirrored vanity, and sprinkles out some of the contents before looking back at me.

"I need something to cut with. Give me your credit card."

Before I can say anything, he's opening the drawer, rifling through, pulling out my hidden case.

"Hold on—"

Kai's holding the cigarette case in his hand. "Is this your wallet? Why is it all the way back there?"

"No. That's not—"

His brows furrow as he opens it, then looks over to me. "Care, what is this?"

My heart stops. *It's exactly what you think, Kai.* I've never told him any of my history with cutting myself, and I'm not starting tonight.

"Oh my God. I forgot that it was even in there. It's been a hundred years since I've seen that. I was so emo when I was thirteen."

He's staring at me, wanting to believe me, so he does. Manipulation is always the most effortless when a person cares about you—because the alternative is that they think you're a monster.

"Caroline the emo cutter—it's almost unfathomable."

I stand looking down at my crystal princess shoes, glimmering in the light, and wishing that today weren't my birthday because then maybe my life wouldn't feel so shitty.

"Everyone's a caterpillar once," I tease.

Kai growls at me, giving me a once-over and spreading his muscular thighs so I can perch.

"Come here, baby."

I hesitate, only for a moment—maybe to grieve the girl I could be if life hadn't made me fight back so hard. But my smile is firmly in place as I sit on his leg, taking the rolled bill from his fingers, and lean down, inhaling the powder, pinching my nose closed as I come up.

"Pink coke," I laugh. "What a ridiculous invention."

Kai's mouth descends on my neck as I stare at myself in the mirror, wiping away any evidence of my sadness and hating myself just a little bit more.

Chapter
Twelve

Liam
Past—twelve years old

Grey's been gone since Monday morning, and now it's Wednesday. He was suspended for the week over what he did, but it's better that way because when his dad found out about what he did, Grey took a beating. Sometimes I think his father looks for reasons.

I, however, didn't get into any trouble. My dad patted my shoulder and said, "Sometimes moments shape us, and sometimes we shape the moment. I'm proud of you, son."

I didn't really get it, but I was happy to not be in trouble.

The bell rings, so I shove my book inside my desk, looking out the windows, wondering how hot it'll be. It's October. It's supposed to be cold—but Mother Nature didn't get the memo. I hate doing PE outside when it's hot.

"Boys, please line up for lacrosse," Mr. Green calls out. "And girls, I believe you will have dance in the gymnasium."

So unfair. I groan, looking around the room as I stand from my desk, noticing Caroline doing the same. Kids are standing up around me, getting ready to line up, but I'm chewing the inside of my cheek, trying to sneak another glance at Caroline without her noticing.

The day after the shit hit the fan, she acted like I was invisible, completely ignoring me. But I still see her.

My feet shuffle behind the kids in my row, taking quick looks as we move toward the front. I survey the boys' line, doing fast math, and grab the kid in front of me.

"Switch places with me," I whisper to the back of his head.

"Why?"

"Because I fucking said."

I tug him back, making him switch, falling into line right next to Caroline. My hands shove into my khakis as I look over and pretend to not care about anything. We come to a stop in the line, and I give myself an internal high five for planning correctly. She's picking at her nail polish. I let my eyes dart over again—light pink nail polish.

"This is stupid," she mumbles, looking up.

"Huh?" I answer, my face darting to her profile. *Too eager, dipshit.*

Her scowl remains fixed on her pretty features as she answers.

"I was talking to myself."

"That's weird." *Dude... why'd you just say that?*

She glares at me, one hand on her hip.

"No, sorry. I meant, why are you talking to yourself?"

Oh yeah. That's better. I'm an idiot.

"Because, clearly, it's the best company."

Ouch. I deserved that. I run my hands through my unruly hair—that's too long according to my mom—and let out a breath. Fuck. I'm nervous—Caroline's scary.

I itch my chin. "Are you always so harsh?"

"Are you always so…" She pauses, motioning up and down. "This?"

A smile grows over my face. She said, "Always." That means Caroline notices me too.

I nod. "If you were going to say awesome, then yeah. I am always this awesome."

Her grin doesn't stay hidden, even though it tries.

The line begins to move, and we walk through the double doors, not speaking, but she breaks the silence, whispering, "It's ridiculous they break up the girls and boys. As if girls can't play lacrosse. It's so antiquated."

Antiquated? I remind myself to look it up to make sure it means what I think it does.

"I know. So dumb. But at least you don't have to be outside in the heat." I'm rambling, feeling the words all sticking in my throat. "It's the worst. It makes your balls all—"

I catch myself, wrinkling my forehead. "I mean, it makes all the balls deflate. It ruins all the soccer balls. And the footballs." I cringe on the inside. "All the balls."

My eyes stare straight ahead because I'm mortified. Why am I like this? But she laughs, and it's a melody, sweet and pure, making me do the same.

Mr. Green gives a sharp "Shhh," and we both cover our mouths, unable to hold it in.

Her eyes meet mine as I look over, and she points to our teacher, rolling her eyes at him. I wipe my middle finger under my eye discreetly, keeping her amused, but it only serves to garner another shush.

We jerk our faces forward, trying harder not to laugh, but I wish I could look at her again. I like her, like really like her, which is weird because she's been ordered off-limits. I don't get it though. The other day she was decent. Why would Donovan hate her so much?

The line slows as Mr. Green stops to speak with another teacher, so I seize the moment and brush Caroline's hand to get her attention.

"Hey," I whisper. "How come you helped us the other day? Because you and Van—I mean, you guys aren't really friends. Right?"

Caroline stares at me for a moment as if she's debating answering, then says, "She hates me. I don't think about her."

I don't know what to say to that. So I shrug, saying, "Cool," and look away, chewing on the inside of my cheek. I've never felt more out of my league in my life. Nobody is like Caroline. Not even Van.

A tap on my arm draws my eyes back to hers. "But to be clear, I wasn't helping Grey. He can take care of himself."

Oh.

"Okay, but why help me?" I question, noticing that she still has her finger on my arm.

"Because," she huffs.

Heat rises in my cheeks as she notices her finger too and pulls it away. "Because what you did was brave. And bravery deserves defending. I read that somewhere once."

She thinks I'm brave. My stomach flips, so I let something dumb fly out of my mouth to distract from the moment.

"So what? You're like a slayer of dragons?"

Just let me die. I laugh—at myself because I'm so embarrassing, but also hoping that she'll join in.

Caroline shakes her head. The line starts to move again, taking her in the opposite direction, so she looks over her shoulder.

"No, Liam. I am the dragon."

My mouth is open, staring stupidly in her direction as she walks away. Now I finally get what my father meant—this girl shapes moments.

***

"All right, guys, go get water."

The heat is beating down on me. I officially hate October. The lacrosse coach claps his hands together, ushering us off the field, expecting us to jog, but I wipe my sweaty forehead as I walk toward the water fountains thinking the same thought I've had in my mind the whole time—Caroline Whitmore.

Boy after boy lines up, anxious for their chance to drown themselves in the fountain, but I'm still in no hurry. Bloody-nose Paul is in front of me, waiting for his turn, and I roll my eyes at his back. He pivots, looking at me, but I cut him off.

"Fuck off, dick."

He flips me off. "It's Paul."

"I don't care. Nice bruise. Want another one?"

He spins back around, pissed off, but like I said, I don't care. The kid's an asshole.

Everyone takes a step up as a kid peels off from the line, wiping his arm across his mouth. My focus shifts to the building he walks past as classical music filters out from the cracked gym door. Girls' PE—damn, it's beckoning me to look.

I glance over my shoulder, not seeing any coaches, so I step out of the line, closing the distance quickly. My hands press against the metal gym door, opening it just enough so I can slip past. I'm immediately hit with the air-conditioning, so I close my eyes, appreciating the reprieve, almost forgetting why I snuck in.

When I open them, I see girls from a bunch of different classes dancing together. They're twirling around in their gym clothes and sneakers as giggles keep erupting between them. I look around, searching the gym for Caroline, but I don't see her, making my brows knit together.

She should be here. Maybe she's in the bathroom.

From behind me, I hear a "Psst. Brooks. Come on. Coach's calling."

I turn and nod at a kid who sits a few seats behind me in class. Slipping back out of the door, I squint at the sun.

"Thanks."

"No problem, dude," he says as we walk. "What were you doing in there anyway?"

"Nothing. Just getting cool. It's too hot outside."

He nods enthusiastically. "Agreed, and the coaches are dicks for making us run around today too."

I give a much less spirited agreement than he did because I'm thinking about the fact that I'm probably going to stink after this. Damn. Turning my head to sniff my armpit, I see Caroline coming from the office. It looks like she's heading back to the gym. Her arms are wrapped around her waist, hugging herself as she looks at the ground.

What the? My eyes follow her, watching her walk. Without a well-thought-out plan, I tap the kid's shoulder. "Hey, tell the coach I felt sick and went to the office."

He looks at me, surprised. "Are you going to puke?"

My eyes lock to his. "No. Dude, just tell him. Okay?"

He nods, mouthing, "Ohh," finally getting it as I jog away. I cut around the building to intercept Caroline in the outdoor hallway. Her back is to me as I slow up, walking next to her, leaning down to bump her shoulder. "Hey. Aren't you supposed to be dancing? Cutter."

She looks up, eyes rimmed in red—confusion melding into hate.

"Go away."

Whoa.

"What's wrong?"

"None of your business. Go sweat somewhere else."

She spits the words at me. Viciously. But it doesn't make me mad or scare me away. I don't know why. It just doesn't. I look down at my dirty hands before wiping them on my gym shorts and reach across her body, taking her hand.

My fingers close around her hand and tug it down as Caroline's gaze darts to mine again.

"What are you doing?"

I shake my head and shrug because I don't really know, but it feels right. Like she needs someone to hold her hand.

"Come on," I say, pointing to a walkway that leads out to the lower school community garden. Caroline doesn't try to take her hand away, but she keeps the suspicion on her face. I lead her over to the garden gate and through until we're hidden. Raised beds full of vegetables and weeds surround us, and the crunching of the pea gravel is all that can be heard until we stop in the middle of the garden. She looks around, hand in mine, finally landing on my face.

"Are you okay?" I ask.

Everything about her says no, but she says, "I'm fine."

I want to speak, but I don't know what to say, so I opt for, "Do you want to go back?"

Caroline frowns. "Why did you bring me here?"

I open my mouth to answer, but I close it just as quickly. Her frown grows. But I stand there, like an idiot. She wipes her eyes with her free hand and smiles—but it's cold.

"Why do you do that? It's so stupid."

I wrinkle my forehead. "Do what?"

"You never say what you really want to say. You lie."

I guess she has been paying attention to me. Suddenly, I don't like it as much as I did before.

"Well? Are you a mute? Or a coward?"

I thought I was brave.

"Neither," I snap back, letting go of her hand, but she holds it tighter.

"Then speak, Liam."

"I'm not a dog, Caroline. God, you're such a—"

Her brows rise, but I don't finish saying the curse word I was thinking. Caroline's voice is so level and intentional that it instantly makes me angry.

"Then if you aren't a dog, Liam, say what you were going to and quit acting like a little bitch."

My eyes grow wide as she smirks. Caroline Whitmore is a viper, a vicious little snake, and right now, I realize why Van hated her.

"No." *And you can't make me.*

She nods as if she's read my thoughts.

"I'm leaving. It smells like dirt, and I don't want to hang out with a liar."

She tugs her hand away, but this time I don't let go because, for whatever reason, I want to hold her hand even more. Maybe to make sure she doesn't run away.

"I'm not a liar," I exhale harshly. "You want the truth? I was going to say you look sad, so I thought you'd want to be somewhere nobody could see that. Sorry for being so nice."

Her nails dig into my hand.

"Liar. You aren't nice—you pretend to be. Just be yourself, Liam. God, I'm so tired of people being fake. We aren't friends. Right? Nobody will even know we were out here. Go ahead, you baby. Use your big-girl voice."

God, she's the worst. My chest feels tight, like I can't breathe. I try to swallow, but my throat is dry. The longer she stares at me, the angrier I feel.

Until all the words I hid away erupt. Because she's right, I did lie.

"Fine. I thought you needed to come out here because you don't look regular sad. You look, like, broken-sad. And I felt sorry for you. But when Grey comes back, I'll never speak to you again. You'll go back to being a girl I don't know. So I wanted to steal this moment and try to do something nice for you while I could."

Her eyes swell with tears, but this time, she doesn't say anything, just keeps her hand in mine without her nails digging into me. Regret hits me like a rock to the face, and I feel bad for telling her all of that. But I also feel like my chest is lighter, and I can breathe again.

Caroline looks down, bringing her fingertips to the ends of her hair, rubbing the strands between her fingers.

"My birthday is tomorrow."

I don't say anything because she speaks it like a confession.

"I hate my birthday. Weird, right?"

My shoulders lift as her hand finally drifts away from mine. She looks around at all the raised beds, labeled with colorful signs, shielding her eyes from the sun.

"Thank you for bringing me out here. I'd say you're a good friend, but that's only for today."

The pit in my stomach roils because now that I've told her the truth, I hate myself a little.

She starts walking around the garden, so I follow her, just a few steps behind, watching her but not speaking.

"Have you always been too chicken to be yourself?" she questions, pressing a finger to the dirt in a section labeled rutabaga.

The way she says it like she's not judging me, instead just making an observation, makes my feet stop moving. I've never really thought about it that way. Sometimes I choose not to say things because I know people will be displeased. Other times, I say what I know people want to hear. Mostly, I keep all my thoughts to myself—especially the ones that make me less of what I'm expected to be.

I ignore her question for one of my own. "Do you always talk like this?"

Her head swings back to mine. "Like what? Honestly?"

"Grown-up," I answer with a grin.

She shrugs and brushes her hands together, ridding them of the dirt.

"Not sure if you noticed, but I don't have a lot of friends, Liam. My nanny, the butler, the driver—those are my peeps."

I laugh as she says *peeps*, looking over what looks like cabbage. "Never say 'peeps' again."

"Deal."

I'm still following her, but we're not really looking at each other as we explore the garden. Seconds feel like minutes as we say nothing, so I fill the silence, wanting to hear more of her voice.

"Yeah, it's hard." She glances up at me, confused. "I mean, yes, being myself is hard. There are so many rules and expectations."

She tosses a leaf at me. "Rules and expectations? You realize following those is the complete opposite of being yourself."

"I guess," I answer, leaning down, sniffing a plant, and jerk back. "Gross. That's disgusting."

Caroline laughs, walking around the box to face me. I scrunch my nose, staring at her, thinking but not speaking.

"You're doing it again, Liam. Just speak. We never even happened today, remember?"

What if I want to remember it? Forever.

I'm not saying that, so I opt for my first thought. "Be honest. Why were you in the office?"

Caroline curls her finger for me to meet her where she stands. So I do. She takes a deep breath, straightening her shoulders, and looks up at me.

"First, I never lie, not really. Second, I was in the office because I cut myself in the bathroom, and I was bleeding."

My eyes widen. "Whoa. Does it hurt? Can I see it?"

She pats my head. "Down, boy. I swear to God—you're so innocent. I cut myself, Liam."

"What?" I laugh, but the expression on her face is serious, so I stop. I'm trying to connect the dots. She cut herself, so what? The more I look at her face, the less it gives away, so I ask another question.

"How did it happen?"

Her lips purse before she speaks.

"It happened because I did it on purpose, and I accidentally made it too deep."

"Why would you do that?"

My heart feels like it's racing, but Caroline seems so calm. But her chest is rising as fast as mine, so I know she isn't. This is why she looked so sad—she cuts herself. My cousin Adelaide did that. I remember my mom telling me about it. She said it was because Adie was depressed and that she just needed to get some help.

Caroline's looking over some wildflowers growing among the weeds, ignoring my question as she speaks.

"I'm fine though. The nurse butterflied it. My parents were unreachable, so the nanny made the call for me to stay. It's a small cut, but I guess the wrist just bleeds a lot."

"Why'd you do that to yourself, Caroline? Is it because you're sad, or are you sad because you do it?"

Her ice-cold eyes fix on me again, saying more than her words could. "Both."

"Can I see it? I won't tell anyone in our class," I whisper, feeling like we should be secretive.

"Promise," she demands.

"On my life."

Caroline pulls her sleeve up, showing me a small bandage wrapped around the side of her wrist. Her finger gently pulls back the gauze, revealing a jagged, bloody cut about as long as a pen cap.

"I was sad because my gym shorts were too tight. And the teacher told me she'd send my mother an email to let her know I'd need another pair. But my mother hates that I'm fat."

I look down at my shoes, wishing I could tell her mom to fuck off as she closes the bandage. Her voice is so small.

"Don't feel sorry for me."

I picked up a pebble off the wooden bed and toss it. "I don't feel sorry for you. I think your mom is a jerk. But I also think you're dumb for doing that shit."

Her face shoots to mine, and a smile breaks out. "Dumb? You're calling me dumb after what I just told you."

"Yeah. But if it makes you feel better, you're also really pretty."

"Are you lying?"

I toss another rock, feeling my cheeks start to burn. "Nope."

Two big teardrops run down her cheeks before she wipes them away.

"Whatever, the sun is in my eyes," she snarks.

I just nod and grin. The bell rings, and we jump.

"Oh shit. We're going to get busted," I laugh, looking over my shoulder, knowing that our stolen moment is over.

She walks past me and shrugs. "It takes two minutes to get back to class through the hallway but probably three if we go the back way."

I walk next to her, wondering which way we'll take, a little sad, but she reaches down and takes my hand, letting me hold hers half of the way back—the long way.

***

"Take your seats, please. Quiet down."

It's the start of Thursday, and Mr. Green is already on the warpath, but I don't care because my eyes are on the girl two rows over. Caroline sits at her desk and reaches inside for her morning journal when she stops and leans sideways to see inside.

Here we go.

She pulls out a small blue Tiffany's box—one I stole from my mom—and a folded paper bag. Her head turns my way, but I'm already looking forward, pretending I don't notice. I wait for a few more seconds and look back over, watching her unfold the bag and pull out the chocolate chip cookie—the cookie I made. Well, made with the help of our chef.

Caroline brings it to her nose, inhaling it, and places it back in the bag. She pushes it aside and opens the box, checking again over her shoulders to make sure nobody is watching her. The top lifts, and the scraps of tissue paper I ripped up fall out. Her delicate fingers reach inside and pull out the

Care Bear sticker I stole from the nurse's office days ago.

I'm staring, watching as her fingers brush over the top of the puffy sticker, and this time when she looks my way, I keep my eyes on hers. I point to the top of the box, and she looks back down, flipping it around, confused until she sees the writing on the inside of the top.

For the girl that feels everything and wears her heart on her sleeve.
Happy Birthday, Carebear.

Chapter
Thirteen

Liam

The black carpet is littered with gold-and-silver confetti that's sticking to my oxford shoes as I make my way to the front door. Camera flashes accompany catcalls, barked at a slew of socialites, begging them to smile and turn around, but I keep my head down, already second-guessing the fact that I'm here.

I knew it'd be a fucking feeding frenzy of who's who and Manhattan extravagance. So I'm not surprised by the reception. Caroline has managed to "PR" her birthday into bed with the likes of the Met Ball. I bet by tomorrow, the list of guests is plastered on every fucking blog and entertainment section in this city. And that bet is why I'm walking on this goddamn carpet going to a goddamn party for a girl that I'm desperate to forget about.

Not showing tonight would make for a much bigger headline. Something Donovan not so subtly reminded me of, again, in a series of texts about an hour ago. Now I'm here to make enough of an appearance to satisfy the loose lips, and then I'm bouncing.

And if I'm lucky, I won't even see Caroline.

I bypass the attention whores standing still on the step and repeat, hands in my black tuxedo pockets, ignoring "Liam" as I make my way up the steps, giving security a nod. The security rope pulls back for me, and I step over the threshold to walk into the house, but I'm halted as an arm snakes through mine.

A purred "Hi" warms my ear.

I'll be damned. My head turns.

"Hi, yourself, beautiful."

Arden Livingston smiles back at me, that whole summer we spent together flashing before my eyes, leaving me smiling. I don't have one bad memory of this girl, not even when we said goodbye—Arden's good like that. No commitment, all fun.

She comes to stand next to me, and I motion with my other arm, letting her take the momentary lead before giving her my arm again. We walk in silence, giving each other quick glances as we head toward the elevator.

"My, my, my. You look good, Liam."

I smirk.

"As do you, Arden. How long's it been?"

She smooths the lapel on my tux.

"Summer before your junior year."

"That's right."

And what a welcomed summer it was. I was mending a broken heart, and she was more than happy to help me find ways to lick all my wounds. Her auburn hair flits through her fingers as she runs them through, cocking her head to smile at me.

"And here I thought tonight was going to be boring."

We stop in front of the elevator, and I bring my face closer to hers. "Boring? At a Caroline Whitmore party? Never. She might be better than you at throwing them. But I'll definitely do my best to make sure you have a good time."

She pushes my face back.

"Better than me? How cruel. I can think of a few things I'm the very best at. Seems someone may need reminding."

Looks like Arden's gonna save the day for the second time in my life. Maybe I'll stay for longer than a minute.

The elevator dings, and the doors open. Two emaciated girls holding cigarettes, both wearing way too much makeup and laughing too loud, step out, practically skidding to a stop when they look up to see Arden and me standing in front of them.

We ignore them. It's easy to do when Arden is around. She's so used to the attention that missing it becomes easy. We walk inside the shaft as they exit, and Arden turns to stare at me. I press the button to take us to the atrium, not taking my eyes off her as the doors close, leaving us alone, with matching grins.

"Didn't you have a date, Arden?"

I realize I saw someone with her after she'd said, "Hi."

She shrugs, letting her fur jacket fall off one shoulder. "Probably, but now I have a new one."

"We'll see." I chuckle, giving her a wink.

Her mouth pops open. "Liam Brooks. Are you playing hard to get?"

"Nah, I'm a slut."

She laughs, pushing my shoulder. "A true whore."

"Takes one to know one."

She laughs harder this time, taking my hand in hers. "I missed that quick wit. Everyone always thinks Grey's the one to watch out for. But nope. I've always known it's you, Liam Brooks."

The elevator stops, doors opening, and I give her my arm, happy for her company. "It's really fucking good to see you again, Arden."

"It's nice to be seen. There's nothing like a DUI and a tiny little nothing hit-and-run to make your parents lose it and ban you from coming back."

"Yeah, but Oxford has to be pretty spectacular."

Arden is a year older and always ran with a crowd even older than her. She's legendary.

"Well, anything's better than Madison Prep. The only thing an all-girls school is good for is learning all the ways to kiss."

Voices interrupt our bubble, growing louder as we get closer. An elegantly dressed pair makes out indiscreetly against a wall, and Arden wags her brows, nudging my shoulder.

I smirk at the salacious pair, music beginning to vibrate my chest. "All the ways? There's more than one way to kiss?"

Arden presses against my body to avoid running into a group of kids milling outside the opened doors of the entrance.

Her chin tips up, beckoning my ear, whispering, "There's more than one place."

I clear my throat and turn to her face, our lips almost touching.

"You'll have to show me sometime."

She twinkles with amusement, puckering her lips at me, making me smile again. I pull back, changing the subject.

"Speaking of the hit-and-run, how is your ex?"

"Eating soft foods without a straw. It's a real comeback story."

My laughter's drowned out by the pulsating music as we stand atop of a dozen or so stairs. They lead to the main floor, but we stay put because I'm awed, same as Arden. I can only describe the scene as a proper "Gatsbyesque" party, like that meme with Leo holding the champagne glass.

This is fucking epic. Caroline outdid herself.

Crystal hangs from the ceiling, girls in shiny outfits are dancing atop black pianos, and it feels like there's glitter in the fucking air. It's a bacchanal, not just a party. She's fit at least a hundred couture assholes into this ballroom, but it doesn't feel cramped.

The glass walls surrounding us let the city lights shine through, and the ceiling looks like there are raindrops set against the night sky. It even makes the black dance floor look like liquid.

"Holy fuck." I smile, looking over at Arden.

"Uh, yeah. Not exactly boring."

Lights shine down, spotlighting us standing arm in arm. The beat drops, and Arden squeals as tiny gold stars rain down on us. This is like a fucking movie.

"Wow. This girl knows how to throw a fucking party. I need to meet her. My PR told me I needed to be seen here…I thought they were full of shit. But damn, they were right."

My brows draw together as Arden pulls her arm from mine, searching the crowd.

"Hey. Is that…?" Her hand shields her face until the lights switch to a different part of the room. "It is." She looks over her shoulder to me, pointing. "It's Grey."

Shit. I'd kind of hoped to avoid everyone by pretending to chase pussy. My gaze follows the line she's drawn, seeing Kai waving us over, Donovan under Grey's arm…and Caroline. I suddenly feel hollow, completely empty inside.

She looks gorgeous, even from here. Perfect for the day she hates most.

Arden taps me with her clutch. "Come on, Romeo, your friends beckon."

I shove my hands in my pockets. "Fuck them. I'll intro you to Carebear later. First, let me get you drunk."

Shit, did I just say Carebear?

Arden shakes her head, joking, "Are you ashamed of me, Liam?"

She takes a step back toward me to grab my jacket, but her smile drops. Arden is staring at me as I look past her, jaw tense. I thought it'd be easier to be here. But I'm bombarded by memories—it's too much. This room. Caroline, Arden, all of it. I need to get out of here.

"Hold on, is this *the Caroline*…like 'Hi, I'm a sad sack, sulking in the Hamptons because of Carebear' Caroline. It is, isn't it? Don't lie, because you just called her Carebear."

All I can do is swallow. I was heartbroken at the beginning of that summer. Arden was older, more experienced, and a good listener. She's the kind of girl that takes shit to the grave—like Donovan. Damn, I never thought about that—both wild, good listeners. I guess Arden was doing double duty that summer being all the girls I missed.

"Arden, come on. We don't need to go down memory lane. I'd much rather get drunk and make terrible decisions—with you."

She lets out a huff, patting my chest. "Oh my God. Hell no. Now you will introduce me." Arden turns around to go down the stairs, but I catch her arm, stopping her. Pressing myself behind her, I bring my lips to her ear.

"Nobody knows about what happened. Or how I felt. Nobody. I'd like to keep it that way. That girl's taken a lot from me. So I'd prefer to keep my fucking dignity."

Arden turns into my arms, smiling, the light beaming down on us again.

"Done, baby. But what fun would tonight be if I didn't help to make her regret that fucking decision? Who knows, maybe she'll see the light and try to steal you back."

I'm searching her eyes, wondering what the fuck I'm doing other than clinging to some delusional need for retribution, as I lean down, diving headfirst into a stupid decision, and take Arden's lips between mine.

Chapter Fourteen

Caroline

My heart's beating out of my chest and not because of the coke. That was a dud. It's because Liam's standing at the top of the stairs with Arden Livingston in his arms, kissing her.

"Grey!" Kai yells over the music, pointing to the stairs. "Guess who decided to show the fuck up."

I pretend not to look, but I can't help it. How can I? There's a fucking spotlight on them, giving me a clear picture. What kind of fucked-up birthday sorcery is this? Now I know how Carrie felt—it's all crowns and glitter until someone throws pig's blood on your face. My pig is Arden.

I guess Liam chose torture as his option.

Laura's eyes grow wide, and she sees what I do, tapping my arm. I brush her off, walking away to grab some more champagne. Fuck him for coming tonight. I'd just made peace with him ghosting, or maybe just forgotten to think about it for the last five minutes, and now he shows up—with her, to make the day I hate even worse.

"The most important person," Laura's words rattle around in my head as I throw my flute back, taking unladylike gulps.

"Caroline," Laura flaps. "She's here. And with Liam. So that means Arden's not just at your party—she's a part of your crew. This is so exciting."

When I don't smile, she adds, "Be excited."

"Eat shit and die," I say against my glass, reaching for the bottle again.

"Huh? I didn't hear you." Her big oval eyes stare up at me.

I give her a tight smile before handing her my empty glass and shaking the empty bottle. "I thought I was the guest of honor."

"Sorry. Whoops. I'll be right back."

Laura walks out of our area to grab another bottle of champagne, and I watch her, feeling a twinge of guilt. *That's a first.* Donovan saunters up next to me, eyeing me like she's going to say something stupid. For her, I won't have any guilt—I dare you, I'm not in the mood.

"Wow, Arden Livingston."

"And?" I snap.

"I didn't know you two were friends."

The fury behind her blue eyes matches the feeling in my chest. I pull my hair over my shoulder, looking at her for more clues.

"We aren't friends. And why do I get the feeling that neither are you two."

She smiles, glancing back to where Liam was standing.

"Because you're smart."

Well, this just got interesting. Liam and Arden make their way down the stairs, through the crowd, and straight for us.

"Care to share why, kitten?"

Donovan glances at Grey and back to me. "No. I just heard a story or two about her. Does it really matter?"

Oh, so, jealousy. Okay, same.

Laura walks back up, handing me a filled glass with champagne, and I smirk as Donovan says, "An enemy of my enemy is my friend. Right?"

Donovan plucks the champagne from my fingers, taking a sip and handing it back as I seal our truce.

"Then tonight, bitch, we're besties."

I finish off the champagne and walk past her to Grey and Kai. Weaving my fingers between Kai's, I see Donovan follows my lead, doing the same with Grey.

Deep breaths.

"I'm not surprised they're together," Grey offers to Kai over our heads.

When the fuck did they meet? I've basically known Liam my whole life. How have I been ignorant of this unholy friendship? My face turns to Donovan, wondering if she knew any of this, but she looks as confused as I feel.

"He's always had a soft spot for Arden," Grey adds, lighting a cigarette.

Oh right. Hate me but love the girl that commits vehicular manslaughter. Technically the other person lived but tomato, tomahtoe. It's amazing what you can find out on the internet. I did my research the moment Laura brought her up. Arden may have paved my way, but I built this goddamn universe. I'm like the Kylie to her Kim, and I'll be damned if she shows up, looking like she's just been blown out on a sex tape and act like she owns what's mine.

"Come on." Kai gives Grey a knowing look. "Can you blame him? I've heard the stories."

Stories? What fucking stories? I elbow Kai, scowling, unable to control my irritation.

"Ow," he complains.

"You deserve that," I hiss.

He laughs because he knows it's not him I'm internally raging over.

"Don't worry, she's not even in your league."

I catalog Liam's hand gripped to the back of Arden's neck, and hers wrapped around his waist as they stop to talk to Ethan, looking perfect together.

Perfect. As if Liam wants Arden next to him. Wants to show her off, not hide her in a fucking closet.

The taste of blood spills into my mouth because I've bitten into my lip, trying to prevent the scream from escaping my mouth.

I hear Donovan ask Grey, "I didn't know Liam knew Arden?"

Looks like Arden's made her rounds. Donovan should understand the motivation. She's kindred. I'm surrounded by girls that have been there and literally done that. And I fucking cannot with this shit anymore.

"I didn't realize you knew her either," Grey counters, sucking his bottom lip between his teeth and drawing his brows together like he's trying not to smile.

"And?" Donovan presses. "Keep going."

Grey's face turns down to hers. "And you were in Spain, Cherry."

Kai leans down to my ear. "Houston, we have a problem. Want to place bets? My money's on Donovan."

Jesus Christ. I yank my hand from Kai's and take a step forward.

"Who doesn't know Arden? She's a legend. Right?"

I don't have to look behind me to know they're all listening.

"But if she's so fucking spectacular, why is she at a high school party? Shouldn't she be in London fucking Jude Law—I mean, since the last time I checked, her parents cut her off, and rumor has it she's been doing duty as an au pair?"

The last part's a lie, but she deserves it. Everyone is quiet as I turn around and see that they're staring at me.

"Meeoow." Kai grins, pulling me back into his arms. "Someone's awfully feisty."

"But correct." Donovan winks at me. "Who is this girl to show up, with Liam, without our permission?"

Kai and Grey both shake their heads, laughing, Grey saying something like, "Poor Liam, two for the price of none."

I scowl, turning my attention back to the beautiful ones descending upon us. Donovan's shoulder brushes mine, her hair hiding what she says as she whispers to me, "Please make her cry."

Oh, I'll do better than that.

"She looks like a Betty," I say flatly, back to Donovan, my irritation reaching its petty pinnacle.

"Like as in Betty and Veronica?" Kai questions, and I nod.

Grey cocks his head. "So, hot?"

Donovan stares at him, shooting daggers, but I shake my head.

"No. Poor and unoriginal."

Donovan quickly covers her mouth to hide her laughter as Liam and Arden come to stand in front of us.

"What's funny?" Arden smiles, lighting up as she sees Grey. My eyes don't leave Liam's face, because he won't look at me.

Arden flips her coiffed hair. "Wait. Don't answer. I have a feeling I probably won't love it."

Kai chuckles, but her eyes shift between Donovan and me, the Cheshire grin never leaving her face.

"Every brunette needs a blonde. Isn't that what they say? You two are stunning together. I'm glad we finally meet. You'd be the new Serena and Blair—if they were real."

"I'm more of a Chuck Bass, plus I hate headbands," I offer, never blinking.

Arden lets go of Liam's hand, and I immediately chastise myself for looking. She closes the distance between her and Grey, glancing at me again but not responding. She greets him by kissing both of his cheeks. So pretentious.

"Hey, stranger. You're taller than I remember."

Grey gives a very tight smile. "Arden. Welcome back."

Her eyes shift to Donovan, but her hands stay on Grey's chest.

"So this is Donovan?"

She says it to Grey, not Donovan. He nods. And I swear I'm waiting for Donovan to rip Arden's hands off Grey's chest. I almost can't wait. So much so that my lips tip up. *Do it, do it, do it.*

"I am," Donovan answers, but before she can pounce, Grey removes Arden's hands. Boo, but of course he does.

"God, you two are red-hot. He's a lucky guy, blondie. Now I know why I lost touch with my friend. Who needs little old me around when he's got you?"

Donovan slides in front of him, letting Grey's arms snake around her as she speaks, "I can't imagine why he'd ever have needed you, but you'll have to forgive me because he's never mentioned you either."

Oh, come on, Donovan, do better than that. Go for the jugular and watch her bleed out.

Arden shrugs, taking her place back with Liam and leaning her head against him. "That's okay. Some memories are meant to stay where you left them. Although there was this one night—"

Liam begins to cough, and Grey immediately laughs.

Donovan pulls Grey's arm from her, stepping forward, "Oh, we're making memories now?" Her voice is raised. "I'm sure I can provide a lasting one."

Grey's laughing harder, pulling Donovan back into his arms to face him. He rocks her in a hug, engulfing her, and whatever he's whispering in her ear thaws the ice that was across her brow because she looks up with a surprised look.

What the hell is going on? I'm still icy. No thawing here.

How come nobody is pissed over how this twat is speaking to Donovan? Or that Arden is throwing out more innuendos than TMZ. I barely opened my mouth to Queen D before Grey was threatening my existence. And Arden gets a pass? What the fuck am I missing?

Arden laughs saying, "She's spicy. I like her," to Liam, brushing off the moment and turning her lackluster eyes on me. I can't even tell the color because she's so full of shit—so brown's my best guess.

"So…" she greets me, waiting for an answer.

I offer nothing—not a smile or a polite introduction. We just stare, sizing each other up.

Kai breaks the tension, leaning over me, shaking her hand. "Hi, I'm Kai. The handsome, smart friend."

I'll kill him for that later.

"Yeah, you are," she growls. "Aren't you delicious."

"If you want him to fuck you, you'll have to get in a long line."

My teeth grind as I look behind her at Liam. I'm speaking about Kai. I think. A part of me isn't actually sure. When Liam gives nothing away, I add, "But while you wait, I'm sure I can arrange for you to attend to me while he watches."

For the first time, Liam glares back, cracking that façade he's trying so hard to keep in place. Kai clears his throat, pressing his fingers into my waist, but I'm not done.

"Aimez-vous la chatte?" Do you like pussy?

She doesn't answer, so I give a laugh, amused over her ignorance. "Who speaks French anymore, anyway? Guess it's only me."

Liam lifts his chin, disdain on his face. He's not so amused anymore. Looks like someone doesn't like me being mean to their little tramp, or maybe he's scared I'll actually fuck her. *Wouldn't that be funny.*

Don't worry, Liam. Eurotrash isn't my thing, and neither is owning this bitch in an unfair fight.

Arden pulls Liam's arm over her shoulder. "What is it with your friends, Liam? They're all so yummy. You've been holding out on me."

The idea that he speaks to her, knows her in some way, makes me feel sinister—like I could commit a murder.

His face softens as he looks at her, and I die a little bit more.

"I suppose what they lack in personality they make up for in looks."

She cackles, and I feel the group relax. Everyone is laughing along. Accepting her. Have I fallen into a coma, and this is some kind of purgatory?

Arden wiggles her finger at me, basking in my frozen stare. "But not Caroline. She's got both. *Et si j'avais su que tu aimais la chatte, je t'aurais laissé m'occuper de moi pendant que je suçais la bite de Liam."* And if I had known you loved pussy, I would have let you take care of me while I sucked on Liam's cock.

Fucking cunt. I snap, turning around, taking an empty champagne flute off the table and fill it, bringing it back to her.

"How rude of me. I didn't offer you any champagne, Arden." I extend it out, hesitating before drawing it back. "Or are you still a part of the program? I know it was sanctioned after that tiny little incident involving your dad's Aston Martin." I suck some air between my teeth. "Pity—it was such a beautiful car. At least from what I could tell from all over the internet. Tell us, how do you deal with such attention?"

Liam frowns behind her, and Kai loudly whispers, "Care." But Arden—Jesus, if looks could kill, I'd be fucking dead. *Welcome home, bitch. We've leveled up.*

Arden takes the glass from me and sips it, smiling. "So sweet of you to ask first, Caroline, but I've never had a problem with alcohol, only cunts."

Oh. I like it when they put up a fight.

She looks back at Liam, lifting her chin. "She's everything you described and more. Reminds me of me when I was that age."

I rip the glass back out of her hand.

"Glad you could indulge in reliving your youth. But you should probably keep your hands to yourself tonight since it's a high school party. Wouldn't want to add statutory rape to that rap sheet of yours."

You'd need a fucking ax to cut through the tension. Kai is discreetly squeezing my free hand, hard enough that I know he's trying to get my attention, but I don't fucking care.

Arden turns, running her nose up Liam's neck, making me sneer. Liam's eyes stay on mine, his face adorned with the meanest smile like he's enjoying every word.

Arden shifts her gaze to mine. "Then I guess I'm lucky because the only boy I'm interested in is eighteen. I'd share like you offered to, but I'm much too greedy."

My stomach drops as Liam rubs his nose against hers, taking her overly injected lips in a lingering kiss before saying, "If you're done making new friends, I'd like to dance, Arden."

Arden looks back at the four of us, wiping a finger under her lip to clean the smeared lipstick.

"Duty calls. But this was nice."

Everything inside of me is rattling, making me feel like I'm vibrating. Arden tugs away from Liam, closing the distance between us, coming so close to my face that I jerk back.

"Oh, and Caroline. Save me a dance later."

She grabs the back of my neck, pulling me forward and planting a hard kiss on my lips before releasing me. "Happy birthday, Carebear."

Carebear. I almost bite her.

Chatter starts behind me, Donovan flooding my ears with a long trail of words I'm not listening to. Kai asks me question after question, but I'm not answering because I'm watching Arden walk away with Liam.

"What the fuck was that?" Donovan's voice booms, finally breaking through.

I grab a napkin off the table and wipe my mouth, tossing it to the floor. "Karma."

***

An hour later, I'm pretty sure that my eyes are permanently glued to the bar where Liam and Arden are posted. They danced, basically fucking on the floor. He kissed her again and introduced her around like she was a trophy he'd won. But watching him now has to be the most challenging part of the night. Every expression he's made—easy, serious, amused, all of them—they're genuine, relaxed, and killing me.

Before Donovan came back, Liam and I played this stupid game. The one where he talked to other girls, and I pretended not to notice because, in the end, I still got a piece of him nobody else got. Beggars can't be choosers because each time we had these moments—ones that were so honest and real—I'd forget that he didn't want me.

But I'm not sure I can endure this anymore because the idea of Liam never stops hurting me. He can't help it. That's the consequence of the pact I made with the devil when I signed my name on the unrequited contract.

Arden laughs at something he says and grabs his leg. I feel sick.

"Hey." Kai slaps his hands together. "Baby, you're being a horrendously bad hostess, sulking around like a poor sport."

"Shut up." I pout.

He cages me in with his hands on the arms of the chair I'm seated in. "Care, if you aren't careful, this whole room, including your Prince Charming, will realize that you've got one major obsession with Liam Brooks."

"Are you always this annoying?"

I let out a heavy breath.

"The way I see it, you have two choices. Tell the boy you are Sandra Dee, hopelessly in love with him—or numb the pain and have some fun with me. Remember when you used to let me take your mind off of him?"

A hint of a smile graces my lips. Kai and I haven't touched more than a kiss here and there since that fateful day in the cafeteria. Something about Liam ripping out my heart when he said he chose Donovan made him too hard to put out of my mind, let alone allow Kai inside of me.

"Door number two, please. I'm not in the mood for rejection and embarrassment. Again."

Kai frowns, then winks.

"Open your mouth. I have amends."

A v forms between my brows, but I do. Kai's lips descend onto mine, kissing me and mixing our tongues together. My eyes close, realizing what he's doing, accepting the drugs passed into my mouth with the taste of Kai.

"Open your eyes," he growls, pulling away.

I do that too.

The music feels like it's slowing as he brings a small round white pill with a red heart on it to my eyes. It's affixed to his finger. He places it on his tongue, sealing our fate with another quick kiss before nuzzling my neck and peppering love up to my ear.

"No more thinking. No more wallowing."

"Okay then. What now?"

He tugs me from the chair, eyes gleaming with devious glee. "Now we dance and fuck and live like gods, Caroline. Because this is your day. Happy birthday, baby."

The music fills my ears as he lifts my arms over my head. The bass bumps the entire room as I'm led to the dance floor, willing to forget it all and live in this moment.

Chapter Fifteen

Liam

Caroline's been falling into a different set of arms with each song, Kai in tow, sandwiching her and grinding her ass. And I could break his neck. I hate that the possession I feel toward Caroline never seems to go away—I've just become good at pretending I don't care.

Because she's none of my business, even if I can't stop fucking looking. I should be numb to this by now. It's been our whole existence—her choosing every other guy around, and me watching her do it. But tonight, being in this fucking room and seeing her this way... *Fuck these memories.* Damn, it's got me twisted.

I run my hand over my head, cracking my neck, uncomfortable in this suit and my life.

"It's like a game of musical dicks," Arden interjects, handing me another shot.

I nod and throw it back.

"Jealous much?" she snarks.

I smack the glass onto the bar and whoosh out a breath. "Nope. I told you I don't care about her anymore. I didn't mind rubbing my humiliation in her face earlier, but this"—I motion to the dance floor—"is none of my fucking business."

She lifts her finger, calling the bartender. "Mm-hmm, right. Except I've only seen your profile since she went out there. You're ready to break necks, Brooks."

I turn my face toward Arden, hating that she's right. When the bartender comes back, she takes the bottle, giving him a wink.

"Liam, I don't know why you're acting like you lost." She huffs. "You won. And she's crazy about you, no matter who she's dating. That girl hangs the fucking moon on you. She all but skinned me alive. It was sheer luck that I made it out of that fight in one piece. I mean, look at how she's acting. Girls only do that shit to torture you guys."

It's working.

"I'm not stupid, Arden. I feel the chemistry, but that doesn't make me the one for her."

Arden opens her mouth, but I cut her off. "Caroline told me back then. Fuck, she showed me—in this very goddamn room. I took my shot, but she blocked it."

Arden's bottom lip protrudes as she reaches for my hand, but I grab the bottle of Jack to pour more shots.

"And like the fucking masochist I am, I just keep proving we're all wrong, over and over, until I gut myself, never learning the lesson. And the kicker is, I have nobody to blame but myself."

I raise the shot glass before tossing it back.

I could say all the rest of the story, tell Arden everything I'm leaving out, but saying it might actually kill me. It hurt that fucking badly, and in the end, it doesn't matter.

"Oh, Liam. You're a beautiful tragedy married to an ideal. When are you going to open your eyes?"

"Can't we just drink, Arden?"

I grab the bottle and pour two more shots, feeling my senses dull.

She purses her lips like she's thinking. "Yes, only because I can't stop you. But give me one honest answer, and then I won't ask any more questions."

She licks her lips and looks me in the eyes as I nod.

"Go."

"Did you know you loved her during our summer?"

I stare into Arden's eyes, tired of pretending. I've never admitted anything aloud, but for whatever reason, maybe the alcohol, the setting, I don't know, but I say the exact thought in my head, for once.

"I can't remember a time when I didn't know."

Arden holds up her shot glass, clinking it to mine. "Brutal."

She sucks it back, slapping it down on the counter, but I leave mine.

"Liam Brooks, I'm thinking staying here is the worst possible idea. Let's go get into trouble together. Maybe we can find a girl for each of us? God knows I need to get laid."

I glance back at the dance floor and then back to Arden. "Just you. I'm done with women."

"Oh God, been there done that—and then I hit her with my car. Well, you remember. Didn't work out too well. But she forgave me when she was going through her vegan Buddhist phase. Lesbians are good like that."

"Vegan? Sounds like you dodged a bullet."

The saying sticks in my throat, remembering what Caroline said to me the other day.

Arden laughs, slapping my chest. "Too bad she didn't dodge the fucking car."

We stand, me shaking my head and her laughing. Arden reaches for her fur coat, but I push her hand away, smiling.

"I got it."

She turns for me to help her put it on, and I look over at the dance floor again, feeling her arms slip in.

"How come it feels like I'm the one that's been hit by the car," I whisper.

Kai's running his hands up Caroline's body as they dance. She spins away from him into some random dude's arms as Kai gets pulled over to someone else. I turn my head, watching Caroline sway with the stranger, who takes her hand and starts to lead her away.

My eyes shift to Kai, but he's preoccupied.

"Dude," I say to myself, immediately looking over to where Grey isn't paying attention either. Motherfucker.

Caroline's disappearing into the crowd, tucked under that guy's arm, and my heart starts to beat through my chest. Who the fuck is he? Anything could happen to her. I don't like this.

"What's up?" Arden questions, looking to where I am.

I don't answer her, mumbling to myself, "Come on, Kai. Pay attention to our girl."

"Everything okay?" Arden questions again, taking my hand.

I nod reluctantly. *She's none of your business anymore, Liam.* We turn, walking back toward the steps to leave, but I keep glancing to where she's now dancing, that dude's hand running up under her dress.

"Goddammit," I growl, stopping us in our tracks.

"Hey." Arden grabs my face, turning it to hers. "You said 'our girl.' But we both know you meant 'my girl.' Just go handle your shit, Liam, and stop waiting for life to give you permission."

Arden barely finishes her words before I'm past her, making my way into the crowd to break necks.

Chapter Sixteen

Liam
Past—sophomore year

February

"**D**ude. You have to get over it," I laugh from where I'm sprawled out playing video games.

I can't stop laughing—Grey's miserable. I would feel bad if his shitty attitude were about his dad remarrying after his mom's death, but it's not. It's got everything to do with his new stepsister.

Caroline Whitmore.

I haven't spoken to the girl since that day in sixth grade, but I haven't stopped noticing her either. She's changed over the years, fake blonde hair becoming sexy brunette, the roundness in her face becoming too gaunt at times. Most of all, the girl that told me who she was in a line to PE has become mythic in her own right—but now she's more viper than dragon.

"Of all the fucking girls," he yells from his bathroom, "Caroline Whitmore's a fucking punishment."

Jesus, he's dramatic.

My hands swerve right, then left like I'm driving the video game car before I crash, groaning, "Fuck," and tossing the remote.

"You can't hate her just because of Van anymore," I yell back. "Van's been gone forever. No messages, no nothing. And Caroline Whitmore isn't replacing Van—last I checked, you never wanted Van to be your sister. Because what little Grey would have eventually done as big Grey is illegal in this state."

A roll of toilet paper whizzes by my head, but I duck.

"Shut the fuck up. I hate that girl for my own reasons," he growls from the doorway.

Sure you do.

I chuckle, leaning back on my elbows. "Whatever. All I'm saying is you can't do anything to change shit, so you might as well make the best of it."

He comes out looking around the room, so I point to the valet stand where his jacket is hung, and he stalks over to it.

"That's another thing. How can I make the best of this?" Grey says with his back to me. "The little tart came on to me. How fucking twisted is that?"

"That's not what she said. I remember the actual version. She sarcastically offered an idea to break up the wedding. Stop reshaping the truth to fuel some fucking need to hate her. You're worse than a chick right now."

Grey stares at me, but I shrug. "What?"

He's pissed over what I'm saying. But I always tell him the truth about himself. It's what brothers do.

He swallows and looks down, letting out a breath.

"Dude, it just…I don't know. It feels like everything is changing. Like my mom is being replaced too."

Now this time, I do feel bad.

"Your mom was one of a kind, Grey. Nobody replaces her. And think about this, in a few years, we'll be out from under these pricks. Doing what we want, eating, drinking, and partying." I stand and walk over, tossing an arm over his shoulder, holding out a hand in front of me like I'm painting a picture. "And on our way through Europe. Specifically, Spain."

I give him a look, and he nods before shrugging me off. He straightens his dinner jacket. "All right, I'm good. Let's get this shit over with."

We walk a step toward his bedroom door, but a chuckle escapes my mouth. I turn my head to look at him.

"I could always entertain your new stepsister. You know, keep her busy?"

Grey swipes at me, but I jump back.

"Come on, dick. Not the face. I want her to see how pretty I am."

He comes at me again, making me howl with laughter as we mess around all the way to the dining room, pushing and shoving each other as we spar, only stopping when the butler clears his throat.

"Sirs." Bradley's tone is reprimanding as he opens the dining room doors, keeping both of us appropriately sheepish.

Once Bradley's back is to us, I lean over, whispering, "Maybe she'll like me enough to give me a handie under the table."

This time my shoulder hits the doorjamb, eliciting a quiet, pained "Asshole."

I'm down but not out, so I nut-check him and smile as he coughs, having to hold himself up with a hand on his leg.

"You okay, Grey? Need some water?"

Bradley turns around, frown in place. "The senior McCallister will join you shortly, and may I remind the two of you that this isn't a mess hall. Please behave, if not for yourselves, at least in front of the young lady."

Grey and I both look behind ourselves, seeing Caroline standing there. *Oh, man.*

She's devoid of an expression, looking bored as she takes us in. She walks in between us but not before she stops and looks at me. "Sit on my left, Liam—since that's my dominant hand."

Fuck me. She heard. I wince as Grey gives me a look like he might kill as she leaves us standing there like the assholes we are.

Bradley motions for us to follow her, so we do, but I whisper to Grey, "Relax, I'm not hitting on your sister."

"Step." He groans to himself.

We're seated, Caroline by herself and Grey and me together on the other side. We're quiet, and it's awkward, only made worse when Evan and his new wife walk into the room. Grey's stepmom is wearing a dress that screams new money, or so my mother would say. It's tight and very deep cut—uncomfortably so for those who are sixteen with raging hormones and have to sit with her.

Don't look at her tits. Don't look at her fucking tits.

"Boys. How's rowing?" she questions with a hint of a French accent, bouncing in her seat as it's pushed in.

I drop my face to my plate, trying hard not to laugh, as she situates. "Evan tells me you both compete for the school."

When neither of us answers, Caroline speaks up. "They're quite the star athletes at our school. Beloved, really."

Grey flips his fork around between his fingers, staring at his father. "I'm surprised you knew what I did after school."

"I had your transcript pulled," Evan counters, leaning back in his throne at the head of the table.

Grey's family is so different from mine, which is why I knew I needed to be here. I couldn't leave him in this shit alone. The rest of the uncomfortable conversation goes just as I expect. Evan counters all of Grey's jabs until all that's left is silence and chewing.

Although I helped when I could, it was Caroline jumping in that shocked me. It's weird because it's as if she really were his sister—the girl's got his back.

"Liam," Evan interjects, "how's your father? I heard he has you on track for Harvard."

"He's great, sir. And yes, Harvard is his plan."

"His plan?" Caroline questions from across the table. "What's yours, then?"

I open my mouth but take a moment, changing course. "Sorry, I meant it was my plan too."

She lifts a brow as her eyes roll.

"Good man. Maybe some of your good sense will rub off," Evan snarks, pointing a fork at Grey.

They begin sparring again, but I'm more interested in what's happening in front of me.

Vivienne, so I've learned, pushes Caroline's plate away from her as she's midbite. Caroline stares down at her mostly uneaten food, placing the fork and knife crossed on her plate, all the while keeping her smile.

"Boys," stepmommy says, quieting the discord. "You should show Caroline a good workout plan since you're so active. I fear she will never be fit. Teenage girls are so lazy. Not like you boys, with all your stamina."

Jesus Christ. She's a delight.

I look at Grey, and he shakes his head, obviously grossed out, but Caroline's face never changes, and it pisses me off.

"I think she looks great." My voice shatters the silence.

Caroline's eyes dart to mine, and I smile. "Sorry, I think *you* look great—but are you looking to put on weight? Because I have a great weight gainer. Grey used it. He used to be so scrawny."

She laughs but stops quickly, clamping her mouth shut. Her witch of a mother just gives me a look before returning back to Evan. I wink at Caroline, looking back at my food, noticing that she's pulled her plate back her way.

We finish dinner, much the same way we started—tense. Evan stands, beckoning his new wife.

"Stay out of trouble" is all he offers before leaving.

A collective sigh sounds, followed by quiet laughter as we look at each other.

Caroline leans over, nabbing her mother's wine, and downs the rest as we watch.

"Great. So you're an alcoholic." Grey grunts.

Such a dick.

"Great. So you're a dick," she tosses back.

I laugh and don't even stop when he glares at me. "What? It was funny. And she's right."

Tossing my napkin on the table, I look at Grey and move my head toward her, but he shakes his, so I do it again.

"No," he mouths.

I clear my throat, looking at Caroline. "So a bunch of us are doing a bonfire down by the river. Wanna come?"

Grey crosses his arms and continues glaring at me.

She looks at Grey intently and then shakes her head. "No. I have better things to do."

"Killing puppies?" Grey throws out.

Her hand shoots to her chest as she gasps. "No. That's terrible. I keep my murder to people, where it belongs."

This time he laughs too. We push away from the table, standing as she does, watching Caroline leave. As soon as she's gone, I smack his arm. "Dude, why can't you be a decent person?"

"That's your job."

"Mark my words. You two are going to love each other one day."

He waves me off. "Unlikely. I'm going to go change, and then we'll go by your place to pick up clothes—since my clothes are too big for you now because of the weight gainer. What the fuck was that about?"

I grin and shrug. "Hurry up. I'm gonna go play pool because we both know you'll take an hour to pick your outfit, princess."

"Fuck off," he bellows, throwing up middle fingers as he leaves me standing in his massive, cold-ass dining room.

I nab a piece of steak still left on my plate and head out of the door. Making my way through the living room, I cut around the couch to the hall that leads to the library where the pool table is. I'm walking down the hallway, minding my own business, hand in my pocket, when an arm shoots out from behind a door and pulls me inside of a closet.

"What the—" *fuck*, I almost say until I recognize my captor.

A small hand covers my mouth. "Shhh. I'm hiding."

I wrap my fingers around Caroline's wrist, gently pulling her hand off my mouth, whispering, "Who are you hiding from?"

"None of your business."

I'm still cuffed around her wrist, amused, enchanted. I don't know which.

"You're still weird."

She shrugs as my eyes begin to acclimate to the dark.

"Incidentally, why can't we turn on the light?"

This time she tilts her head from side to side, saying, "Umm. Because the dark makes everything easier to say."

And I decide on amused.

I let go of her wrist and put my hand back in my pocket. "Are you about to tell me that you're going to murder me?"

She laughs again. "No, idiot. I want to say thank you for what you said to my mother. You know, about—"

"I know," I answer, cutting in. "She's a bitch. Does she do that a lot?"

Caroline gives a deep inhale, answering as she lets out the breath.

"Depends on what you mean by 'that.' Do you mean taking my food away, then yes. If you mean insulting me, also yes."

"I'm sorry…and don't take that as pity—I know you hate that."

She pokes my hard stomach.

"So you do remember me, Liam Brooks."

Never mind. I'm enchanted.

I lean down toward her, bending at the waist. "Who says I could've ever forgotten."

My name is bellowed out, breaking the moment, so I open the door, letting in some light, and assault her with a quick peck on the cheek.

"See ya around, Carebear."

***

March

Caroline

"**E**xplain to me again why you're all wearing this getup," I ask, astonished at the sight of Grey, Liam, and Kai in white T-shirts and girls' school skirts as they crawl into the back of the limo.

Liam takes a swig from the flask as he settles in next to me. "Because, Carebear. We're going to Red Oak's St. Patrick's Day party."

He says it like it's supposed to make sense, making my shoulders shake.

Over the last month, Liam's taken to calling me that nickname and to smiling at me the way he's doing right now. But when anyone asks about my nickname, he says it's because I wear my heart on my sleeve, as long as you can make it past my bite.

It's a play on the truth from the moment that "never happened," so I've adopted the same lie. Being conspirators feels good. I like being something to him.

Grey chimes in, "You drop us, Caroline, and then you can meet your friends at that dress thingy."

"The Tom Ford showing," I correct as the car pulls into traffic.

"Whatever." Grey shrugs, reaching across to take the flask from Liam. "Like I said, dress thingy."

I look at the three of them, already half-drunk, and despite myself, I'm entertained.

Liam groans, "I think I'm already wasted," lying sideways, putting his head in my lap and twisting onto his back.

My heart stops as he looks up at me. "Can I lay on you?"

I swallow, giving him a nod and feeling flush—everywhere. My eyes shift up to Grey. "Hold on. Why are you dressed like Scots if you're going to a St. Patrick's Day party?"

Grey's face brightens the way it does when he has a tremendously wicked idea.

"Because the Scots hate the Irish, so we're going to disrupt the party—and this time, the Scots will win the war."

"Ah," I say, narrowing my eyes down on him, "so you're going to start a fight."

His smile grows, and Kai laughs, "We're going to finish a fight. They started it."

I look down at Liam. "Asinine. And you're supposed to be the future. It's tragic, really."

Kai puts his finger under my chin and brings my gaze to his. "Come with us. You could be our Mary, Queen of—"

"Pass," I laugh, turning back to Liam, whose eyes are closed, now sleeping in my lap.

Grey and Kai start talking, laughing about the trouble they'll cause, ignoring me and the fact that I've brought my fingers to Liam's wavy wheat-colored hair. Hesitantly, I run my fingers through it so gently as to not wake him, savoring the feeling.

The car begins to slow. Grey looks behind himself, out of his window. Kai joins him, leaning over, placing a hand on the seat. My face points in the direction they're looking until I feel warm lips press against the scar on my wrist, sending goose bumps over my whole body.

My eyes dart down to Liam, who's awake and smiling up at me.

"I always regretted not doing that the first time," he whispers.

I draw my bottom lip between my teeth, trying not to squirm as my heart races so fast that I'm scared I may pass out.

"Thanks for the lap, Carebear," he breathes out, sitting up with a grin on his face. The boys start filing out of the car, Liam last. He looks back just before he exits.

"I never realized how nervous I make you. Your heart was beating a mile a minute."

My eyes are wide. How could Liam know that?

"No, it wasn't," I lie.

His eyes dart to my lap, then back to my face.

"I could feel your heartbeat, Carebear."

Liam gives a wink, and then he's gone. The door shuts, and my mouth falls open as understanding settles. My hand shoots over my center, knowing my body betrayed me.

I've never been more embarrassed and turned on at the same time in my life.

***

April

Liam

I got to Grey's early, but he hasn't made it back from the gym yet, so I'm sitting in a living room that never looks used, waiting for him.

Caroline's mother's voice carries down the hall, and although I don't understand her, I can tell what she's saying isn't cordial at all. Her heels come to a stop as she snaps her fingers, pulling my attention, an embarrassed look spreading over her sharp features. Because she's not barking at me.

"Oh. I apologize, Liam. I was unaware anyone was here."

Caroline's standing next to her, in a pair of jeans and a white sweater that has little colorful polka dots all over it. Now that I think about it, I've never seen her so casual. Caroline's always presentation ready.

Vivienne huffs in Caroline's direction, making me frown. "Go change. This is exactly why I said what I said. We have a guest, and you look…" She searches for the word, so I cut in.

"You look perfect." *Shit—too honest.* "Perfect for where we're going."

I'm suddenly on my feet, walking toward Caroline's wide eyes and her mother's confused expression.

"She didn't tell you?" I ask, running my hand over my newly shorn hair. "I asked Caroline to go with me to the park today. I have a boat that I'd like to sail on the pond."

Vivienne takes in my casual appearance, much the same as Caroline's, minus the polka-dot sweater, and nods.

"Oh. Well. Have fun, then, I suppose."

Caroline doesn't look as her mother walks away, opting to keep her eyes on mine. I take her hand and grin. "Ready to go?"

She narrows her eyes. "You little liar. What about your plans with Grey?"

"He'll live. But your mother may eat you alive. Come on."

***

Caroline

"It's going to crash, Liam. Go right."

I'm hopping from foot to foot as he races against another boat. The tiny wooden sailboats zoom past each other in the glossy water, creating ripples.

"Shut your pretty little trap," Liam yells back. "I'm going to take him. I'm not losing."

The excitement I'm feeling over this race is ridiculous, but I want us to win so badly. Being here today with Liam has felt perfect, even if it's a fake date. And now I want the icing on the cake.

"Liam," I shout, pointing to the rock peeking up from the water. The one he's sailing directly into.

"I got it" precedes "aw, fuck!" as the boat crashes, upending into the water, and Liam tosses the remote to the ground.

He's such a sore loser that it's hilarious, but I like it because I'm the only person that ever gets to see Liam this way—imperfect.

"Well…" I say, somberly looking out at the other boat as it crosses the finish line. "You can't win them all?"

Liam drapes an arm over my shoulder and exhales a hard breath. I follow his gaze, and we stand together, watching our boat slowly sink underwater.

"Carebear. This is a dark day, but we'll come back."

I stare up at his profile, pleasantly occupied by our dramatics, pushing my shoulder into his ribs. "Well, I won't say it. But I told you so. You were warned."

His face turns down to mine. "I thought you weren't going to say it?"

"Oh no, you being a pathetic loser is what I'm refraining from saying."

Liam twists around, grabbing my waist with his other hand, and begins tickling me mercilessly. I scream and try to squirm to get away, but he holds me close to him as I laugh.

"Stop, Liam," I protest. "You're going to make me pee my pants!"

He wags his brows, his fingers moving across my stomach. I bend forward when he reaches an especially sensitive spot by my hip, causing his hand to move higher and duck under my sweatshirt, accidentally brushing the underside of my breast.

I gasp at the contact and straighten, but his large hand stills, keeping me in place, splayed too close to where he unintentionally touched me. Liam's so close that I feel the heat rippling off his body. My nipples pebble, and his fingers press into my skin, swallowing my rib cage.

Our bodies are almost flush against each other as his chest rises and falls, matching my breathing. I'm nervous because I don't want whatever is happening to stop, but that's how I know it has to. Liam's reputation with the ladies has become his brand—he's known for his friendly cock. And this is the most I've ever been touched. We aren't the same.

Liam closes in on me, pulling me flush, whispering into my ear, "Your skin feels softer than satin. It's unfair to ask me to never touch you again. So don't."

A slickness rushes between my thighs. I don't answer him, but I want to because I haven't stopped thinking about Liam since we met *again*.

A voice calls out behind him, "Hey you!" breaking our connection.

Liam lets me go, but I feel his eyes on me as I step back, a bit flustered and still in a haze by the unexpected intensity of what just happened.

"Hey, dude. I want what I won," I hear.

Liam begins grinning, holding up a hand. Confusion befalls my face as I crane my neck to see who is speaking.

A short little tyrant that looks all of nine or ten stomps toward us.

"Carebear. Listen, don't hate me."

Oh, this sounds ominous. Liam turns to face the little four-foot sailing champion.

"And why would I hate you?" I press, standing next to Liam.

He grips the back of his neck. "Because we lost."

I shake my head up at him. "We?"

"Don't be glib, sweetheart. You're losing in this too."

Before I can ask any more questions, the little guy grabs my hand, tugging me with his chubby fingers. "Come on."

"Let go of my hand, you little monster. Where's your nanny?"

The kid doesn't answer as he tugs me to a bench a few feet away. Liam's following behind, laughing, as I take my hand from the pushy little monster and watch as he crawls up, making us about the same height.

I look around for a parent or someone that looks in charge of him.

His cherubic little face fixes on mine. "Your boyfriend said that whoever won got to kiss you."

"You said what?" I shriek, looking back at Liam.

He shoves his hands into his pockets and shrugs. "I could've never predicted he was a ringer, Carebear. I thought I was a shoo-in. I'm as upset as you in all of this."

He's so dead.

"Let's do this, beautiful," the tiny little terrorist demands in his thick New York accent.

My head shoots back to my toddler Romeo. "Excuse me. We will not be doing anything of the sort."

"But he promised."

"Hey. Be a gentleman," I snap, before looking back at Liam. "And you. You wagered my lips with a child? You're a degenerate. Truly foul."

Liam's laugh cracks like thunder through the sky, and I can't help but join in.

It's at this moment that it dawns on me that he wagered a kiss—and thought he was going to win. Liam's face is bright and happy. He's amused and giddy. I love it when he's like this. It makes me want to find ways to stay in his light.

"Come on already," the little shit whines.

I grab his face and turn it sideways, kissing my fingers and pressing them to his cheek. "There, now run along and hustle someone else."

The kid jumps off the bench, less than pleased, complaining, "That sucked," as he walks away.

I turn back to Liam as his hand finds mine, pulling me away.

"Are you mad at me?"

"No. I expect you to be a court jester."

He swings our arms, giving me a wink. We walk down the pathway that winds through the park. The chill in the air relieves my hot cheeks. I don't think I've stopped feeling flush since I realized Liam wanted to kiss me.

"Today's been—" he offers, not finishing the sentence.

I look up at the trees, at the clouds that are gathering. "Yeah, it has been. I'm glad we're friends—unless you still aren't allowed to be."

It's a stupid joke, but I can't blurt out, "Do you like me too?"

But over the last few months, it's all I think about because of all the time we spend together, now that Grey and I have found ourselves as allies—it only took him witnessing my mother's behavior and some less than outstanding moments from his own father to turn me into someone this little crew protects rather than just tolerates.

Which means I get time to ogle Liam, and be ogled, a lot.

"Are we friends?" he answers, making me nervous.

I take in his profile while we stroll. "I think so. Do you think so?"

He stops, turning to look at me, and cradles my face with one hand. "Are you friends with Kai?"

This question feels loaded, but I answer honestly, "Yes."

"Then maybe I don't want to be your friend."

We're staring at each other as the sky opens up and drops of rain begin to sprinkle. I blink as one hits my eyelash, forcing my face toward the clouds.

"Oh my God."

The rain compounds, pouring down.

"Liam. Let's go," I squeal, tugging his arm.

But his white teeth go on full display as he hauls me in the opposite direction toward some swings.

"Are you crazy?" I shout as we start to get drenched.

"Maybe. But only about you. Stay here with me."

He picks me up and sets me down on the bright yellow seat. Liam pulls me back until my feet aren't touching the ground and then lets me go. The air and rain whip over my face and I close my eyes, leaning back, before tipping my body forward. I feel his hand on my lower back as I career forward again, enjoying the sensation.

"Hey, Carebear. Let's be 'not friends' forever."

The smile on my face feels permanent. *I don't want to be your friend either, Liam.*

***

May

Liam

Kai tosses Caroline into the water, a splash making Grey and me laugh from the dock. We're laid out on our respective striped beach towels, propped up on our elbows. We've been at my family's lake house all day, soaking up the sun.

"You think he likes her?" Grey questions, watching Kai swim around with Caroline.

It's a question I've been asking myself. I know they're friends, and it's not like I've followed up or locked her down, but I want to. There just never seems to be a perfect time to bring it up to Grey.

"Would that bother you? If they dated?"

He shakes his head. "Nah, Kai's good for her."

The toothpick in my mouth wiggles—it's something I traded out so that I'd stop eating the inside of my mouth. All my nervous habits seem to worsen when I'm stressed, which appears to be all I feel lately.

A dripping wet Caroline walks up the planks, accepting the towel Kai holds out to her. She comes to stand over Grey and me, casting her shadow in between us, before laying her towel down and lowering onto her stomach.

Kai calls to Grey to race him to the buoy, so he stands, taking the challenge, leaving Caroline and me alone. Her head switches its position, bringing her eyes to mine as I relax down. We're lying there, not saying anything, staring at each other.

"Hi," she mouths.

"Hi," I mouth back.

She moves to lie on her side, and the bottom of her bathing suit pulls, making it dip around her hip and drawing my eyes.

An almost indiscernible white scar shines on her skin, just above where it had been hidden.

"You still do that?"

Her finger hooks around the material, righting it.

"No. I do therapy now."

My tongue presses against the back of my teeth, wishing I could kiss her.

"Good. Your skin's too pretty to mark up. Unless it's by my mouth."

She releases the breath she's been holding. "You're insane."

If she knew how fucking serious I am, it would scare the shit out of her. The more time I spend with Caroline, the more I wish I could hide her away and keep her to myself.

She sunbathes on her back, letting out a tiny moan. "My week was so shitty. I wish I could bottle this moment."

I push up to sitting and flip over to stand, jogging off.

"Where are you going?" she calls, but I don't answer.

Opening the door to the house, I run into my room and grab my sketch pad and a pencil, making my way back to her.

Her face is full of questions, but I offer no answers, sitting back down.

"Just lay there and be you. I'll handle the rest."

"The girls must swoon when they hear that."

I laugh and jerk my chin at her. "Be still, and you'll get your memory."

She closes her eyes again, enjoying the sun as I start. My eyes caress every line and dip on her body. I take my time, making sure I commit every fucking inch of her to memory because I'm making a memory of my own.

"Still planning on Harvard?" Her voice is conversational even though that statement is accusatory. "Or have you grown a pair and started looking at art schools?"

Like I thought. My pencil stops moving as Caroline asks, but I start again, shushing her.

"Still a mute, I see."

"And you're still mean. Some things never change. Sit still."

She rolls over, making me sigh and frown at her. "Look at me, Liam. Nobody will ever see you unless you step out from behind the crowd. Aren't you tired of carrying everything?"

"What are you talking about? Roll over."

She gives a frustrated groan and rolls over but doesn't shut up.

"You stand behind Grey and your reputation. Behind your father and his legacy. Sooner or later, you need to be your own man."

I know Caroline, but I can't say that. The idea alone feels impossible. It's weird to think she's the only person who's always seen me for exactly who I am.

When I don't answer, she sighs, changing the subject.

"Okay, draw me, Brooks, but make sure I look perfect."

"Not a problem, Carebear. I draw it like I see it."

***

"Do you ever wish you could disappear? Like, get in the car and drive—no destination or purpose?"

Caroline's never looked so carefree, dancing around the grass, like a child playing with a sparkler in her hand as she asks me the question.

The guys and I had gone into the town earlier, and for whatever reason, I'd bought a dozen packs. Not necessarily with her in mind, but now I'm making a mental note to buy a trunkful tomorrow.

"No. What's the point of no destination?"

Caroline freezes, turning to stare at me for a moment like she's pondering how to answer. Fuck, I wish I could read her mind in moments like this. She shrugs as I take another swig of my Coke before turning back to the night sky.

Her hand lifts, and she begins drawing letters against the dark backdrop of the lake with the sparkler. *Tell her, Liam. Tell her she's the one. Tell her you would leave and never look back, but only for her.*

"Aww," she breathes out, turning around and tossing the burned-out sparkler into the fire. She extends her hand to me for another, and I grin as I oblige but not before I lean forward and light it using the bonfire.

"Thank you." She smiles.

Sweet Caroline is my favorite. Not because she's polite but because she saves that version for only me. I rub my hand over my head, looking down at the sand before lifting to stare at her back.

"Why would you want to escape our world? Life's only worthwhile because of the people in it, Carebear. I'd never leave them behind. Those people, you know, they mean everything to me."

Fuck. I'm such a pussy.

She looks over her shoulder, back to the house where Kai and Grey retreated to a half hour ago. A sly smile draws out on those red lips.

"That's your problem, Liam. You're so fucking codependent on Grey."

I'm talking about you. Just fucking say it. But I know why I can't— because what if Caroline doesn't feel the same anymore.

"And you aren't attached to anyone?" I counter. "What about Kai?"

She glances at me like she's lost in thought again. "Kai's like my best friend—that's different. Who would I have to be attached to?"

My eyes drift to the fiery streaks she creating in the background. I chew the inside of my cheek because I've long run out of toothpicks since this morning, as I watch her make loop after loop. *Is that?* A grin grows before I tamp it down. Son of a bitch.

Taking another drink of my Coke, I tilt my head. "Mmm. I think you underestimate what you feel. Maybe you're more attached to someone than you realize."

Caroline looks over her shoulder, almost irritated, rolling her eyes at me. "Unlikely."

"Then why have you been drawing my name in the sky for the last few minutes?"

She freezes before glancing back at her hand that's still extended in the air, then chucks the still-burning stick into the ocean.

Gotcha, Carebear.

Letter after glorious letter repeated absentmindedly, over and over— that's what I saw.

She brushes her hands together as if wiping herself clean, and I chuckle as she coolly walks back to her chair, lowering down. We lock eyes, and the way she looks at me tells me I hit the mark.

She's rubbing her finger as if she burned herself, as she says, "Dangerous little things. If you aren't careful, they'll burn. Better to get rid of them before they get too close."

I lean in and capture her fake burned hand, bringing my lips to her fingers, pressing a kiss.

"Don't worry, Carebear. It might hurt, but I'll always kiss it and make it feel better."

***

Caroline

The party's raging. Apparently, Grey's idea of celebrating the end of our sophomore year was to invite everyone from our school. Red cups litter the floor as people dance in the main living room, filtering out in the halls, and God knows where else.

I walk through my house with my friend Laura in tow, looking for the guys. I haven't seen them since this insanity began.

"Gotcha—"

I yelp as I'm nabbed by Kai and spun around. "How's my favorite girl?"

I pretend he's joking, but I know he isn't. His affections have become more apparent over the last few months. Maybe because we've been spending so much time together, just him and me. At first, I wasn't interested because my sights have always been set on Liam, but now I'm starting to think Liam doesn't feel the same.

"Where's everyone else?" I question as he sets me down.

"Over there."

Kai points to some chairs over by a fireplace, and Laura and I follow him over. Grey gives Laura a half-interested once-over as she begins to fawn all over him. *Never happening, Laura, move on.* Everyone around is talking and drinking as a familiar pair of hazel eyes stare at me over a red cup.

I look around for a place to sit, but all the seats are taken. Liam's still staring at me as a smirk grows over his face, and he pats his leg. The memory of him telling me he could feel my heartbeat pulls forward, so I shake my head.

He raises his brows, then spreads his legs wider and taps his foot.

Flirt.

I lick my lips, pulling down the black bandage dress that's daringly short, and turn to Kai. I touch his bicep, letting his arms wrap around my waist as I stand on my tiptoes.

"I'm going to go get a drink. Do you want anything?"

Before Kai can say anything, Liam jumps up. "I'll come with."

We walk in silence, people parting for us, me glancing up at him. He's holding my hand like he always does, but most people just assume it's because I'm protected—like he's my brother by proxy. I know that's not true. Not with the way it feels when he holds it.

Liam pulls me past the keg and down the hall, but I don't say anything or stop him. We weave around people until we get to the empty hall that leads to the library. He's like a man on a mission, never once looking down at me. He reaches out, opening the closet, the one I pulled him into the first time we re-met, and guides me in. The door closes behind us with a thud, and my heartbeat trades place with the sound as we stand in silence.

"Why are we in here, Liam?"

"Are you dating Kai?"

"What? No…maybe. Why?"

I run my finger over the scar on my wrist. It's like a blankie, making me feel strong even when I'm weak. "I don't know what I'm doing with Kai. But I know he likes being around me, and he's not hot and cold."

"I like being around you," he counters.

"So then be around me."

Put up or shut up, Liam.

"It's not that simple, Caroline."

He lets out a groan attached to his breath. *Yes, it is, Liam, for people with a spine.*

I reach for the handle, wanting out of the closet, but Liam's hand on my waist stops me as he says, "Don't see him anymore."

"Why?" My voice is so quiet.

The warmth of his body invades my space. "Because I want you. All for me."

His finger trails up the side of my body, making me shiver and want things from him.

"Is it true that you slept with Gabriel freshman year?"

The way he asks like he's preoccupied with another thought feels predatory. I feel as if I'm being readied, played with.

My head shakes no, but I answer, "Does it matter?"

"No."

Liam's hand splays over my back, sealing our bodies. I let out a tiny gasp, answering his first question.

"I'm a virgin."

He says nothing, and neither do I. We stand in the silence, waiting for the other to speak first.

"Have you ever touched yourself?"

My cheeks are beyond red as I whisper, "Yes."

Liam bends down, running his nose across my jaw to my neck, inhaling. My head falls back, carried away by the sensation.

I lick my lips. "Why don't you ever kiss me?"

We've come so close so many times.

"Because I won't stop, Caroline. Once I get a taste, it'll never be enough. Come get me at midnight. We'll sneak upstairs to the atrium."

His words are spoken against my neck.

"I'm supposed to go out with Kai."

"Then I guess tonight at midnight you'll make your choice."

His thumb runs over my bottom lip, dipping inside my mouth and making my entire insides quiver. Before I recover, he's gone, and I'm thoroughly turned on, alone, in a closet.

I stand there for a second, piecing myself back together because I feel unraveled. A rare smile graces my lips, and I lift my fingers to my mouth. I open the door, looking around before leaving the dark closet and heading straight up to my room.

***

I changed into a hundred different bra and panty sets, ultimately choosing to go bare. My lips press together, trying to hide my excitement. The thought makes me pause. It's a rarity in my life that I get what I want. There are plenty of situations I manipulate in my favor. Still, I'm never chosen by life for the happily ever after, but tonight—tonight, I'm going to lose my virginity and give my heart to the boy I've loved since I can remember.

He chose me and asked me to pick him. It's almost inconceivable.

I trot down the stairs in my same dress to rejoin the party and tell Kai I can't hang out tonight. My phone in my hand reads eleven o'clock, setting off more butterflies in my stomach.

Laura comes bounding over to me, drunk and giggling.

"Oh my God, Care. Where have you been? I've been looking for you for like an hour."

I shrug. "I had something to do. What are you drinking?"

The liquid sloshes inside the cup, and she waves it. "Something purple." Her arm shoots out toward me. "Here. Try."

I accept the plastic cup and take a sip. It's not bad, tropical, so I keep it.

A few other girls I know make their way over, and we stand drinking and chatting before a girl, whose name I've never bothered to remember, stumbles over, hysterically laughing.

"You guys. You have to see this video I just took."

She holds up her phone, facing the screen our way. Some girls are dancing super provocatively in the foreground before they start to kiss, but I'm not looking. It's what's in the background that has my eyes.

Liam with a girl on his lap, laughing and high-fiving Grey. He smacks her ass as she stands. My brows draw together, having seen enough. I push through the group, ignoring my name called, and walk through the crowd to where the guys are holding court.

Grey and Kai are sitting, drinking, surrounded by girls, but Liam's a no-show, and neither is an electric-blue mini dress.

"Where's Liam?"

They look at each other and laugh before Grey offers, "Becoming a legend."

"What does that mean?"

Kai stands up and pushes me backward, confusion marring his brow. His lips grace my ear to speak over the music. "It means he's about to break Grey's record for the number of virgins slept with."

I feel numb, like everything moving in slow motion. The music fades, and everything goes silent as I close my eyes.

That's why he asked. It was a game. A means to a victory. All of it, bullshit. God, I must have seemed so pathetic, such an easy target. The pathetic puppy that follows Liam around.

My palms lift to Kai's chest, my perfected smile leading the way.

"God, he's so gross, but it's not unexpected. That's not why I was asking though."

Kai grins as I continue. "I was hoping he'd keep Grey company so we could slip away."

His grin grows as he nods. "Yeah. Okay."

"But do me a favor. Don't tell Grey—I don't want his opinion about anything. Just wait like fifteen minutes and tell him you're coming to find me because I disappeared. 'Kay?"

He takes a drink from his cup. "Whatever you want, gorgeous."

"Atrium. Fifteen minutes."

I give a small wave and walk backward before turning around, walking out. The girl I just became is permanent and almost unrecognizable to the one with a broken heart.

***

Liam

The girl under me wraps her legs around my back, running her hands up the side of my body.

What the fuck am I fucking doing?

"I can't do this," I rush out, tapping her legs to unhook.

The moment she does, I stand from the bed.

She sits up, pulling the sheet over her chest. "What do you mean you can't do this?"

I shove a foot into my jeans. "I mean, put your clothes on. We're done here."

"You're supposed to take my virginity."

I stare at her, pausing my redress. "Are you fucking serious—trust me, in a few years, you'll be glad it didn't happen."

Buttoning my jeans, I sit down on the bed's edge to put my sneakers on.

"Liam, people are going to think there's something wrong with me."

I spin around, grabbing my T-shirt and pulling it over my head. "Then tell the world I fucked you, ate you, and thoroughly used you up."

I'm back on my feet, throwing the door open and leaving her on the bed. I storm down the hall, berating myself for being so fucking stupid. When I reach the stairs, I take two at a time, heading back to where Grey is. My eyes search the crowd for Caroline, but I don't see her.

I can't fucking believe that I almost fucked another girl because I couldn't just tell everyone that I'm crazy about Caroline. I'm an asshole who couldn't turn down the salacious reputation he's built because I don't know how to be my own man.

Girls are dancing on the chairs around Grey as I come up. "Hey. You seen Caroline?"

He nods. "Yeah, she was over here looking for you earlier. What's going on?"

"Nothing," I rush out, noticing Kai's missing too before I ask my next question. "Where's Kai?"

Grey shrugs, taking a drag off his cigarette, then looks at me. "Oh wait, he went to find Caroline."

There's a rock in my fucking gut. He's going to tell her what I was doing. I tug my phone from my pocket and look at the time, 11:50. Fuck.

Grey shoves my arm. "What the fuck is up with you, dick?"

My eyes come level to his. "Did you tell Caroline what I was doing?"

"No. I mean, I said you were becoming a legend, but—" Grey's words bounce off my back because I'm already headed to the atrium.

She knows. I can't make my feet move any faster without calling way too much attention to myself, but my heart is in rapid movement. The moment I'm up the stairs and out of sight, I book it, hoping I beat Kai from finding her.

The massive glass doors to the atrium are closed, a heavy blanket of darkness behind them, any picture I could see also hidden by the intricate iron pattern over the top half. I run down the long hall, begging inside to find Caroline. The closer I get, the more the moonlight shines in from the ceiling, illuminating what's behind.

My feet skid to a stop, all the breath in my body sucked out. The picture I see through the patterned, metal-framed glass is broken and mangled like a Picasso painting, or maybe that's my pride because what I see is the girl I'm in love with, locked in a kiss, with Kai.

***

I waited through the moans, the panting, and her undoing. I waited, standing in my place, feeling like I could break every wall around me. But I waited, so when she walks out, she'll know that I know.

This was her choice, and it's what I fucking deserve, but I can't help but hate her just a little.

The door opens, Kai coming out first, shirt untucked.

"Whoa. Hey, man," he says, surprised to see me.

My eyes land on hers, not acknowledging him. "Give us a minute, Kai?"

She pulls her hand from his and nods at him. He leans down, kissing her lips before saying something I don't hear and walking away.

I wait again, but this time I can feel the knife in my chest.

"Did you see us?" she questions, but her voice doesn't sound like hers.

She doesn't look like her anymore either, and not because she fucked Kai. There's something cruel about her.

My jaw tenses. "I guess I should say, 'Congratulations.'"

Stop being a dick when this is your fucking fault.

Her eyes narrow. "What do you want, Liam?"

For you to erase this and let me be the one. Or keep it and still let me be the one.

"I came to tell you that I think we should just be friends."

Pussy.

She huffs a laugh, bringing her hair over her shoulder as if she's poised to go in for the kill.

"We're 'not friends,' remember? So let's stay that way. Forever."

She's throwing my words back at me, but that's not how I meant them. She's using something pure as her weapon, and before I can stop myself, I say something meant to hurt.

"I was only being polite, Caroline, but honestly, I'd say I dodged a bullet."

She turns to walk away, but I grab her hand, instantly regretful. I don't know this version of us, and I don't like it.

"I'm sorry I said that."

Her bright, violet-blue eyes land on me from over her shoulder. "Well then, let that be your lesson, Liam. Always say what you mean."

Her hand slips from mine, and I watch her go, only glancing back once before Kai wraps his arms around her, and they walk away.

Chapter
Seventeen

Liam

The music is blaring, but it's my pulse I hear in my ears. Goddammit. I see Grey stand and point in her direction. He's just noticed. So I hold up a hand, like I got it, moving into the crowd.

"Move," I bark, barreling through people.

The dude with Caroline leans in to kiss her, but she pulls away, leaving him to land his sloppy fucking mouth against her neck. My fist hurts from the pressure I'm squeezing into it.

Caroline's laughing, obviously high, as that asshole keeps pulling her closer to him and touching her with his soon-to-be-broken hands.

"Hey," I yell, immediately getting the dude's attention. "No."

He releases her instantly but doesn't leave as I stand behind Caroline. Taking her arm, I spin her around. I'm mad, so fucking angry, that I'm not thinking about anything that's gone down between Caroline and me.

All I see is this prick with his hands all over her. In this fucking room, mixed with all my memories, and all I think is, *"He looks like a good enough punching bag."*

"Time to go back to the table, Caroline."

She laughs, reaching for my face, trying to squeeze my cheeks. "Grrr. So serious. Go away. I don't want you. I'm busy."

The asshole reaches for her waist, and I look at him like he should know better, shaking my head. "Don't do that. Don't make me break that hand."

He doesn't even feign bravery or press for her attention, walking away. Smart guy. My lips find her ear, trying to keep our conversation private because I can already tell she's ready for a fight, preparing to scratch my eyes out.

"You're fucked-up, Carebear, and you wandered away from Kai. Time to listen to me, or you're calling it a night."

She glares at me, ice in her veins, pushing a finger into my chest.

"You don't tell me what to do. You aren't my boyfriend. Remember?" *Boyfriend—yeah, whatever that means.* "Go hang out with your trollop, Liam Brooks."

Damn, she's good at giving tiny little jabs meant to compound until I break. I'm already teetering on the edge, so it won't take much to tip me over.

I shake my head, trying not to let her words stick. "You're right, I'm not your boyfriend. He'd happily share you… Just shut your mouth and move your ass."

Frustrated, I hold my hand out in the direction she should start walking, but she doesn't move. People are beginning to pay attention, clearing out space around us and staring, so I step in closer, placing a hand on her waist.

"Caroline. Don't make a scene. I'm trying to be a decent friend."

She laughs, but it's filled with anger. Shoving my hand away, she steps back. Caroline looks around at our audience before stealing the drink from the person next to her.

"Friend?" She tips the beveled tumbler back, taking big gulps before firing the glass down, shattering it on the concrete.

A loud crash sounds, and shards fly, eliciting some screams as people scatter. As they should because Caroline just rang the fucking bell, and now that we're here, there's no turning back.

"Since when have you been my friend, Liam? Since we were twelve? Oh, but that didn't count though, right? We never happened then." She motions around the room. "Or how about all the times we hid around this house together. Do you remember those since we weren't friends then either?"

"Enough, Caroline. Just go sit down before you say something you'll regret."

She laughs harder before closing the distance between us, but her eyes are sad.

"Were we friends when you told me to meet you in this very room?" I look over her, unable to meet her gaze. Caroline's palms rest against my tailored tuxedo shirt. "Or have you forgotten the plan to take my virginity as a trophy? Was that you acting like a decent friend, Liam?"

She doesn't know what the fuck she's talking about. I reach for Caroline's hand, wanting to put an end to the words spewing from her mouth, but she moves away, hurling her next sentence like knives.

"You don't get to hold my hand. Ever again. You've ruined my party, my birthday—my goddamn life. Go away. I thought I made it clear years ago that we weren't friends. Or do I need to arrange to fuck Kai in front of you again?"

My mouth drops open. Arrange? She did that shit on purpose. Any last shred of love I had for Caroline dies at this very moment. All these years, I thought she'd just made a choice. I'd sat around pining for a fucking monster while she delighted in my misery. Everything feels like a lie—it was all a lie.

My voice is low, so low I'm not sure she'll even hear it, but I've never felt so much rage.

"I ruined?" I shake my head, staring at the ground. "I ruined your life? That's a goddamn joke. You've made me miserable since we were fucking sixteen," I growl, looking up. "The only thing you got right is that, yeah—I fucking hate you."

She crosses her arms, eyes beginning to shine. "Good."

I nod, stepping back, genuinely meaning what I say, "You're fucking diabolical."

"And you're a coward."

Donovan and Grey stand next to me as Kai tries to put his arm around Caroline, saying, "Care, people are watching. Think about the Debs. You don't want the rumors."

But we're committed, no turning back now. I'm in a haze.

"I don't care," she cuts. "Everyone should know he's a bastard."

Every bit of anger I feel begins to bubble to the surface, and the more I try to hold it back, the more I can taste the curse in my throat.

"Fuck you," I spit, stabbing a finger at her, making Donovan gasp. "I've been here. Through everything, right next to you. When Grey hated you—I was there. When you hated yourself—I was fucking there. Always. And you let me be even though I was just a fucking game you played for fun. You deserve nothing—least of all my loyalty."

I can't even finish, my voice dropping out as my hands lift to my head. My chest feels tight, like I can't breathe. All her smiles, the times when I traveled over her face and got lost, the moments when I saw her so clearly that it felt like I could never unsee that kind of beauty again—it was all a fucking lie.

Her face draws in. "What does that mean?"

I laugh, empty, disgusted at her. "I should've seen it. It was right in front of my face. You never said you were sorry—to me, for me in that goddamn cafeteria. You let my best friend think I betrayed him—sent him off the rails, with Laura on his fucking lap. You let people believe I'm a monster. That I would fuck my best friend's girl, when of all people, you know I would never do that to Grey. Because. I. Haven't. To. Kai."

She blinks against my punctuated shouts.

"You fucking used me for your shitty revenge, like I was something to discard because you were jealous of Van. But I told you the day she came back that you were my girl—and I meant it. Never again. Because I finally get it, Caroline. You don't fucking care. You never did. Caroline the cruel, long may she reign."

Her hands are fisted by her side. Her mouth opens, then closes, but nothing comes. I turn, leaving, feeling like I've been punched in the gut.

I need out of here and away from her, but Grey grabs my shoulder. "You gonna be okay, man?"

The way he asks, it makes me feel raw. He knows I'm not. We've never spoken about that summer, the glances I've been caught in. The fact that I love his sister. But he knows, and if he didn't, he does now.

I hear Kai call Caroline's name behind me right as hands smack my back. "Fuck you, Liam Brooks. *You* broke *my* heart."

My head swings over my shoulder, watching Kai lift her and step backward, but she keeps yelling at me, "And I won't feel bad for you. Not when you cared more about your reputation than my feelings. You keep being the perfect son, friend, and Hillcrest manwhore. Because we both know you're just a liar!"

I rush forward, pissed, as Grey's hands on my chest stop me.

"Appearances? Lies? Are you kidding? You're one to talk."

This is why we're toxic. Because we take out our hurt on each other, slicing over and over, always giving back as good as we get. But in the end, all we do is destroy each other.

Caroline may have stopped cutting herself with razor blades, but she replaced it with me.

My voice roars over the music, "You want the truth? You're a spoiled little fucking brat."

Grey's pushing me back now, telling me to shut the fuck up, that it's gone too far. But I'm way past that.

"Oh poor Caroline, she has a hard life—nobody fucking cares about her."

"Shut up!" she shouts, confetti beginning to rain down.

I'm shoved another foot. "Poor Caroline, she's just mean because her mom's a bitch."

"Liam. Stop it," Donovan yells, rushing toward Caroline.

But I don't stop as the bass drops in the music.

"Poor Caroline, she never eats because she hates herself. Poor Caroline. Poor Caroline. Come on, gorgeous, show us the scars."

"I hate you!" she screams.

Kai pushes in front, blocking me from seeing her, but I laugh. "What the fuck are you going to do? Nothing."

He shakes his head. "Liam. Stop. Dude, this isn't you."

"But it is, and it's her fault."

Caroline shoves the concerned hands off her, steeling her spine as she walks around Kai. I'm sucking in the hot air, enraged and irrational. I feel like a monster, uncomfortable in my own skin.

She stops in front of me, searching my eyes, then slaps me hard across the face.

I don't move, remaining fixed on her as she does it again and then a third time. Her palm is red, probably as much as my cheek.

Bending down, I bring her face to mine. "Poor Caroline, she spreads her legs for everyone because I never loved her."

Her spit hits my face as large hands toss me away. Kai and Grey are bellowing profanities at me, but I don't care. I don't care about anything anymore.

"I'm done. Get the fuck off," I yell, shoving at the hands and arms on me.

If I can't destroy her, I might as well destroy myself.

I point my finger at her. "You got what you wanted, right? I told the truth. No running."

Caroline's body is shaking, arms wrapped around herself as I look around at the faces of my friends. They're all staring at me like they don't know me.

They don't.

She's the only one. Always has been. I guess we hurt the ones we love most.

Caroline's eyes lock to mine. "I wish I could blow out my candles and ask to have never met you."

I shrug. "I wish the same. Happy birthday, Caroline."

Chapter Eighteen

Caroline

The light bleeds out of my room as I shove the door open. It makes a lit path for me to walk, but as I enter, I hit the dimmer switch, wanting the darkness to swallow me whole.

"Hey." Donovan's voice is hushed as her hand touches my arm. "Let me help you."

"Just go. I want to be alone."

She whisked me away the minute Liam left, protecting me from everyone and bringing me to my room. She even told Grey to handle the party and make sure people kept having fun. She might be blonde, but she's not dumb. The more fun they have, the more that what happened tonight between Liam and me becomes a highlight rather than the whole night.

My feet feel like lead as I walk toward my king-size bed. With my hands on the mattress, I balance, stepping out of my Cinderella shoes and discarding them behind me. Donovan's hand touches my shoulder.

"Care, let me help you out of this dress."

I shake my head, pushing her hands away, wanting only to crawl into my bed and never wake up. I grip the blanket, bunching it, as I tug it down. All of Liam's words keep battling for dominance in my mind, not giving me any kind of reprieve, playing on a loop. *"Poor Caroline"* ... *"I fucking hate you"* ... *"Spoiled brat"* ... *"You're diabolical."*

My fingers curl around the fabric, feeling too much. It's like a dam burst, and now I can't make my emotions stop flooding. I'm overwhelmed, and this ache just won't fucking quit. My head drops down, feeling my hair fall over my cheeks.

"I never loved you."

My hand shoots over my mouth, suddenly tasting bile.

Donovan grabs my shoulders—"It's okay. I've got you"—rushing me to the bathroom.

I beeline for the toilet door and push it open. Cold marble hits my knees as I fall forward, gripping the porcelain, trying to hold back my tears.

Donovan's stroking my hair, pulling it back, but I can barely feel anything as I stare down.

Don't cry. Liam doesn't get to have that. Don't you fucking cry.

My rippled reflection stares back at me, eyes smudged with too much eye makeup, lips smeared by red gloss, cheekbones hyper defined. A tear streams down my face, bursting free, falling into the water, distorting my view.

"I hate you," I whisper. "You deserve this."

My stomach begins to heave, contracting my muscles and forcing my breath to hold. I vomit, coughing up nothing but bile because my stomach is empty.

"Poor Caroline. She doesn't eat because she hates herself."

I wretch again, so violently that my body lifts, trying to exorcise my own hatred. My knuckles turn white from the force I'm exerting to grip the seat as my stomach turns over again. Each time I heave, his words play through my mind. Over and over, until no more comes out.

"Come on, show us the scars."

This time I dry heave so hard that my eyes burn, blinking back tears from before as I fall back onto the floor, shaking. My back is against the wall, hair blocking my face as I fight, trying not to cry anymore. I don't want to feel this. I won't survive it.

"Caroline. Don't you dare hold on to this, goddammit."

Donovan's rubbing my arms. I look up into her eyes, trying to speak, but all that comes are stuttered breaths followed by guttural sobs until all I'm doing is screaming my sorrow.

"Make it stop. Please. Make it stop. I can't—Donovan. Take it away."

She throws her body over mine, engulfing me in a hug.

"Shh. Shh. It's okay. I'm here, Caroline."

I cry so hard, making sure I won't have any tears left. Donovan's arms stay wrapped around my body as she sits on the floor, reminding me I'm not alone and keeping me from disappearing any deeper into myself.

We sit for what feels like hours, reliving all of Liam's words, as I purge a different part of myself empty. I suck in air through my nose, wiping my eyes as Donovan finally releases me. My whole body seems to wake up, feeling the cold floor and the hardness of the wall behind me. I lean forward to pull some paper from the roll.

"No, here, let me," Donovan whispers, tearing some off and folding it, wiping the sides of my mouth.

I grab her hand and take a breath.

"Why are you being so nice to me? I've been nothing but a cunt to you."

She lowers the paper with the kindest eyes and smiles. "Because you're letting me and because you deserve it, Caroline. We all deserve someone to be there when we need it."

My brows furrow, unfamiliar with what I feel as I say, "Thank you."

I'm spent, stomach cramping as I try to push off the toilet, but I can't. She helps me to stand and walk to the sink, where I brush my teeth and rinse. She stands behind me, catching my eyes as I look up into the mirror, taking my hand and motioning toward my room. "Come on. Let's go to bed."

I follow her out. It's fitting that it's Donovan who's here. She's the only other person that could understand my grief. She knows what it's like to love someone you can't have and hurt them only because they might love you back.

Donovan walks me back to my bed, helping me in, not bothering with my dress, and pulls the cover over me. I sigh, wondering how long she'll stand there at my back, secretly wishing she doesn't leave.

"Are you going to be okay? Do you want to talk? Or sleep?"

I pull the blanket up to my neck, answering with a lie. "I'm fine. You can go."

Please stay.

"Care—"

"Stop, Donovan," I cut in. "I'll be fine. I just need to sleep."

The mattress dips, and Donovan gives my back a small pat for me to move over. I scoot, making room for her, feeling her lie down and spoon my body. Her hand strokes my hair before she wraps an arm around me, squeezing. The inside of me literally shakes. I don't want to need her hug, but I do so badly.

"Okay," she breathes out. "Let's sleep."

I can't answer because my body curls into itself as my chin quivers.

"I'm scared I'll disappear, D, because it hurts that much."

My voice is stuttered and cracking as I say it, but she only pulls me closer.

"Shhh," she whispers. "You're not disappearing because I see you—sweet, broken, mean, hopelessly in love, Caroline, I see you. And I'm sorry it took so long."

I pull Donovan's arm tighter around me and let my sorrow escape my lips and fill the room.

"I wish I could go back and tell him I'm sorry—when it mattered. I wish I could make us unmeet, so all of the hurt and the lies never happened. I turned him into this monster—I ruined the only precious thing life ever gave me."

She says nothing as I cry for myself, for Liam, for the future we'll never have. I cry because I love him so desperately, but now that we've done so much damage, we're unrecognizable.

I love him, so I hurt him because poor little Caroline hates herself so much, she doesn't believe anyone could ever really love her—that could only ever be a lie.

We were over before we even began.

My eyes close in between my tears, eventually winning the battle and bringing sleep, and along with it, all the haunted memories I want to forget.

Chapter
Nineteen

Liam

I t's three in the morning. The party's long over, and I'm sitting in the dark, staring across this room, unable to leave.

I ran from Caroline, and myself, walking the streets and looking for trouble but finding nothing. Good thing because there was already enough of it inside of me that I didn't need any help beating myself up. But no matter the path I walked, I ended right back where I started—here, sneaking inside as people left. I waited in the shadows, watching as Donovan quietly shut Caroline's door behind her before slipping inside.

Of all the fucking places I could go, the beds that would welcome me, here is where I sit, watching the girl I tried to crush sleep. Praying that she'll let me try to put her back together because of what I did. What I said—it's unforgivable.

Caroline's body stirs before rolling over and tucking the blanket under her chin. She looks peaceful, but I doubt she feels that way. I haven't taken my eyes off her since I sat down, listening to every soft breath, wondering what I'll say if she wakes up.

I think I needed to prove that she was still whole because it feels like I took a chunk from her broken heart—straight out of her chest.

My head hangs in my hands, elbows on my knees, as I stare at the floor. *If God is real, I hope he knows that I'll do any penance to set this right.*

"What are you doing here?"

Her soft voice lifts my face, big eyes staring back at me. All my words get stuck. Until the truth tumbles out.

"I don't know."

Her eyes narrow, thoughts flitting over her face. She has every right to be angry—to hate me. I can't blame her. What I did—fuck. I can barely stand the thought of living with it, and it's not stuck on me.

"You should leave."

I nod but start speaking before I lose my nerve. "I needed to make sure you were okay. The things I said—"

Words begin to fail me, so I take a breath.

"The hate that I drowned you in tonight. I don't know how to make that right. I didn't even mean it. I don't know why I said it all. I just hated myself so much for all the things I was too much of a fucking pussy to say—all the reasons it was never me you chose, that I think I wanted you to hurt just as much."

I clear my throat, trying to keep my emotions at bay, as Caroline's fingers wipe over her cheeks.

"All you did was tell the truth, Liam. The words are meaningless. It only hurts because *you* said them."

My hands wipe down my face as I let out a breath.

"No, Caroline. I lied. There is no world in which 'Poor Caroline' exists. But I hate myself because the truth is, I needed you to be as empty as I feel. Sorry isn't enough for what I've done because now I'm just another person who hurt you."

Caroline pushes the blanket back, her party dress still on. She wiggles off the bed, padding slowly across the distance before stopping between my legs, wrapping her arms around her waist. I want to drop to my knees and beg her to forgive me, but I owe her words, not actions, yet.

"And I don't hate you. I was a coward. I was mad you chose Kai. Even madder finding out that you did it to hurt me. But tonight, I walked the city trying to put myself in your shoes. I've never given you a reason to believe in me. All those months, I wanted to be with you, and I made you wait around. You must've felt like a fool."

She gives away nothing behind her mask as I continue.

"I was too scared to admit my feelings because I didn't know what Grey would say, and back then, I didn't know how to navigate the world without him. I was scared. So I fucked random girls and held your hand. Acted like a prick while I was trying to be your prince. I sat around, hoping something magical would happen to let me have you, all the while making you feel like shit. I'm sorry, Caroline."

Her hand lifts, running over my head, and I close my eyes, leaning into it.

"How is it that I can *love you* and *hate you* with the same heart?"

I rest my forehead on her stomach, hands coming to her waist. I've never understood anything more. We can't walk away because love brings us back, but all the goddamn hate we feel for ourselves, each other, creates our tragedy.

I swallow down the lump in my throat as my eyes close.

"Hate me, like you should for all the other villains in your story."

My eyes lift to hers, my chin against her stomach as she pores over my face.

"We're all sinners here, Liam. Welcome to the club."

Her chin trembles, but I shake my head, reaching up to wipe her cheeks. "Please don't cry. I don't deserve your tears. Because you're right. I've always been a liar and a fucking coward. Baby, don't cry."

I can feel her stomach dipping and pushing out as she breathes. She gazes down at me, pressing her hands over mine onto her face.

"Liam. That night. I knew what you were doing. I *am* diabolical—but I knew it was all a setup to be a notch in your belt. A wicked little game you and Grey were playing. So I beat you at it by seducing Kai, knowing you'd see. I wanted you to hurt as much as I did too."

Oh fuck. She doesn't understand. All this time, this is what she thought—the reason why she did that. She's not diabolical—that was survival, and my Carebear has carried that broken heart on her sleeve since.

"No. Baby." I pull her toward my face, whispering my words into her lips. "I wasn't going to touch you in the atrium. I swear. You were never a game."

I hear her suck in a breath, and my own tears spread over my cheeks as we come eye to eye.

"I wanted to ask you to be mine, Caroline. To kiss you in the dark—because you're right, it makes everything easier, and I was a fucking pussy."

She pushes against my shoulders, straightening, her face staring at the ceiling. My hands find her waist, wrapping around and kissing her stomach. "I just wanted to steal another moment."

I feel her crying, and I hate myself for what I've done to her.

"We're so ruined," she breathes out.

"I know."

Even with my answer, I stay as I am, holding on to her for dear life. I feel her hands wrap around the back of my neck.

"Too maimed."

"I know."

She's right. Too much has happened to ever fix. There are too many unsaid sorrys for our unholy deeds, but I still can't seem to remember how to fucking stand. Let alone walk away.

She brushes her fingertips over my brow, and I ask the only thought on my mind. "Just give me tonight, Carebear. Let me have you, just for tonight."

Even though I don't deserve you.

We're frozen, moonlight dusting the room, bathing our bodies in just enough anonymity to make us brave. Caroline's hands slide down over my shoulders, leaving me, and reach back behind herself.

The click of the eyehook cracks the silence, and I feel drunk. Caroline opens a second button, and I blink before replacing her hands with mine, stilling them as her arms slip down by her sides.

Her lips part as I unhook her dress one button at a time, all the way down her back, stopping right above her ass. My hands splay against her skin, relishing the feel of her, as I run them up her back, fanning my palms over her shoulder blades, slowly dragging the material away. I'm holding my breath, scared she'll run away.

The black lace material around her shoulders falls away, exposing more of her milky skin, calling for my lips as her chest rises and falls faster. Caroline's tongue darts out over her bottom lip, drawing it in between her teeth as she stares down at me.

I take her hand, bringing her fingers to my lips, kissing each one before tugging the sleeve from her arm and repeating it on the other side. The dress pools at her waist, leaving her standing in a black strapless bra.

"You're the most beautiful creature I've ever laid eyes on."

My palms swallow her ribs as I lean forward, pressing my lips to the skin just below the middle of her bra, savoring it and letting myself linger as my heart starts beating again. I can't help myself. I want more. So I draw her in closer, kissing her again in that spot, never wanting to stop. Caroline's hands run over my head, skimming her nails over my scalp as she lets out a small whimper.

The sound is the most erotic thing I've ever heard. I raise my hand, tearing the cup of her bra down, bringing my mouth over her pert nipple, sucking and running my tongue over the pebbled surface.

I can't stop myself—I'm all in.

"Liam," she breathes, dropping her head back as I run my lips over the perfect surface of her body to the other breast. "This feels like goodbye."

My fingers are clawing at her, demanding her body come closer because I know she's right. This is goodbye. It's the one thing I can give her to protect her heart. Caroline's palms cradle my face, forcing me to look up at her as her mouth crashes down on mine.

This kiss is fevered and insistent. Caroline's lips slide between mine as our mouths open and close around each other, heads tilting and pressing deeper. I want her, and it's all I know anymore.

"I want you. Inside of me," Caroline whispers into my mouth.

The tulle bottom of her dress bunches as I lift it, dragging it up her legs, guiding her onto my lap. She wraps her arms around my neck, mouth never leaving mine, kissing me back with the same desperation I feel. Her hands drop down, fighting with the fabric and lace of her dress, trying to unbutton my pants.

"Fuck," I growl against her lips.

I stand, knocking the chair over, taking her with me, with an arm around her waist. I'm holding her up as I jerk the dress down, taking her panties with it. Fabric rips and tears as I discard the now worthless couture. Caroline's legs wrap around me as I carry her over to her bed, dropping us down, kissing with the kind of indulgence for those hoping to die in one another.

I suck her bottom lip between mine before I stand and pull the end of my bow tie, letting it fall open. Her hands run up her legs, drawing my eyes to the small bandage on Caroline's hip, and my heart breaks again.

"Is that one because of me?"

"No. Me," she rushes out.

Caroline comes to her knees on the bed, running her hands under the shoulders of my jacket, slipping it from my body. It hits the floor as she begins to unbutton my dress shirt.

We don't speak because there's nothing left to say.

She methodically unbuttons the black circles, her fingers brushing against my bare chest hidden underneath, making my dick strain. She tugs at my shirt, untucking it, pushing it open, and leans forward. Her lips touch my chest, and I suck in a breath, head dropping back, overwhelmed by the feeling of Caroline kissing me.

"Heaven," I whisper.

All my senses feel like they're exploding as I drop my eyes back to hers.

"Fuck me, Liam. Make it so nobody else ever existed."

My hand wraps around her throat, squeezing enough to get her attention.

"Nobody else ever has, Carebear."

My lips mold to hers as I undo my pants. Our tongues swirl as I move forward, letting go of her throat to support my weight. She spreads her beautiful goddamn legs, running her hands up my biceps, never taking her eyes off mine.

I love you.

It's my singular thought as I shove inside her, almost dying from the hit.

Chapter
Twenty

Caroline

My back arches off the bed, overpowered by the sensation of Liam filling me, stretching me as he relentlessly thrusts inside of me, each time whispering how beautiful I am as he kisses every fucking inch of my body.

I'm breathless, alternating between gripping the sheets, then hands on his back, then back to the bed as he holds one of my legs in place and circles his hips. God, he hits just the right spot, as if my body's road map had been committed to memory.

"Look at me, Caroline."

My eyes are obedient, cutting to his, watching him hovering over me, mouth agape. He's so intense, so connected to every piece of me that I'm devastated. Liam licks his lips, bringing them to mine again. His tongue sweeps around my mouth, teasing and exploring, serving up the best kiss I've ever experienced. He may be kissing my mouth, but I can feel it everywhere.

My arms snake under his, gripping his shoulder and holding him close to me.

"It's so much more," he whispers into my mouth.

He doesn't need to explain. I understand. This is more than I could've ever imagined it to be too, and I almost can't take it.

I flip Liam over, straddling him, slapping my hands down on his chest. His fingers dig into the fleshy part of my ass, rocking me into him, still fucking me, even though I'm on top. I stare at his throat, watching a vein throb under his skin, unable to look him in the eye.

I'm scared he'll see that I don't ever want us to end.

He shoves himself up to sitting, wrapping his arm around me, pressing my cheek to his own.

"Stay with me in this moment, Caroline. Don't run yet."

He's taken the lead, thrusting inside of me over and over, fucking us into our goodbye. As I bring my eyes back to his, Liam's mouth descends on my neck, sucking hard, leaving a mark, I'm sure. But I want it, so everyone will know that I belong to Liam, and only him—always.

"How can I say goodbye?" I breathe out with a shaky exhale.

I'm tossed onto my back, Liam back inside of me before I can take a breath. He grabs my wrists in his hand, drawing them up above my head, and stares at me, stilling.

"I'll do it for us."

I dig my heels into the bed, anchoring myself and pressing my pelvis into his, begging for more of his cock. He moves slowly, at first, letting his words sink in. But I nod, holding back tears, hooking a leg around him as he picks up speed. We're like animals, grunting and moaning, the sounds of skin hitting skin filling the room as the build begins.

Sex fills the room, as much as our grief, heightened by our passion.

"Say something, Liam. Say something that I can keep, long after you disappear."

The desire grabs hold of me, forcing my eyes closed, owning me, but I force them open. I don't want to miss even a moment.

Liam looks lost as if the words won't come. Maybe he's as scared as I am, or maybe he can't handle saying them out loud. But he doesn't have to because I know them all.

I love you too, Liam.

A heady sensation, like tiny fireworks exploding inside of me, begins to fire as his mouth covers mine. Liam devours my pleasure while I climb higher and higher until I'm coming harder than I ever have before as he growls, moving as if he's going to pull out. I wrap myself around Liam tighter, desperate to have all of him.

"I'm on the pill. Stay."

His body tenses, hesitating, before pushing deeper, saying nothing as he releases inside of me.

Liam's full weight falls onto me, warm and safe, as his lips graze my ear. "I will never feel like this for anyone else, Caroline. You've always meant more."

I clutch him, wrapping my legs around his sides, depleted, inhaling his scent—but not missing that he didn't say *love.*

We lie that way until it starts to hurt too much, not just physically. My legs fall away, and I suddenly feel so naked as Liam rolls over, putting a hand on his chest and letting out a breath. I start to speak, to take it all back, but he sits up, giving me his defined back.

"No more hurting each other, Caroline."

I nod even though he can't see me. He bends down, grabbing his jacket off the floor, and stands, doing his pants back up. I'm lying on the bed, exposed and raw as he pauses, looking back over his shoulder but only to the point of showing me his enviable profile.

"Goodbye, Carebear."

Liam walks away, not looking back, but this time I don't want to cry. I want to run after him and beg, but I don't because that's what got me here in the first place. The bedroom door closes, clicking with finality. A shiver runs over my body as I stand and walk to my vanity, opening the silver case that's still on top.

A neat pile of small band-aids and Neosporin rest next to each other. They're organized alongside my razor blades—an ill-fortuned necessity for those who can't feel.

But I do now. I feel it all.

I reach inside of a satin pocket, hidden in the case, and pull out the Care Bear sticker that doesn't stick anymore, placing it on my vanity and tossing the rest in the trash, whispering to myself, "No more using you to hurt me anymore, Liam."

Chapter
Twenty-One

Caroline

"**W**ake up. You've overslept, and God, you smell, Grey." My face scrunches up in disgust. "How much did you drink last night? It smells like a bar in here."

Grey grumbles into his pillow, making no move to actually wake up. Donovan's long gone, so he's lying alone, still drunk, I'm sure. I wish I were doing the same, but life doesn't stop just because my heart's broken. I gave myself a moment to spiral out over the repercussions of last night, but now I have my big-girl panties on.

"Grey," I press.

"For fuck's sake, Caroline. I hear you. Your voice is like nails on a goddamn chalkboard. Why are you torturing me?"

He sits up, hair askew, and my hand shoots to my mouth, trying not to laugh.

"You look worse for wear, but we have our hellish brunch, dearest brother. You need to clean up."

"Cancel," He grunts, pulling the blanket over his face.

I roll my eyes, stalking over to his drapes and tugging them back to allow the light in.

"We can't. They're downstairs."

A pillow hits me from behind, and I spin around. "Asshole! Get. Up."

He throws the blanket down to his waist, sitting up and shaking his head. "No. Tell my father I said to fuck off and to get out of my house."

Good God, he's an actual toddler. If the girls at Hillcrest could see this—with his luck, they'd find it adorable. I, however, do not.

I raise my brows, but he shrugs.

A burgeoning sense of panic begins to take hold. Grey never leaves me alone with his father, not since an uncomfortable moment when our parents were first married. I don't think Evan would ever step over a line, but that doesn't mean he didn't consider it for a terrifying moment.

That day is just one of the strings that weaved themselves into the ties that bind Grey and me. He promised me two things that day. The first that we'd take care of each other—even if we didn't like each other very much because we're the same kind of beast in this world of ours. Second, that he'd never tell when I had a human moment. He's kept both.

"Grey," I sigh, standing at the end of his bed. "Please don't leave me alone with them. After last night—I can't do this by myself today. I'm trying to 'brand-new day' my mindset, and my mother is a big fucking cloud."

The moment I say it, I hate how weak it sounds.

"Was that positivity from a Pinterest quote?" he teases, turning and giving me his back. "Hell has officially frozen over."

Grey stands from his bed, and his bare ass has my head turning away as I counter, "Even the devil has optimism for her success. And ass."

"How am I an ass—" His question cuts short because I suspect he's looked down. "Well. That's a whole new take on rise and shine. Okay. Get out, monster, and let me get dressed for this fucking debacle."

I turn, walking toward the door, and as my hand hits the handle, Grey throws out, "Did I see Liam sneaking into your room last night?"

"You did. We're fine. And I'm not talking about it."

"Good. I didn't want to hear about it."

The smile is ever present in his voice, and it makes me want to do the same, but instead, I say, "Thank you. You're the worst brother," quietly, hearing his chuckle as I walk out.

***

Two hours later, I'm sitting at a table in the middle of Grey's father's club, tense and wishing I'd canceled when Grey suggested it. My mother's said no more than ten words to me—none of which were *happy birthday*.

I don't know why I'm so fixated, but it seems like the easiest thing to say to another person. People say it to strangers on fucking social media, at restaurants when a cake is delivered, but she can't bring her mouth to form the syllables—in English or French.

"The house seems to be running well in my absence, Grey."

As if you did anything before.

Even her compliments sound like insults. I suspect that's on purpose— what a tragic personality trait of an insecure expired fauxcialite.

"You sound surprised," I answer in Grey's place.

"I am," she levels, before slicing into her food. "But not about *his* ability."

Evan's fork makes a light scrape against the plate before he drops his utensils and shakes his head. He immediately motions for the waiter. My eyes shoot to Grey, who was over this brunch before it began.

"This frittata is flat. Make it again."

But before the waiter can leave, Grey adds, "Oh, and Louis, give my compliments to the chef for this quiche, *c'est magnifique*. Truly brilliant."

The waiter tries to hide his smile, taking Evan's plate as I huff an empty laugh. Grey shoots me a smirk before rolling up his shirtsleeves. It's funny, he's always just been Grey, stepbrother/pain in the ass, but for the first time, he looks like a man too. There's nothing imbalanced between him and his father. Not anymore. He isn't afraid of disappointing him or even going to battle.

What I'd give for that kind of confidence.

My gaze shifts to my mother, taking her in. I stare at the fine lines diminished by Botox and that damn cold demeanor that's always lingering in every expression.

What's so scary about you? Or is it that I fear all the shit she says to me is true—that I'm unlovable, less, ugly, stupid. *But Liam loved me, just as I was.*

He loved me when I was chubby and a fake blonde and even now, when I'm ugly on the inside.

"So, what do we owe the pleasure of this visit, Evan?" Grey speaks, breaking me from my thoughts.

Grey's voice is laden with so much sarcasm that it draws a furious look from Evan because we all know why Evan's here—to grovel because Grey signs his papers tomorrow.

I pick up my fork, riveted by the fight about to happen, stabbing a slice of strawberry. My mother glances at my plate, but I roll my eyes and take two more bites before I smirk.

Fuck you, Maman, I'm hungry.

After last night, I probably won't be getting a golden ticket anyway, so I might as well bulk up so I can be an even bigger disappointment. Bitch.

Evan counters with a challenging remark, and Grey does the same, but it's worse—at least that's what Evan's face displays. My mother leans over, tapping her long nail on the table to get my attention.

"We came to celebrate, Caroline. I don't want the day to become ruined before we're able to do that. Say something. Change the subject."

My eyes dart to hers, disbelieving. Celebrate? Some of the ice thaws from behind my glare.

"Caroline, take control," she whispers. "Grey will listen to you."

Butterflies flutter inside my stomach, soothing the anger I was harboring. *She wants to celebrate.* Her eyes are insistent as I nod.

I look back between Evan and Grey, wondering what the fuck I should say, ultimately interjecting, "Evan. Has Grey told you that he qualified for the Olympic rowing team?"

Both men's faces shoot to mine, but it's Grey's that makes me second-guess what I've just said. Shit. Donovan told all of us days ago; I didn't think it was a secret.

My mother clasps her hands together. "Amazing. What an accomplishment. It seems we have two things to celebrate today." She nods to a waiter, who approaches with a bottle of champagne.

Was that planned?

I lean over to Grey, whispering, "I'm sorry. I didn't know what to say. She wanted to toast my birthday."

I want this moment more than I can admit is what I don't say, but he gets it because he gives me a wink. "You owe me one, Caroline."

Evan fixes his suit vest, exchanging looks with my mother as the silver champagne bucket is set on the table, the cork popped. Our glasses are filled, but Grey waves it off, opting to pick up his coffee mug.

My mother lifts her glass, urging Evan to do the same, then smiles between Grey and me.

"To Grey. Your father and I are so proud of you and very excited for what the future brings—with the company and now rowing."

I'm paused, frozen midair. I lower my flute as my mother tries to clink mine, recoiling as I look down at the table, my voice quiet.

"You wanted to toast Grey. Of course, how silly of me to think otherwise."

Grey sits up a bit taller, watching me, as I laugh to myself, staring at the bubbles swirling like little tornadoes in the crystal, thinking that it's exactly how I feel—like a fucking tornado.

Lifting my eyes, I stare at my stepbrother, who looks like he'd ruin the lives of every person in this room if I asked. So much is communicated between us with just a look.

We really only have each other and the people we've made family—Grey, begrudgingly Donovan, Kai…Liam.

"Caroline," she hisses. "What is wrong with you? Don't be stupid. Of course that's why we're toasting," she laughs. "What other reason would there be?"

My head swings to hers. "My birthday, Mother."

She doesn't even have the courtesy to look guilty as she waves a hand in the air, dismissing what I've said.

There was a time when I hung on her every word, and when I was much younger, I'd hoped I could convince her to love me. Later I just aimed to please. Jesus, all of my achievements are aimed at gaining her respect, even if she never deserved mine. And here she is, proving that point. I smooth my hair back to where it sits in a low ponytail, hearing my mother's guffaw.

"Caroline, excusez-vous *maintenant.*" *Caroline, apologize now.*

Grey smacks a hand on the table, commanding everyone's attention.

"Vivienne, your daughter is set to graduate with honors. She'll receive early acceptance to every school she's applied to. Her birthday party got an honorable mention, not only on Page Six but by Anna fucking Wintour. The social ladder you've been climbing since you got off the goddamn bus ends with Caroline now. You'd be wise to remember that and lift your glass."

Shocked, worried, nervous—all are appropriate descriptions of her face, but I'm smiling. *He's the worst.* Grey grabs the champagne bottle, filling his glass and clinking it to mine.

"Happy birthday, Care."

Fuck you, Vivienne Rycroft Whitmore.

She turns her fake smile on me, turning on the accent as I take a sip.

"Chérie, of course I was going to include you in my speech."

I lean in closer on the table, keeping my voice low, placing my flute down.

"No. You weren't. I haven't mattered to you since my father left you."

Grey reaches back, taking his suit jacket from the chair and giving me a nod. Time to go. Her face shifts back and forth, panic setting in. Even Evan looks nervous—I guess this isn't what they expected today. I slide my chair back, but she darts her hand out over mine.

"Caroline. Think about where your loyalty lies."

My brows rise. Is she serious?

"So much has happened over the last twenty-four hours that I barely have room for this. But a word to the wise." I lift my chin to Evan and then back to her. "*C'est un bateau qui coule.*" *That's a sinking ship.* "You may want to invest in a life vest because when you drown, your husband won't help you. And neither will I."

Her nails dig into my hand as she sneers.

"*Faites attention à la façon dont vous me parlez, petite salope. Vous me devez—je vous ai cette vie.*" *Be careful how you talk to me, little bitch. You owe me—I got you this life.*

"Don't you mean little pig? What is it about me that you hate so much, Mother? Is it that I have the life you wanted without all the sacrifice? You do realize that you didn't have to spread your legs so fucking wide, don't you?"

"You know nothing of sacrifice," she snaps, her calm façade chipped away.

My lips tip up, but I don't know why I smile. Maybe because I'm happy everyone gets to witness this moment, or perhaps because I finally decided that I don't care what she has to say anymore.

"How's this for sacrifice?" I pull back the sleeve of my sheer black blouse from the hand she's holding in place, exposing the scar on my wrist.

"This wasn't the first time. Just the first time I didn't care if it kept bleeding. I've given a pound of flesh in the name of your disappointment. But I don't have to anymore. I've decided to be free of you. It took me letting go of the most precious person I've ever loved to realize that if I can do that and still have a pulse, well then—"

I don't bother to finish. She understands.

Tearing my hand away, I stand as her eyes narrow. "Don't forget who controls the purse strings."

Grey stands next to me, buttoning his jacket, as he interjects, "Brunch is over." He directs his attention to his father. "I'll have your belongings sent to a storage facility—on your dime. And just for fun, I'm directing the company's lawyers to look into Caroline's trust. If even one penny is missing, it'll be a headache you don't want."

"Is that a threat, son?" Evan spits, tossing his napkin down on the table as my mother sits back, face ashen.

"No, it's a promise, Evan. If you don't fall in line, I'll destroy everything you touch. Then, just to be a prick, I'll fuck your wife and make her tell you how much better the younger version is."

My mother gasps, and I laugh, shocked and thoroughly entertained. Grey holds out his hand for me, and I accept, smiling at my mother.

"It's always a pleasure spending time with family. Call again when you're in town."

Grey and I stroll out of the club directly to the valet, who immediately calls the car over. We stand stoic, looking forward, but my punch to his arm breaks our silence.

"Ow."

"You couldn't have left out the part about fucking my mother?" I snap, shaking my hand, "You're such a degenerate."

He shrugs, grinning. "Don't tell Donovan. She'll kill me. But it was a good jab."

Our car pulls up, and Grey opens the door for me, allowing me to slide inside. He follows, plopping down onto the leather seat next to me, searching his pockets for a cigarette.

"You okay?"

I shrug, holding out my hand. He scowls but places a smoke in my hand before rolling down the window. The flame of the lighter flickers as he extends it over, and I take a drag, releasing with a long exhale.

"I wish I'd been the one that put her in her place—said meaner things."

He smirks and nudges his knee into mine, drawing my eyes.

"Caroline, she may have raised you in her image, but you're a much nastier version. You'll get your sea legs with her."

A silent laugh moves my chest as I take another drag and throw the cigarette out.

"That might be the nicest thing you've ever said to me."

Chapter
Twenty-Two

Liam

I only slept because my body forced me into it. There are three times in my life when I've felt altered, known that a decision I made would leave me forever changed.

Once when I placed myself between Grey and our sixth grade teacher. The other when I stood outside a door watching Caroline fuck someone else.

And now.

Now feels like the worst time. This time, I don't know if I've changed for the good or the bad. The ceiling feels like it's coming down on me as I stare up, thinking a thousand thoughts. *Did I do the right thing? Should I run her down and say, "fuck it, let's just be together"?*

I already know the answer because nothing's changed. It doesn't matter that I said I was sorry for the million little wounds I've inflicted. We're still at the place we began. I'm still a guy who can't choose his future or tell the girl of my dreams that I loved her when it mattered.

But saying the word makes it something real that I have to then do—

and how can I? How am I the man she needs when I can't even stop myself from hurting her.

Caroline deserves everything, not just bits and pieces I forfeit as I stumble around fucking everything up. My door swings open, jolting me to sit on my bed as my mom breezes in, heading straight for my curtains.

"Mom, "I grumble. "Why? Just leave me in the dark."

"Time to rise and shine, little prince."

The light assaults my eyes as she sweeps the fabric open, turning to smile at me. "Darling, it's noon."

A yawn muffles my words as I rub my head. "I've been awake, but I'm staying in bed. All day."

She's staring at me, arms crossed, and I don't like the look on her face.

"What's wrong?" she levels with narrowed eyes.

Great, this isn't what I need right now. I don't have it in me to have a fucking kumbaya with Babe. No way.

"Nothing." When she frowns, I add, "I swear. The party took it out of me."

"Mm-hmm," she hums.

I huff a laugh. "Come on, it's Sunday. Leave me be, Warden. I'll come down later, and you can feed me and tell me all about your benefit next week."

I lie back, pulling the covers over my head, adding, "'Kay?"

But she makes no attempt to leave, walking over to my bed instead and sitting.

"Are you sure that's all there is to it?" Her voice is quiet. "Because you look like shit, darling, and you're sulking."

Fuck. Can I get one day off from everything? Why does she have to know me so well? I raise my voice from under the covers, trying to derail this fucking conversation with humor.

"Babe Brooks. Did you just say 'shit'? Language. What would your ladies that lunch think?"

"Liam. Look at me."

I pull the blanket down and let out a breath, but she pats my cheek. "Are you and Donovan fighting again? Because this is a lot of déjà vu. Or is it something else?"

Who am I not fighting with?

Shaking my head, I lie, "Mom, I'm tired. Seriously."

I can tell she doesn't believe me, but she knows I won't tell her. The thought of how she'd look at me, if she knew what I did, the disappointment she'd have—it feels crippling.

She sighs and looks away.

"Okay. Fine. Don't talk. But get up. I have a chore for you. Maybe that'll help you shake off the doom and gloom on your face."

I frown, lifting the side of my lip in a sneer. "You're torturing me. Your only son. This is borderline child abuse."

"Good thing you're a man and not a child."

She stands, shaking her head with a laugh, heading back toward my bedroom door before stopping and turning around. With her hand resting on the frame, she winks. "You have a package to deliver down to my office, and as a reward, there are some gorgeous palettes on my desk that you can grab for your paintings. That is unless you've given that up in favor of Harvard."

Jesus, Babe. She's pushing all my buttons today. Not going there either.

I groan, ignoring her pointed remark about my conversation with my father, and throw my blanket back, feet hitting the floor.

"Don't you have an assistant for this?"

She grins. "Yes. I do. But you and Kai are free labor."

My face goes blank. Fuck. Babe said Kai. He's here to throw down. Can I blame him? I'm surprised it's not the entire cavalry.

Adjusting my basketball shorts on my hips, I say, "What do you mean, Kai?"

"He's downstairs. His mother donated a piece for the Nudes benefit. I don't think she wanted to risk a courier taking a look, so she sent him to deliver it."

The frown I feel must be evident on my face because she grins. "Funny, that's the same look he made when I told him you'd go together. Now hurry because I don't like to wait."

Fan-fucking-tastic.

***

Kai managed to remain polite only until my mom closed the front door behind us.

"I should put my fist through your face. Right here on your front steps."

"Probably." I nod. "I won't stop you."

Kai and I are about the same size. I'm not scared of him, nor do I think I'd ever lose to him in a fight. But I deserve to get my ass kicked for what I did to Caroline and, depending on what he knows, to him too.

He blows out a breath, turning and taking the steps quickly. So I begrudgingly follow as his voice raises. "You're a fucking prick, you know that? That shit you pulled last night was not cool. I don't care if she started it"—he spins around at the bottom—"she's Caroline. We don't treat her that way."

"I know."

But he clearly doesn't.

Anger vibrates off Kai, justifiably so. I did hurt Caroline. But I don't want to hear about it from anyone but her.

"What the fuck were you thinking, Liam? Since when are you such a dick? That's Grey's department."

Since I lost the only girl I've ever wanted and with her my mind.

I don't know how to explain what it's like to continually eat your words until nothing else will go down, so you fucking spew it all up. And with Caroline, I can't hide—she won't let me.

I open my mouth to try, but all that comes out is, "I don't want to talk about it."

Kai's brows pull together like he's fighting with himself before he turns toward his maroon Mercedes G-Class. He pops the trunk, stepping out onto the street where he's double-parked, and places the small, crated photo in the back. Another look in my direction has his head shaking again as he clicks the fob to shut the door.

"Well, are you coming?" he shouts, walking around to the driver's side.

Fuck. Why me. This shouldn't be awkward at all.

I open the door and slide inside, rolling my shoulders because the confined space feels even smaller. Or maybe it's because of all the tension filling it up. Kai stabs the address that he has on a piece of paper into the nav, tensing his jaw.

"Look, man—" I start, but he cuts an Acura and me off as he begins to lay in.

"No. No 'look, man.' You hurt her. We may not be conventional, but that doesn't mean I don't love her or want to protect her."

"Stop," I breathe out, feeling my chest get tight again.

He doesn't listen, still ranting. "You don't get to speak or act like that. Caroline's fragile, Liam. I know she puts up an act and pretends to be mean, but it's out of survival."

"Kai, stop."

His shakes his head. "If you knew her the way I do... If you really knew her, you'd know that deep down Caroline's—"

"Stop," I shout, smacking the dash.

Just fucking stop.

I take a deep breath, feeling it rattle around in my chest as I stay focused on my lap.

"Don't fucking tell me what I'm supposed to know. Trust me, I know her better than anyone. I made my amends with the only person that matters—Caroline. So drop it."

My hands run over my head as I stare out of the windshield, silence hemorrhaging the car.

"What the fuck do you mean amends?"

I don't answer.

He hits the steering wheel. "This is bullshit, Liam. Did you see her, since the party?"

The way he says it sounds like panic, not like jealousy. Because that's who I've become—the person that hurts her. He doesn't trust me anymore, and I can't blame him. I don't trust myself.

This time he asks quietly as the car pulls to a stop at a red light.

"When?"

I turn my head to look at him because I'm pretty sure he just figured out why he wouldn't know about it.

"I left her this morning. But am I having this conversation with her boyfriend? Or her friend? Because all I'm going to say is don't put us in this place, dude. I didn't. For three fucking years."

Kai tugs his seat belt off, staring at me like he's about to do something.

His eyes bore into mine. "Did you two…tell me you didn't fuck with her head like that."

My chest rises and falls faster because I can't tell him that—I fucked with both our heads because I couldn't stay away from her anymore. No matter the aftermath.

Kai's head shakes. "You don't see her anymore."

"She can make her own decisions, Kai, but I don't think you have to worry."

My head lies back against the seat, feeling exhausted, as horns begin to blare around us, intensifying when we don't move.

I point to the road, looking at him. "Are you gonna go?"

"That's it, dick? Don't worry about it. I don't want to talk about it. You destroyed her, and according to you, you already know that because you know her best. But this is all you'll say? Some bullshit line about whether or not I'm acting like a boyfriend or a friend." He huffs, turning toward the front, and pulls his seat belt back. "For your information, I'm acting like a person who loves her."

I try to take a breath, but it's hard. It's the way he said "a person who loves her"—as if I don't—that's making me feel paralyzed.

I've spent my whole life being what everyone expects, needs, fuck— just prefers. I'm Tucker's Harvard-bound son, Babe's artistic charmer. I'm Donovan's partner in crime and Grey's rationale, but I will never be the guy that doesn't love Caroline.

The car starts forward but jerks to a stop because we sat through the green light.

"Fuck," Kai growls, adjusting his sunglasses, but I start speaking, lost in the idea of Caroline.

"You think I don't know that she's a masterpiece, Kai? The best note in every song, a mean little snake that should never be tamed. That girl's owned me since 9:17 a.m., on October 31, 2015—when I gave her a goddamn Care Bear sticker that I'd stolen."

His face turns, eyes searching mine, and then his expression shifts. Kai's head draws back ever so slightly as he points his finger at me.

"I can't believe I never saw it before. I mean, how could I? A month ago, you were chasing after Donovan. Last week you were dipping into the freshman pool. But all this time, you've loved Caroline."

I don't look at him, just stare at the goddamn roof of the car. Everything inside of me wants to demand, threaten, hurt him—just to ensure he never touches her again. I want to say, *"Now that you know, all you get is her friendship because she's mine, always has been and always will be."* But I lost that right when I tore out her heart the first and second time.

Screamed obscenities come from outside the car as someone passes us, pulling both our eyes. The light's green again, and we're still here.

"Shit," Kai breathes, just as we're met with a sound of a siren and one of New York City's finest on a loudspeaker.

"Pull over. Now."

This fucking day's getting better and better.

***

I've been hiding downstairs in my art studio all night. My mom had it built for me years ago, much to my father's dismay, but this is always where I come when my head feels too loud, and today it's like a full-on concert in there.

After Kai and I sat on the sidewalk, receiving a lecture and some threat from the cops, we were released, but I opted to walk home, and he went to my mom's office. I couldn't get back inside the car and hash out what I'd said or done to Caroline. So I walked away without a word and slipped back inside my house, coming straight here.

The toothpick in my mouth is wearing down as I lean sideways on my stool, sweeping my brush over the faint pencil line of my sketch, feathering the paint. I pull back, looking at the lips I've drawn—her fucking lips.

My head drops to look at the ground as I jerk the toothpick out of my mouth, and a wave of thoughts flood, but I try to shake them off by raising my gaze back to the picture.

But all I see is Caroline.

"Fuck," I breathe out, tossing the paintbrush onto a nearby table, and interlock my fingers behind my head, staring at her perfect pout.

This is so fucked.

Buzzing sounds from where I left my phone on the couch. I stand and head over to see that there must be another dozen texts from Donovan. I'm not answering her or anyone; it's a dick thing to do, but I can't, not right now.

> **Van:** Why are you ignoring me?
> **Van:** Answer your phone.
> **Van:** Kai said you guys were held by the cops longer because you kept running your mouth. WTF, Liam!
> **Van:** Are you serious rn? This is how you're going to be? Real nice.

Blowing out a breath, I pick up my phone. My thumbs hover, debating what to say, what not to say, and all the shit in between.

> **Me:** Get off my back…

Delete.

> **Me:** I'm sorry…

Delete.

> **Me:** I love h…

Delete.

The door to the studio opens, drawing my eyes in surprise as my father walks through. He's staring at my face with a look that tells me I'm not going to like whatever he has to say. I type quickly, responding to Donovan, and hit Send before pocketing my phone.

My father comes to stand, facing me, from the opposite side of the dark leather couch. He places his hands on the back, leaning forward. "We need to talk."

Shit. He can't know about the cops. Or maybe he does. The man has friends everywhere. It's not as if it was a big deal, but I'm sure this will all circle back to fucking Harvard.

I point toward the door to indicate I'm going up to my room, saying, "Okay, but let me clean up first?"

"No, Liam. Now."

He shakes his head while holding up a thick white envelope, one I didn't even notice he was holding. I look at him, confused.

"When were you planning on telling me?"

What the fuck is he talking about? My eyes drop to the envelope, catching the one word that bottoms out my heart—Columbia. Holy shit. It's my acceptance letter.

"Where did you get that?"

"From your room. The housekeeper left it for you."

"It's addressed to me."

He says nothing. Jesus, he's not even embarrassed by his behavior. I close my eyes, trying to calm myself.

"Columbia isn't the plan, Liam. Your future is brighter than this. The connections you'll make and the legacy you'll continue at Harvard is more important than this hobby—"

He's talking, but all I can think is *push, push, push*. That's all he ever fucking does. Be the best, do what I choose, toe the line. I can't anymore—I'm too far underwater to be in this race. Caroline's words fill my head, taunting me.

"Have you always been too chicken to be yourself?"... "Sooner or later, you need to be your own man."

I swallow, knowing what I should say, but it feels like my body's physically rejecting it as my honest thought tumbles out.

"I wasn't aware I needed your permission to apply to a school. Or did you want to call in a favor for Columbia too?"

Goddamn, the look on Tucker's face makes me want to take it back, but I don't. I keep my mouth shut, choosing to let what I said stay out there between us like a battle line.

"You don't need any permission, but your attitude tells me that you're still too immature to direct your own future. Which, in case I've been unclear, is more than just yours." His voice rises. "Your last name dictates that."

My jaw tenses as we stare at each other.

"I, of all people, know my responsibilities. But is it so hard to believe I could become successful in another arena?"

He laughs before frowning. "Yes." His head shifts around as he waves an arm. "All of this is the product of a spoiled little prince—your mother's influence, I'm sure. But it doesn't amount to a legacy, Liam. They're just pretty pictures from a boy. I'm trying to help you to become a man."

Fuck you. I am my own man. It's on the tip of my tongue, but I can't get it to leave my lips, waving him off instead and starting toward the door.

"Liam. We aren't done."

I spin around, this time without the filter.

"What the fuck do you need me here for? Looks like you've got it all figured out, Tuck. I'm gonna go do some immature shit while you direct ship."

I can't even look at him. My chest is heaving as if I've run a mile as I walk down the hall. Taking the stairs two at a time, I make my way outside and shove my hands into my hoodie. I stand on the sidewalk in front of my house without a purpose other than to get away. It's dark, lit only by streetlights and a few front windows. But I don't care. I stand there, trying to catch my breath, looking down each way, not knowing what I'm doing or where I'm going.

What do I do? What the fuck do I do? I just keep looking back and forth, knowing that I'm not thinking about the direction I should walk but about my fucking life.

I pull my phone from my hoodie, swiping it open, finger hovered over Donovan's name. I need to hear a voice I can trust, someone I know will understand. But her text reply comes through from the one I'd sent earlier.

Me: I need space.

Van: Then you'll get it, dick.

I throw my arms out, punching the air as a growl turns into a yell. "Fuck."

Everything is so mangled. My friends hate me. I hate me. And

Caroline… She breaks my heart.

I need a vacation from my fucking life. Opening the contacts in my phone, I choose a random direction and stalk down the street. The third name on my list stares up at me, bright on my cell phone's screen like a temptation—the kind you know you should probably avoid but won't, especially when you're feeling self-destructive.

Without thinking twice, I hit Call, and it only rings once before the husky voice answers amongst loud voices in the background.

"Liam. I was just thinking about you. Come out."

"Love to. Tell me where you're at, beautiful."

"I'll text you. Ciao, baby."

"Ciao, Arden."

***

Van: I'm sorry. If you need space, take it. I was a shit.
Love you, Brookie.

Grey: Don't be a dick. I get it—but don't hurt Cherry
too.

Kai: I know what I said but dude—let's talk, for real,
no bullshit.

"Liam, your phone is buzzing like crazy."

"Turn it off." My throat burns as I take a hit from the blunt passed to me by some random guy sitting on my right.

The smoke lingers inside my mouth before I blow it out, feeling the tightness in my chest begin to relax for the first time in a long time.

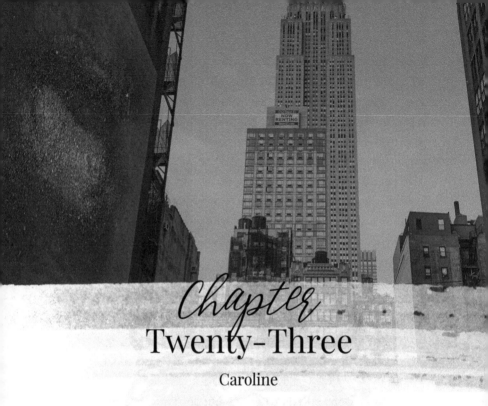

Chapter
Twenty-Three

Caroline

I shift, looking at myself in the mirror, closing and reopening my pink tweed Chanel blazer.

"This jacket makes me look like Elle Woods. Grab another one or buy me a Chihuahua."

"The horror." Kai grins, diving back into the massive pile of clothes that have taken up residence on the floor of my closet.

"This outfit needs to be perfect," I yell so he can hear me. "I have one shot to impress these Upper East Side bitches and become one of the chosen few. I didn't even think I'd get a fucking invitation to interview after—" *the party* is what I don't say.

After two weeks of all these damn feelings, I try not to avoid it because Liam is still all I want to think about.

Kai's voice carries. "They'd be fools not to want you. You are the social scene, Caroline. What about the taupe Calvin Klein?"

My head shakes. "Too suburban. I want a classic look, not something that screams, 'I have a husband embroiled in a Ponzi scheme and two kids via surrogate because I couldn't give up the wine.'"

I hear him laugh as he peeks his head around the corner. "Miu Miu?"

"God, no. Too Tribeca."

"I've got it," Kai shouts, emerging with a fucking classic trench with perfect lines and just the right shade of champagne.

"Yes. Herrera to the rescue."

Kai walks over to me and slides it over my shoulders as we both stare in the mirror. His arms wrap around my waist, cinching the belt.

"This is a statement. You look stunning, baby."

I smile, but it quickly fades as he leans down to kiss my neck.

"Stop," I whisper, dodging his lips. "It's still a no."

He lets out a breath and stares at me through the mirror, removing his arms to grip the back of his neck. I know he's pissed, but I'm not his playmate. *Not anymore.* My eyes dart away as I turn to walk to my jewelry table. Kai follows, grabbing my elbow, turning me around.

"Is it ever going to be a yes again?"

No. But I don't say that, opting to stare back. I think a part of me is scared that if I answer Kai truthfully, we won't be what we are anymore. I know he loves me, but would it be a little less until it wasn't something I don't recognize anymore?

The thought hits me like a brick because suddenly, I understand Donovan in a whole new way.

Kai cradles my face, forcing me to look up at him.

"It's been two weeks, Caroline. Liam's all but ghosted everyone, including you. Does he even go to Hillcrest anymore? Because I know he doesn't row."

"So?" I push back, tugging my elbow from his grip. "What does that have to do with me?"

"I'm starting to think you'd rather pine away for him than live in the present with me. Let me take your mind off of him."

I don't want my mind anywhere but on him.

"I'm not pining—"

"But?" he cuts in.

I haven't told Kai that I slept with Liam. I told him I was too hurt over what happened, then that I had my period. All excuses to spare both his ego and his feelings. Because if I tell him the truth, then I have to admit that I despise the idea of him inside of me, that it makes me feel sick because I refuse to lose my last tie to Liam. God, it's so twisted but all-consuming.

I wrap my hands around his wrists, telling him another considerate lie.

"But nothing. Right now, my focus is solely on becoming a Deb, and your dick does not take precedence. Come to think of it, dick never prioritizes itself over my own need. What can I say? I'm a feminist that way."

His eyes narrow. "Or maybe you don't want to tell me you fucked him." I pull back, but he holds me in place, looking me over before letting go. "That's what I thought."

My fingers come to the scar on my wrist, blinking up at him.

"How long have you been holding that in?"

Kai waits for a beat before answering, "Since the day I almost got arrested with Liam."

Liam told him. The idea makes my heart beat faster. Kai said they fought, but he didn't offer details, and with Liam missing in action, I'd assumed Kai laid into him about the party.

"Is that why you aren't speaking? Not because of what happened at the party."

Kai walks past me over to the bed, sitting down on the edge of the mattress. His big hands splay over his knees, the black polish on his nails shiny.

"Partly, but mostly we aren't speaking because he's acting like none of us exists. He's hiding, hanging out with Arden and her party squad. He's self-destructing, Caroline, and none of us can stop it. Grey's the only one that's been able to get Liam to text back."

"How come nobody said anything to me?"

"Care—how could we?"

I wave a hand. "I get it."

And I do. I may be getting on with it, but that doesn't mean I'm good. Not by a long shot.

I turn around again, heading toward my jewelry that's sparkling on the table. Looking over the pieces I've laid out, I try and hide that I wish that I didn't care so much—that everything inside of me didn't want to track Liam down and bully him into getting his shit together. I rub my chest, remembering the way he couldn't look at me before he said goodbye, but the way he did, for me.

My voice is so quiet that it's almost as if I'm speaking to myself.

"Liam is stronger than he gives himself credit for—but he's also stubbornly insecure and takes forever to see the things right in front of his face. He just needs a minute. Give it to him and be there when he comes back." I lift my eyes. "Promise me, Kai."

He frowns, standing and making his way over to me, taking my hand in his.

"I'll promise, but only if you answer something for me." I nod as he adds, "Why?"

"Why what?"

Kai's eyes skitter over my face before he answers.

"Why give him a pass? You invited him into your bed without ever kicking him out of your heart, Caroline. Why is that? How does he deserve your kindness? Because as your best friend, I have to say that this reeks of that shitty self-esteem you do such a good job hiding."

I raise his hand to my lips, pressing a kiss to it. "Don't worry about me, Kai. I'm familiar with my demons. It's Liam that's meeting his for the first time."

Kai's jaw tenses. "What he said to you—that was all meant to cut you, deep."

I smile, giving a small shrug, looking away.

"Yes. It was. But Liam's problem's always been his refusal to have a damn voice, and he finally spoke. I'd much rather it be about me than anyone else." I shift my head to look him in the eyes. "We're all terrible fucking people that sometimes do terrible fucking things, Kai. Careful with your judgment. I've found that it comes back to bite you."

Because how can I hate someone for being just like me? I understand all that's wrong with Liam—it's why we fail because two wrongs don't make a right.

Kai's shoulders relax as he lets go of my hand, shoving his into his pockets.

"Okay. I promise to be there. But no more secrets."

My fingers brush over a pearl necklace, nervous about what I'm about to say.

"Agreed. No more, but that goes for you too because that's what friends do. And that's what we are now—*friends* that tell each other all the shit, good, bad, and Mila."

Instant understanding passes over his face. Kai has secrets too, but I've never pressed because why would I. Kai's never really been mine, just a placeholder for the boy I didn't think loved me.

But if he thinks I didn't notice months ago at the lake house, when he went missing as I was being kicked out after masterminding Donovan's towel drop, he's wrong. Or when we were at the club, he had Donovan take me home because he had to stay back. I even knew about Mila when he missed out on the whole cafeteria debacle.

His lips tip up as he stares at me.

"Fucking Caroline Whitmore. There'll never be another like you, not even Mila."

His arms wrap around me, chin resting on my shoulder from behind. "I hope you two get your shit together because you deserve to get what you want, little queen."

I mouth, "Me too," into the mirror, feeling his kiss on my cheek.

***

The girl seated next to me turns her face to mine. "Are you nervous?"

Dying and ready to pass out. Who knew this morning that this trench would require Botox injected into my armpits so that I didn't sweat so damn much.

The thought in my head stays there as I smile, ankles crossed, back straight. "No. Nerves are for the unprepared. I take it you're nervous though."

She blinks, then looks away.

We're seated in the entryway of a post-war classic Fifth Avenue apartment that overlooks the park. A home that belongs to Barbara Wells, co-chair and oldest living matriarch to the social calendar for New York. She *is* the International Debutante Ball.

I've never been more nervous, but I'm never telling that to a girl named Pip.

Pip adjusts in her seat, brushing my arm and garnering my attention again as she says, "Sorry, Caroline."

Of course she knows who I am, just like I know who she is.

"Pip, correct?"

She nods, and I sweep my long chocolate locks over my shoulder.

"Why Pip? What I mean is, why'd your parents name you that?"

Her dewy face brightens, and one of her fingers winds around a strand of her overly processed hair as she begins explaining.

"Oh, it's a family name. My mother says it means attractive or beautiful. It's silly, really."

I raise my brows, and Pip laughs as if it's just too embarrassing to admit that she's so pretty.

I look her up and down before offering, "It also means a hard seed from a fruit." She frowns as I add, "The kind you spit out."

"Oh."

It's a short answer but adequate enough to prove that Pip's just realized this is a competition, and she's sorely unprepared. I smooth my hands over my skirt, letting out a sigh and looking forward.

A woman emerges from the rug-lined hallway with a clipboard in her hand and looks at me.

"Caroline Whitmore."

"Good luck," I offer a pale Pip before standing and following my guide down the hall.

As we walk, I let my eyes drift, mentally taking notes about the art on the walls and the procured antiques. We stop at what I assume is the chair's office door, and the woman that led me looks back over her shoulder, smiling before she knocks.

"Come in," I hear from behind the door.

I stand a bit taller with my best smile in place as the heavy door is opened. But what I see isn't at all what I expect.

Big brown eyes stare back at me, attached to a haloed braid atop her head.

Arden fucking Livingston.

She relaxes her arm across the back of her chair as she sits sideways, smiling from ear to ear. Internally, I'm losing my shit, but outwardly, my smile never dims.

Did she maneuver this? Why the fuck is she here? Is this some kind of revenge for what I said? Oh my God, she's here telling the sordid details about my birthday. Fuck.

But even amid all those swirly thoughts, it's my last thought that has me sweeping my hair over my shoulder and feeling vicious.

What the fuck are you doing with Liam?

"Caroline, please take a seat," the chairwoman offers, extending a hand.

"Thank you."

I glance at Arden as I walk to my chair, sitting and keeping my eyes forward.

The chairwoman takes one more look at the file on her stark white desk before closing it and looks up. "I hope you don't mind. Arden asked to join us, and since she attended your party, I thought, why not. I can never say no to my niece."

I never read that. How did I not know this? Fuck, fuck, fuck.

My polite laughter spills from my lips. "Fantastic." I shift to look at Arden. "I didn't realize you were related to the chairwoman." I add in a teasing voice, "You kept that a secret on purpose."

"How could I tell you, Carebear? Surprising you is everything I thought it would be."

Bitch.

***

My bag hits the floor as soon as I walk through the door, slamming it shut. Grey's feet slow as he bounds down the stairs, staring at me like I'm crazy.

It's appropriate. I am. I've just endured the worst half hour of my life. Everything I said was countered by fucking Arden while she tried to gaslight me nonstop, driving me to mentally configure how I'd hide her body.

Grey crosses his arms. "I take it that the interview didn't go well?"

I scowl, pushing off the door that I'm leaning against. "Well, let's recap, shall we? Your summer fling was there. So that was fun."

"My what?" he answers, furrowing his brow.

I stalk past him toward the kitchen, hearing him follow as I rant.

"Arden. She was there—as my guest fucking interviewer. Imagine that? A girl I all but flambéed shows up to ask me questions for one of the most important moments of my life."

I throw the door open to the walk-in freezer, beelining for the vodka and jerking it from its spot. I don't even bother to walk out or get a glass, opting for pulling the cork and tipping it back.

The bottle drops to my side, and I lick my lips, staring back at Grey.

"So yeah. It didn't go well."

I take another swig, and the burn tightens my throat. Grey steps inside, gripping the bottle. We play a game of tug-of-war, me losing.

He holds out his hand for the cork, and I scowl as I drop it into his palm, as his shoulders shake.

"I don't want to have to carry you upstairs. And I bet it wasn't as bad as you're making it out to be, Caroline. There's no way she got one over on you."

My eyes roll as he continues, even though it's a compliment.

"But I bet what's pissing you off is that you know she's seen Liam. And that imagination of yours is running wild."

I sneer, biting down a few times, making a clacking sound with my teeth, before confessing, "Maybe." My eyes narrow. "Kai told you he told me, didn't he?"

Grey nods. I throw my arms up, walking past him out of the freezer.

"Do you know how hard it was to be nice to that twat?" I spin around.

"Knowing she's gallivanting around with Liam. Blech, I hate everyone."

Grey follows me, now leaning his hip against the butcher block countertop. I hate how amused he seems.

"Today was important, Grey. Stop grinning. It isn't funny."

I was going to be everything I never feel.

Grey's grin grows into a full-fledged smile, making me cross my arms.

"Then tell me, Caroline, what's the appropriate response for hell freezing over?"

I let out a tiny growl, punctuating my words, "What the fuck does that mean?"

"It means that for the first time in your life, you put someone above your own self-interest. And that, my twisted sister, is why hell is fucking chilly today."

My body shivers involuntarily, and he tips his head back, laughing loudly.

"Shut up. It won't happen again. Trust me." I let out a long exhale, letting my lips flap. "The whole time I was in that room, I wanted to excuse the chairwoman and threaten the hell out of Arden. So that she'd know that if she helped Liam self-destruct, I'd personally make sure she'd never be welcomed back into this city again. I will wipe her existence off the fucking social map because—"

Grey cuts me off. "Because you can't actually murder her?"

A chuckle shoots out, but I stamp it down, stomping my foot.

"Yes! It was all I could think, Grey. This is what I've come to. It's pathetic."

It's almost as if Grey can read my thoughts because he lowers his gaze to meet mine.

"Do you want to know what they're doing, Caroline?"

"No." *Lies—fuck yes, but I'll never admit that.*

Grey sets the bottle of vodka down, motioning with his head toward some glasses in a cabinet.

"How would you know, anyway?" I snark, grabbing two tumblers and handing them to him. "Liam would feed you exactly what was needed to keep you off his back."

"Is that still a 'no'?" he challenges, pulling the cork on the Grey Goose.

He pours two slight shots and slides the glass my way. I wrap my hand around and stare at him.

"Speak."

All I get is a quiet laugh before he does just that.

"Nothing. Arden's a lesbian, Caroline. Liam might be acting like a bitch, but he lacks some important characteristics—like a vagina."

Um, what? I gulp my drink back as flashes from the party begin to make sense. That's why the guys thought the whole exchange was funny. Son of a bitch.

I scream-growl, smacking my glass down onto the counter, and punch Grey in the stomach.

"You're such a dick. The whole time I was acting like a jealous little—oh my God. You knew and let me make a fool of myself?"

He grins, rubbing a hand over his abs. "You hit harder than I expected."

I ignore everything he's saying, fuming, shaking my head. "Why would you do that to me?"

"It was entertaining."

Grey's enjoyment's pushing me over the edge. He takes a polite drink of his vodka before adding, "And it was about time for the shit to hit the fan."

My eyebrows shoot to the roof. Grey drags his hand through his hair, placing his drink on the counter.

"For fuck's sake, Caroline. You and Liam have been in this ridiculous holding pattern since we were kids. Get over yourselves. You needed a push, and Arden was fate providing an opportunity."

"A push? How dare you—"

Grey interrupts, putting a hand in my face—"Zip it, princess"—before lowering it as he adds, "Yes, Caroline. You needed a push to stop buying into the idea that somehow, you're an imposter. You belong in this world—just as much as you belong with Liam."

I hate him. Because that's exactly what I feel like—an imposter. The Debutante Ball, the parties, the mentions on Page Six—it's the only way I know how to prove I belong.

All this time, I've been worried about my mother, along with everyone else's opinion. I've been living to disprove all the fucking condescension and insults instead of asking myself if I even want to do half of the shit I do.

Grey pours another shot into my glass, placing the bottle back on the counter.

"Arden is everything you've been vying to become. Seeing them together, a real piece of competition—I figured you'd go nuclear. I didn't factor in that Liam would lose his shit though. Although I'm proud. Take it from me, Caroline. Love doesn't request permission to happen—so stop with the melodrama and get on with it."

My mouth hangs open, trying to process his words or my own, but I can't, so I snap my jaw shut. I let my shoulder hit his arm as I push past, swiping the bottle and yelling over my shoulder.

"You burned down a fucking tree. Maimed a kid and beat up your best friends. Don't talk to me about melodrama—you were an episode of a telenovela."

I look back as he shrugs, uncaring, so I scowl. "I expect an apology."

But he yells back.

"Lower your expectations."

My feet stomp up the stairs as I uncork the bottle again. "You are literally the worst brother."

His laugh is all I hear as I hit the top of the stairs to get very drunk and forget about this fucking day altogether. What Grey doesn't understand is that loving Liam isn't a problem. It's knowing that I'll still hurt him that I can't live with.

Chapter
Twenty-Four

Liam

"L iam."

I look up from my bowl of cereal, which I'm having at two in the morning, to see my mother standing in her robe glaring at me. Shit. Cereal drips from my lip, so I slurp, wiping the back of my hand over my mouth.

"What are you doing up, Mom?"

"Looking for proof of life. It's nice to see you still live here. I'd begun to wonder."

Fair. My nights have been late and my days fuzzy these last two weeks. I've been hiding, crashing on Arden's couch, down in the art studio, or locked in my room, avoiding everyone, including Babe. I know I shouldn't blame my mom for the bullshit between my father and me, but anger is all I seem to feel anymore, and it's currently strong enough to replace my reason.

Babe shoves her hands in the robe's pockets, staring at me with that fucking look—the one she reserves for people she's about to fire. Am I about to be fired as her son? *There's a good chance.* She starts toward me as she speaks.

"I had a fascinating conversation with Grey today, then with your coach, and finally the dean of Hillcrest. Do you want to guess what they all had to say?"

Not really. Because I already know, and I'm going to kill Grey. He threatened to rat me out to my mom if I skipped another week of practice, but I'd told him to eat shit. Looks like he made good on his promise to *"spoon-feed my words back to me."* Motherfucker.

She takes a seat on the barstool next to me, anger ablaze in her eyes, jabbing a finger into the counter as she levels her words.

"Tomorrow, you will attend every single class for the rest of the goddamn year, without so much as a tardy. And two—you will stop smoking weed and eating all the cereal at 2:00 a.m."

"I don't smoke—" I protest because it's only been twice, but she closes her eyes like she can't bother with my voice, so I stop speaking.

God, this is worse than with my dad. At least with him, I was prepared for his disappointment, but seeing that same sentiment behind her eyes is fucking me up.

Babe reopens her eyes, her hand coming to cradle my face as she adds quietly, "And three—" She reaches inside the pocket of her robe and pulls out my Columbia acceptance letter, placing it on the counter. "—you'll prove your father wrong."

I let out a heavy breath, one I think I've held on to for the last two weeks. The thing that's fucked me up so much with my father is that a part of me knows he's right—I don't know how to be my own man yet. I'm not like my father, or even like Grey. They always seem to know exactly who they are and what they want, but I only know who I am to the people around me.

Babe pats my cheek and smiles, sitting back, her eyes glistening.

"When you were little, people would ask, 'What do you want to be when you grow up,' and while other kids named superheroes or princesses, you always said, 'My father.'"

My eyes drop to the counter, feeling off-balance, knowing that I haven't spoken to him since he left on business. I wasn't afraid or cowardly. There just wasn't anything left to say.

Babe's hand comes under my chin, lifting my face to meet her eyes. "Liam, all the other kids grew out of their fairy tales. It's time you did the same. You owe him nothing more than your happiness. That's it. So I ask you, what does your future look like?"

Petite, brunette, pouty lips. I hope.

"I don't know, Mom. But I know I want it to be mine."

"Then get back to *your* life—I, for one, am truly excited to see how it unfolds."

Even though I kind of want to say thank you, I don't. Mainly because the lump in my throat would expose how much this moment means to me. My mom turns around on the stool, hopping down, and heads back the way she came, without another word. I don't know how she does that—punches right through the wall and hits me where it counts.

The last two weeks started as me escaping, partying, and trying to numb the memory of what I'd done. But then it just became aimless, and night after night, all I could think about was Caroline and Columbia art school. Each feels like a reality I'll never accomplish but one that I can't stop craving.

My eyes dart to the goddamn elephant in the room. Pushing my bowl out of the way, I slide the letter toward me, taking a deep breath. The sound of the paper ripping feels intrusive in the silence, but I pull the folded letter out, opening it, and read to myself.

> *Dear Mr. Brooks,*
>
> *On behalf of Columbia University, I am delighted to congratulate you on your acceptance into the incoming freshman class. As you know, Columbia University has a rich history of academic excellence, and we review the many hundreds of applications we receive with only the highest standards.*

My eyes scan the paper, looking for information about the School of Fine Arts.

> *We are pleased to offer you consideration for*

acceptance to one of the few spots in our highly competitive Painting concentration. Please schedule your interview by—

My hand hits the counter—"Yes"—catching myself as I do, looking around.

Fuck me. I did it—or at least got an interview. A relieved sigh leaves my body as I smile, tilting my face to the ceiling, and wipe a hand over my jaw. Babe's words sit heavy on my chest, keeping my feet on the ground, even though I feel like I'm flying. I'm going to prove him wrong, but more importantly, if I do, I'll prove to myself that I deserve Caroline.

***

Books close, and the sound of papers shuffling snaps me out of my daydream. People begin to stand, grabbing their bags, and I feel like I'm on a delay.

All I can think about is my interview today. It's making focusing damn near impossible, but on the upside, it's offered an out with my friends. Being back this week after avoiding everyone is exactly as awkward as I thought it would be.

Thank God it's Friday because the only person that's not giving me shitty looks is Grey—because he's Grey. Donovan's mad, only because she's trying to hide her sadness over being ignored, and Kai—well, we're still not speaking, so practices are awesome.

I lean down to grab my backpack, catching a glimpse of Caroline doing the same. She half-smiles before I look away, feeling stupid that I did. *Idiot.*

Our eyes met Monday morning as I walked up the front steps, but neither of us gave anything away. Since then, it's been sweet glances, distance, and me thinking about her every night.

I'm standing behind a line of people, all shuffling to leave. It's slow-moving, and without thinking, I look over at Caroline again because I'm greedy for even a glimpse. But she's not where I expected. My eyes dart ahead, seeing she hasn't got anybody in front of her, so she's making it to the door faster.

Before I know what I'm doing, I tug the kid's backpack in front of me, jerking him out of the way, and walk around him, doing the same to the next guy so that Caroline and I will be at the door at the same time. But I just miss her, watching her walk out.

Damn. I don't know what I thought I was going to say anyway. I run a hand over my head, walking through the door, heading to the left toward my next class.

"Brooks."

I swing around to see Caroline's petite frame standing across from me. *Fuck me, she waited.*

"Hey," I answer, brows pulling together because those violet-blue eyes are grabbing me by the fucking throat.

We're standing on opposite sides of the door as she gives another small smile that I tilt my head to see as someone passes between us. I scowl, irritated that I'm blocked, and close the distance.

Caroline's name is called from the other side of the hallway, but she ignores it, poking a finger to my stomach as I come to stand in front of her.

"I heard you're going in for an interview with the Columbia art department today."

I'd just barely made the cutoff date. The only person I told was Grey, even though I'm still holding a grudge that he fucking told on me like we're twelve. But he's also the only person that understands my head right now. It's like when we were kids, and he'd freak out. I'd sit with him and just be quiet; now he's doing that for me in his own way—the pushy, irritating way.

"Only one other person knows that information. Were you eavesdropping again, Caroline?"

She rolls her eyes. "The level of self-importance—it's an ugly trait for such a pretty face."

"Mm-hmm."

She bites her bottom lip, and my eyes drop to them, wishing I could replace her teeth with mine. Some kids pass by too close, rowdy and laughing. Instinctually, I move her aside with a hand on her waist, closer to the wall.

Her eyes dart down to my hand, and I swallow because—fuck. It's the first time I've touched her since… Her body's so warm, and I swear to God my fingers don't want to let go. She's looking up at me through those impossibly long lashes, making me wish I could bend down and run my fucking tongue between her lips—both sets.

Every. Single. Goddamn. Moment from that night ticks through my mind. Caroline naked. Legs spread. The perfect shape of her breast and how one is slightly bigger than the other. The way she whimpered the closer she got, like she was begging for it.

Guess I know what that sounds like after all.

Holy shit. I just sunk into Caroline, like she's quicksand. It's like each time I fight this feeling, she swallows me faster into my death. My mind is scrambled, ruined as we stand there staring at each other, connected at this moment. I clear my throat, dragging my eyes away, and let her go, taking a step back.

"Yeah. Um. I do have an interview. Today, right after practice, actually."

She's nodding as she brings her hand up to fidget with the bottom of her hair and lets out an audible exhale.

"I wanted to say congratulations."

The first bell rings, and we both look up at the speakers, two minutes until the final one. She's already starting to step backward, so I follow, not wanting this moment to end.

"Shouldn't you say good luck?"

She smirks. "You don't need luck—you're pretty decent at the whole art thing."

I laugh. "Only decent, huh?"

She's not looking where she's going, not that she has to, because I snap my fingers at the idiot standing a few feet behind her, who's not looking.

"Hey, pay attention, dude. Move."

The guy looks up and shuffles out of her way as she passes him, with her eyes fixed to mine the whole time, answering my question.

"Yes, decent. Stop fishing for compliments. It's embarrassing and beneath you."

I close the distance, quickly making her eyes grow wide, and her feet stop moving as I bend down, saying quietly in her ear, "Well, a compliment from Caroline Whitmore is worth its weight in gold, so—"

She giggles. *Whoa. I've* never heard that before. Her mouth clamps shut, looking embarrassed as I pull back, but I fucking love it.

"Was that a giggle, Carebear?"

She narrows her eyes, then hooks a finger over her shoulder. "Eww. I have to go hang out with my real friends now." She spins around, looking over her shoulder. "See ya, Brooks."

So mean. And I'm hanging on every goddamn word.

"Fine. Go," I say, licking my bottom lip. "But don't be mad when I watch you leave."

She doesn't look back, not even once.

I don't know what just happened, but I want it to happen again, even if sirens are blaring in my head, saying, *Don't fucking do it.* I take a few steps backward before turning around and hightailing it to my next class, replaying that giggle in my mind over and fucking over.

***

It's hot. That's all I can think of sitting in front of the man about to decide my future. This interview couldn't have gone better. We talked about art, other people's and my own. He asked me about where I saw myself in five years, to which I gave a perfect textbook answer.

I've nailed this damn thing, but I'm still so fucking nervous. I just want to hear the words: "Welcome to the program."

"Well, Liam, I think that wraps it up. I want to thank you for coming in today. The Painting concentration is a highly coveted track within the Columbia School of the Arts. We only have four spots to offer this year."

I'm nodding. "It's incredible to just be considered." I sound like an Oscar nominee. *Shut up, Liam.* "I know you probably get this a lot, but when should I expect to hear the committee's decision?"

He folds his hands on the table and looks down for a moment. It's long enough that my stomach drops.

"I'll cut to the chase, Liam. The committee doesn't feel your work is ready for this particular program. Although we happily welcome you to the undergraduate art program, we're declining your acceptance into this concentration."

"I don't understand."

I'm telling the truth. I don't. The ringing in my ears is too loud, and I feel incapable of blinking. What the fuck. Everything I worked for, all the months I prepared—the years I've poured my heart into painting, all of it, for "we're declining your acceptance."

Fuck that. "Why?"

His hands flatten to the table. "We feel your work lacks real-world experience. There's no honesty in it. Go out and have your heart broken, live a little—"

"Been there, done that."

He looks confused. "I'm sorry?"

I rub my forehead. "I don't understand. I researched my ass off. I know you gravitate toward impressionism, while three others on the committee prefer paintings with a contemporary flair. Fuck, I even know that last year you admitted more applicants that painted with oils over acrylic. I paid attention. I did the work."

His face is somber. "No. You didn't, Liam. We don't care about medium or style—we care about the statement. We want to know what you have to say."

I can't breathe. Fuck. I can't breathe.

"—your piece said nothing, son. It was just another pretty picture."

My eyes jump up to meet his because, for a second, his voice sounded exactly like my father's. I feel like I've bottomed out as I hold my head up, refusing to look as battered as I feel.

He gives me a tight smile, rapping his knuckles on the desk. "We hope to see you back next year, once you've explored more mediums and styles. You do show promise. But you need to find your voice, Liam."

He stands, so I do the same, but I'm on polite autopilot, saying goodbye as I walk out of the room. I haven't even formed a thought as my phone rings, and Arden's number comes into view.

"Hey."

Music blares in the background. "Liam. Where have you been? Meet us. I'll text you the address. There's someone here you have to meet. He's an artist too."

I should go home. Keep my head straight, but to hell with it. I could use a distraction.

"Yeah. All right."

Twenty minutes later, I'm slung back on a vintage couch somewhere in the middle of Chelsea, listening to a girl tell me a story about how she once met one of the British princes and how she could've easily been royalty. This was a dumb idea, coming here. It's not working because I don't want to be numb anymore.

A much deeper voice from beside me calls my attention as the girl turns hers to someone else.

"Arden says you paint."

Some dude with curly black hair and designs tightly cut into the sides of his head stares back at me.

"Sometimes."

He nods, scratching his chin with paint-stained fingers. Not paint though—spray paint.

"Cool, us too. I'm Matias."

Us?

"Liam."

He rolls his eyes, pulling a blunt from his pocket.

"Yeah, I know. Arden told me. She also said you were going to art school."

My head falls back on the couch, staring at the ceiling. "I'm still undecided. What about you? Are you applying somewhere?"

He laughs and sucks in a heavy pull off his blunt, extending his hand to offer it to me, but I shake my head.

"Nah," he says with a held breath before releasing a whoosh of smoke. "I'm not going to college, but everything you need to know about art is on the streets anyway."

I start thinking about that, wondering if he's right as he adds, "You should come with us sometime. Banksy over there does some dope-ass pieces if you wanna check 'em out."

My head lifts over my shoulder to look at who he's speaking about because I know it's not the real Banksy, only to see this dude's mirror image coming toward us.

"You two wouldn't be related at all?" I joke.

He laughs. "Yeah, we get that a lot. That's my brother, Mac. So you down or what?"

My forehead wrinkles. "For?"

Mac joins in, sitting on the back of the couch. "Making a statement. Live a little, or are you only about those rich-boy paints and easels?"

I can't help my grin. "You're talking about tagging."

They look at each other and laugh before the dude sitting next to me mocks me in a shitty impersonation saying, "Yeah, we're talking about tagging," making me sound like I should be on a yacht.

Now I laugh, "Fuck you," but the brothers stand, staring down, Mac shrugging.

"You down, or are you exactly what you look like?"

Matias finishes. "Boring."

My head shifts between them. Matias doesn't mean boring. He means the same thing everyone else has said—lost. But it's about fucking time I figured out what kind of statement I want to make. I push off the couch to stand, accepting their challenge.

"I'm down, but stop standing next to each other and finishing each other's sentences. It's too redrum for me."

They smile, slapping my hand. Matias pulls the hood of his black puffer jacket over his head. "Dude, stick with us. You won't regret it—and maybe you'll learn a few things. Get less undecided, right?"

I grin, pulling my jacket on, just as my phone buzzes in my hand, but I pocket it, ignoring the text, following the brothers out to get some of that real-life experience I'm lacking.

***

I step back from the cement wall in the alley, staring at the colorful picture. Mac looks over at me.

"You sure you never did this shit before?"

My head shifts to Matias as he says, "Yeah, he's new...look at his boots. Spray off be real."

I laugh, feeling light. No burdens, no worries, no fucking regret. These two were right. Fuck, even the Columbia chair was right—I've been living in a box. My mind may be expanding, but some things will never change because the wall of my father's building looks like Caroline gave it a kiss.

Mac nudges my shoulder. "Hot lips."

"Your girl's?" Matias adds.

I lift my phone, taking a picture of my creation, and smile. "Yeah. My girl's."

***

My knife slices through the turkey on my plate as my parents politely chew their food. The tension's thick enough to suffocate us all. The day after my father and I exchanged words, he left on business, but now he's back for Thanksgiving, and it's everything I expected it to be.

Tense. Polite. And fucking irritating.

My mom looks up over the table at me and smiles before shifting her gaze to my father. "Tucker, did you hear the boys won their last race? They're undefeated."

He grunts in answer while chewing, his way of saying, "I'm still pissed." I choose to ignore it, discreetly pulling my phone from my pocket as it vibrates to check the message under the table.

Matias: 11 p.m. Same building as last time. Good call
on that, btw.

Taking them to my father's building was immature, ridiculous, and yet I'm not remotely sorry because there's some kind of poetic justice in it.

I start to close my phone but stop short, scrolling up to Caroline's message from a week ago. I've thought about how to respond a hundred different ways from Sunday, but in the end, Caroline and I shouldn't go there, not after how I felt in that hall. Touching her wasn't just physical. That girl left a lasting impression that's impossible as fuck to shake.

Not that I'm trying too hard. But I promised Caroline I'd walk away for the both of us. Pocketing my phone, I go back to eating in silence, this time with a smile on my face. My father dabs the napkin to the sides of his mouth before speaking.

"I understand the Crimson Crew is having open rowing sessions over the Christmas break. You may want to attend to solidify a spot on the team for next year. Especially now that you're undefeated."

Is he fucking serious? *Of course he is.* I huff a laugh and keep eating, stabbing the tines into the turkey roughly.

He clears his throat. "And why is that funny, Liam?"

That's it, Tucker. The sound of my fork dropping clangs against the china as I stare at him. I lean back into my chair, crossing my arms, stretching my legs out in front of me.

"Well, it's funny for two reasons. The first is that you think I'm still attending Harvard. You had to know that I'd get here—to manhood, albeit a tad late, but nonetheless, here. It's what you've been trying to teach me, right, Father? And two, and really the main reason it's funny, is because you think I'd need to try out for any crew team. I'm second in the country to an Olympian, Tucker. And my second isn't anyone else's first."

He's staring back at me, locked and loaded, ready for battle, but my mother snaps her fingers at the both of us, holding us at bay.

"No. Absolutely not. Must I remind you two it's Thanksgiving?"

My father tosses his napkin on the table, looking away, as I shake my head because this bullshit is ridiculous. How is it that the man I held above all others has become the villain in my story? Regardless, I won't deconstruct my spine to fold myself back into the box I was born into. Not for him, not for anyone. Never again.

The silence stretches out, blanketing the room in discomfort. Nobody's eating or even looking in the same direction. We're just sitting uncomfortably at the table, counting the minutes until the end of dinner.

Fuck this. I'm out.

I scoot my chair back to stand. "Dinner was delicious, Mom, but I have plans downtown."

She frowns. "Liam. Sit down." Her face twists to my father's. "Tucker. Say something. End this nonsense."

He says nothing, not even looking at my mother as she presses, "Are you really going to dig your heels in, Tucker? This is our son."

My eyes drop to the table as I button my jacket because a part of me can't believe it's actually come to this, but it has.

My father stands, looking me in the eye. For the first time in my life, he's just another man standing across from me. His shoulders somehow seem a little less broad, and the set of his jaw is less intimidating. But I suppose this is what adulthood brings, the diminishment of heroes.

"Have you accepted Columbia?"

"Yes."

"Then we have nothing more to discuss."

He turns and walks out of the dining room as my mother sits stunned. I walk around the table and kiss her cheek.

"Hey, he's stubborn. It's where I get it from. Everything will be okay. I'll see you later. Thank Simon for the food."

She pats my hand before I walk out the room and directly out of the front door.

Chapter
Twenty-Five

Caroline

Music pulses, vibrating my chest, and the crowd sways. My eyes lift to Kai from the table we're all seated at, watching him look like a fucking god as he spins record after record. He's so wholly in his element.

Donovan leans over. "Can you believe he booked a festival this summer? It's amazing, right?"

I nod, not looking at her. I'm not trying to be rude, but the idea makes me a little sad. The more popular Kai gets, the more deejaying will take him away from me. But I wouldn't want anything less than adoration for him, so I'll suck it up. Which is why I'm here in this godforsaken Brooklyn hotspot on a Sunday night, hoping I don't catch anything poor.

Plus, I wouldn't want Queen D jumping on another opportunity to coax me into liking her. My birthday party was enough.

Donovan lifts her arms, encased by Grey as she sits on his lap. Now that he's officially signed the papers for the company, they're even more annoyingly attached to one another. He's basically her shadow.

I grimace over the jealousy I hear in my thoughts as my eyes wander down to my phone—again, for the thousandth time since I texted Liam.

Me: I really liked hearing Carebear out of your mouth today. xx

He never acknowledged it all last week, keeping his distance.

I shouldn't have sent it. It was a momentary slip of the finger—but we'd felt like us again. Whatever the fuck that even means. Friends, with an asterisk, I guess? The asterisk being heavy sexual tension.

I know we did the right thing by walking away, but I never thought about the aftereffects. Clearly, there's no magic pill I can take to compel this Liam high to stop feeling so fucking good. Truthfully, it'd be the only pill I'd give a pass because I'm just a strung-out bitch, picking the scabs on her heart. *For fuck's sake, I'm problematic.*

Strumming my red nails against the table, I'm fixated on the dark drink circles stained on the wood, letting that thought sink in.

"Liam," I hear Grey bellow over the crowd, and my head snaps up.

Speak of the devil. My eyes search the crowd, past baseball caps and slicked-back hairstyles, until Liam comes into view. *Fuck me.*

He's wearing all black, doused in one of his signature hoodies with a beanie cap that he's dragging off his head as he walks. Jesus H, he's hot. Right out of bed—makes you want to crawl into his—is a look only Liam can pull off, and really fucking well.

Liam's eyes meet mine but look away quickly as he greets Grey in one of those guy hugs before staring down at an icy Donovan for a second before gently kissing the top of her head. I don't miss the smile on her face. She's trying really hard to hold a grudge for him disappearing on her, but Liam makes it hard to hate him. And she's a pushover.

"What are you doing here?" Grey asks, sitting back down and tugging Donovan back onto her throne.

Liam pulls the chair out next to mine, taking a seat as everyone looks between us, but I glare back, making Donovan and Grey smile in return before looking away. This doesn't have to be weird, even if it feels that way.

"I'm here with some guys I know," Liam offers, pointing over at two guys I've never seen. "We're heading out, actually."

Other friends. Brooklyn friends. Interesting. Grey doesn't seem to care, Donovan frowns, and I turn my head to meet Liam's gaze.

"Carebear."

His lips barely move as his eyes drag down the front of my body.

"Don't call me that."

The words fly from my mouth out of habit, but I don't mean them. Doesn't matter, though, because Liam's grin gives away just how much he liked it. His arm drapes over the back of his chair as he stares at me, bringing his thumb to wipe across his bottom lip.

"Mmm, say please."

If the devil had a brand, it would be Liam. And I would wait in line for it—in the rain. The tip of his tongue runs over a sliver of his side teeth that peek from behind his grin. I think I know what Little Red Riding Hood must've felt like—except I want to be eaten. And with that thought, I need to get out of here.

"I'm going to the ladies' room."

My statement is left in the middle of the room as I push from the table and walk away, picking up a tiny bit of speed once I'm out of sight. The bathroom door closes behind me as I let out a whoosh only to scrunch my nose, looking at the dirty one-room stall. So gross.

But desperate times and all.

God, I felt knocked stupid. He smiled, and my knees got weak—while I was fucking sitting down. I'm disgusting.

My head drops to look at my pussy. "Weak bitch. Get it together."

We should've never fucked that night. It was quite possibly the worst way to say goodbye. Even when we do the right thing, we end up doing the wrong one. We're doomed.

But what is he doing, being all fuck-boy attractive toward me?

My hands stay glued to my side, careful not to touch anything as I walk to the cloudy mirror, checking my lipstick and hair and allowing myself to gather the self-respect I need to go back out and slay without being slayed.

The longer I stand here though, the more all my thoughts drift back to the bedroom and then to the feel of Liam's hand on my waist. And to the way he chews on those toothpicks. My eyes close as my back arches. Oooh, I bet he's good with his tongue.

For fuck's sake. It's like I'm in heat.

I tear open my eyes, ripping off a rough paper towel from the dented silver machine on the wall, and turn around, walking the few steps back to the door, using the paper to cover the handle. The music instantly smacks me in the face as I open the door and step out into the dark hallway, heading back the way I came.

Without warning, I'm yanked backward, a squeal escaping my lips as I'm spun around, meeting Liam's green-hazel eyes. My hands grip his biceps as I stand scowling.

"What the fuck."

Both of his hands are on my waist, except this time, they're affixed to my skin. It's sending goose bumps up over my body. Liam looks down at me, a toothpick lying on his bottom lip. I'm so fucked. He feels electric, lighting up all my senses.

Coupled with the music and the shadows, it's as if we're standing on the cliff's edge. *Push me over, Liam.*

"I had to say goodbye, Carebear. Wouldn't want to be rude and all."

Jesus, he's heavy on the asterisk right now.

"So now you remember your manners? I guess it's better late than never."

One hand leaves me as he draws the toothpick from his lips. But I can't help but notice his nails are painted.

"Your nails are black? New look?"

I'm not complaining. It's hot. Liam gives me that sexy charmer with enough bad-boy you can't catch your breath smirk, and I'm wet.

"It's paint and all over my hand. By the way, I liked your name on my lips too."

I can count the number of blinks I make because my whole body stops functioning. Liam steals his other hand back, bringing it up to push my hair back over my shoulder.

"You should go back to the table. It's dark in these halls, strangers everywhere. Wouldn't want someone taking advantage of you in the shadows, Carebear."

There's that grin again. Liam looks down at his phone and then back to me.

"I have to go."

I'm frowning. *Stop it, Caroline.*

"Where?"

Liam offers no answer, just boops my nose. "I like your shirt. But I hate that other people get to see you in it."

God help me if my lips don't tip up in the face of his honesty. This version of Liam is dangerous, and I haven't seen him in a while. *Welcome back.*

He jerks his chin to whoever's behind me. "Make sure she makes it back to the table safely. This crowd isn't allowed near something, so"—his face dips closer to mine—"pristine."

Asterisks are exploding like fucking fireworks.

Liam turns and walks out the back way, out through a door I didn't know was there. I spin around, flushed, dumbstruck, to see Kai behind me, accessorized with a frown.

"You're playing with fire, Caroline."

Jesus, he's so CW-drama serious.

"Oh, am I?" I mock. "I'm playing with fire. Why? Because Liam's so hot—is that what that cliché means? Do you wish you could play with fire, Kai, maybe blow smoke up his—"

Kai's hand clamps over my mouth. "Wretched whore. Say less."

I shove him off, raising my shoulders in a little dance. "Calm down. I'm not playing with anything, including Liam's dick. But like—fuck. Me. How much did you witness?"

Kai reaches for my hand. "Enough to know why you're blushing. Come on, let's do as Daddy says."

My eyes squeeze closed as I grin at the way he says *Daddy*—because, hell yes.

***

slide under my blanket, getting comfortable as my phone buzzes on the nightstand. It's too late to be anyone I know because we all just parted ways after Kai's set, intent on crashing before school today. Staying in place, I stretch out my arm and nab my phone, pulling it under the cover.

Liam: Did you burn that top yet?

My lips press together, holding back my laughter.

Me: No. I made sure to have it cleaned so that I could wear it tomorrow.

I picture him laughing as the bubbles appear and then go away. *No, come back.* My fingers type quickly.

Me: Are you ever going to tell me what happened with Columbia?

Liam: They passed.

Ah. So that's what Liam was doing with his new friends—self-destructing. Although, he didn't seem destructy. I'm well versed in that emotion, and it doesn't fit the Liam I saw tonight.

Me: I'm sorry?

Liam: Why the question mark?

Me: Because I almost want to say—good. I mean, when is exploring your options a bad thing? It could lead you to something you never expected.

Silence. No bubbles, no anything, so I type.

Me: Night, Liam. xx

I set my phone back on the nightstand, rolling over. As I close my eyes, Liam's face pops into my mind, looking at me the way he did tonight. Everything about him is always so alluring and vivid. It's like the rest of the world is in black and white, but Liam lives in color. His smile is brighter than other people's, his eyes are greener, and his lips—fuck, his mouth is heaven.

When he kissed me, it was as if nobody had ever done it right before him. I pull my lip between my teeth, sliding my hand down over my stomach. I can't help it. I haven't been able to shake him off since earlier tonight.

The craving I feel seems insatiable. My back arches off the bed as I dip my fingers under my panties, feeling wetness. I drag my middle finger down and up between my folds, letting out a quiet moan.

Slow circles become faster, and my hips push into the pressure. I squeeze my thighs together, drifting in and out of every single Liam fantasy I have until my body quakes, and I'm gripping the sheet, calling out his name into my pillow.

I'm huffing stuttered breaths as I hear my phone buzz and shoot my hand out to grab it. The screen is bright, punctuating his words as I lick my lips.

Liam: No exploring needed. I know exactly what I want. Night, Carebear. Oo

O's to my X's.

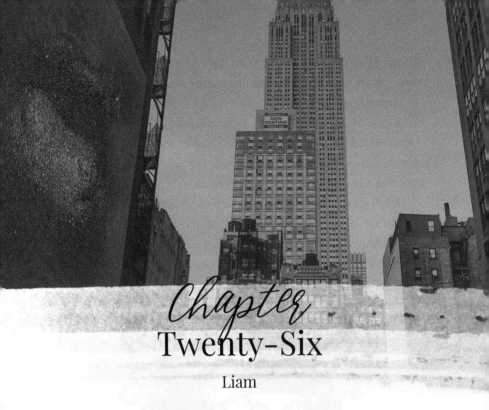

Chapter
Twenty-Six

Liam

Matias: You coming tonight?
Me: Can't. I have a race next week. Practice times run late.
Matias: So, rich dude shit. Lame.

My laugh is cut short, and Kai walks inside the boathouse. I tuck my phone inside my duffle and stand, looking at him.

"We need to end this shit between you and me. I'm sorry I was a dick to you. My head was fucked, not an excuse, just an explanation, and honestly—"

"Your balls hadn't dropped yet?"

The grin on my face spreads. "Fair. Yeah."

Kai hangs his bag on the hook next to his locker and sits on the bench, stretching out his legs. He offers me a tight smile before he speaks.

"The last few weeks were weird. First, you disappeared after being a version of you I didn't even know existed. Then Care and I became something different to each other. It was like all my best friends told me to fuck off. I don't know. I wanted to be there for you because you're like a brother to me, but when you acted like that, I got mad too."

I lean my shoulder against the wall as my arms cross.

"I'm sorry for all my bullshit in the car, man. And for almost getting us arrested. But especially for not talking to you. I just didn't know how. I know that sounds crazy, but I'd spent so much time being angry or jealous that it was all I could feel—until I stepped away."

He's nodding, matching the somber look on my face.

"But my head's clear now, and I'm sorry."

He shrugs, smirking. "I was kind of a dick too. I could've tried understanding more. It's cool you had Grey though—anger's his love language."

I laugh, and so does Kai as he stands and walks over to me.

"Are we good?" I offer, meeting his outstretched hand.

"We're good, Brooks."

He pulls me in for a shoulder-to-shoulder hug, giving me another nod as we separate. But I shake my head, still smiling.

"Wow. That's so much more reasonable than the conversation I had with Grey months ago in this very spot."

Kai turns, saying over his shoulder, "Well, think about who you're talking about," as he heads back to his locker, and I start to stretch.

The boathouse door opens with a thwack against the wall as Grey strolls in. "Think about who?"

Grey tosses his bag my way, landing it in front of his locker that's next to mine. He looks between our smiling faces with an approving look. "I like this better. Now, what are we talking about?"

I turn my back to rifle through my bag as Kai offers, "Caroline."

My head shifts over my shoulder with raised brows, and Kai grins. "Well, Liam being an asshole, but ultimately Care."

Dick.

Grey lifts his arms overhead, yawning. "Ah, has Romeo admitted he loves Juliet?"

"Not yet. Or is there something you'd like to add, Brooks?" Kai pushes slyly as they both stare at me.

I should've quit being friends with these two bastards when I had the chance. I lift both of my hands, flipping each the bird.

"One for each of you. I'm not talking to either of you about her."

Grey shakes his head, grabbing a water bottle from his bag. "Why not? We're the perfect audience. I'm her brother, and well, Kai"—he motions to him—"knows her biblically. No two better people to talk to."

Kai's head hangs, hiding his laughter, but I fake Grey out, making him flinch as I act like I'm going to toss my shoe at him.

"Too soon?" he jokes, holding up his bag to hide behind.

My ass hits the bench, amused at the ridiculousness of my reality. It doesn't bother me that Kai and Caroline had sex because I know the piece of herself Caroline gave me was only for me. That's all that matters. Plus, I like that she's knowledgeable—it's more fun.

"Fine. You want honesty?"

Grey and Kai get serious as they wait for me to speak, seeing that I'm about to tell them shit I never say.

"I'm trying to figure my shit out so that I can make her an offer. But I made the first step and turned down Harvard for Columbia art school."

Grey puts his hand on my shoulder, and Kai taps his knee with his fist, saying, "Oh shit. Brooks for the win. Grey, 'our baby's all growns up.'"

"It's about fucking time," Grey levels, giving my face a light tap before sitting back with his hands behind his head.

My brothers are proud of me. A weaker man might pretend that didn't matter, but I'm not weak anymore, so I smile to myself.

We're silent for a few more moments until having feelings begins to make it uncomfortable, so I clear my throat and add, "I'm so ready to kick St. Simeon's ass today. What do you think we'll beat them by?"

"In seconds or minutes?" Grey laughs, diving into his duffle and pulling out his gear.

Kai stands. "Fuck that school. Although, I did meet a stunner named Sutton there once. Damn, legs for days."

More crew members begin to filter in as the chatter continues, my moment all but forgotten until the coach blows the whistle, and we all start to make our way out. Kai grabs my shoulder, holding me back as the others leave. His eyes meet mine as he jumps right to the point.

"Do Caroline and yourself a favor, and don't cross the line anymore. Not until you're ready to stay. You understand what I mean?"

"Yeah, dude. I understand."

And I do. But sometimes, *knowing* what's right and *doing* what's right are mutually exclusive and uncontrollable.

***

Carebear: Heard you and Kai made up. Was there kissing involved because that's hot.

Me: Just me kissing his ass.

I laugh as soon as I hit Send, typing again.

Me: That joke played out differently in my head. But yeah, we're good.

Carebear: Good. So tell me, is Donovan the next stop on your apology train?

The elevator dings, but I don't look up, stepping out into Donovan's penthouse entrance. Her mean-ass butler, Vic, doesn't smile as I look up and say, "Sorry, just sending a text. But I know where to go."

Me: I'm on my way to her room now—with cookies.

I wait for a minute, starting toward Donovan's room, but stop again in the hallway when Caroline doesn't text back.

Me: Carebear, don't be like that…I know what your face is doing rn. You're always my favorite—there, now you can screenshot it for proof.

Carebear: xx

There are my kisses.

Me: oo

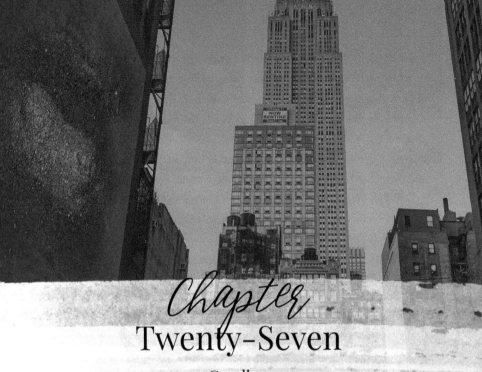

Chapter Twenty-Seven

Caroline

The sound of lockers closing around me muffles the sound of my own. Everyone that goes to Hillcrest is losing their minds today because it's the crew race day. The minute the St. Simeon buses began pulling up in the parking lot, boys started acting like dogs, barking as a sign of their loyalty, while the girls started primping.

I wasn't surprised. Crew hoes have no commitment to a team. They're only loyal to the wood. Speaking of crew hoes, Laura slides up next to me, pulling her backpack higher onto her shoulder. "Jesus, you'd think it was a pro game. People are going crazy."

"Well, St. Simeon is number one in their division, like us, so I suppose people like a good fight."

I button my blazer, already feeling a chill coming down the hall as the doors keep opening. Laura looks over her shoulder, waving to some girls I don't care about, then looks back to me.

"We should go get a place before the hill gets too crowded. I brought a few blankets. I'll run by my car and grab them."

My phone buzzes, making me press my lips together before I release them with a pop. "'Kay. Bye. I'll meet you there."

She smiles, turning around, and heads toward the door as I pull my phone from my blazer. It's been a week since Liam and I began secretly texting. During school, we give each other nothing but a stolen look, here and there, but late at night, we talk about everything and nothing.

Kai was right when he said I was playing with fire because I think my idea of friends is going up in flames. *Oh my God, he has me repeating that dumb saying in my head.*

> **Liam:** I don't see your face. Carebear...
>
> **Me:** Don't text that tone with me. I'm still deciding if it's worth my while.
>
> **Liam:** It's not. But come anyway. I always put on a good show.

The smile on my face is too broad. It's happening a lot lately. I debate what to text back as a raspy voice says, "Hey."

My eyes lift, blinking at Donovan standing in front of me. Closing my phone screen, I slip it back into my blazer pocket and wrinkle my forehead.

"What?"

She motions with her head, saying casually, "Let's go," while pulling the sleeves of her cardigan down halfway over her hands.

My head draws back. "Where?"

Her head does the same, and then she laughs.

"The race, Caroline. Be less salty. We're expected."

He did not send her to collect me. I narrow my eyes. "Pass. I have other friends to sit with."

But as I turn, she does the same, and we begin to walk in step. It's hard not to notice the people's reaction left milling about in the halls as we walk by them. This is priceless. It's the moment in a movie when they pan from our heels to our faces, playing some badass girl power music in the background.

"Wow," I say, turning to look at her as we walk. "We could rule the world if only we liked each other."

She rolls her eyes. "I don't completely hate you."

As we walk through the doors, I counter, "Aww, kitten, I don't completely like you either."

But she grabs my arm, stopping me at the top of the steps that lead to the grass, shifting to lock eyes.

"However...I trust you, Caroline."

I hold my breath because we aren't making sarcastic jokes anymore. Donovan picks at her bracelets under her sleeve as she speaks.

"I didn't know, back when we had our little confessional in the limo that night, that I could trust that you wouldn't break Liam's heart. But I do now. And I'm not in your way anymore unless you hurt him. Then I'm in your face."

What the fuck? Why is she saying this? I wonder if she and Liam spoke about me the other day when they made up.

"Is this your idea or one of his?"

She grins, knowing precisely what I'm asking.

"Mine. And this is our little secret. Liam doesn't talk to me about you, Caroline. But that doesn't mean he isn't thinking about you. It's obvious that whatever's going on between you guys isn't done—because he doesn't want it to be. Just don't hurt him—I think you're the only person that really can."

There are so many things I want to ask, even more I want to say, but I opt for the one that's the most honest.

"Stop being the *you* I like. It's unnerving. I prefer your actual personality—trite crew ho with an annoying laugh."

She smiles, and I roll my eyes before we turn and create more buzz, making our way down to the waiting blanket and a shell-shocked Laura.

***

Me: Nice win. I'm sure Grey did all the work, though.
Liam: So mean. Keep going, see what happens,
Carebear.

I stare down at my phone, heat creeping up my neck. What does that mean? Whatever it is probably isn't any one of the things running through my imagination, but a girl can wish.

The guys are inside the boathouse while everyone waits for them to emerge. It's a tradition to have a rally after a win, so I sit here because I'm all for a ceremony and another opportunity to indulge my addiction.

"There they are." Donovan points as the people scattered on the hill start cheering and clapping.

The boys are walking up the dock, donning their Hillcrest hoodies over their long uni's. I like when the water gets this cold because Liam in spandex pants is clit bait.

As they walk, he reaches behind him, tugging the sweatshirt off and holding it in one hand as he pulls a strap of his uni off his shoulder, switching hands to do the other side.

The top of the unitard hangs around his waist, putting his bare tan chest on display as he rubs a hand over his head, laughing and pushing an arm against Kai's shoulder as they walk before putting his sweatshirt back on.

I swallow, chancing a quick glance at Donovan to make sure she didn't see my drooling, but she's too busy eye-fucking Grey. Liam holds up his phone and wiggles it.

My head shifts around to make sure neither Laura nor Donovan is looking before I discreetly swipe my phone open.

Liam: Did you like that little show?

Me: Huh? I didn't notice anything special. If you want
my attention, you'll have to try harder.

Liam: Noted.

My gaze shoots back to his again. With a grin on his face, Liam snakes his hand up the inside of his hoodie. It lifts just a bit over his abs, making me bite my lip. His hand moves up, his chest peeking out of the top as he winds it around the side of his neck and drags his tongue over his lips.

Oh. Fuck.

The rally keeps going, but I'm not present. I'm in a game called try not to look at Liam because each time I do, he smiles as if he was expecting it. The goddamn arrogance makes him even that much more attractive, and he knows it.

"When is this ridiculous spectacle over?" I snark, adding, "How long do we have to sit here adoring them? Jesus."

I feel hot. I open my wool coat and unbutton my blazer, hoping the cold will cool me off.

Donovan laughs, looking to Laura. "Is she always like this?"

Laura giggles but stops the minute I glare at her. I push off the blanket to sit on my knees, brushing my hands together. "I just mean, I'm over it. I'm leaving. I'm supportive, but I can't groupie." I wink at Donovan. "That's all you, kitten."

Donovan rolls her eyes. "Well, you're in luck…" She motions with her head to the guys.

They're making their way back to the boathouse as people begin to gather their stuff. Thank God.

"Guess I'm lucky," I answer, as a deep voice comes from beside me.

"Caroline, right?"

I look at the guy standing next to me, feeling Laura and Donovan do the same. My hand lifts to shade my eyes.

"Yes."

"Wow," the handsome stranger says. "You're even more beautiful than I remember."

Remember? Who the fuck are you?

"Glad I can live up to the memory."

He laughs before squatting down, making him too close, which forces me to lean back to sitting.

"You don't remember me, do you?"

My brows rise in surprise. "No. Are you going to start giving me clues, or am I to assume I'm the only one of us that's unforgettable."

He extends his hand for me to shake, but I look at it and then back to him.

"I know we lost today, but you're really the only reason I wanted to race here anyway. I couldn't wait until I saw you again this summer."

Oh. My. God. My head shifts to Laura, who's staring at me with big eyes because it went right over my head.

"Hunter," I reply, turning back to him and smiling sweetly. "Am I right? Hamptons, last year. You followed me around like a puppy."

He smiles a toothy grin. "Yeah. That was me. I'm all grown up now though."

"Hunter. If you have to tell a girl, is it really true?"

His face drops, trying to make out if I actually just insulted him or if I'm kidding, so I make it clearer.

"How's the baby mama, Hunter? Shame she's not here to watch you compete. But I hear crabs can be extremely debilitating, what with all the scratching. Interestingly, I thought you boys shaved your junk. I guess you missed that memo because it would've saved you both some trouble."

Laura clamps a hand over her mouth, trying not to laugh as Hunter frowns before standing.

Donovan giggles behind me, saying, "Bye, Hunter," as he shoves his hands in his pockets and walks away but not before turning around and calling me a bitch as he flips me off.

Laura stares at me. "Oh my God. That did not just happen."

I push my hair over my shoulder, leaning back on my one hand, grinning. "Hunter may be a gutter whore, but he isn't a liar, Laura. I am a bitch."

The three of us laugh as I turn my head back toward Donovan, catching some commotion out of the side of my eye.

What the fuck?

Liam's stalking forward angrily up the dock, a sneer spread across his face.

Whoa. What did I miss? One of his crewmates tries to pull him back with a hand on his stomach, but Liam has too much momentum. Calls for Grey and Kai begin echoing as more crew members jump the pony wall by the boathouse. Everyone's running toward a pissed-off Liam.

"What the hell is happening?" I breathe out, not taking my eyes off the scene.

Everything speeds up, and the energy ramps up like there are live wires tapped into the ground. I jerk my head to Grey, running head-on into Liam, lifting him off the ground and walking him back a few feet.

"Oh my God."

Laura's tapping my arm as I scramble to a stand, along with everyone else watching and gasping, eyes glued on the guys.

Kai starts speaking animatedly to Liam as the guys surround them, making it impossible for me to see.

"Can you see what's happening?" Laura questions as she joins me, lifting her chin to try to get a better look.

"No." I point to the drama and look at Donovan. "What happened while I was abusing Hunter?"

She doesn't answer as her eyes grow wide, and she covers her mouth, laughing.

My eyes dart back to the guys to see Liam hoisted into the air by the group, laughter erupting as he curses loud enough for the world to hear. The crew ignores him, walking toward the end of the dock.

They aren't.

One. Two. Three is chanted before Liam is launched into the air. The word *fuck* echoes long and drawn-out until he lands in the cold water, making a huge splash.

I gasp, looking back as Donovan continues cackling like the witch she is.

"Good. Maybe that'll cool off that hot head of his. It's funny. Liam's always been the sweet and rational one."

"Except when…" I press, annoyed at her ambiguous statement.

She doesn't look at me as she answers.

"Except when you fuck with what he loves. Then you get a much different version."

"Who got fucked with?" I push again, narrowing my eyes at her.

Donovan turns her blue eyes to meet mine.

"You did, Caroline."

The pieces slowly fall into place, and my head shifts toward the direction Hunter just walked and back to the satisfied smirk on Donovan's face. *No.*

"He's out," Laura squeals, tapping my arm and calling my immediate attention.

Liam pulls himself out of the water, wet, still mad, and staring straight fucking at me.

***

Liam: You left.
Me: You seemed busy being a moron.
Liam: I'm only stupid when it comes to you, Carebear.
OO
Me: XX

Chapter
Twenty-Eight

Liam
December

My lips tip up into a smirk. I'm standing in the expansive marbled foyer of Grey's house. The noise grows louder from the outside of the glass double doors as shadowed forms near the entry, kicking the energy up a notch.

Tonight's going down in the books as fucking epic.

I watch through the glass, hands behind my back, as our rowdy crew team make their way up the outside steps.

The heavy doors are pushed open in greeting by two stoic butlers, and the guys playfully shove at each other as they enter, laughing and celebrating, dressed to the nines, complete with top hats, tails, and white gloves. It's the attire of the night.

We may look like proper gentlemen, but we're far from it.

Grey, Kai, and I wait, amused, for the twenty or so of them to pay attention as they walk inside. Their mood is already revelrous, hinting at the fucking debauchery they anticipate.

Still, as they gather in the foyer, eyes land on the three of us, standing side by side, formidable, and a hush falls over the group.

It's appropriate. That's the kind of respect we command and deserve.

Tonight's a night that's been in the making since the beginning of the year. It's the last official night as a crew—as a brotherhood.

We've rowed with some of these guys all through high school. So this night is important because if there's anything I've learned, it's that the guy who stands beside you now will be the same man who stands by your side later.

Grey and Kai are proof of that.

The last two months of my life have been bumpy, but Grey never wavered, even after losing my shit on Caroline and when I disappeared for two weeks. He stuck by me, forcing me to stop hiding. And Kai—he took me to task, justifiably so, then forgave me.

These guys are my brothers. They had my back when I spun out, and even now, while I find my footing. I'm starting to realize that the things I hate about this world of traditions, responsibility, and name are also why I have a family of brothers like this. My life is a double-edged sword.

There has to be a balance I can find between feeling suffocated and respecting legacy.

"Fellas," Kai's voice booms from my left. "Welcome to the circle. The last night you get to act like complete fucking idiots, and it doesn't matter…"

Quiet laughter filters out amongst the guys, but I don't crack a smile as Kai continues. "Because next year, you will be responsible for carrying out what those before you accomplished. And we *will* hold you to that standard. It's the privilege that was given to us, the men before us, and so on."

Grey steps forward and holds up his phone, waving it at them. "But before the party begins, each of you will turn in your phone." My eyes sweep over a few frowns as he continues. "There could be a future president amongst us, after all. The last thing he'll need is a photo to surface from tonight."

Howls and yells erupt from the group as I chuckle and glance over my shoulder, saying, "Beauties," calling out to three scantily dressed girls with velvet sacks.

I don't give a shit about these girls. It's the one standing out of sight at the top of the staircase, looking back at me with those violet-blue eyes, that I give a wink to before raising my voice over the ruckus.

"Put 'em in the bag, boys, and get ready for the fucking time of your life."

***

Wet feet slap against the indoor deck as we run around the Olympic-size pool to our designated table and take shots of whiskey.

Shouts and clapping fill the space as I sloppily gulp mine back, glancing at the opposing side as they run toward their own table. Grey throws back the amber liquid, and I shove his shoulder, already turning, gaining two steps ahead of him to dive back into the pool.

There's a splash a second behind me as I swim to our boat that's idly floating where we left it.

"Get in the fucking boat," I call out, laughing as I try to pull myself up and fail miserably.

"Fuck you. I'm trying," Grey yells back, laughing as hard as I am.

My hand slips just as I pull myself up, and I sink quickly back in the water, too drunk and unwilling to keep at it. Nobody ever beats us in real life, but I think tonight's their night.

"I'll do it alone," Grey growls, hooking his leg over the side and crawling in. "Move, asshole, before I hit you with the oar."

I smack the side of the boat, pushing myself away and floating on my back. "Let's go, McCallister! Don't let us down."

Letting out a ceremonious howl, he digs in and begins rowing away. Our side of seniors goes wild, cheering him on as I backstroke, spitting water into the air.

Because he's so far ahead of the other team, he decides to stand and take a drunken bow toward the applause. It's a premature celebration because the boat tips, and he falls in.

"Fucking loser!" I yell.

Laughter fills the room, and the boys break out in song, holding up shot glasses, arms draped over various bikini-clad girls as I swim away back across the pool, coming to the edge.

I raise my torso out, straining the muscles in my arms, and turn to sit on the edge. My stomach hurts from the amount of laughing I've done, so I run my hand over my defined abs.

The towel girl dangles the white fabric next to my shoulder, where beads of water drip down my bicep. I drag my gaze up, feeling the heaviest sense of déjà vu. Damn, this is like that dream I had the other night that ended up with me fucking Caroline but started with some random girl flirting with me. What was her name? It started with a *B*.

I let out a breath, remembering. "Your name isn't Bridgette, is it?"

"No. Stacey," she answers, walking away to give a towel to some other guys.

I look away, hiding my smile but not before catching a glimpse of Caroline by the pool doors, speaking to Kai. My eyes won't leave her as I watch the way she smiles at whatever he's saying.

She's wearing a pair of shiny black leggings—they look as if she was dipped in the material—and she has on that fucking crop top I hate.

The one thing this moment and my dream have in common is that I'm on my feet, making my way to where Caroline's standing, but when I get to her, instead of taking her into a corner and asking if she fucked herself today, I offer an "Excuse me" and walk past.

The towel around my waist begins to come loose, so I tighten it as I walk down the hall, past the alcove that draws my eyes and pulls pieces of that dream forward in my mind.

"What are you doing?"

Her voice is husky as I turn her body and push her back, slowly, into the dark alcove, hiding us away from prying eyes. My fingers knead into her waist as I lower to her ear, skimming my lips over her lobe and placing the only chaste kiss I'll give on her neck. The words I shouldn't speak drift out of my mouth, tinged in whiskey, and soak into her skin, making goose bumps bloom.

"You know exactly what I'm doing. I just said, 'I want to taste you,' Caroline. And I think we both know you want that too. No more games. You want to fuck me. I want to fuck you."

She doesn't answer, but she doesn't move either. I lean back, letting my eyes drift over her body, down past her nipples that are pushing against the silk of her thin-strapped tank, further down, stopping at her pussy. My tongue glides over my bottom lip involuntarily as I stare.

"I wonder if you taste like that expensive vanilla shit you bathe in. God, the idea makes me want to fucking drink you in."

Footsteps sound behind me, drawing my eyes over my shoulder and snapping me out of reliving my dream.

Caroline's about twenty feet behind me, walking the hall, alone, biting her bottom lip. My face jerks back to the front, hyperaware of her. Fuck, I want her. So goddamn bad, but we promised. I said I'd walk away—then I went about blurring every new line with each text I send. Fuck.

The reality is that I don't know how to walk away from Caroline. And I don't fucking want to anymore.

I pass a closet door, the one she first pulled me into when we were kids. Without another thought, my hand reaches for the handle, turning the knob, and I slip inside.

Fuck. This is one of those moments when you know you're about to make all the wrong decisions, and your stomach flips because there's still time to change course. But all I want is to crash into Caroline.

I've accepted that I'm probably going straight to hell over what I'm hoping will happen, but I can think of worse ways to get there. I close my eyes, trying to focus on any sound other than my breathing. *What if she just keeps walking by?*

The moment I think it, the light filters in, giving a glimpse of the tiny brunette shutting the door behind her.

Neither of us speaks, barely breathing as the sound of my heart beating feels so loud that we wouldn't be able to talk anyway. Seconds tick by, and we say nothing, but I can feel everything—her anticipation, mine, and all the things the darkness allows.

I reach out slowly until my fingertips brush her skin, making her gasp. The sound makes me feel like a fucking animal because my dick pushes against my board shorts. My fingers slide inward over her arm, feeling their way to her stomach and tucking up underneath the crop top.

My body jumps, surprised by the light touch of her fingers connecting with my abs. She runs her hand up my stomach, her palms brushing over my chest.

"Liam."

Her voice is arresting. *You keep saying my name like that and I'm going to lose my mind.* I close my eyes in the darkness so that I can live in the sweetness.

The sound of her feet shuffling closer makes me feel lost to this moment. I can hear her breathing faster, in quick succession.

Fuck, she's breathless, and I swear her body's getting hotter as my hands rub up and down the sides of her waist.

Her delicate hands explore my chest as one of my own splays against her rib cage. It moves up her body until my thumb rests under the fullness of her breast. Caroline arches her back, pressing her tits forward, letting out a whimper as my thumb brushes over her nipple under her shirt but over the soft lace bra.

The gorgeous pink bud begins to harden as I swipe back and forth, languidly, taking my time.

"Oh my God," she whimpers, leaning her head sideways. I know because her hair tickles my arm.

Wetting my lips, I try to keep myself calm because all I want is to run my tongue over that nipple until it glistens and feels rock hard. The hand still on her waist holds her in place as I sweep back and forth over her nipple, roughly now, listening to her body respond.

Caroline's hands reach up to my shoulders, gripping the muscles, as she whispers, "We shouldn't."

A growl rips from my throat as I grab the fabric of her bra, pulling her closer. The hand that was on her waist now grips her jaw, holding her in place as I bring my lips so close to hers that I don't know who's inhaling or exhaling.

"Are you looking for permission? Or are you saying no? Be clear, Carebear. Because you're right, we shouldn't, but I don't give a fuck about shouldn't anymore."

Her breath flutters over my mouth as her hands drop to my waist, undoing the towel and letting it fall as she whispers, "We said we wouldn't hurt each other anymore."

"Then say no."

I wait in the silence before running my tongue over her lips, hearing her sigh.

My hands slide over Caroline's face, weaving my fingers through her hair as I kiss the side of her mouth. "Say no. Don't let me hurt you."

But she doesn't say anything, just grips my hips, jerking them against her. I let my tongue dip inside her mouth, swirling and teasing. I take turns between our tongues dancing and sucking her bottom lip between mine.

I can't get enough of her. Kissing isn't enough; fucking her won't be either.

Caroline's arms snake inside of mine, wrapping around my neck. Our bodies smash together, secured even as I stand, taking her with me.

"Carebear, say no." I groan, kissing her faster, feeling her legs wrap around my waist.

I'm almost begging her because I know I'm going to fuck her regardless of the aftermath. With one arm wrapped around her waist and my other hand gripping her ass, I rock her center up my cock.

"Fuck me, Liam. I want it."

A deep guttural groan rips from my chest as I snap, spinning us so she's up against the door. I grind so hard into her she shudders. I'm holding her up as my lips sweep down her jaw, attacking her neck and sucking on the delicate flesh. Unladylike moans fall from her lips.

I love her this way—filthy, vulnerable, and mine.

"I'm fucking starved for you, Caroline."

She sighs into my mouth, scraping her nails over my head as my lips travel down past her collarbone.

"Off," I snap, hating the T-shirt that's in my way.

She tugs it over her head quickly as I dive back down, sucking hard on the spot just above the bra line. She sucks in air between her teeth, diving a hand between us into her pants. Jesus, she's rubbing herself as I mark her. I adjust her, giving her body a lift up, hearing her whimper.

My tongue runs over each spot I suck, her hand moving faster and faster while I bruise her alabaster skin. I scrape my teeth over her skin, tilting my head to pull her nipple into my mouth through the fucking bra. Caroline's hand slaps down on my bare back, breathing out, "Fuck yes," as I pull away.

I feel like I've run ten miles. I can barely catch my breath as I look at her silhouetted face. My fingers grip her working hand, pausing it and dragging it from her pants. I bring her hand to my lips, running my tongue over her finger before sucking on them.

She draws in a breath, exhaling her words.

"Take it all. Fuck me, lick me, hurt me. Just don't stop."

Tasting Caroline is like hearing music for the first time. It's like the first time I picked up a paintbrush, or like rain on a summer day—a perfect slice of fortune that should be exalted.

I'll never be strong enough to walk away. I know that now.

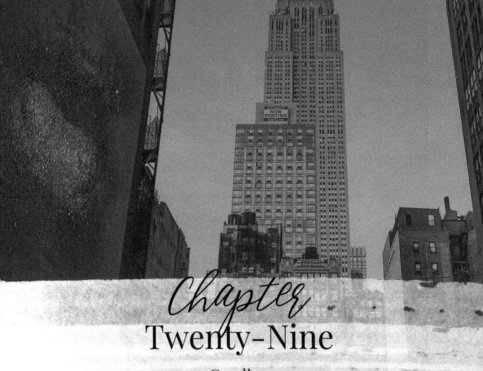

Chapter Twenty-Nine

Caroline

My body writhes against Liam's cock. I've never wanted something so much in my life. I knew I was walking into trouble the moment I followed him down the hall, and when he stepped inside the closet—our closet—my fate was sealed.

His lips are on mine, kissing me, teasing with his tongue as I run my hands over the muscles on his shoulders.

"Mine."

His words are whispered into my jaw as my head falls back against the door. *Did he just say...?* I pull his face to mine, smiling even though I'm sure he can barely make that out.

"What did you just say? Repeat it. I dare you."

His nose brushes over mine.

"No dare needed. You're mine, Carebear."

My lips press together, holding back the words I don't want to escape. Because *I love you* isn't something you share inside of a closet, secretly fucking a guy you're supposed to be staying away from. But I do…love him. And now I know it'll never go away. No matter how long we stay away from each other.

But love doesn't erase hurt, and if I do one decent thing in my life, it'll be to not hurt Liam. Donovan may trust me, but I'm not sure I feel the same way about myself.

I can't do this.

Liam's lips meet mine again, but I bring my hands to his chest just as I hear Kai's voice from outside the closet. My hand shoots over Liam's mouth, forcing him to stop kissing me as I listen quietly.

"Hey, have you seen Care?"

"No," Donovan answers. "Why?"

Speak of the devil. It's like we're hiding from our parents.

"Eh, I saw Liam walk this way, and Caroline followed. I just don't want him fucking with her head again because he can't help himself. But mostly, I worry she'll let him. Keeping that girl clear of her addiction is daunting, to say the least."

Donovan laughs. "I'm sure. But maybe they'll be different this time around."

"Maybe, but come on, beautiful, which one of them has actually changed? I'm crossing my fingers for them too, but Liam's still figuring his shit out, and Caroline's still avoiding it all."

I can't hear what Donovan says, but it suddenly grows quiet. Everything they just said feels like ice in my veins. I don't have to be able to see Liam to know that he's staring back at me. His face squirms out of my grip as his hand comes to cradle my face.

It feels like we'll never be able to escape ourselves long enough to start over. Liam leans his forehead against mine.

"Say no, Caroline."

My arm stretches out past the door, clicking the light, keeping my eyes closed as I whisper, "No."

Liam lets me slide down his body, smoothing his hands over my hair as my feet steady on the ground. He presses a kiss to the top of my head, but I can't look up because I want to hide. His hand presses to the small of my back, moving us backward, before reaching behind me to open the door. As Liam's body slides past mine, he stops in the doorway, turning me around too, bringing a finger under my chin.

My eyes meet his as he says, "I meant every word, Carebear."

***

The alarm on my phone blares through my room, but I'm already awake, staring at the ceiling. I could barely sleep. All I thought about was, did I push Liam far enough away that he indulged in the booze, girls, and whatever other kinds of fuck-boy behavior that crew touts as their mission statement?

How can I hate him if he did? He has zero reasons not to embody every tenet. *I said, "No."* I should've gone back, hung out with Kai, but I couldn't. Instead, I came up to my room and watched reruns of *Unsolved Crimes*—research for when I run into Arden again.

Throwing back the cashmere blanket, I sit up. I'm right back where I started. Finally plummeted into the depths of basic bitch that I'd hoped to avoid. I'll need to start wearing beach waves, drinking Starbucks, and watching the Hallmark movie channel.

Fuck. "No," I growl to myself as my feet hit the floor, and I make my way to the closet.

This melodramatic girlshit is precisely why I did what I did last night. Liam and I haven't changed—maybe individually, we're growing. *Wait, am I growing?* Because I feel like I'm still sixteen, wondering if I'm enough, acting jealous and petty. And he's still the same guy that didn't say the word *love*.

Still didn't miss that, Brooks. Why am I so dumb?

I grab the first dress I see, going on autopilot as I change and do my makeup, painting myself into a pretty picture. My feet are halfway down the stairs as Bradley stands at the bottom looking up, pensive. A frown blooms on my face.

"What is it?"

"The staff would like to know what to do with the clothes left behind by the young ladies from last night."

Are you fucking kidding me? *I have no right to be mad. I have no right to be mad.* Maybe if I keep chanting it, I'll start to act accordingly. I close my eyes for a moment, reopening and smiling at Bradley.

"Young and ladies don't seem applicable. Burn them." I stop at the bottom of the stairs. "Where is the degenerate?"

Bradley never smiles or gives anything away as he says, "Last I checked, in the billiards room. You may also want to ask the young Mr. McCallister where we should store the crew boat that's still in the pool."

I give a tight nod, crossing my arms as Bradley takes his leave. I'm so irritated. I stalk down toward the billiards room, shoving the heavy double doors open, hoping to exude the bravado I wish I felt. All the while secretly hoping not to see anything that'll burn itself into my brain for life.

"There you are," I hiss at Grey, rolling my eyes. "Why is there a crew boat in the pool? What the hell happened in here last night?"

My eyes discreetly scan the room, eyeing a pair of cheap red panties on the floor before Liam's voice comes from the pool table. He's laid across it, back in his tuxedo pants, shoeless with just the top few buttons undone on the shirt.

Grinning at me, he pushes to sitting. "What didn't happen? I think hell might've frozen over with all the nos that became yeses."

What the fuck is that supposed to mean? Because it's not funny. My stomach drops because, during my spiral over last night, as I weighed out what would happen between Liam and me, I never considered that he'd be angry.

Or that he'd turn back into the same guy who used that well-worn charm against me. *Don't be douchey, Liam.* But that grin on his face, paired with those words, is proving otherwise. *Guess old habits die hard, huh, Liam.*

I narrow my eyes at him, saying, "Shut. Up," before walking past and turning my attention to Grey's half-awake face.

"Make your feet stop." Grey groans, rubbing his head.

Good, I'm glad Grey's hungover. He deserves the pain as a consequence of being one.

"You've destroyed the room," I snap.

My hands find my hips as I look around at the floor that's littered with empty bottles, and cigarettes. Eww. I glance over my shoulder at Liam, who's leaning back on his elbow, letting his eyes roam over my body.

Is he fucking serious? I roll my eyes, ready to spit venom, when footsteps from behind call my attention. Donovan's in the doorway, holding two lidded coffees. Our eyes meet for a second, and then hers dart to Liam before she saunters past me, stopping only to do a double take at Kai.

"Looks like I left just in time last night." She giggles.

I follow her gaze to Kai, seated in a high-back leather chair, and my brows hit the roof. For fuck's sake, he's wearing a top hat, boxers, a red bra, and a fucking monocle. How didn't I notice that when I walked in?

"Jesus. You look like a perverse Monopoly character."

He grins back at me, amused over his costume, and winks. I almost laugh, but I'm too on edge with Liam behind me.

Grey motions to his chest. "That must belong to the owner of the mystery panties on the floor. Wanna share with the class?"

A small breath leaves my body in relief, relaxing my shoulders. Dammit. I'll hate myself for that moment, for at least a few months. Liam huffs a laugh, but I refuse to look back at him. *He didn't notice that, did he?*

Grey pulls Donovan onto his lap, laughing. "Dude, you'll need a penicillin shot if it's the girl I think it was."

Kai tosses an empty beer can at him, and I scowl because they're acting like Neanderthals, or more truthfully because I'm losing my mind with Liam staring at me. I know he is because he hasn't stopped since I walked in. *Time for me to go.*

I turn to leave, saying, "Clean up your mess, Grey," but as I head toward the door, I'm halted by a set of broad shoulders filling out a wrinkled tuxedo shirt as Liam jumps off the pool table.

He stumbles toward me, rubbing his head and licking those fucking lips. I bite my bottom lip, letting go immediately and steeling my spine, remembering that everyone is watching. His arms stretch overhead as he yawns, and every muscle ripples under that damn shirt. Each step he takes toward me reels me in because Liam's so flawlessly easy. He has all the charm in the world within just a goddamn yawn.

"How come you didn't bring *me* a coffee?" he rasps, rubbing a hand over his stomach.

God, his voice is all husky and deep.

Say something. Shut him down.

"I'd assumed you'd choked on your own vomit." I press a finger against his chest to move him, adding, "Byeee."

He lets out an "oof" that only I can hear, encircling my wrist and bringing it to his hip, adding, "Are you my Grumpy Bear today?"

His Grumpy Bear?

"Come on, Carebear"—Liam's fingers drag up my arm—"please." His eyes meet mine, and he pulls his bottom lip between his teeth before adding, "Grab me some coffee."

Oh, he is one hundred percent not talking about coffee, and I will kill him because I'm confident that I'm blushing, but I still don't move. Because I am here, in this moment, not at all struggling against being held hostage by that innuendo.

"I told you not to call me that anymore."

I say it with absolutely no strength behind it because I'm only playing along for the sake of staying in this bubble for as long as I can. Hopefully, this hit will last longer than the others have in the past.

"You told me a lot of things last night, Carebear." He tilts his head, staring at my mouth, whispering for only me to hear, "But I'm not a particularly good listener."

I swallow, feeling my chest rise and fall faster. Liam glances down at my chest and back to my face, giving me a wink. Oh my fuck.

"I didn't see you at the party last night, Caroline," Donovan butts in, ruining our moment with her voice. "When were the two of you hanging out?"

Oh, shut up. We were two feet away, almost fucking.

I only think it as I look at her, my face blank, trying to get my bearings. Liam weaves his hand through mine, but I pull it away quickly, swallowing and trying to stay calm.

"Have you hit your head?" I whisper so only he hears.

Liam's brows draw together, eyes dropping from mine down to my hand and then back to me before he turns his attention to Donovan.

"Before you got here, Van. Caroline helped me with some of the decorations." He looks at me. "Right, Carebear?"

I nod, crossing my arms and turning around, using the moment as an escape. Liam whispers something as I pass, but I don't pay attention, trying to get out of the room as fast as fucking possible.

What the hell was that? Jesus. I exhale harshly, walking down the hallway and shaking my head. *He tried to hold my hand—in front of everyone. Why would he do that?*

I'm halfway down the hall, knee-deep in my thoughts, as footsteps come bounding down, surprising me. I jerk my face over my shoulder to see Liam bounding down the space toward me. *Absolutely not. I am not doing this right now.* My feet begin moving faster, but he laughs.

"Carebear. Hold up. You can't outrun me. Not in those fuck-me heels."

I spin around, mad at him. I hate Liam for making me like him, only to remember I shouldn't do that anymore.

"First off"—I stab a finger at him—"we have to stop meeting in hallways. Second, what the fuck was that back there? It wasn't funny, Liam. I am not a game, and we aren't some kind of joke. Last night hurt. But then today, you're trying to hold my hand?"

"I know we aren't a joke. But Carebear, I always hold your hand. It's only different because you've felt my hands in other places."

I blink back at him, letting those words sink in. He's right. He did use to always hold my hand, but now when he touches me, I don't wonder what they would feel like on my body—I know. And I'm scared everyone else can see that too.

A pathetic girl that can't close the deal with the boy she loves.

"You don't have to admit that I'm right." He grins, hovering over me as he takes one of my hands.

He's staring down, tracing his thumb over my fingernail as he says, "You're so pretty when you're mad," under his breath. My eyes drop, watching him lift my hand, bringing my fingers to his mouth, slowly kissing the tips. Liam's making it impossible to keep a clear head. *Why do you have to do things like this?*

"Like what?" He grins, lifting his sparkling eyes to mine. "Get lost in you? Because I am, Carebear."

I don't think I'm breathing as I stare back at him until he speaks. I don't have time to freak out about what I thought was said in my head was actually said out loud because his answer's rendered me speechless.

"I thought about us the whole night—well, mostly just about you. I almost came upstairs, but I knew if I did, I wouldn't be coming back down. So I've been waiting to have this conversation, sober."

Liam smiles, letting go of my hand, and tucks my hair behind my ears before cradling my face.

"Don't be mad at me, Carebear. I woke up wanting to kiss you, and it made me a little frisky." He brings his lips closer to mine, rubbing his nose over mine. "I meant everything I said. I don't give a fuck about the shouldn'ts. And after debating every fucking con, I realized that you can't do anything to make me stop needing you. It's me and you, Carebear. And you know it."

I push his hands away as I take a step back. Part of me is disbelieving, and the other part is afraid that he's really this determined. Both scare the shit out of me.

"What Kai and Donovan said, Liam. They're right. We're toxic."

"So?"

A v forms between my perfectly manicured eyebrows. *So? How is that an answer?*

"So?" I look up at the ceiling and back to him. "Liam, we're damaged goods. Neither of us knows how not to be. I'll hurt you, you'll hurt me, and we promised not to do that anymore. Jesus, let me be decent—once."

He closes the distance between us again, reaching up and taking a strand of my hair around his finger.

"I like you better indecent." I try to sweep my hair back, but he bats my hand away, continuing to play with it. "I'll never break you again, Caroline. And even if you try to hurt me"—he smirks—"I won't let you."

My heart is beating so fast. Why is he doing this? It's almost mean. I grip his chin, tugging his eyes to mine.

"Every odd is stacked against us, Liam."

"I like a challenge." He shrugs, dipping his face to kiss the inside of my wrist.

"Why are you doing this?"

I groan, trying to turn away, but he growls, bending to cage me in his arms around my waist. My hands grip his shoulders as I look around to see if anyone is witnessing this spectacle. Liam leans in, kissing the hickies that he left on me last night, hidden under my dress.

"What are you doing? Liam, stop."

"No." He rests his cheek on my chest, holding me like a prize he's won. "You don't fucking get it. All I see is you, Carebear."

His head pulls back, speckled green-and-amber eyes locked to mine. "I walked out of that closet only to sit in a room full of people and think about kissing you. Everywhere I look, it's you. Tell me how I walk away from that?"

"We can't just start over. It's not that simple."

His face nuzzles my neck, breathing the words into them, "It is that simple. Be my New Year's date. Let's do our midnight over again."

I'm staring down at him, trying not to squint because he's so fucking bright. *There's no saying no to this Liam.* It's impossible. But is it selfish to let him try to love me when I know I'll only disappoint us both?

My lips press together, but he scrunches his nose and starts to shake me gently from side to side.

"Don't do that. Say it. Come on, Carebear." His smile spreads over his face. "Come on. Say yes."

I laugh. "Goddammit. Okay, fine. But don't tell anyone; I don't want to deal with the peanut gallery just yet."

"Deal."

His lips push out, and he jerks his chin at me, so I give him a quick peck.

"That's all you get. Now go brush your fucking teeth."

I'm spun around, ass smacked, making me squeal as I look back.

"This is silk, Liam. You'll wrinkle it."

I don't give a fuck about the silk. But I also refuse to melt into a puddle in front of him. Liam sticks his tongue out at me, walking backward before turning around and pointing at the closet as he walks by, yelling, "I love that room."

My hand covers my mouth as I watch him leave, wondering how I'll survive if we actually make it this time. I've never tried on happiness. I always just coveted it on others.

But maybe this time…

***

Liam: Did you think of me today?
Me: No
Liam: Lies come with punishments.

"What's with the smile? You're doing a great impersonation of someone happy."

Laura laughs at her own joke, immediately rendering it unfunny, as she flips through a magazine sitting on the couch in my room.

"Shocker," I answer, tucking my phone away. "I am happy. Hurry, call Page Six."

The look on her face is priceless; she's staring at me dumbfounded, so I go back to the subject we were speaking of before Liam's text came through.

"You were saying? Your interview."

Her eyes search my face, the lightbulb finally going off.

"Oh yeah, I don't think I'm getting a ticket. From what my mom says, they go out right after the New Year. But it's worthless to be hopeful. My mother wasn't chosen when she was my age, and honestly, I'm not relevant like you."

Her choice of words assaults my senses. Relevant? I'm staring at her, watching as she eats one of the cookies she brought over.

Perspective and irony are friends with benefits. Sometimes you get fucked, and other times you're reminded about the things right in front of your face.

I spend all my time repeating back to myself that I'm irrelevant or an imposter in this world of ours. But to someone who really is a void in these social circles, like Laura, my life is enviable. I'm getting perspective fucked, and ironically, by someone I'd never touch.

"I had to apply too," I offer as a consolation.

"That's just a formality—because you're not a legacy. But Caroline, you've always been a shoo-in. I just went along with what you were saying because you seemed to believe that you weren't. And I've learned my lesson on disagreeing with you."

I don't answer. Instead, I take a black-and-white cookie, pondering what else she's just gone along with. I'm not stupid—I know our "friendship" is transactional, but I'd thought that she was at least partially honest. I take a bite, chewing before I speak.

"I have a plus-one for the New Year's Eve party at the Campbell. Kai's mom is hosting. It's a who's who of celebrity twats, coupled with New York socialite whores. A real orgy of importance."

She's staring at me, not connecting the dots.

"If you want the ticket, it's yours. Consider it a gateway to relevance."

Laura bounces in her seat, rushing me like she's going to hug me, but I hold up my hand.

"I do one nice thing a year. It hadn't been used, so—don't make me regret being nice to you."

She nods in rapid succession, scooting back into her seat as I turn away, taking another bite of my cookie and swiping the message open again on my phone.

Me: Stop threatening me with a good time, xx
Liam: I want my kisses in person, Carebear.

Chapter Thirty

Liam

My mom pushes the door open to my room, walking inside, eyeing me adjusting the collar of my crisp white dress shirt.

"You look handsome. I can't remember the last time I saw you in a suit. It's been all tuxedos lately."

I grin. "Yeah, but it's nice to not have to wear those penguin suits. You can blame the celebrity crowd for the party being less highbrow tonight."

She brushes her hands over my arms. "Celebrities. Gah, they're the worst," she jokes as a smile peeks out. "So. Who's the lucky lady?"

"Who says there's a girl?" I tease, reaching over to grab my jacket off the valet stand. "Maybe I just like to look nice, Mom. Geez, can't a guy dress for himself—why does it have to be all about the girls?" She's staring at me, rolling her eyes as I grin. "When am I enough?"

She smacks my arm and laughs.

"You're ridiculous. And the fact that you showered gave it away."

She helps me put on my jacket and stares at me through the mirror.

"I'm happy to see you so happy, Liam. It's a nice change from—"

I nod, looping the buttons through the maroon blazer. "Yeah, I know. I think I'm starting to find my footing. How's the other Brooks doing?"

"Sulking. Regretful. Stubborn. But let's not talk about your father. I want to hear more about Caroline."

My head jerks to the side to stare at Babe, mouth hanging open.

"What?" she says casually.

"What? Oh, you are sneaky. How'd you find out I was taking Caroline tonight? Do I have any secrets, or is my life a lie?"

My mother walks back toward the door, picking up a box she'd placed on a table next to a chair in my room. Her smile is far from hidden as she walks back, handing it to a confused me. It's a small square box, reminiscent of the size a cookie would come in.

Oooh, food. I'm starved.

I lift the lid, peering inside to see a single white rose. It's for my lapel. My shoulders shake as I begin to put it all together.

"This came with it," my mother says, handing me a small white envelope that simply says *xx Caroline* on the front.

I stare at the note, giving my head a shake, and shove it into my jacket pocket. But my mother scowls at me. She's so nosey. It makes me laugh harder as she takes the box from me, opening it and pulling the flower out to pin to my lapel.

"If a girl goes to all this trouble, you should read it, Liam."

I turn to look at myself once she's pinned it, countering, "Not in front of you."

My mother's eyes grow wide as I walk past her to gather my wallet and phone from the bureau.

"So she's that kind of girl, huh?"

She's teasing. She knows exactly who Caroline is, but I play along for fun.

"I hope so."

Her gasp is priceless, and the "Liam!" that follows makes me howl with laughter.

Babe points her finger at me. "Be good tonight and be a gentleman."

"I wouldn't be anything less for my Carebear."

She gives me a look of approval before leaving me to finish gathering the rest of my things. I walk inside my closet, grabbing the black trench coat. Folding it over my arm, I glance back over my shoulder to ensure I'm alone before pulling out Caroline's note.

> *Brooks,*
>
> *I read somewhere in an old 1950s guide to dating that when boys buy girls flowers, it means they expect them to put out. I thought I'd take the opportunity to set our boundaries now. Here are your flowers, I expect dick.*
> *xx Caroline*

This fucking girl.

Swiping my phone, I pull up Caroline's number, shooting off a text.

Me: I'm just a piece of ass to you.

Carebear: Never discount the power of a good ass. An entire Kardashian fortune was built atop one.

Me: You know what I want to be on top of tonight?

Carebear: Interesting...I always pinned you as a bottom. Good to know. Now hurry up. I miss you.

A whoosh of breath leaves my body as I read the last words—*I miss you*. When Caroline's vulnerable like this, so delicate, so much of the "real" her, it almost crushes me.

The feelings I have for her are so fucking intense that when she says stuff like that, I want to love her, protect her, be a monster on her behalf. I would literally do anything for her.

I'm trotting down the stairs with a smile on my face as my phone buzzes in my pocket. I reach inside my suit jacket, pulling it out, bringing it to my ear.

"What's up, man."

Matias's voice fills my ear. "Richie Rich. We got a problem."

I frown.

"What problem?"

"Someone marked over your shit. Not too bad. I mean, it's fixable, but Mac said I should call you first before I did it."

Fuck. I look at the time on my phone. It's only nine, and I'm not meeting Caroline until ten. And the warehouse is on my way.

"Hello? Liam?"

"Yeah, yeah. I'm coming. And also, way to keep that fucking wall our secret."

I hear Mac say, "I told you to shut up," in the background, and Matias responds, "I only told like one guy in my hood, but I guess he told a few more."

"Like I said, I'm on my way—but you owe me a new wall."

"Done," Matias laughs.

Smiling, I hang up, sliding into my limo, and go back to my text with Caroline. The door closes, and I redirect the driver as I type.

> **Me:** I have a stop to make. Go with Kai? And I'll meet
> you there.
> **Carebear:** I better like this gift you're getting me.

I smile down at the phone. Oh, Carebear, you're gonna fucking love it.

> **Me:** oo
> **Carebear:** I want my hugs in person, Liam.
> **Carebear:** And don't forget you owe me dick
> because…flower.

***

I look up at the wall, cluttered with bright paint and initials that belong to people trying to make a name for themselves. It's no different from a gallery, really. We're all artists—my medium is usually a paintbrush, theirs is a can of spray paint. Different and yet the same.

I shrug off my suit jacket, handing it to Matias, who puts it on, making me laugh because he's about six inches shorter than me and probably seventy-five pounds lighter too.

Mac nudges my shoulder. "My brother looks like he's twelve."

Matias flips us off as I reach down to grab a can of paint from the few on the ground, turning my head toward him as he speaks.

"So, what's the plan tonight? With all this and your girl?"

I roll up my shirtsleeve before shaking the can, before teasing him. "I'm not telling you. Why? Just so you can show up and try to steal her?"

Mac laughs. "Good call. Matias is a sneaky fuck, always trying to be a player."

We're all laughing as I make quick work of respraying Caroline's lips, switching to another color to add definition. I can't believe I never got to see the world this way when I was younger and learning about art.

"Sweet," Matias breathes as I step back.

I glance down at my white retro Jordans, hearing the boys say, "Aw, shit."

Mac drops a hand to my shoulder. "You finally arrived, Richie Rich. No spray off."

I shove Mac's shoulder, chuckling. He takes a playful swing at me, and I dodge, but as I do, the can in my hand drops to the ground, making us all jump back, trying not to get hit with a shot of paint.

"Aw, fuck," I laugh, turning toward the wall, wincing, preparing to get tagged up.

The can clangs against the pavement as it lands, rolling a few feet away. I turn around, relieved, as Matias and Mac both look amused. I open my mouth just as a bright spotlight blinds me.

"Bro," "Fuck," and "Don't move" echo around me as my hand shields my face. A whoosh of air sounds from my sides as both brothers break in separate directions, yelling, "Go. Go. Go."

Oh shit. My sneakers dig into the pavement as I start to bolt, but the click of a gun has me freezing in place, already breathless, slowly raising arms. Two cops walk toward me, each with a gun aimed straight at me.

Fuck. Fuck. Fuck. Fuck. No.

Caroline.

***

Caroline

Ten, nine, eight, seven...

The countdown's happening, but time's already standing still. It doesn't matter how much longer until midnight. Because I'm standing in the middle of the room—alone, empty, and stripped of all my hope. He never came. I waited. Smiling and hoping the whole night that he would walk through the door, apologize, and sweep me off my feet. But he never came.

Six, five, four, three...

I believed him.

I trusted him.

I loved him.

Fuck, Liam.

One.

Chapter
Thirty-One

Liam

"Liam Brooks, you're out."

My eyes dart up, scooting away from the drunk guy who's using my shoulder as a pillow, and stand quickly. The metal bars slide open, and I let out my first official breath as I walk back into the world and out of the holding cell I've been sitting in since last night.

"Follow me."

The cop waves me over to a counter, where I'm handed a Ziploc bag of my belongings and asked to sign some paperwork by a surly, rotund officer.

"Bail's been made. Go to the doors."

By who? Nobody knows I'm here. God, let it be Caroline by some form of sheer fucking luck. The same feeling I've had since last night blankets me again when I think about how pissed she's going to be.

She's going to slit my throat. I just need to explain before she grabs the knife.

Grumpy cop stamps some paperwork, not looking at me, as he shoves it my way, closing the file. But before I can ask what anything means, he's already arguing about a Giants game with another cop. My head shifts around, unsure about what I'm supposed to do, still trying to get my bearings.

Yet another cop snaps his fingers at me, standing by a metal set of doors, so I grab my shit and head that way as they're opened to a new hallway that leads to yet another set of doors. Those are opened as well with a buzzing sound, only to click behind me as I find myself standing in a lobby staring back at my father's face.

"Liam."

Aww, fuck.

"Tucker."

He motions with his head before turning so that I follow. We walk silently, making our way out of the precinct to the waiting limo—parked in a red zone. The driver opens the door for my father, but I stand back as he slides inside.

"Get in the fucking car, Liam" is bellowed from the shadows.

"No," I say calmly as I unzip the bag and take out my wallet and watch, putting one on my wrist and the other in my pocket before continuing.

"Let's walk. I've been cooped up in one hellhole for most of the night. I'd like to be free of being stuck inside a small space with more bullshit."

I barely finish my sentence before my father's standing face-to-face with me, angry but compliant. He buttons his jacket, pointing to the driver.

"Take that."

My head turns to see the driver walking back toward us, holding out a jacket for me. It's the same trench I left in my own car before I'd gotten out last night.

My father clears his throat. "You'll probably need this too at some point today."

He's pulling out my cell from his breast pocket.

I take it. As I toss my Ziploc in the back of the limo, I try to swipe my cell open, but the screen stays dull. Fuck, it's dead.

Caroline's going to be a goddamn mess—mean and hateful. With how mad I know she'll be, I may have to hold her down to get her to listen. But first, I have to do this—my dad and I are long overdue.

Tucker tells the driver to go back to our home since we aren't too far. He looks at me for direction, so I turn and begin to walk down the sidewalk. It's quiet outside, no people, only noise from the city because it's only around six in the morning.

Neither of us speaks for almost a block. I know he's wondering where to start too. But then his voice disrupts the peace.

"Why didn't you call me, Liam? You get a phone call."

He sounds almost hurt, and that takes me off guard. I exhale, putting my hands in my jacket pockets.

"I can't believe I'm saying this, but I'm a tragic story of technology—I couldn't remember anyone's number by heart. But honestly, you wouldn't have been a call I'd have made."

Tucker stops, attracting my attention as I slow my feet and shift to look at him.

"How did we get here, Liam?" He motions between us. "To this place where your father isn't a call you'd make when you're in trouble."

I don't look at him, letting my head hang heavy in thought. Words have never been more important than in this moment. The fucking irony of that—needing him to understand me, but not knowing how to explain myself. *Damn, I thought I was past this.*

As I stare at the concrete, wondering how I'm going to say anything and everything, a grin grows on my face because I suddenly remember a piece of advice he gave me as a kid.

"Say what you mean and mean what you say. There are never any right words for the truth. Only the true ones."

I laugh, lifting my eyes to his. Maybe he's not so removed as my hero, after all.

"We're here because you forgot you trust me."

His cheeks fill with air before he blows it out, but I don't stop talking.

"My life is my own. My legacy is for me to leave. Dad, you forgot that you could trust me with our last name. I'm never going to disappoint you because you raised me to be a leader, and now it's my turn to decide where the Brooks name goes."

His hand lands on my shoulder as he nods, jaw tense.

"I just bailed you out of jail, Liam."

"Yeah. You did."

I chuckle as he clears his throat again. I swear if I didn't know Tucker better, I'd say he's trying not to get emotional. His free hand falls heavy onto my other shoulder.

"You skipped school for almost two weeks, doing God knows what. Making your mother worry."

"Yep. I did that too."

We're staring at one another as he says, "You walked away from Harvard, son. From the place I made for you and your grandfathers before that."

I let out a frustrated breath, stepping back out of his grasp.

"Fuck." His eyes grow wide as my hands smack together. "Yes. All of those things are true, Dad. But you're not asking the questions."

His arms cross over his chest, brows arching.

"And what should those be, Liam? What am I missing? Because I'm trying here, son."

My hand rubs over my head as I speak.

"Ask me why I skipped school—because I'll tell you it was because I was a coward. I was bogged down by all the responsibilities of who I thought I should be that I forgot it was all mine to decide. I decide who I am, not who I am based on you, or Mom, or my friends. Knowing I was a coward makes it so I'll never be one again. I needed to get lost to find myself—as cheesy as that sounds."

He opens his mouth, but I shake my head. "Ask me why I got arrested. It was because I finally figured out what I had to say—which was that I love Caroline. The tagging started with me trying to figure out my place in the world. But that's the thing. She is my world. And I would've never gotten the courage to tell her that if I hadn't tagged up a hundred walls with her lips. She's kissed this whole damn city."

I laugh, tipping my head to the sky and back to him. "Because when I was stripped of everything—the Columbia program I wanted, your respect, my friends, even my own backbone… She's the one fucking thing that stuck. Being out here taught me that all the other things fall into place as long as I know mine is with her. So I wouldn't do any of this differently or apologize for finding my way."

He looks down, running his hands through his salt-and-pepper hair as some people pass between us. I step in closer as they clear.

"Now, ask me why I walked away from Harvard."

I've never been more ready to be my own man. To not ask for permission or even his respect.

"No," he breathes as he lifts his head.

I frown with a deep pull of my brows.

"No? Are you even making an effort to hear me?"

He smiles. Actually fucking smiles.

"Yes. Yes, I am, Liam."

I'm dumbstruck. I don't know what to say, but I don't have to speak because he doesn't stop.

"I don't need to hear any more because what I hear is that my son has a passion he's willing to fight for. That would make your grandfather incredibly proud. I hear that you're in love, and I know what that feels like. And I hear my son speaking like the man I raised him to become."

A lump in my throat keeps me silent. I may have been ready to live without his respect but fuck if it doesn't feel good to have it again.

Tucker grips the back of my neck. "I failed you, son. I'm not perfect, but I hope you can forgive me. I am ridiculously proud of the man you've become and that you were brave enough to become that man, on your own, while I was busy being a narrow-minded prick."

He pulls me into a hug, squeezing me tight, and my arms wrap around him. My dad kisses my cheek, giving me another squeeze before pulling back and looking at me.

"'It matters not how strait the gate. How charged with punishments the scroll.'"

I cut him off. "'I am the master of my fate. I am the captain of my soul.'"

The "Invictus" poem on his office wall.

Patting his arm, I smile, stepping away toward the curb, lifting my arm to call a ride.

"Thank you for bailing me out, and I love you, but I have to go. I need to get to Caroline. Can we rain check the rest of this conversation?"

He nods. "Go. I understand. And once you charge your phone, hire someone to clean up my fucking building. I'm not paying for Caroline's lips. I already paid for your mother's."

I laugh as I open the cab door and slide inside as he continues down the street. Caroline's address leaves my lips as I tap my knees like a set of drums, wishing this cab driver would go faster, which isn't something that's usually a problem.

The moment we pull up, I'm paying and out of the car, taking two steps at a time to the door. The doorbell gets a workout as I knock, waiting for someone to open.

Come the fuck on. There must be twenty people that work in Grey's house. Is everyone off for the damn day?

I'm knocking over and over as Bradley's disapproving face comes into view, but I'm already slipping through the door as it opens, ignoring anything he's saying.

Speaking over my shoulder, I head toward the stairs.

"Bradley, where's Care? Upstairs? Her room?"

My feet hit halfway up the stairs as Grey's voice comes from behind.

"Where the fuck have you been?"

I glance over my shoulder, still bounding up the stairs, yelling back, "Jail. I'll explain later. Where's Carebear?"

"Gone."

I skid to a stop and turn around, racing back down.

"What do you mean gone?

Grey crosses his arms. "As in, she left about an hour ago. Something about wanting to start the year off in better company. I thought she was just being Caroline. But now. Explain."

I don't explain, asking instead, "Where'd she go?"

Damn, if this isn't Grey and me about to stand off. There have only been a handful of these moments in our lives. Once when we were kids. Once when he lost his shit over Donovan, and now. Now because he's not getting in my way. He's telling me where my Carebear is, or I'll beat it out of him.

He shakes his head. "You'll need to explain first."

Dick.

"No. We've been here before, Grey, and I let you have an opinion. This time you don't get one. I love her. That's all you need to know. Now tell me, or we're throwing down until you do."

Our eyes are locked, both of us ready as Donovan comes from behind Grey, making us immediately cool as she lifts his arm to drape over her shoulders.

"She's at the house on the island. Have fun. She's pissed. Not that anyone could tell, but I'm smarter than most when it comes to being in love with a dickhead."

Grey looks down at Van. "Thanks. And he was supposed to have to work for that, remember?"

She shrugs, blowing a kiss up at him. "I think he's earned her."

I don't wait around, just yelling as I run out, "Bros before hoes, Van," hearing her yell back, "Ride or die, Brookie."

My feet slide in the doorway as I grip the door to stop my momentum. "Hey. Don't tell her I'm coming."

Grey smirks and nods, bending down to toss Van over his shoulder as I head out, hailing a cab back home. I need a shower, some clothes, and to let my parents know that I'll be out of town for a few days.

***

I reach for my ringing phone in my pocket, brushing the paper-wrapped bouquet of peonies on the seat next to me in my town car.

"What? Are you calling to give me more shit?"

I hear Van laugh. "You're on speaker. We're calling to be nosey and find out what the hell is actually going on."

Grey's voice chimes in. "Caroline just texted and is none the wiser that you're on your way. Now tell Cherry what she wants to know so she'll stop torturing me with all her unanswered questions."

Donovan cuts him off. "Oh my God. Shut up, Grey. But since we're playing accomplice to all this, we want to know the whole enchilada. Spill it, Brookie."

I growl, hearing them laugh.

"All right. Fine."

They're silent as I retell the whole damn thing, leaving out the more private details. But fuck if it doesn't feel good to talk about this. I go all the way back to when we were kids, as Van keeps saying, "Aww, so romantic."

Grey knowingly laughs every time I tell them something that made me jealous or crazed because I'm sure that bastard identifies. Cars pass, and buildings become trees as we drive out past the Hamptons to the ferry that leads over to St. Simeon Island.

I take a breath, finishing the entire journey, sitting silently as Donovan says, "Wow. You've loved her for so long, Liam."

"I have," I answer, looking out the window as the car pulls onto the ferry.

"See," Grey offers. "I told you I was the only one that loved you."

Van giggles, and I laugh. I know he's joking, but in a way, he's right. In the absence of Caroline, I looked for anything to fill that void, but nothing ever fit. Not even Donovan.

"Don't listen to that dick. I love you, Van. But what I feel for her—"

Grey's voice cuts me off. "Are you crying? Cherry…"

Wait a minute. What?

"Why are you crying, Van?" I say, trying to be gentle.

She sniffles. "Be quiet, both of you. It's romantic and perfect. And I love it."

A smile breaks out on my face. *Thank fuck.*

Grey laughs, saying something like, "Great, now you two are *The Notebook*, and I'll have to buy a house to renovate," before I hear a smack in the background. Van's always a feisty one. I take a deep breath, saying my words on my exhale.

"All right. I'm getting off the phone now. Don't call me anymore. I'll be busy trying to get my Carebear to not eat me alive."

"Good luck, Brookie." Donovan's voice beams through the phone, accompanied by Grey's sarcasm. "Yeah, good luck. You're gonna need it. Dick."

"Real nice. Bye, asshole…and Van."

Chapter Thirty-Two

Caroline

The sun feels warm through the window even though it's freezing outside. I love this island. The Hamptons is a city-dwellers destination, but St. Simeon is different. It's not touristy or overindulgent; it's all gorgeously landscaped beach homes, set on the water, banked in wealth and privilege, without some bullshit celebrity throwing an all-white party making the place low rent.

My phone rings, Kai's face showing up on the screen.

"Hey. I thought you were on a plane to LA?"

Chatter in the background grows quieter, leaving me to assume he's walked away from the crowd that is his mother's entourage.

"My mother left her Critics Choice dress at home—we're waiting for the courier. How's the house? Everything you remembered?"

Faint laughter in Kai's background makes me smile. It sounds like his mom—a woman just as beautiful as she is badass. I want to feel more like that today.

I drag my hand over the all-white kitchen island, nestling onto a stool as he speaks. Turning my head, the white froth from the waves comes into view through the french-paned doors.

"Yes, actually. More, even. I think this is exactly what I need."

"I don't like you all alone. Are you sure about staying the week because you could be bicoastal? I'll let you ride on my jet."

I grin at his dirty joke, trying to muster the energy for this banter, but all I come up with is, "I'll leave the bi life to you. And yes, I am completely sure. Plus—who's lonely? I'm my own best company."

Kai chuckles. "Little witch. Hey, have you heard from Liam? Grey said he never texted back last night. Same for me. I can't believe he didn't show. Donovan was mad, I think."

My shoulders tense. I didn't tell anyone Liam was supposed to be my date. The whole night, I sat waiting, dying inside but smiling and rolling my eyes as if him ghosting was so annoying instead of devastating. Only Donovan seemed to eye me suspiciously. I'm growing awfully tired of her being so good at reading me—and me secretly feeling comforted by it.

I'm shaking my head, mindlessly rubbing my finger over an imperfection in the marble as I answer.

"No. I haven't spoken to him. I'm sure Liam found someone warm to fall into for the night. Not my concern, remember? Anyway, have fun, and tell your mother I said congratulations once she wins."

"And if she doesn't?"

I can picture the devious smirk on Kai's face. Such a shit.

"Then tell her I said the other actresses clearly fucked their way to the top and that we'll find out who for next year."

He laughs loudly, making me grin and spin on the stool to stand.

"Call me when you land?"

"Of course, gorgeous," he levels with that deep voice of his.

I wish I could lose myself in it, but all I feel is empty. Depleted of fucks and tears. A knock at the door grabs my attention.

"Hey, my breakfast is here. Safe flight."

I hear him smack a kiss as I hang up. Sweeping my hair over my shoulder, I only make it three steps before the door swings open, and a set of goddamn hazel eyes stare back at me.

Oh my God.

"Sorry I'm late, Carebear."

Liam's holding flowers, peonies, actually. My favorite. He leans sideways, setting his bag on the ground, before holding out the flowers toward me.

I glare at the dusty-rose-hued blooms and then back to Liam's face as he grins that puppy dog sweetness.

"They're peonies. Your favorite, Carebear."

My entire body short-circuits as every bit of anger I felt explodes to the top.

"No, they aren't—they're called audacities."

Before I even register what I'm doing, a vase flies at his head, forcing him to duck as it hits the wall, shattering into a million pieces.

"Fuck, Carebear. What the hell?"

I growl, swinging my head around, grabbing a piece of driftwood that's used as a paperweight off a console table, and chucking it as hard as I can at him.

"Jesus," he yells, dropping down trying to cover his head, "that's my head."

"Then off with it."

My hand lands on a tall candle amassed in a bundle, and I wind back to toss it at him, but Liam's rushing me. His arms wrap around my waist like he's going to tackle me. But instead of hitting the ground, I'm lifted into the air and right over his shoulder.

"I hate you," I grind out, smacking him as I drop the candles as I squirm, but he doesn't seem fazed at all. "Put me down. Right now. I can't believe I ever tolerated you."

He's holding me firmly in place with an arm around my legs as I keep yelling, but his deep bellow shuts my mouth.

"Carebear. Shut up."

My eyes grow wide as my lips press together. *He yelled at me. He fucking yelled at me.* Is he kidding? I crawl my hands up his back so that I'm almost upright, making him have to let me slide down a bit so that we're almost face-to-face as I snarl.

"Do. Not. Take. That. Tone. With. Me."

The lopsided grin on his face makes me want to bite him. That is until he licks his lips and leans in close to my face.

"Then be quiet, Caroline."

I arch a brow, but he shakes his head. "I didn't stand you up, you little viper. God, I was in my own personal jail. You have no idea how low I was feeling."

One blink, two blinks, then a swallow. Is he fucking serious? Does he expect me to feel bad for him?

"Who cares, so was I. And frankly, I have no interest in some bullshit brooding from you. Find a new metaphor." I put on a baby voice. "I was in a jail of my feelings. Gross." He shakes his head, but I'm not done. "I'm sure you can think of a better metaphor for this fucked-up nonrelationship while you're heading back into the city. Put me down and fuck off."

Liam's chest vibrates as he leans in, running his nose up my jaw, inhaling.

"You smell good."

I pull my head back as far as I can, shaking it to rid myself of his breath on my skin and his goddamn charm.

"Eww, off."

He growls before pressing a kiss to my collarbone, making me hate my body because his lips—fuck. *It's fine.* I can love his body and hate everything else about him.

"Carebear." He says it like a request, but I don't look at him as he adds, "Look at me."

When I don't, he lets out a frustrated breath. "You weigh like three fucking pounds. I can stand here all day if I have to. Put your fucking eyes on me. Now."

Begrudgingly, I do, ensuring that my goddamn look could kill. *Die.* Liam rolls his eyes at me.

"I said it in the literal sense. I was in jail. The real kind."

What the fuck? My mind races, going through a thousand scenarios where Liam is lying to me, but one look at his smug face tells me different.

But it still doesn't douse the flame raging inside of me.

"Why wasn't I the phone call?"

"I left my phone in the car," he counters back just as quickly as I asked. *Convenient.*

"What the hell were you doing to get arrested?"

"Graffiti."

Who. What. When. Where and fucking why. This is a lie.

My mouth opens, then closes because I'm arrested by a thought as I stare at him. Why am I actively trying to wallow in disbelief? As I think it, I already know. How am I supposed to trust him? To honestly believe that this twist of dumbass fate is the cause of my heartbreak, rather than the big bright shining truth.

If he'd told me he loved me, I could believe him because I would know where we stood.

Last night wouldn't hurt so much because that would be our truth. Not that we missed another opportunity because maybe we're actually wrong for one another—life keeps proving it. We just don't listen.

"I don't care. You weren't there, Liam. This is just another example of fate telling us to run."

His eyes darken with the irritation present on his features.

"Bullshit. This is the reason why I missed our date. Nothing more."

My eyes narrow, squirming in his arms to be let down.

"You said we'd do midnight over, and even our do-over failed. We failed, Liam. Put me down and go."

Turning toward the door, he carries me a few steps, stopping to look at the ceiling. I can feel his frustration vibrating off him, but I don't care.

I'm right. And he's leaving.

Liam's eyes drop back to mine as he chews the inside of his cheek before letting it go with a pop. "Fuck that, Carebear. You either give in or cool off."

My head draws back as the grip on his shoulders tightens.

"What does that mean?"

He leans in close to my face, dead fucking serious.

"It means I'm here for the week. Kiss me, and then we can get on with it… Or I'm tossing your gorgeous little ass in the pool to cool off. It's effective. I know."

Fuck you. I grit my teeth together so hard they may break, staring at his stupid damn smirk as sarcasm rolls off my tongue.

"It's heated."

***

Liam

I give Caroline a pop, chucking her sarcastic little ass back over my shoulder, and turn to head outside. Her hands are pushing against my back as she yells profanities, but I've tuned her out. This is what she gets. I showed up with her favorite flowers and a reasonable fucking explanation, and still, Caroline's trying like hell to deny the both of us this moment.

I'm done. I want my girl, she wants me—this bullshit is over.

The chill from outside is on us for only a moment until I open the atrium door that houses the pool.

"Liam Brooks. I swear to God. Don't you fucking da—"

The rest of her sentence is a scream because I launch her slight frame into the water. She better hope it's fucking heated. The splash makes me chuckle as I cross my arms, standing at the side of the pool as a wet Caroline pops up, spitting water, but it might as well be fire. Oh shit. She's growling a scream—I love it when she does that—as she swims back toward the edge with daggers in her eyes.

Here we go. I squat down, locking eyes with her.

"You ready to talk now? Or do we need to try the ocean next?"

Her hand grips my sweatshirt, tugging hard, jerking me right into the pool. *Dammit.*

As I come up, she's halfway out, flipping me the bird, stomping back toward the house. The smile on my face might be permanent because I swear as fucked-up as it sounds in my head, I know my thought is correct.

I would rather fight with Caroline any day of the damn week than be with anyone else.

"Nice try, but I'm not going anywhere, Carebear."

She spins on her heel, walking back to where I've swum to. I prop my chin on my arms that are folded over the edge of the pool.

"You are such a dick."

I reach for her ankle, but she kicks at me.

"How are you trying to stay mad? It wasn't even my fault. I'm sorry. Stop being salty. Let's kiss and make up. You can choose where I kiss first."

Her hands smush my face, pushing me back in the warm water.

"I hope you drown."

Caroline stalks away again as I pull myself out, weighted down by my soaked clothes. I toe off my sneakers and socks as I call out to her.

"Carebear. Can we talk? Please? Stop being such a—"

Her hair slices the air as she spins around, towel around her, glaring at me.

"Say it. I fucking dare you."

My face softens as I reach to where she's standing and grab a towel from the bin.

"A brat. I was going to say *brat*. Stop treating me like the enemy. Why are you so fucking mad—it wasn't like I ghosted you on purpose. I was sitting on a concrete slab next to a guy that smelled like piss. Not exactly the night of my dreams either."

Caroline tucks the towel to hold around her wet clothes as she walks out of the atrium, me following, and back inside the house. She throws her arms in the air, groaning.

"God, this is so like you. I sit in a room full of people feeling completely devastated, and you waltz in here with a twinkly smile and some flowers, and I'm supposed to what? Lie down, spread my legs? Say thank you?"

I drag my wet sweatshirt overhead, tossing it on an Adirondack, standing just outside the house, uncaring about the cold.

"Yes—without the thank-you. You should forgive me because I never meant to leave you last night. I missed you too. And I know you're pissed, but—"

"But nothing," she yells, facing me in the doorway. "This is exactly why we don't work. You can't be serious."

"So now us not being together is because I can't be serious. Is that why? I'm losing track, Caroline. Or is this just a convenient excuse because you're scared."

"Fuck you." She scowls.

Goddammit. I didn't think she'd be this damn pissed. This is not going the way I thought it would.

I reach for the buttons on my jeans, tugging them open and dropping the wet mess to the floor, leaving me in my underwear as I dry off a bit more. I rub the towel over my boxer briefs before wrapping the towel around my waist.

Her eyes run over my chest as she grits out, "Why are you getting naked? I'm not fucking you."

"Because I don't want to track water inside. I'm polite. Stop fucking around. We aren't playing this game anymore. Tell me why you are *so* fucking angry."

Her chest rises and falls, and I don't miss that her fingers run over the scar on her hand. She's a shitty poker player because that's always her tell when she's scared to say something that makes her feel vulnerable. *Come on, Carebear, meet me here, baby. I'm not leaving until you do.*

A delicate force of air releases between her pursed lips before she says in a voice so quiet, I'd miss it if I breathed.

"I was devastated last night, Liam."

Suddenly the world becomes smaller, locking me to her as I step closer, shutting the door behind me. Because the way she just said what she said was honest, not melodramatic like before, and it fucking guts me. But if I'm honest, I don't really understand why she was devastated instead of worried about me. I had one missed text from her. That's it.

"Why?"

Her head lifts, confusion marring her features as she looks at me with those violet-blue eyes that hit me straight in the heart.

"How does that go over your head, Liam? You left me waiting for you. Again. I trusted you. But there I stood, like a goddamn fool, and you were in jail? So you say. But you could've been anywhere because I don't have anything to hold on to that makes me believe you. I'm still a fool."

"What are you talking about? Make sense."

I reach for her, but she steps back, water pooling around her, making a puddle on the wood floor.

"Carebear. You know how I feel about you. Why would you just toss that away to believe the worst? Come on, you know how I feel."

"Do I?"

I blink back at her, silenced as her arms wrap around her middle. She looks fragile enough to break. But I'll never do that again—break her. I swore it, so I answer gently.

"Don't you?"

She swallows, gathering all her courage.

"You've never said the words."

There it is. I almost laugh because here I thought all these years that the girl who sees through me also saw through me when it came to her. But it seems even love needs a voice.

I drop my head, slowly closing the distance as I say, "I've never been great with those—words."

She stands stock-still as I reach for her face, brushing the back of my fingers over her smooth cheek as she locks eyes with me.

"Be great for me, Liam."

I'll give you everything you want, Carebear. Trust me.

"I will. But you're so goddamn blind. I've been fucking showing you since as far as I can remember. I've drawn like seven hundred damn pictures of just your mouth—it's what got me fucking arrested."

"You drew me?" She whispers it almost to herself.

I can't help but chuckle. "I draw you. I've probably drawn another eight hundred of that beauty mark on the inside of your knee. I told you— you're all I see."

My other hand cradles her face. "I forgive you for everything, even when you're wrong. I never let anyone overstep, including punishing myself when I did. I don't do that for anyone else."

She's staring back at me, blinking faster but finally listening.

"I always make sure that the cafeteria has at least one of those cookies you like since sometimes that's all you eat. I pay attention to that too—to make sure you have a better day when you haven't taken enough bites at lunch. I watch when your eyes are sad and make jokes to cheer you up even when you snap at me to stop. I know when you're scared because you rub your scar—"

She looks down at her hand and back to me as I keep going. "—and I protect you. Always. From everyone, including yourself. I'm here, Carebear. I'll always be here. And like I said, baby. I'm sorry I'm late."

Her eyes are brimmed with tears as I lean down and wrap my arms around her waist, lifting her so that we're face-to-face.

"But the thing I do most is give you everything you want. So make sure you're fucking listening. I love you, Caroline Whitmore. Always have. Always will."

Her arms wrap around my neck as a smile peeks out. "You brought me flowers."

I nod, rubbing my nose against hers.

"I thought I'd set the expectation early."

Chapter
Thirty-Three

Liam

Caroline wraps her wet legs around my waist as my arm moves to hold her ass while walking back toward the bedrooms.

She skims those delicious lips over mine as she whispers, "I want you to fuck me, Liam. No stopping this time."

There's no fucking way I'm stopping. This moment is happening. Right now.

I run my tongue over her neck, sucking and nipping the skin. "Then don't say no, Carebear."

She smiles against my mouth as I speak the words onto her lips. "I'm going to do every filthy goddamn thing I've fantasized about since my dick was old enough to notice you."

Her nails come over the top of my head, scraping my scalp lightly.

"I'm holding you to that."

I set her to her feet, smacking my palm on the bedroom door to open it. Strained hinges from the antique door creak as I motion with my head for her to enter. With her bottom lip between her teeth, she takes backward steps into the room, eyes locked to mine.

"Out with it. What does Liam Brooks fantasize about?"

My tongue swipes over my lip as I run a hand over my head, leaned against the doorjamb. Her bright eyes stare at me, enjoying the way I'm letting my own drag over her body.

A hint of a blush blooms on her face as I lazily point a finger up and down her body.

"Take your clothes off, Carebear."

She bites the tip of her tongue before she speaks. "You're not going to undress me yourself?"

My head shakes slowly. But damn, the way she said that, it was like a tease. The fabric's still clinging to her, in parts, creating windows to her skin as she gathers the material, dragging it up over her head.

The shirt smacks to the ground, her hair left to stick to her chest as she stands there fixed on my gaze.

"Be a better listener, Carebear. I said *clothes*."

I drop my eyes to her pants, crossing my arms over my chest.

She undoes the button, lowering the zipper as she bites her lip. Her hands fit just inside the sides of her pants, wiggling them past her hips before stepping out.

Caroline stands in the middle of the room in her sheer bra, no underwear, and wet hair—I couldn't have invented a better fantasy.

A deep hum of appreciation rattles my chest as I push off the doorframe, her breath hitching as I begin walking toward her.

"No underwear. I like it."

I hover over her, bringing a finger to the strap of her baby blue sheer bra and sliding it off her shoulder. Her head turns to watch as it dangles before fixing her eyes to mine.

"So are you going to tell me? What did you fantasize about me?"

I'm lost to her form, her lips, her fucking voice. I bend, running my tongue over her shoulder before sucking on her skin, letting go with a pop. Caroline jumps, gasping quietly. Shifting my mouth to her neck, I bury my lips against her skin, kissing, licking, and sucking every fucking inch. I want me all over her, marks for the world to see.

Her hands reach for my towel, but I nab her wrists, pulling them away and lifting my head to look down at her.

"Unh-uh."

With her hands placed back to her sides, I go about removing the other strap, slower this time, watching goose bumps bloom as I let it hang. She's flawless alabaster, wrapped in dirty thoughts.

My first two fingers run over her collarbone as I speak. "When I was younger, I dreamed about holding your hand." I let my fingers dip down the center of her chest, through her cleavage, then down her stomach, smiling as she shivers, before weaving my fingers through hers. I bring her hand up to my lips, pressing a kiss to the top.

"Then, when I got older, I thought a lot about kissing you."

She's on her tiptoes as I bend, drawing her bottom lip between mine, switching to her top lip before pushing my tongue inside her mouth. Our tongues marry, swirling, dipping in and out as our heads move slowly, savoring the taste of one another. I reach up with the hand not holding hers, brushing between her breasts to caress her neck, letting my thumb stay just under her chin.

The moan elicited from my touch vibrates her throat against my palm, making me smile before I pull away from our kiss.

She blinks slowly, getting her bearings as I whisper onto her lips.

"But now, all I think about is ruining you. I want you fucking spun on me the way I am on you. I don't want you to be able to think about anyone or anything else. I want to fuck you and eat you whenever I choose—like I'm entitled to your goddamn body. Tell me I can have you like that. Tell me I can have you for forever, Carebear."

Caroline's eyes close as she heaves a stuttered breath against my lips. Her hands grip my face, pulling our foreheads together.

"Be obsessed with me, Liam. Because I am with you. I don't care how unhealthy that is—if I have to die someday, I hope it's from loving you too much. I love you, Liam. I fucking love you so much."

I'm an animal, ripping at her bra as she stumbles backward. The towel around my waist drops as I spin her around, giving her a rough shove so that she falls onto the bed, bent over, me behind her.

My cock grinds against her ass, hand splayed over her spine, holding her firmly in place.

"Tell me who I belong to, Caroline."

Mewls become moans as she breathes, "Me. You belong to me."

I gather a handful of hair, pulling it, forcing her chin to lift as I push against her ass again.

"Now tell me who you fucking belong to."

"You, Liam. It's always been you."

Her words are delivered within a breathless voice. She slaps at me from behind, squirming to flip over, spreading her legs, and jerking my dick against her center. Intense eyes on me make the grip I have on her thighs tighten as she makes slow undulations, rubbing herself against me.

Goddamn. My hands leave Caroline's legs, dropping forward to flank the sides of her head, depressing the mattress. One side of my lips tips up as I rub my hard cock up and down her clit. We're so fucking connected at this moment, staring into each other's eyes, feeling each drag and pull, feeling the goddamn friction that feels like we might explode.

I exhale, walking my hands back so that I'm standing. I can't wait anymore. If I don't sink into this girl, I may die. Her tongue lays a glisten over her top lip as she drinks me in from her back, propped up on her elbows.

Fuck, she's sexy—unabashedly ogling me, comfortable with her sexual appetite. One of a kind and all mine.

"Take me out, baby."

The room is devoid of sound. All I can hear is our hearts beating and the sound of Caroline scooting to the edge of the bed, tugging my briefs down enough to release my dick.

She wraps her hand around my cock as much as she can, tugging upward, evoking a hiss from between my teeth.

Violet-hued eyes tip up to mine. "You want to know what I fantasized about?"

A bead of precum rises to the tip, and as my eyes drop to look at her, she sweeps her tongue over the head, licking me clean.

"More."

Her eyes stay on me as her mouth opens, blanketing my dick in warmth as she lowers her head over me, sucking.

"Jesus, your fucking mouth should be weaponized."

I swear to God, it almost feels like I'm going to lose consciousness. My palm on the back of her head battles with my mind because I want to fuck her mouth, hard and fast. I want to see her gag on my dick and swallow me down, but I'm trying to restrain myself from being an animal.

Her nails dig into the sides of my ass, urging me toward her face as she sucks faster and harder, bobbing her head. My breath comes out in short huffs as I brush Caroline's hair away so that I can watch her hum around my cock with sweet sounds like she can't get enough.

"Caroline," I groan. "I don't want to control myself."

I inhale harshly as she takes me deeper, looking down at my every fantasy come to life. Tears spill from the sides of her eyes as she goes lower on my shaft, hollowing her cheeks with each pass. Fuck, she's beautiful. Her face shoots to mine as my dick leaves her mouth with a pop.

"Who said I fucking wanted you to?"

The smile on her lips blooms, only for a second, before she goes back to sucking me fiercely. *Yes, baby.* My palm on the back of her head squeezes a fistful of hair as I begin tugging her head down faster, dominating the motion. Her hands brace against my hips to give her support as I start my assault on her throat.

"Relax your throat, Carebear. And tap my leg if it's too much."

Partnered with a tug of her head, rough movements guide my hips, fucking her goddamn perfect mouth. Jesus, it's everything I'd hoped it'd be, but the filthiest part of me still wishes I could feel her throat. My head drops back, the ceiling coming into view as Caroline's tears mix with her spit, gagging on my length.

"That's it. I'm almost there."

Dropping my face back to hers, I blow out a heavy breath, coupled with a deep, husky groan.

Fuck, she feels good, mouth suctioned onto my dick as I slide in and out, pulling her face almost to the hilt.

"Come on, baby, take it all."

Her nails double up on the crescent marks along my hips as she tears at my skin, wanting everything I'm giving her.

My stomach begins to tighten, and my eyes blink slowly, feeling the sensation building inside me. Caroline's thighs spread, commanding my eyes to her hand that's now between her legs, rubbing that swollen, hungry clit.

Fuck me. Sucking me off is getting her off.

That's all it takes. I shatter, balls drawing up as I hold Caroline in place, releasing cum into her heaven-sent mouth.

"Fuck" is drawn out long and gutturally as my body spasms.

I'm panting, my hand still strangling her hair, with my dick in her mouth. I close my eyes, feeling her lips dredge over my length as I let her go, feeling the soreness in my hand from how hard I was pulling her hair. Her tongue circles the head of my cock, making my body jerk before she swallows.

Caroline pulls my still-damp briefs back, taking care to tuck me back inside before she stares up at me. All the rest of my breath is stolen from my lungs. The way she's looking at me, like she loves me, wants to please me—it's precisely the way I'm looking at her.

This moment was her gift to me. A way to show me how much she loved me. It's not just sex, not for her. I'm fucking leveled. There are first loves, great loves, and then there's Caroline—she's both.

I grip the back of her neck and muscle her to stand, kissing her like she needs my breath to live. My mouth rips from hers, and I hook my hands under her armpits, tossing her back on the bed.

"Let's do you, now."

Her squeal echoes through the room as I pounce, covering her body with mine. But we slow, amidst our laughing, staring at each other before I bring my lips to hers.

I kiss her chastely, moving to her cheeks, then her forehead, nose, chin, and eyes. She's beaming, smile so wide she'd be unrecognizable to anyone that knew her, except me. This is my Caroline.

"I love you."

She closes her eyes like she's trying to capture the moment in memory. When she opens them, I repeat it.

"I love you."

"I love you too," she whispers, "with my whole black heart."

I'm pulled to her lips as my leg dips between hers. I can feel how wet she is as she rubs herself up and down, squirming under me. Oh fuck. Caroline smeared over my thigh is the sexiest goddamn thing I've ever experienced. I'd reapply her every day if she'd let me.

Her arms wrap around my back as she creates more friction, moving faster against my leg.

"Feel good, baby?" She can't speak, only giving little whimpers as I talk. "Like this or with my mouth, Carebear? Tell me what you want."

Teeth press to her lip, and I know she's getting close to coming. Caroline's fucking herself, using my body, and all I can think is—sex and candy. She's going to explode her sweetness all over me. But I'm not done with her. Not by a long shot.

"Come, baby. Let me hear you."

She sucks in a breath, saying, "Liam. Oh my God."

"Make sure you come hard because I'm going to lick you clean."

Her whole body is sliding up and down my leg as she tenses, teeth finding their way to my chest as she lets out a scream, biting down.

My dick jumps, trying to get hard again because every instinct I have is demanding I sink inside of her balls-deep until I make her scream like that again. But I can't. Not yet, so I do one better.

I shove down, bringing the thick of my tongue to her fucking clit, lapping her wetness and earning a gasp as her body sits up and folds over me only to fall back down.

"Oh my God. Liam."

Not stopping. I run my tongue between her folds, lapping up every bit of pleasure until her body begins to quake again. She's her own unique flavor, sweet and decadent—and unmistakably addicting. I won't stop until I've had my fill.

"Liam, I can't. Holy shit."

Flicks of my tongue against her clit have her thrashing on the bed, trying to crawl away, but I hook my arms around her creamy thighs, keeping my mouth locked on her pussy. Her body begins to relax into my mouth, seeking out the pleasure instead of bucking it.

Caroline's hand latches onto my head as I eat her, bringing her back to that delicious place where she's willing to fucking beg.

"Yes. More. It feels so good. Lick me, Brooks."

I hum, vibrating the sensitive flesh, and she shivers.

"Make me come, again. I want to. Please."

Like fucking music to my ears because I'm a monster, and hearing Caroline beg is like hearing fucking church bells in the morning. It's a spiritual fucking experience.

I lick slower, deviously waiting to hear her plead again. She presses my face into her pussy, growling.

"Liam."

My eyes lift to hers, seeing her mouth agape as she looks down her body at me.

"Beg me," I whisper, spreading her pussy wide with my fingers and placing a peck on her clit.

That Mona Lisa smile graces me as she shivers, licking her lips.

"Eat me. Please."

I blow on her clit, moving my head around to hit in different spots, as her head falls back to the bed.

"Make me come, Liam. Please," she begs haughtily.

My tongue sweeps up her pussy, teasingly making her body shudder and her knees open wider.

"Please," she pants. "Fucking please."

I flick my tongue in slow, languid motions as she snarls at me.

"Eat my pussy, or I'll fucking kill you, Liam."

My teeth clamp over her clit, and she yelps, slapping my shoulder as her back arches from the bed. Her face shoots to mine as she breathes heavily.

"Do it again."

I circle my tongue, soothing the sensitive piece of magic before doing it again and watching her eyes roll back into her head.

"You're a beautiful monster, Brooks. Oh fuck. Make it hurt just enough."

That's my girl.

My palms slap against her inner thighs, forcing them utterly and divinely open as I attack her fucking pussy, eating it like it's my calling in life. I devour her, egged on by Caroline's moans and pleas as she arrives in front of the gates of satisfaction—screaming my fucking name.

The only name that'll ever leave her lips for the rest of her goddamn life.

Chapter
Thirty-Four

Caroline

I stretch my arms above my head, faintly hearing a voice growing louder in my ear. My eyes blink open as two realities smack me in the face.

The first is that Liam's a foot away from me, sitting on the bed smiling, and the second is the smell of the coffee from the mug he's holding.

I yawn out my words. "How long did we sleep?"

"Not long. A few hours, but we have plans. So get up."

He presses the warm coffee mug into my hands before pushing off the bed to stand. It's then that I notice he's fully dressed, donning another signature hoodie and gray sweatpants, along with that yummy beanie he had on that night in the club.

"Why are you dressed?" My head shifts to the window, realizing it's pitch-black outside. "And why am I drinking coffee when it's dark outside?"

He winks, raising a toothpick to his lips. "Because I need you to wake up quickly. Like I said, Carebear, we have plans. Throw something warm on, and let's go."

We fucked our morning and afternoon away, becoming insanely acquainted with each other's bodies before we ordered food and ate. Liam also caught me up on all the details about his jail sentence, the last month, and even Arden. Then we fucked again.

So why he's waking me up in the middle of the night is a mystery—sleep, that's what we should be doing.

"Again, I ask. Why?" I push to sitting up, taking a sip of my drink.

He scowls at me, but not really. It's more of a pout on a beautiful face atop a sexy as hell body. Fuck—this combo might be my kryptonite.

"Because I said. Now get up."

I stare back at him, holding my coffee with both hands as I take another sip, contemplating whether or not to challenge him even more. It's like he knows because he smirks as he walks back toward me, removing the toothpick before crawling onto the bed. Liam dips his head under my arms, forcing them to break apart as his lips land on mine.

"Be a good listener, Carebear, and you'll be rewarded." He winks before pushing back off the bed, leaving me flushed.

Oooh, those eyes and that smile.

"'Kay," I answer, trying not to smile.

Liam wags his brows, disappearing back out of the doorway, bellowing, "Ten minutes" from down the hallway, kicking me into high gear.

I set my coffee down after taking another big swig and throw on the sweats he's pulled out of my bag. I don't think he's really ever seen me this dressed down—the no-makeup, sweatpants version I usually only allow when I'm alone. Like I thought I'd be for this week, which I'm glad he ruined, but still, I'm kind of...shy—dear God, he's ruined me. How is this what I care about?

He's been inside of me. Seeing me without a full face of makeup shouldn't feel more intimate. And whatever, this is what he gets for waking me in the middle of the night. Weirdo.

What are we even doing?

I rush, putting my clothes on, laughing to myself over my dumb thoughts, and head quickly into the bathroom to wash yesterday's makeup off my face. Once I'm done, I throw my hair on top of my head and trot out to the living room. Liam's standing at the counter, stuffing something inside of a bag. So I clear my throat to garner his attention.

"All right, this better be worth the loss of my beauty sleep."

He chuckles, not looking at me. "You're already ready? I thought I was going to have to yell again."

"Well, apparently, I didn't have to dress for an occasion. So—"

I raise my brows as he looks up at me, but he doesn't say anything, just stands there staring at me. The longer he looks at me, the more self-conscious I start to become until he shakes his head like he's coming out of a daze.

"Sorry. It's just... You're so fucking pretty. Sometimes it takes me a minute to come back from that reality."

I roll my eyes, pulling on the strings of my black hoodie, fighting the urge to say, *"Shut up. You're dumb,"* because when he says things like that, I instantly want to die. I'm pretty sure nothing will ever feel better than Liam loving me back.

"Ha. Ha. Nice line. Charmer."

Liam closes the distance, prying my fingers off the strings, and lifts my chin to look at him. "I'm not trying to charm you, Carebear. When I look at you, sometimes it feels like I can see my whole future, and that takes a minute to snap out of."

My brain stops working. Liam's robbed me of the response I had readied—my wit, bested by his sincerity.

He takes my hand, leading us toward the back patio. "Come on, I have a surprise."

I let my feet drag, making him tug me because I can never just go easy. It would ruin my rep.

"If you throw me in the pool again, it won't end with you getting laid this time."

He's laughing, letting me pass through the door before he puts his hands on my waist, directing me from behind me as we walk from the deck to the sand. A flicker of orange catches my attention, so I crane my neck as we take the sandy path, passing through tall grasses on either side of us until the flickers of orange and red I saw reveal themselves as a bonfire.

I look back over my shoulder. "What did you do?"

He spins me around, bending closer to my face.

"I made us a New Year's Eve party. I thought we could redo our redo." His arms wrap around me, kissing my lips.

I pull away, truly surprised. "Wait, what time is it?"

It's funny. I didn't even check when Liam woke me up. I was too busy thinking about him to even check my phone.

Liam chuckles. "We have about ten minutes, and this time, we're together, and I love you, and"—he leans in conspiratorially—"I have sparklers."

My hand shoots over my mouth, squeaking out between my fingers, "Sparklers."

He nods. Only him, only Liam, would remember that night at the lake house.

"Come on," he offers, taking my hand, so I follow him to the warmth of the fire and the blankets he's set out.

It's perfect. Liam takes out his phone, setting the alarm so we don't miss our countdown, and scrolls through his playlist before settling on a song.

"When did you do all of this?" I say, lifting my voice enough over the sound of the tide for him to hear.

"While you snored in your coma."

Liam reaches inside the bag he brought down, pulling out my favorite champagne. My shoulders jump as he twists the cork, hearing a loud pop. He laughs again, and my body warms, even though it's cold outside, maybe because I'm already hot watching him from over the fire.

My mouth pops open, mainly because I'm ogling him, but I play it off, countering, "Take it back. I don't snore."

He shakes his head, pouring two red cups, extending one to me. "You absolutely snore—like a fat old man. It's fucking adorable."

My head shifts to the darkness of the ocean as I take a sip, giggling as the bubbles tickle my lips before I turn back to him.

"This is kind of amazing. You're kind of amazing."

He takes a much bigger gulp of champagne than he should, licking his lips after narrowing his eyes at me.

"Kind of? How can I make that a statement of certainty?"

I give him a look like *duh* as I say, "Sparkler me, Brooks."

He grins, reaching back into the bag, and pulls them out, saying, "Do you remember that night at the lake house? When we were sixteen, and you drew my name over and over."

Of course I remember. I wanted him to tell me that he liked me too, so badly, that I sat up all night contemplating sneaking into his room. But I'll never admit that, so I roll my eyes.

"You're so full of yourself. I was writing *lame*, not *Liam*."

He lets his eyes drift over my body as he mouths, "Liar." I shrug, pretending to be unfazed, but this game is the most fun one we play. Liam lights a sparkler for me, walking around the fire to give it to me. I dart my hand out, excited for my present, but he draws it back as it crackles and flickers.

"Carebear…" He draws it out like it's a reprimand. "Use your manners. What do you say?"

I stare up at him, my palm coming to his chest. "I love you."

His lips press to my forehead as he hands it to me, adding, "Now be a good girl and go draw my name again."

I give a coy smile, breaking away from him to streak the crackling stick against the sky. Music soundtracks the moment as the silver and gold waves back and forth, leaving black spots in my vision from the glow. The night he talked about is clear in my mind, and I start thinking about younger us as a thought tumbles forward.

"You know what's weird? To think we've spent most of our lives together, and now we're finally figuring it out."

"Better late than never, I guess," he laughs.

My brows draw together as I draw hearts in the sky. "Why do you think it took us so long though? Because what's really changed?" The words keep falling from my lips without thought. "I mean, other than your felony." I laugh to myself before continuing. "We're still basically the same people. What about *now* makes this our time?"

Liam doesn't answer, and the silence calls my attention. I look over my shoulder at his pensive face as he stares back at me.

"What?" I shrug.

He shakes his head. "Are we back there? You doubting us again. Don't make me chuck you into the ocean, Carebear."

"Shut up," I answer, rolling my eyes. "No, Neanderthal, it was just a thought."

One that's putting a knot in my stomach now that I've said it aloud. Because what has changed, other than Liam?

My sparkler fizzles out, so I chuck it into the fire, wishing I could throw my thoughts in too as I shift to face him. I hold out my hand for another, but it's Liam's palm that slips into mine instead.

He hovers over me, our arms minutely swinging between us. The fire crackles with a pop from the wood, making me blink down to look at his hand encasing mine.

"Hey," he calls to my downturned face, forcing my eyes to his. "I'm sorry it took me so long to get my shit together. It was my fault we were apart. But I'm right where I belong. You are everything I want, Carebear."

I'm staring at his face, listening to his honesty, my mind running on repeat with the same thought—*it's not all your fault.*

He tilts his head. "Why does it feel like you don't feel the same?"

Because I haven't gotten anything together. Not like Liam. I'm still a goddamn mess of a person. Mean and occasionally insecure. Desperate for a seat at the Upper East Side table—his table.

This is Liam's world, and even though everything feels perfect when I'm with him, eventually, the real world will seep back in. And then he might wake up one day to realize that me, stripped down, no backbone, no clout, isn't worth the headache. He'll eventually get tired of my survival because he'll want me to live for him.

But I can't do that. It's not that simple.

My reality is a constant game of choice between what I want versus what's expected to stay on top. With what's expected always having a vicious uppercut.

God, just when I thought not having Liam was the worst feeling I could feel—knowing I'll eventually lose him is even worse.

But I don't say any of that, opting for the easy out.

"Of course I feel the same. Kiss me before I change my mind about you for real."

His mouth opens to speak, but the alarm goes off, so I pat his chest and shrug. "Introspection be damned by the bell. You owe me a countdown."

Liam takes my hand, kissing it before leading us back to the chairs. He pours more champagne for me and lifts his cup, so I do the same as the seconds on his phone begin to count down from ten.

"Here's to figuring out what's important, Carebear. And choosing to be right where we belong."

***

Liam

Caroline's dancing around the fire, yelling at the sky, singing a song, drunk. And I can't stop laughing because I'm not on her level—higher tolerance.

"Come here," I yell as she skips my way, plopping right down onto my lap.

Her hair sweeps across my face as she brings her eyes to mine. She looks so carefree and happy that I wish I could memorize this moment. Caroline leans down to kiss my lips, lingering.

"Let's fuck outside."

I laugh against her lips. "And if someone sees?"

She shrugs as she pulls back, bringing the red cup to her lips, chewing on its edge. I love how dirty she is. My hands come to her waist, lifting her to stand as she squeals. I yank her bottoms down, making her scream and her laugh drown out the music.

"It's a full moon out," I tease, reaching my hand around to grab her ass.

My other hand wraps around her hoodie strings, tugging her down to my lips, pushing my tongue inside her champagne-flavored mouth. She tastes divine.

Our mouths are working overtime as she takes tiny steps, attempting to rid herself of the fabric bunched around her ankles. But they're caught around her shoes, so all she's managing to do is kick up sand.

"Help, dick," she whines, so I stand, hooking an arm around her waist, picking her up so that she's folded over, ass up.

I muscle her up and bite her ass, hearing, "Liam!" screeched between her giggles as I rip the damn sweats off and set her to her feet.

When I look down, she's a fucking mess. Hair mussed, no makeup, nude from the waist down—perfect.

I don't want to forget this. That's all my drunk-on-Caroline head can process, that is until I remember something I've always wanted to do. I hover over her, forcing that elegant neck to stretch up to my face.

"I want to draw you."

My voice is deep, husky, and full of every fucking intention I have. And Caroline feels it.

Her eyes blink rapidly, a shiver spurring her words as she shoves her hands inside the front pocket of my hoodie.

"What happened to fucking me?"

"Who said I wasn't."

God, she's so cute, standing ass out in the middle of the beach. I pick her up like a football, smacking her ass as I carry her back to the house, drunk laughter floating over the tall grass. The minute we're back in the room, I toss her on the bed, opening the curtains so the moonlight filters into the room. Leaning down to my bag, I pull out my notepad and pencils.

As I turn around, the sight of Caroline laid out, toeing off her sneakers, with her arms above her head, makes my dick grow.

"Freeze."

Caroline's face presses against her arm. "What? Do you want me in a different pose?"

"No. Just like that. Don't move."

I walk to a desk in the room, grabbing the chair and slapping it down directly in front of her—all of two feet away. Shadow and light dance over her body, creating a streak of light that reaches all the way up to those deadly eyes.

Goddamn. I sit, propping one foot up against the bedframe, and open the pad of paper, hearing only her breath and the waves crashing onto the shore. The scratch of my pencil against the paper feels more like a gunshot that starts a race, because my adrenaline shoots through the roof as I tilt my head, dragging my eyes down her body.

"You look divine. But I want to see more of you."

She laughs, "So then top off?"

I nod as she drags the hoodie over her body, revealing her teardrop breasts. Caroline winks at me just before tossing it my way, making me smirk. Her arms go back above her head, creating the most delicious curve to her body.

"Like this?" she breathes out, waiting for my answer.

My pencil swipes over the paper faster in short strokes, the answer readied as my eyes drop to the paper.

"No." I lock eyes with her. "Open your legs for me, Caroline."

Her breath hitches as she stares back, unmoving. "What are you drawing, Liam?"

The way she licks her lips tells me she's hoping for exactly what I'm about to do.

"I said, open your legs. Don't make me ask again."

The coy smile stays on her lips as her milky-white thighs begin to separate, her feet coming to the bed as she scoots into place, baring her beautiful wet pussy to me.

My tongue sweeps across my bottom lip. "I can almost still taste you on my tongue. The memory is that potent."

I motion with my pencil for her to open further. The fabric of the comforter rustles as she does. My eyelids slowly fucking blink as her lips part, revealing the soft, glistening piece of heaven. A shine of her desire is drawn directly between her beautifully manicured folds, highlighting her swollen pink clit.

Swallowing takes a concerted effort because I can barely close my mouth. I feel primal.

"Liam." The way she says my name sounds as if she's hoping it'll touch her in the places she needs me most. "I like the way it feels when you look at me. But I want you to touch me."

I click my tongue against my teeth before saying, "Begging won't help this time. Patience. First, I draw."

My eyes don't leave her as I lean in closer, enjoying the erotic portrait before me: Caroline opened, turned on, and on display. Her back arches, making the muscle around her entrance contract, and I have to clench my jaw because I want to dive forward and thrust my tongue inside of her. Fuck her with my tongue until she's a quaking mess.

Her hips press up ever so slightly as she whimpers, needing me to satiate the craving.

"Don't move," I growl, causing a whoosh of breath to leave her lips.

My eyes lift from her loveliest spot back up to her face, which is full of agony. Caroline's so fucking ready that she may explode.

"Oh, baby, that look on your face. I want to memorize what it looks like when you explode."

She's nodding. *So hungry.*

"What do you want me to do?"

Mindlessly I reach out, slowly dipping my middle finger inside of Caroline, drawing out a long gasp from her. I drag it in and out, faster each time, twisting my finger and relishing the warmth tightening around it.

"I want you to touch yourself, and let me watch."

Caroline's hand runs down the front of her body, breath shaky as I pull my finger from her. She obediently dips into her wetness, rubbing small circles on her needy clit.

"Like this?" she purrs.

I bring the coated finger to my lips, sucking it clean as I watch. "Yeah, baby. Just like that."

Caroline's panting, her eyes on me. "Tell me what I look like, Liam."

My hands are stilled, unable to draw because watching her is more intoxicating than all the champagne we drank.

"You look drenched, soaked in fucking desire. Each time you move your finger around your clit, the entrance of your pussy clenches like it wants my dick inside."

"Oh God. I do," she moans. "Fuck me now. Draw me later."

My cock is so hard that it hurts. There's no fucking way I can draw her now. The notebook in my lap hits the floor as I stand, ripping my hoodie off and tossing it to the floor. Her head lifts, eyes on me, but she doesn't stop her motions as I toe off my shoes and shove my pants down, stepping out and directly between her legs.

Caroline reaches for me as I crawl over her, lining my cock up at her entrance and holding just outside where she's trying to swallow me in.

"You have the most beautiful pussy, Caroline"—I look down at her with a smirk—"but I'm gonna murder it, now."

She laughs, wrapping her legs around me as I thrust inside, groaning.

"Goddamn."

"Mmmm, yes," she hums, kissing my neck as I pull out to the tip before thrusting back inside.

Caroline runs her tongue over my neck as we start a slow, teasing tempo of fucking. I reach back, gripping her thigh and pulling it up to my hip as the muscles on my ass indent with each thrust.

We're locked to each other. With every rock forward, Caroline raises her hips to meet my push. My hips roll, gliding my cock inside of her drenched pussy, still stretching her with every thrust.

"It feels so good, Liam," she pants, hugging me tighter.

I'm buried in her neck, fucking her faster and faster, pounding into her pussy, my hand weaving into her hair to grip it. Her nails scrape my back, trying to pull me closer and feel me deeper as we pick up the pace.

I tighten my fist in her hair, clinging to her as the smell of sex fills the room. Our bodies rub, delicious tension building within the friction of my thrusting. I grip her leg harder, pulling it higher, sinking deeper inside her.

"Fuck. You own me, Liam."

I pull out of her, growling, "Over," as she lets go of me so that I can flip her onto all fours. My hand clenches her shoulder as I thrust back inside her tight pussy, jerking her backward until she's seated against me.

"Yes," she screams.

I pound into her mercilessly, bodies smacking with the contact faster and harder with each thrust.

"Fuck, you feel like heaven."

My fingers dig into her porcelain skin, knowing I'll leave a bruise. But this need is all I know—I want her more, harder, deeper. I want her cum dripping over my cock and my name screamed from her perfect mouth.

Caroline's all moans and whines mixing together in a string of gratitude. *I got you, baby. I'll give you what you need.* She drops her head as I fuck her with unrelenting force. Her elbows buckle, dropping her face to the bed.

But I don't stop. I fuck her needy pussy harder until the words coming out of her mouth don't make sense anymore. My dick pounds into Caroline over and over. Faster and faster. Until all that's left is growls and pleading mewls as she grips the blanket, clenching around me like she's going to strangle my cock.

"I'm coming, Liam," she says between held breaths.

My free hand grips her ass, spreading her perfect cheek as I spit, a guttural moan vibrating from Caroline's body, growing even louder as I bring my pinkie to her ass, pushing inside.

"Fuck," she screams, contracting so hard that I double up over her back, shoving my dick to the hilt as we come together.

Chapter Thirty-Five

Liam

Caroline's still sleeping, wiped from last night. It was as close to perfect as it could get, mainly because I didn't push back about what she'd said. But it's still on my mind. I tried to give her an opening to tell me what she felt—because I already know.

I know Carebear like the back of my hand. For all her lovely bravado, a part of her wishes she was more palatable, easier to digest so that she won't be the one who ruins us. *As if I'd ever fucking let her.* That streak of insecurity is most definitely because of that bitch-ass mother of hers. I'll have to remember to tell my mom about Vivienne—get that cow banned from every committee my mother chairs. Which is every single important one.

Carebear's not the only one who knows how to wield a sword. And fuck anyone that ever makes my baby second-guess her worth again.

My eyes shift to Caroline's serene face, listening to the soft breaths she takes as words leave my lips in a whisper.

"I'll be here right next to you, holding you up, until you can do it for yourself, Carebear."

She doesn't have to be perfect. That's her expectation—not mine. I'm okay with both of us being a goddamn work in progress.

The sooner she realizes we work outside of us, only because we are an us, the better. But until then, I have a feeling I'm going to need to strap in for the ride.

A heavy exhale leaves my body as my phone buzzes on the nightstand. I stretch my arm to nab it, looking at the screen, wincing as I do. *Shit, I forgot to send cleaners.*

"Dad. Hold on."

"Why are you whispering?"

I slip out from under the blanket, trying not to disturb Caroline before standing. Keeping quiet, I tuck the blanket back around her and turn around.

"I don't want to wake Caroline," I answer, padding quietly toward the door.

"Well, while you're on the lam playing house, I thought you'd like to know the charges were dropped."

I chuckle after shutting the door behind me, treading down the hall, barefoot in search of coffee.

"Good to know. The owner of the building must've really liked the artwork to drop all the charges."

He laughs.

"More like the owner's wife threatened his life if he let them stick. And he might like his kid a lot. There's also the part about feeling guilty for dropping the parenting ball."

I stop opening the empty cabinets in search of food to give him my attention.

"We're good, Dad. Really. And I swear I'll get everything cleaned, but I'd like to leave it up until I can show Caroline. Seeing as my plans were ruined that night."

"Done. When you're back, I have a proposition for you. I know you are studying art, and that's fantastic—"

I can't help but laugh as he continues because he really is making a hell of an effort.

"—but I'd love for you to learn about Brooks Industries by way of an internship—so that way when I'm dead and gone, you will be skilled in choosing someone to lead the company. Think about it, Liam."

Study art and honor my family. It's a fucking no-brainer.

"I don't have to think about it, Dad. I'd love that."

"We'll talk soon, son. Your mother says to send Caroline her love."

"Will do."

The line disconnects, and I set my phone down because fuck if life doesn't just keep getting better. Now I just have to convince my little jerk in the bedroom to stop doubting herself so that we can bask in our love and maybe go to the damn store for food. Because I'm fucking hungry.

***

"How about these?" I ask, holding up a box of crackers. "Are these good?"

"Amazing." She smiles, browsing the spreads and dips.

I'd ushered her downtown almost the very moment she woke up. My stomach was growling, I didn't get coffee, and I was fading fast. But I forgot what this place is like. Downtown isn't the word. It's more of a village with posh French bakeries and upscale markets flanked by five-star restaurants than a city with a corner store. But we needed food, and I couldn't survive another day of snacking on leftovers.

So here I am browsing shit my mother serves during cocktail parties. I'll die on this island. Why can't they just have a fucking bodega?

"Who eats this?" I ask, looking at the box of crackers she just approved. My head shifts around, glancing up and down the aisle. "Where do you think they keep the cereal? I don't want these bland-ass crackers, Caroline. I need boy food—milk, Cocoa Puffs, Red Bull, salt-and-vinegar Lay's. The staples."

She laughs, "How would I know? I've never been inside this store—let alone done my own shopping, ever. The Real Housewives of New York I am not."

I grab her hand, letting out a groan, dragging her behind me as I hold the basket with my other hand. We go down the next aisle, her laughing and me getting grumpier by the second until I see the familiar little bird on some packaging.

"Bingo."

I grab three boxes of cereal and then look back, reaching for a fourth.

"Oh my God, Liam. How many boxes are you getting?"

She takes one out of the basket, putting it back, but I grab it, tossing it back to where I put it in the first place.

"Enough to keep me full." My hand darts out, grabbing a handful of the front of her hoodie, dragging her close to me. "I plan to take you home and fuck you for the rest of the day. I'll need my strength."

Caroline looks around as if she's embarrassed someone might hear. Goddamn, she's cute when she's shy. But I don't give a fuck if anyone does hear. Tightening my grip, I force her back against the stacks of cereal, bringing my face close to hers.

"Are you blushing, Carebear? Here I thought you'd like it if people watched."

Caroline sucks in a breath as I let go of her hoodie and dip my hand down, further south, until I skim over her leggings-covered pussy. She pushes against my chest, biting her lip.

"I'll kill you. Quit it."

"Make me," I whisper back, sucking on her neck.

The act draws out a small whimper before she catches me off guard, shoving me hard as she laughs.

"You're a degenerate. I'm not fucking you in a grocery store." She takes two steps away, smoothing her hair, before counting on her fingers, a smile beaming on her face. "One, my ass is too posh to come next to a fucking box of Cocoa Puffs. And two, orange is not the new black—that gets to be your reality, not mine."

I snap my fingers, then point to the floor, beckoning her back to the spot she's walking away from.

"Get fucked," she whispers. "You're crazy."

My head tilts as my eyes narrow. "Carebear. Don't make me chase you."

A laugh bursts from her lips before her hand covers her mouth.

"Liam," she says, hushed, "get a grip. Not happening. Wipe that look off your face."

Her hair swings over her shoulder, with the pickup in her step, humor all over her face as she flips me the bird. I thrust the basket to the ground, making a thwack, watching her jump.

"Don't say I didn't warn you, Carebear."

The look on her face is fucking priceless as she turns and speed walks away. I rub my hands together as I give her a head start because there's nothing better than fucking with Caroline.

Chapter Thirty-Six

Caroline

O h my God, he's the worst. My cheeks are burning as I cut around the corner, leaving Liam behind with all his bad ideas. I'm walking just not fast enough to draw attention as I turn down another aisle and run straight into a body. *Jesus.*

"Oh. Goodness," a polite and oddly familiar voice rings out.

I take a step back, immediately embarrassed. "Excuse me. I didn't see you."

My eyes lock to the well-put-together woman standing before me, and my heart arrests. No, no, no. The checklist for everything wrong with this situation begins to ticker tape in my mind.

I look like a hobo. I'm wearing the same sweats from last night for the love of God. My hair is a mess, and I'm positive I probably smell like a whore since I fucked Liam right before we left the house.

Oh my God. This isn't happening.

"Miss Whitmore. How nice to run into you. Metaphorically speaking."

"Oh my goodness, Chairwoman Whitney. I apologize."

I reach down, grabbing a baguette from the floor as she shakes her head. Of course, who the fuck eats bread off the floor. Oh my God.

I smile, tucking the bread under my arm, trying to save the moment. "I enjoyed my interview so much. So, it's wonderful to see you again."

What am I saying? This is the moment I will be remembered for amongst circles of women that tell the cautionary tale of being a dumb whore like Caroline Whitmore. If I want to save myself, I'll need to die. Please, something, someone, kill me.

"As did I," she answers. "And you can call me Mrs. Whitney, Caroline. We're past the formalities. The invitations are sent."

Faint, borderline hysterical laughter leaves my lips.

"So I hear. Fingers crossed."

I clear my throat and smile, but she doesn't return the gesture, opting to purse her tangerine-stained lips before speaking.

"I have to say, I'm surprised to see you here. Most girls are waiting at home for their tickets."

There's no point in lying. I've clearly not gotten a ticket. And frankly, missing midnight with Liam took precedence to my hopeful excitement.

"Your decision was made. Me waiting around doesn't affect the outcome. If I was privileged enough to receive an invitation, it will be there when I return home."

Fuck. Was that too much?

Her brows rise, and a smile peeks out. "Looks like my niece was right about you."

Great. Arden. As if this moment wasn't already shit.

I swallow. "How is Arden?"

"Back into the kind of trouble she frequents. But before she left, Arden had plenty to say about you."

I answer politely, keeping my cool, "Oh. I didn't realize I made such a large impression."

Considering we only threw daggers at each other for five minutes. Then again, I'm confident I drew blood. *Fuck you, karma.*

"You did. She told me that you're the kind of girl to never follow the crowd because you prefer to set the standard."

My surprise isn't well hidden because this is one of the more shocking moments of my life.

"She said that?"

Mrs. Whitney smiles. "She did. She also said that if we passed on you, you'd be the kind of woman that would never forget. Especially when you sat on the top of this society's social ladder looking down at the rest of us."

Fucking Arden for the win. Maybe I'll stop plotting her death.

"Well, she's a very intuitive young woman. I always liked that about her."

The chairwoman smiles, letting her eyes drift over my appearance. "My niece is fearless—it's her downfall—but you—you scare her. That's a powerful quality, Caroline."

I'm silent, smiling politely, but internally I'm starting to freak out. Is she taking this where I think it's going?

Her arms cross over her chest. "Society needs powerful women. Also, women that understand the dress code. Perhaps on your next outing, you'll remember that you never know who you may run into."

My head's nodding. "Of course, Mrs. Whitney."

Holy shit. Holy shit.

"After all, it's rule number one for a debutante," she adds with a coy smile.

Did she just say...? No.

I let out the breath I'm holding, opening and closing my mouth twice before I speak. "I apologize. Did you just say debutante?"

"Yes, Caroline. Your golden ticket arrived by courier today."

It takes everything within me not to scream, keeping a pleasant, non-self-congratulatory smile on my face as I answer. *I did it. I fucking did it.*

"Thank you. I'm honored. I'm looking forward to the ball."

"Glad to hear it." Her entire demeanor relaxes. "Will you be accompanied by Mr. Grantham? Choosing the perfect escort is top on your list." When my brows rise, she smiles. "We do our research, Caroline. A girl's associations speak volumes about her character."

Before I can answer, Liam's voice accompanies his footsteps. My eyes grow wide, reality barreling its way back into this dream moment. I dart my head over my shoulder, seeing his face come around the corner, and his voice feels louder than I wish it was.

"Carebear, I'm going to get thrown back into jail. Forced to spend another night with pissed-his-pants Pete. Because I'm about to desecrate your fucking body in front of the pasta."

My eyes squeeze closed as Liam skids to a stop, immediately shutting his mouth. Thank God he's reading the room, but it's not soon enough.

I turn back, smiling, hoping the chairwoman will politely disregard what Liam's said, but the discerning look on her face says differently. She takes a step closer, leaning in so only I can hear.

"A word of advice, Miss Whitmore. This isn't the finish line. I suggest keeping better company, immediately, because there is a long list of girls that would like to see you fall from my graces. And dating a criminal would do just that."

I'm nodding as she walks away. Oh fuck. I feel like I can't catch my breath. Liam's hand touches my arm, making me jump as I turn around, seeing that she's gone and we're alone.

"Damn, she seemed serious. Who was that?" When I don't answer, Liam tries to grab my hand, but I pull it away.

"Can you just go get the basket? And check out? I'll call the car and meet you outside."

He reaches for me again. "Care, what's wrong?"

I shake my head, taking another step away.

"Nothing. Just do it. God." My voice is like daggers, and by the look on Liam's face, he doesn't like making its acquaintance again.

"All right," he answers.

I turn around, walking down the aisle, past the register, and straight to the sidewalk. What have I done? This is everything I feared.

What I want—to be Liam's girlfriend. What's expected—Caroline fucking Whitmore.

I know I'm dialing for the car and speaking to the driver, but I'm on autopilot. Lost in my thoughts. God, why did I have to come to this store? This fucking island? And be with this boy?

The last part of that selfish, terrible thought makes me sick to my stomach. Goddamn me. Being a Deb is the culmination of everything I've worked for. I fought hard to become a member of the most prestigious societal presentation. I won't give that up.

Now nobody can deny me anything, ever again.

Not the goddamn girls that tormented me in my boarding school. Or the bitches like Donovan that glide through their lives, unharmed by my realities. *Not even my mother.*

I would finally become the girl I've tediously crafted over the years, with my blood, starvation, and tears. I'd belong.

Except.

Fuck. My hands run through my hair as I look around, feeling more lost than ever. I glance over my shoulder, seeing Liam at the register checking out.

He's taking quick looks at me, worry on his brow. It should be disgust on his face.

Shaky breaths push between my lips as I look back to the street, trying not to cry. Why did he do this? Come here, telling me he loves me? And let me love him back, knowing who I am. Because now it all feels meaningless without Liam. I hate him.

How do I fix this? This can't be the choice I'm left with because it's the cruelest kind of fate.

Me or Liam. Me or Liam. Me or fucking Liam.

The lump in my throat catches as I look to the sky. God, I despise myself for allowing this to be an actual choice. Our black Mercedes pulls up in front of me as I wipe my hand under my eyes just in case any of the leftover mascara's running, sucking up some air as I do.

"Caroline," Liam calls from behind me.

I look over my shoulder, watching as he stalks my way. The driver opens the door before taking the grocery bags, allowing Liam to follow me inside the car. We say nothing as we sit side by side, the driver taking his place and pulling the car away from the store.

Liam's hand encases mine, but I don't look at him, turning my head to stare out of the window.

The house isn't far. It's a damn village. Nothing's far from the beach. But it feels like an eternity. Liam's gaze stays on my profile the whole way. I can feel it. But if I look at him, he'll see it behind my eyes, and then we'll be over.

I can't hide from him. Loving me is his superpower.

He should leave me. Stat. It's what I deserve. I know. But that doesn't stop it from stinging.

The moment we pull to a stop in front of the beach house, I tug my hand from his and scoot out, heading straight inside the house. But Liam's on my heels, slamming the door behind him.

"What the fuck is going on, Caroline?"

I'm frozen in my place, staring out the windows toward the ocean, my chest already heaving. Liam's voice raises again. "Caroline."

I don't turn around.

My eyes squeeze shut, wanting to make it all stop—the anger, the sadness, the self-hatred. I just want it to stop. Because this is what I do. I ruin everything and everyone.

Strong hands turn me around as his beautiful face stares down at my tearstained cheeks.

Please don't hate me, Liam. I don't mean to be myself so often.

"Carebear. What the fuck is going on? Talk to me."

"You'll hate me. And I just wanted one more minute of you loving me."

"I could never hate you. That's impossible."

If he realized that I'm about to win this challenge, he would've never made such a bold statement. I take a step back from his hands, lifting my chin because there's no point in looking pitiful when I don't deserve the pity.

"That woman. The one in the store. That was Chairwoman Whitney. As in Tabitha Whitney—head of the International Debutante Ball. She was informing me that I received my ticket today. I did it, Liam. I'm in."

His face softens, a smile gracing me.

"That's amazing, Carebear—"

I hold up my hand, cutting in. "She heard you, Liam, and reminded me that a girl is only as good as her affiliations."

He blanches. And I feel like the terrible person I am. His face drops to the floor for only a moment before he looks up, colder, crossing his arms over his chest. I'm happy he's protecting himself—nobody deserves what I'm about to say.

"I love you, Liam—" I begin to say, looking to the side for a moment.

He takes my chin between his fingers, pulling my face back to his.

"You're a lot of things, Caroline. A coward isn't one. Let me finish for you... But I'm a liability? Is that what you're going to say?"

The silence stretches out as his hands leave my face, but my eyes stay on his. And then I finally say the thing that will break us.

"Yes."

He blows out a harsh burst of air, hands coming to his head. I take a step back, needing space from him to say what I have to.

"The worst part of that statement is that for a moment, I hated you. Because you became another horrible Sophie's choice I had to make to crawl my way up this fucking social ladder. But the good news is that I hate myself more."

"Why?" he demands, shoving his hands inside his pockets. "Tell me why you hate yourself more."

My head shakes because I don't want to answer or acknowledge the profound dark truths that hide behind my eye rolls and faux indifference.

Liam pulls his bottom lip between his teeth, roughly letting it glide out before speaking.

"Tell me. You owe me that much."

I grab my wrist, rubbing the scar, not knowing how to answer. Liam steps closer, placing his hand on the counter.

"Tell me, Caroline."

I shake my head again, tears beginning to fall down my cheeks. Liam's hand smacks the counter as his voice punches through the silence. "Tell me why, Caroline."

My shoulders jump, tears bursting off my lashes as I blink.

"Because I love you," I scream. Cries take over, muddling the rest of my words. "Because I fucking love you always."

He walks toward me, but I shake my head. "Stop. You deserve better than me, Liam. Survival will always be my default. I hate myself for letting the 'choice' be a 'choice.' Because, in the end, it's always you. But every goddamn time, I have to stop and remind myself that—you'll resent me a little bit more until *we* aren't anymore."

But he doesn't stop coming to stand in front of me, his big hands cradling my face as I speak. "I love you, but I don't know if I'll ever stop doing this—weighing me over you. How fucked-up is that? I'm selfish and sad, Liam. I'm so fucking broken that even the boy I've loved almost my whole life loving me back isn't enough to fix me."

"So that's it," he levels, staring down at my tear-filled eyes. "This is your, what? Your goodbye? You letting me off the hook? Do you think I don't fucking know you, Carebear? Because I have news for you. I don't need you to choose me. I choose you. All of you. Every fucking twisted and broken thing about you—I choose it. Because you are what I'm good at. That's what I figured out during the last few months. Everything else in my life will always fall into place as long as I mind my duty—you, Carebear."

He blows out a shaky breath as two tears stream down his godlike face. I bring my hands up between his arms, wiping his cheeks with my palms. How can he love me so much that he'd let me ruin him?

"I don't deserve happiness, Liam. People like *me* don't deserve it."

In the end, that's what it boils down to. I fight for all the clout and the appearance of belonging because that's all I'm allowed. But Liam—he's true love, and I'm not entitled to something so special.

Liam's lips fall on mine, kissing me like he's trying to make me take it all back. He pulls away, staying close to my face as he whispers, "We don't end, Caroline. You're my Love-a-Lot."

The breath catches in my chest. *What did he just say?* The memory attacks me like a goddamn lifeline—me sitting on the floor of my room as Julia lays out my dinner clothes.

"What's that you have?" Julia questions, holding up a cardigan to me as I shake my head.

"The other part of my birthday gift from today."

My finger runs over the puffy belly of the cartoon bear sticker, still thinking about how much he smiled at me.

"That boy must be very fond of you, Miss Caroline."

My eyes lift. "What makes you say that?"

"Well," she offers with a smile. "That's a Loves-a-Lot Bear, or is it Love-a-Lot. I can't remember, but it's from the Care Bears—*I watched it as a kid. So I'm guessing he must loves you a lot."*

My eyes narrow on Julia, looking for a hint of humor, but there's none. She's serious.

"Is he very nice?" she asks, turning toward my jewelry box.

"Yes."

Julia holds up a pretty silver necklace, and I nod as she adds, "And smart?"

"Very."

I lean back on my elbows, watching her.

"And good?"

I'm nodding. "The best."

"See what I mean?" she says like I'm supposed to know the answer.

I wrap my hands around his wrists, tugging them from my face as I turn away from him, rushing toward my purse, zipping it open.

"Stop walking away, Caroline."

My hand rummages through my Valentino as Liam comes up behind me, trapping me with palms on either side of the granite countertop.

"Why can't you believe in us?" he pushes. "You don't have to be perfect. You and me—we don't work without each other."

A bunch of shit spills from my purse as I search frantically for the thing I need, hands shaking as my whole heart spills out too.

"Oh my God. Where is it?"

I'm spun around just as my hand grabs what I've been searching for.

"Make sense," Liam says, gently staring down at me.

"This," I whisper over unsteady breath.

Liam looks at me, confused, then follows my gaze down to the bunched tissue in my hand. Everything around us stills as I unfold the tissue carefully until the only evidence of my heart lies exposed in my palm.

"Is that—" Liam reaches for the old, worn sticker he gave me when we were kids.

I shoot my hand to my chest, pressing the sticker to my heart, staring him in the eyes.

"I kept this forever. It was special because it was something from you. And just now, when you called me by the name of this damn bear, it reminded me of something. Something I never understood until now."

It's hard to speak, so I take a deep breath as Liam tucks my hair behind my ears.

"It reminded me of the day I got it. I was with my nanny, Julia. She told me that you must love me. But I couldn't believe that. Nobody loved me. You were everything good in the world, Liam, and I was—"

He scowls. "Don't talk shit about the girl I love."

I smile, closing my eyes for a second.

"That's the thing. It's so much easier to believe the one bad thing someone says about you than the hundred good things. I don't think I deserve you. But you want me." I shrug. "You loves me a lot. So how bad could I really be? Right?"

He kisses my lips. "Right."

My hands come to his chest, squeezing the sticker.

"I'm going to fail a lot."

"But you'll try," he counters.

A bit of relief finds my shoulders as he kisses my lips again, pulling away to touch his forehead to mine.

"Caroline, I'll lose my nerve sometimes."

"I'll force you forward," I breathe out.

My arms wrap around his neck as his hands dip to my ass to pick me up, holding me close like I'm koala'd onto him.

"I'll be selfish sometimes," I whisper against his neck.

"But you'll be mine."

I will always be his. Even if I'm a work in progress because nobody in this world is rooting for me harder than the boy that gave me a cookie and Care Bear sticker along with his heart for my twelfth birthday.

Chapter
Thirty-Seven

Liam
February

"**Y**ou look beautiful."

Caroline's standing in my bedroom examining herself for the hundredth time. But the color of her dress matches her eyes, so all I really want to do is rip it off her.

"You have to say that because you love me."

I raise my brows, crossing my feet at my ankles from where I'm lying on the bed.

"No. What did I say, Caroline?"

She smirks in the mirror, understanding what I mean. "Thank you."

Every day she gets better at listening to only the good stuff. Baby steps.

I shift, getting off the bed, and walk over to her. My arms wrap around her waist as I bend to put my chin on her shoulder.

"Let's fuck."

She laughs and presses her lips together, smearing her lip gloss, before saying, "No. I've already smelled like a whore once when I saw the chairwoman. Save me my dignity today. But if you're a good boy, I'll let you fuck my ass."

I groan, biting her shoulder gently before standing tall again.

"That's a deal I can't pass on. Now, let's get this shitshow over with. I have a chairwoman to impress. And a Carebear to defile."

I tug at her waist as she gives herself one more look before I drag her from her reflection and out of my room to meet up with everyone who's waiting. My mother's laugh hits my ears as we walk down the stairs, and I look down at Caroline, who's smiling too.

Caroline and my mother have become close. I love it—both my favorite girls, friends. Now, if I can get Caroline and Van on the same page, life would be perfect. But at least Van's here when Caroline needs her. They seem more allies than friends, and I guess I can get behind that.

"It's about time," Grey levels as we walk into the room. "The old witch will be here any moment."

Donovan shakes her head but laughs, standing with Babe. I slap his hand as a "hello" while Caroline makes her way over toward my mother. She's embraced and immediately fawned all over.

I'm not the only one that loves her. The thought makes me happy.

Grey nudges my shoulder. "You realize you're married up. Babe's chosen her future daughter-in-law. I hope you're in love because it's over for you."

I laugh, pushing Grey's shoulder. We're too young to get married— and that's the only fucking reason I haven't asked her. Because I am in love. Wholly and completely.

I motion with my head toward Van. "You're one to talk, dick."

He shrugs, the smile on his face shifting into one of thought as he stares at Donovan. *Oh shit.*

"Earth to the bastard," I joke, interrupting his deep dive into bad ideas. "Did you hear we have to stick around the first week of spring break to work over some fucking newbie from Georgia?"

He's nodding but not listening, so I add, "I hear he might be better than you."

Grey's face jerks to mine. "Eat a dick. I'll smoke him. But I heard he's good too. Jackson something, I think. It's fine, though I don't have plans until the second week. I'm taking Van to Paris. What are you and Care doing?"

"Eh—"

My attention's called to Simon announcing Tabitha Whitney, shutting my mouth. My mother greets her, taking Tabitha's hand and shaking it, saying all the right things.

Grey leans over. "She's old but not decrepit. You should've just fucked her. Then she'd realize Caroline's been doing acts of charity by dating you."

I try not to react, keeping my face still as I lean in. "The minute this hag leaves, I'm going to throw you from the second floor."

"Men," my father greets, walking by and giving us a knowing look as the crowd begins making their way into the dining room.

Grey and I look at each other, chuckling as the girls join us because some things never fucking change. We're still fucking around on the edge of trouble.

My mother directs everyone where to sit. Tucker's seated at the head, with my mother and Tabitha across from one another on either side of him. I'm next to my mom, while Grey is seated next to the chairwoman, the girls next to us respectively.

The brief disdainful look that Grey doesn't even try to hide almost makes me break into laughter. But I hold it in because today is my time to shine. I need to make a good impression so that Tabitha Whitney stops holding me over Caroline's head.

Over the last few months, I've been used as ammo to keep Caroline on her toes, and, so, like any Upper East Side war, this lunch is a peace negotiation.

I glance to Caroline, who's sitting straighter than I've ever witnessed, as the polite conversation ensues.

Grey is brusque enough to deter any kind of lengthy discussion but not impolite. My mother is complimentary, and it seems as though the chairwoman is enamored. I'm not surprised—my family's powerful. I'm surprised it took her this long to figure out who I was.

Caroline leans into my shoulder, whispering, "It seems to be going well."

I nod and give her a wink. The day she opened up on the island, I promised her we'd get her everything she's ever wanted. And if this fucking ball is it, then that's what my Carebear gets. It's hers until she realizes she doesn't fucking need it.

She rules this world. Always has.

Babe laughs at something Tabitha says, and I smile, as does my father. Doting as always. Even Van pinch hits, asking a question about the ball, smiling at Caroline.

"A live orchestra. Wow, that's classic elegance," Van's raspy voice offers as Grey looks at her like she's lost it.

But one look from her has him back on track. This time I laugh and make a whip gesture at him. To which he scratches his brow with his middle finger.

Caroline's hand lands on my thigh, so I look at her as she smiles up at me. "Thank you for this. I loves you a lot."

It's the silliest, most ridiculous way to say I love you. But it's ours, and the fact that she does it unabashedly makes her mine.

Tabitha sets her fork down, lifting the napkin politely to the corner of her mouth.

"I have to say"—all eyes on her—"I'm thrilled you invited me here today. Seeing Caroline's choice of escort with his family, so grounded and exemplary, brings ease to my thoughts."

Give me a fucking break.

Tabitha looks to my mother and father. "I'm sure you can understand my hesitation. The hand of a debutante is only for the most outstanding of young gentlemen. And now that the situation has been taken care of—"

Insert swept under the rug. Or never made the papers.

"—and I've met with you—"

Insert I want on your short list of acquaintances so I can ask for donations.

"—I believe we can proceed as usual."

Babe and Tucker smile, but I know they're irritated. Tabitha basically called me a reformed piece of shit. But it's okay. I don't give a shit what she thinks about me. If this gets Caroline her peace of mind, then so fucking be it.

It occurs to me nobody is speaking as Van locks eyes with me from across the table, darting them to Caroline and then back to me.

What the fuck?

I glance at Caroline and back to Van, who jerks her head again, so I draw my brows together, shrugging with a slight lift of my hands. What the hell is Van doing?

Grey clears his throat, answering my shrug, a shit-eating grin on his face. "Daggers are shooting from *that* Carebear."

My head swings to Caroline, who's tapping her finger against the silver knife and staring narrow-eyed at the chairwoman. *Shit.*

"What are you doing?" I whisper discreetly, but she doesn't answer, so I press, "It's not worth losing what you worked for. It's fine."

Caroline's hand presses against my chest to move me back against my chair, giving direct sight of her target.

Van's laugh is quieted by her hand as she turns her head. Fuck. This is about to become a fully engaged war zone.

"Excuse me. Tabitha," Caroline hisses, and I know we're fucked.

The chairwoman turns to stare at her, surprised at hearing her first name. My father starts to interrupt, feeling the shit about to hit the fan, but my mother pats his hand, never taking her eyes off Tabitha.

"I'm curious," Caroline continues. "What about Liam made him less than outstanding? I'd love for you to explain. And be specific."

Again my father clears his throat, but Grey and I both shake our heads, with Grey adding, "Tucker, we just sit here and look pretty."

This isn't the kind of party the boys are invited to. It's too mean for us.

Tabitha looks flustered, glancing at me and then my parents before shifting in her seat to face Caroline.

Jesus.

Caroline's fingers curl around the handle of the knife, so I place mine over hers, biting the inside of my cheek so that I don't smile. I know my baby, and she's already imagined the woodchipper.

Grey laughs, and I look at him like, "Shut the fuck up," but he doesn't care. His arms cross over his chest as he looks back and forth between Tabitha and Caroline, way too amused.

Van interjects, "I'm sure you didn't mean that Liam wasn't outstanding. Correct?"

I can't read Donovan's face. Is she trying to help, or have we gone full anarchist? The questions cluttering my mind are answered as Donovan adds, "Because that would seem ill-fitted for a prior Deb—to criticize someone with a last name like Brooks. I can't think of anyone more outstanding, other than perhaps McCallister, Kennedy...and Whitmore."

Caroline faces Donovan as Van winks at her. Son of a bitch. My smile finally breaks free. *Ride or die, Van.*

Tabitha places her napkin on the table. "Yes, Miss Kennedy, it would be unkind of me to criticize the Brooks name. But I'm only judging the information I was given. A fall from grace is still a fall, no matter how shallow."

Fuck. Tabby's doubling down. Caroline sweeps her hair over her shoulder, and Grey and I both look at each other, eyes wide. If this moment had a soundtrack, it would play out to LL Cool J's "Mama Said Knock You Out." *Dun-dun-nuh a comeback* plays out in my head before I smirk. I have to remember to tell Kai about this later. He'll appreciate my reference. Fuck, he has no idea how much he lucked out by having plans with Mila.

Caroline's voice is calm, steady, and direct, drawing my focus.

"I ask because I know Trish Vanderhelt's father served a lengthy sentence for his participation in an extortion and fraud scandal. And yet, he's invited."

Tabitha's mouth opens, then shuts. *That's the best idea she's had all afternoon.*

"And then there's Tiffany Astor," Caroline offers, narrowing her eyes. "Her escort frequents real escorts. It's probably where she got the crabs. Because we know that's where she got the baby. Thank goodness for an empire waist."

Tabitha cuts in sharply, "Miss Whitmore, I would like to remind you of your place."

Caroline's hands slap onto the table, bringing her up out of her chair. "And I would remind you of yours."

"Fuck," Grey mouths, and I nod.

But Tabitha asked for it.

"Do you remember when you told me to end my acquaintance with Liam? I paid attention to the wrong part of that lecture."

I lean back in my seat, enjoying watching my little viper eating the mouse.

"You were right, Chairwoman. A girl is only as good as her associations. It's a shame you no longer have mine. Society needs powerful women, correct? Well, I'm here."

Grey holds up his glass to me, and I do the same as we both sit with smiles on our faces. Fuck you, Tabitha.

Tabitha pushes from the table to stand. "I believe we're done here."

Caroline stands to her petite height, smoothing her hands down her dress and smirking. "Don't be silly. This isn't the finish line. I've just gotten started."

Grey sets his glass on the table. "Does this mean we don't have to go to that circle jerk of elitism anymore?"

"Language," Babe chastises to a winking Grey. "And yes, I believe we'll all be skipping the ball this year."

I take Caroline's hand, bringing it to my lips, watching Tabitha stare at all of us. Her red face turns out of sight as she's led out of my home, leaving everyone to let out a collective breath of air and start to laugh. I stand, taking Caroline's bright face in.

"You sure?"

She boops my nose. "I've never been surer of anything. Other than you."

Epilogue

Liam
Spring Break

Caroline glares at me like she hates me from where her sweet ass has been seated all night. We've been playing this game since the party started. The one where we pretend to hate each other only to fuck like animals later. It's her favorite.

I walk over to her and the court of mean girls, reaching out to tickle her side. She jerks her body away, leveling me with a look. Her friends never know what to do with us. One minute she's my soft cuddly Carebear, and the next, they see shit like this. We must look so fucking unstable—joke's on them. Caroline and I are rock damn solid. And neither of us give two shits what anyone else has to say.

Caroline tosses her long brown hair over her shoulder.

"The expression you're wearing is as ugly as the shirt you have on, Liam. What do you want?"

I stare down, thinking about a bevy of dirty shit to do to her. Especially since she picked this fucking shirt out. I hold out a red cup.

"Carebear. Drink this so you can be more of a Funshine than a

Grumpy."

She swats at the cup, but I move it away before she connects, and spills the liquid on my jeans. It almost makes me break character because she's such a little shit. I love these pants.

"I hate you," she spits.

I wink. "You wish that were true. I'm going to hang out with my real friends now."

Walking away, I head over to where Grey and Donovan stand, picking Van up, playing around, making her squeal. I glance over my shoulder at Caroline's scowling face and move my eyes to the door, seeing her minute nod.

Game on.

***

Grey hands me a shot that I throw back quickly as he smirks.

"I thought you were going in for the kill, tiger?"

I grin, crossing my arms over my chest. "That kid from Georgia." I squint, thinking before I say, "Jackson. He's still flirting with Caroline. It's fine. I'll drown him later for being a cockblock. Or I'll watch her do it."

Grey's shoulders shake. "Don't let Caroline kill him. He's going to lead this crew to victory next year. I'm glad I stayed this week to race him. Plus, I think he has eyes for Laura's cousin, Ava. He's been looking at her like he's been waiting for this moment his whole life."

My eyes drift to Caroline holding court, noticing Jackson's are on the door. Grey taps my shoulder.

"Told you so."

Jackson tears out through the party, making his way toward where the girl he clearly has eyes for is leaving.

"Poor bastard. He's a goner." Grey laughs.

I cheers him with another shot. "Aren't we all."

But my eyes aren't on the next generation of Hillcrest's lives. Mine are right where they belong. My Carebear.

***

Caroline

"What took you so long?"

Liam laughs, strolling around the corner of his lake house. "I had to entertain people. Miss me that much, huh."

It's disgusting how accurate that statement is. I hate being away from him.

He leans down, not slowing as he reaches me, grabbing my ass, lifting me. My legs wrap around his waist, arms around his neck, as he backs us up against the house.

Liam stares at me, his bottom lip pushing out. "Say you're sorry for calling my shirt ugly."

I grin, leaning in and sucking on that damn lip before I answer.

"I love your shirt. I'm sorry, that was too low."

He snarls before diving in, locking our mouths. Kissing him never gets old. Ever. It always feels like the first time, butterflies and all.

"Wanna fuck right here? Roll the dice?" he breathes against my lips.

God, he knows me too well. We're not entirely hidden by the shadows, so anyone could walk out and find us. Liam rubs his cock against my center as I push my tits forward into him. We're dry humping for the world to see, like the fucking degenerates we are.

"I almost attacked you inside," he moans quietly. "You were so fucking mean."

I nod, already breathless. "God, I love it when we fake fight. Gets me so hot."

Noise from the porch draws both our faces, but he looks back, not stopping what he's doing. He kisses my neck, sucking on it. I swear I've had a hickey on me somewhere since the day he showed up on the fucking island. But I love them.

With one hand on my ass to hold me, the other fists the back of my leather pants, using his grip to force me to rub up and down against his hard length. The material cuts against my clit, giving just enough bite as Liam guides me, slowly pushing into me each time.

"Oh fuck." I gasp, and he smirks.

"We have to improvise because of these fucking pants. Also, you look too goddamn edible—remind me to burn them."

He's making me stupid because I have nothing witty to say. Holding my breath as I bite my lip, I'm overwhelmed by the sensation in my center.

My head tilts back, my mouth agape as I suck in the air. Liam moves me faster, locking his eyes with me. "Are you going to come for me? Like a dirty little Carebear?"

I'm nodding, eyes wide as the sensation begins to compound, climbing higher and higher.

"Do you hear that?"

Liam smiles, mouthing, "They can hear you."

My hands smack against his shoulders as I bounce up and down quicker, digging my nails into fists full of Liam's shirt. I'm panting so loud that I barely hear the next voice.

"It sounds like someone's fucking around the corner."

Liam's lips come to my ear. "Don't go silent now, Caroline. Let them hear how good it feels."

That's all it takes. The wicked, sweet release floods my body as a raspy "yes" catapults toward the sky.

Liam's mouth drags up my neck, biting and licking on the way up as he says, "You're beautiful. I love you, baby."

He lowers me to the ground, lifting my chin for one last kiss. "Now, let's say our goodbyes. I want you in my bed, naked and all for me."

"Done."

His strong hand engulfs mine, giving me an anchor as I lean against him, walking back to the party on slightly wobbly legs. We round the corner, seeing two guys staring back at us, holding beers in their hands. Looking up at Liam, I laugh, knowing they've connected the dots, and the smirk on his face gives away the fact that he's about to say something salacious.

Liam tilts his head, staring at the guys, who look incredibly nervous.

"Did you hear anything?"

They both shake their heads quickly, swallowing.

"Good men. But I have to tell you, she tastes just as good as she sounds."

I almost scream through my laughter as Liam wraps an arm around my waist, picking me up and rubbing his nose against mine as we walk away. He's a maniac, and I love him.

"Hey," he whispers. "I loves you a lot."

"What a coincidence. I loves you a lot too. Guess that makes me yours forever."

Liam kisses my lips sweetly. "And ever, Carebear."

***

Thank you for reading Caroline and Liam's story. Don't miss out on Ava and Jackson…and Holt. Two is always better than one in this naughty little Hillcrest novella.

Read Dirty little Secrets Now!

Everyone has a dirty little secret...I just have two.
One secret I met at a party I didn't want to go to. We lied about our names, trespassed onto a Ferris wheel, and he made me see stars while I stared into the night's sky.
The other secret wooed me with picnics in an orchard and the taste of honey on his lips. He held me close until I had to say goodbye, even though I wished I could stay forever.
The worst thing about having these dirty little secrets is that where one goes, the other follows.

USA Today **Bestselling author, Trilina Pucci, gives you a naughty little novella, introducing:** Jackson, Holt, and Ava, with guest appearances by some of your favorites from Filthy Little Pretties and Vicious Little Snakes. Dirty little Secrets

vicious *little* snakes

Also By Trilina Pucci

Contemporary New Adult

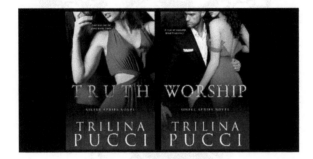

High Steam Anthiheroes

Dark Mafia

About the Author

Trilina is a USA Today Bestselling Author who loves cupcakes and bourbon.

When she isn't writing steamy love stories, she can be found devouring Netflix with her husband, Anthony, and their three kiddos. Pucci's journey into writing started impulsively. She wanted to check off a box on her bucket list, but what began as wish-fulfillment has become incredibly fulfilling. Now she cant's see her life without her characters, her readers, and this community.

She's known for being a trope defier, writing outside of the box and creating fictional worlds that her readers never want to leave.

Connect with Trilina and stay up to date.
www.trilinapucci.com
facebook.com/trilinapuccibooks
twitter.com/trilina_pucci
instagram.com/authortrilinapucci
amazon.com/Trilina-Pucci/e/B07BQFYLKB

Crisis Info

This book is a work of fiction, but your life is not, so if you're dealing with any of the mental health issues in this book, or others, below are some avenues for help, or just an ear to listen. Much love, Trilina.

The Crisis Text Line
https://www.crisistextline.org/
Text HOME to 741741 to connect with a Crisis Counselor
Free 24/7 support at your fingertips
US and Canada: text 741741
UK: text 85258 | Ireland: text 50808

Teen Mental Health
https://teenmentalhealth.org/

National Institute of Mental Health
https://www.nimh.nih.gov/health/find-help/index.shtml

vicious *little* snakes

Acknowledgements

I'm so fortunate to have a village of people dedicated to my baby. Vicious Little Snakes is one of those books that you need your hand held to write. I was so nervous. I second-guessed myself too often, but these people pushed me, supported me, and championed me.

Christine: You are amazing, and the amount of laughter we share has earned us eight-packs. Thank you for keeping us on task and making sure this whole shebang was smooth and amazing. Erica: You slay me. I'm so happy we connected because I'm never letting go! Becky: Honestly, I almost threw it away, but you kept me sane and make me better. Love you forever for that. Ride or Die. I know—awkward phrasing. LOL. Sandra: What can I say except I'm not sure I could ever actually hit publish without you saying yes. Actually, I know I couldn't. #facts Rumi: I'm so lucky to have you and your sharp wit.

Gretchen: You drug me through the finish line, sometimes kicking and screaming. Thank god for that. To my betas: Your thoughts and insight mean so much to me! There aren't enough thank-yous. Grey's Promotions: Thank you for your hard work and all the support you gave. You're top notch. Lou: Why do you put up with me? I'm glad you do because this paperback is beautiful. Ashlee: You. The master of turning my mood into a vibe and giving me the courage to leave the vision where I wanted it. I heart you, forever.